W9-BGF-704

THE BLEEDING STATUE

I took the remains of the path through the garden to the place where we'd spoken with Jusik Porath. The silver arc in memory of Kade was gone, but there was a white marble statue in its place. And somebody was sitting where Jusik had sat, in a tangle of silk robes. He stood up, looking past me. It was Ran.

He turned toward the statue. I called ''Ran!'' and heard the sound echo in my head as though it only existed internally. It was the kind of sound you hear through ear coverings, though my ears were open. I walked toward him.

The statue was of me! That was somehow the most horrible touch of the night, and I felt shivers run up my arms. It wasn't a classical statue, there was no noble look on my face; it was me in one of my street outfits, looking as though someone had tipped a thin sheathing of white over my head and trapped me in a passing moment. Ran put a hand on the crook of the statue's elbow. A surface of red pooled up beneath it.

The statue was bleeding. I was vaguely aware that I was watching this from some other place, and was sorry that I'd come. More wounds appeared. Ran stripped off his outerrobe and his shirt, and tried to clean the statue off. But the blood was inexhaustible. It pooled at the statue's feet, soaked through the shirt, and left stains on Ran's face and hands and clothing.

I wanted to leave here. I wanted to leave here *now.* I didn't live here, right? I came from some other place. This was just a picture, I could go back if I wanted to! . . . If I could remember how.

I started yelling. It echoed in my head without disturbing the air around me. I was completely alone.

The finest in DAW Science Fiction
DORIS EGAN'S
IVORY NOVELS:

THE GATE OF IVORY

TWO-BIT HEROES

GUILT-EDGED IVORY

GUILT-EDGED IVORY

DORIS EGAN

DAW BOOKS, INC.

DONALD A. WOLLHEIM, FOUNDER

375 Hudson Street, New York, NY 10014

ELIZABETH R. WOLLHEIM
SHEILA E. GILBERT
PUBLISHERS

Copyright © 1992 by Doris Egan.

All Rights Reserved.

Cover art by Richard Hescox.

DAW Book Collectors No. 890.

First Printing September 1992
1 2 3 4 5 6 7 8 9

DAW TRADEMARK REGISTERED
U.S. PAT OFF. AND FOREIGN COUNTRIES
—MARCA REGISTRADA.
HECHO EN U.S.A.

PRINTED IN THE U.S.A.

With appreciation
and thanks to the spirit
of Cao Xueqin

Chapter 1

Assassinations are so inconvenient.

It wasn't as though there weren't plenty of other things to occupy my attention at the time. Another summer in the capital, and I was supervising a good cleaning out of the house there, wishing we could spring for importing a Tellys dustcatcher (just an idle wish—the hole it would put in the House budget would never be worth it). My tinaje healing skills were rusty, so I'd signed on to an apprenticeship with a big-name tinaje artist who had offices in the Imperial Dance Academy. And I was taking some trouble to make a clandestine appointment at a Tellys medical clinic (we'll get back to this one later).

And to top it all off, my sister-in-law Kylla was be-having very strangely.

She swept in one afternoon when we were rolling up the carpets from the second floor and taking them down to the courtyard to be beaten. There were no clients in the house, of course, since the place was a mess; and my dear husband had taken himself as far away from manual labor as he could, remembering a sudden appointment in Braece. Danger means nothing to Ran when weighed against duty, but the prospect of actual physical work sends him scuttling like a rabbit caught on a landing pad.

Kylla invaded this prosaic scene like some exotic bird of paradise, all bangles and gold facepaint. Her black hair was caught back in a velvet band rimmed with tiny metal dangles that made a sound like distant bells; her dark eyes were rimmed with midnight blue, clear as the borders of a new map. Since her marriage she'd taken full advantage of the relaxed dress code for respectably wedded women, relaxing it to the point where her grandmother probably would have had a heart attack if she'd seen her grandchild wandering around in public this way. People as gorgeous as Kylla can get away with a lot, though.

"Where's Ran?" she said to me, without preamble. Her robes swished over the head of the stairs.

"Braece," I said.

She looked around at the servants carrying down the huge carpet from the upper office, the tables pushed against the walls, the clouds of dustmotes, and nodded as though she understood. The sleeves of my worst robe were tied back, and I wiped the sweat from my brow with a bare arm, aware that I looked every bit as messy as my surroundings. "The pillows are all outside," I said apologetically.

"I'll stand," she replied. There was a jingling sound behind her, and her four-year-old daughter Shez peeked around, the bracelets on her arms slipping.

"I want to sit," said Shez.

Kylla sighed, lifted her, and deposited her atop the carved blackwood table against the wall. Shez sat regally and surveyed her domain from this new height.

"What's wrong?" I said. Kylla was not usually this preoccupied, or this morose-looking.

She started to pace. "Has Lysander called here?"

"Lysander? Why would he call here? I mean, he's always welcome—" Ran and I got along well enough with Kylla's husband, but we only tended to see him when they were together. Ran was still close to his sister, but I suspected that Lysander was accepted mostly on the grounds that he'd married Kylla.

"He might have called Ran on the Net," she said.

"If he did, Ran hasn't mentioned it. What's going on?"

Just then Shez started to chant, "I want to see them beat the rugs! I want to see them beat the rugs! I want—"

Kylla said, "Please, darling, mother has a head-ache."

Mother has a headache? Kylla had the constitution of a workhorse, and nothing in the universe fazed her.

"Good gods, Kylla."

"Why? What did I say?" She looked distracted.

"What is it, what's the matter?"

"Why?" She was suddenly alarmed. "Do I look bad?"

"Do you look b— You are a glorious vision of sun-rise, as always, but you are driving me crazy. You look worried, is what you look. Do you want to tell me what the problem is, or do you want me to harass you with calls every hour until you crack?"

She smiled suddenly and patted my hand, still en-crusted with dirt. "I'm so glad you married Ran."

It was out of left field but warming, typically Kylla; not every barbarian who marries into a good Ivoran family can expect the kind of sweetness she's shown me from the beginning. You see why nobody can stay mad at her? However— "You're off the point, Kylla."

She nodded but didn't seem disposed to go any fur-ther.

"I want to see them beat the rugs! I want to see them beat the—"

I hauled Shez down from her perch, took her to the head of the stairs, and gave her to the housekeeper who'd come out from Cormallon to help us. "She wants to see them beat the rugs," I explained.

The housekeeper took her hand and led her away. I returned to Kylla. "Speak," I said.

"I thought Lysander might have called Ran for ad-vice."

"What sort of advice?" Lord, this was like pulling nails from stone.

She took a deep breath. "The council wants him to get married again."

I blinked. "Whoa! The *Shikron family council?*" She nodded. "Wants him to divorce you?" She shook her head. "Wants him to take a junior wife?"

She burst into tears. "They, want, him . . . to take a new *senior* wife, and make me a junior!"

Good heavens. I put my arms around her, not easy considering I only come up to her shoulder. "Sweetheart, that can't be. You were married first, you'll always have seniority rights."

"Not if . . . not if she outranks me."

"How can she outrank you if you were married first?"

"They want him to marry Eliana Porath!"

The Poraths were one of the six noble families. They outranked everybody.

I said, "I thought it wasn't customary to take any extra wives until middle age. Lysander's still in his twenties."

"But the council wants the *connection*, and the Poraths want the *money*."

"Oh." Lysander's family was rolling in it, from everything I'd heard. I guessed the Poraths weren't doing so well. My mouth hardened. And for this they were going to screw up three people's lives.

I said, "They can't force Lysander to marry, can they? He's First of Shikron."

"Lysander says they can make his life a living hell. But he also says that Eliana Porath has a face like a mud pudding, which I know isn't true. I went to school with her cousin."

"Oh, come on now. I'm sure he doesn't want this marriage any more than you do. He worships the ground you walk on, Kylla, everybody knows it." This last part at least was true.

Teartracks ran through the gold swirl on her cheeks. "I'm getting old," she said. "I'm losing my looks."

For the love of— "For heaven's sake, Kylla, you're twenty-five standard. You're a year younger than me! If there's a wrinkle anyplace on your body, point it out to me. I'll give you a hundred in gold for it."

She sniffed. "I think my fanny's falling."

"My fanny fell when I was twelve. At this point we'd need a hoist to— I fail to see why that's amusing, gracious lady Kylla.'' She'd smiled behind the tears. ''Say, Ky, why don't we see what Ran's got stored in the way of Ducort wine?''

''It's the middle of the day.''

I made a rude noise with my tongue that I'd learned from a bunch of outlaws in the Northwest Sector. ''Better yet—let's go to the Lantern Gardens and see what they've got on their list of new drinks. We'll stay for the matinee and watch the naked floorshow.''

She laughed. ''Do you know something? I've never had the nerve to actually stay for the show.''

''You amaze me. Wait, I'll check on Shez.'' I went into the other room and looked down through the back window to the courtyard. Lines were strung from one side of the house to the other, crisscrossing among the leaves of the coyu tree. A fortune in Andulsine carpets hung in a thousand brightly colored threads. Six men and women stood there beating (carefully) and Shez stood on the cobbles beside them, whacking away with enthusiasm. ''Wham!'' I heard her voice float up from below. ''Wham! Zam! Ham! Tam!'' Her face glowed.

''She's busy,'' I assured Kylla, returning. ''I think we can safely get away for an hour.''

''She won't be a problem to anybody?''

''Oh, they'll find things for her to do. There's still the floor cleaning, and the unrolling of the clean rugs, and hauling down the tapestries. . . .'' I grinned wickedly. ''All that domestic stuff she probably never sees at home.''

Kylla laughed. I was glad to see it. If you've never met her before, let me assure you that Kylla is a tower of strength as a rule. *I* usually go to *her* for comfort. This junior wife stuff must really have gotten to her, I thought.

But she must have been pulling herself together, because as we descended the stairs she said, ''So how are things going in the offspring department for you and Ran?''

I groaned. ''Gods, Kylla, you've only just stopped bugging me about the *wedding.*''

"That was a full year ago.—So how is it going?"

We barged out the front door, into the summer sunlight, and I signaled for a wagon-cab.

It was midway through the evening, just edging into darkness, the trees outside blending into shadows and the heat finally lifting a notch, when Ran entered the house. He entered tentatively, glancing around the downstairs parlor.

I said, "The floors are all clean and the rugs are back in place. It's safe to come in."

He nearly jumped a foot. I put down my book and stood up from the divan behind the shelves where I'd been reading.

"Uh, Theodora. I thought you might have gone out." Imagine a male version of Kylla, with shorter hair and without the facepaint. When I got next to him, I could smell the expensive perfume that he bought in an exclusive shop three streets away. When I got next to him, he kissed me. He put some extra effort into it, as well he might under the circumstances. Ran is no fool.

Once I could breathe normally, I said, "How was Braece?"

"Oh, much the same. Any new client appointments while I was gone?" he asked, changing the subject instantly.

Well, if I'd wanted a furniture mover I would have married one. I let it go. "As a matter of fact, there were. Two Net messages left while I was out with Kylla today."

"Kylla was here?"

"Wait, you'll like this. One of the messages was from the gracious sir Kempler Taydo. He'd like an interview tomorrow, with a, quote, 'view to possible employment of your services,' unquote."

Ran looked amused. "Taydo of the Department of Sanitation? Is this the same Taydo we were asked to assassinate three days ago?"

"The very." I put my arms around his waist. "Summer silliness."

"I'll say. Three groups of vultures circling over the same piece of budget. And with the Imperial Auditor looking on, the first one to move will be the first one executed, once the dust settles."

"I swear, Ran, I don't know how anything official ever gets done on this planet." We walked back to the divan. "Are you hungry? I saved a bowl of grapes and some seed cake."

"That's very nice of you, considering I—considering how busy I was in Braece."

I started toward the larder, then turned. "What is it about this summer, anyway? This is the fourth assassination we've been offered."

"And every single one of them too hot to touch. Never mind, we'll get a good commission soon."

"That's not what I mean. Don't people come to you for anything else any more?"

"Sweetheart, people rarely ask a sorcerer to do nice things. They rarely ask trial lawyers to do nice things. They rarely ask soldiers to do nice th—"

"I know what you're saying. Hazards of the profession. But whatever happened to love potions and luck spells? Why don't we get a nice newly wed couple asking for the blessing of random chance on their first year?"

Ran lay back on the divan and put his hands behind his head. "Is it nice to confuse someone into thinking they're in love with you? As for the newly wedded couple, it's a well-known law of magic that luck can only be bunched in one place by taking it away from someplace else. Practically all sorcery is at somebody else's expense."

"Then why do it?"

He said simply, "I was brought up to do it." Then he added, "And I'm very good at it." He was, too, the top of his profession. Ran doesn't make idle statements.

I sighed and went down the hall to the larder. His

voice called after me. "And it brings in money for our House."

"All right, all right."

He said something else while I was cutting the seed cake, but I missed it. I went back inside with the plate and handed him a large glass of water, which he drained at once. It's a long ride from Braece. "What did you say?"

He wiped his mouth on the sleeve of his robe. "I said, how's Kylla? I didn't know she was coming over today."

I sat down beside him. "Oh, Ran, I think you should talk to her. She's upset."

He put down the bowl of grapes. "What's the matter?"

I told him about Lysander's wedding options.

"No sister of mine—nobody from the first branch of Cormallon—is going to be anybody's junior wife."

I nodded, unsurprised. "Kylla said you would say that."

"I'm going to call Lysander right now—" He got up, took a few steps, then stopped, as rationality took over from the sting of what he would consider an insult. "No. No, I'd better find out what kind of pressure he's under, and all the details. Yelling at him won't get us anywhere."

"You want to run an investigation?"

"I hate to take the time. If they're really pressing him—I'll call him, courteously, and ask him, courteously, if he'd like to discuss the matter. How do I look? Do I look upset?"

"You look courteous."

"Good." He headed for the Net terminal in the downstairs office, and I followed. I settled myself in the stuffed chair in the corner—one of six in our house Ran had had made just for me—so that Lysander could see me when he came on. Family allies use the visual circuit as good manners, and manners required me to match them by not hiding the fact I was listening.

The call found him in the Shikron office building, I

recognized the surroundings. Why was Lysander keeping such late hours?

"Hello, Ran. Hello, Theodora." He looked tired. "Can I help you with something?"

He could be forgiven the phrasing; we'd never gone out of our way to call him, individually. If it were a social occasion, we would have left a message with Kylla at their house on the canal.

"Lysander, we're sorry to disturb you, we didn't realize you were at work. Uh, Kylla came by today . . . Theodora says she was a little upset. . . ."

He nodded, like a man receiving a sentence. "It was about Eliana Porath, wasn't it?"

"Yes," said Ran in a neutral voice. "We were hoping you could tell us more about what's going on."

Lysander let out a long breath. "Do you know why I'm still at work? I'm avoiding my relatives. I've got a flag on for every Shikron caller, telling them I'm busy handling an import crisis." He opened a drawer, pulled out a half-empty bottle of wine, and set it firmly on the table beside him.

"Imported Ducort," noted Ran.

Lysander nodded.

Ran said, still neutrally, "Do you want to talk about it?"

Lysander ran a hand through his dark hair, cut in fashionable capital mode, and opened his blue embroidered outer robe, now full of wrinkles. I'd always thought of him as a nice fellow, but rather forgettable; Kylla, however, had been in love with him for years. She'd succeeded in marrying for love alone in a world where that was rare. Perhaps more impressive, I understood that she'd engineered an affair with him on Cormallon territory back when her grandmother was still alive, a feat of planning and sheer nerve that wartime generals would be lucky to match.

He said, "It's politics, of course."

"Of course."

"Kylla won't believe that. I haven't even *met* Eliana Porath. I've been negotiating with her brother Kade—"

"You've been negotiating?" Ran's voice was sharp.

"*Talking*. I should have said talking. To keep them satisfied and the council off my back. Ran, I am in *kanz* so deep—"

His voice cracked with stress, and he covered it with an obviously false throat clearing. Ran said, more gently, "My brother, I'll be happy to help you any way I can, but you have to make it clear to me: You really don't want this wedding to go through? You'll pass up an alliance with a noble family?"

Lysander threw a paranoid glance around his empty office and stepped nearer to the Net. "Are you joking? If this goes through, *Kylla will torture me for the rest of my life.*"

Ran and I looked at each other. There was some truth to this.

I spoke up. "Where do things stand now?" Ran was doing pretty well with this man-to-man stuff, but I wanted a practical view of what we were up against.

Lysander said distractedly, "The Poraths are giving a house party on Greenrose Eve. Supposedly it's a holiday celebration, but considering they haven't given a party in about ten years, it's got to be so that I can get a look at Eliana without anybody's honor being officially at stake. That doesn't meant they won't take it personally when I turn her down," he added in a lifeless tone.

I said, "They're pushing this ahead pretty quickly, aren't they? That's just four days away."

"I understand their treasury's practically empty. —Don't hint about that to anyone, though! I'm not supposed to know it!"

"Lysander, of course not." I allowed the tiniest note of offense to creep into my tone. He was under a lot of pressure, but there was no reason to treat me like a typical barbarian when it comes to House secrets.

"I beg your pardon. —Wait! Ran, I can get you both invitations! You can get the lay of the land. . . ."

Ran was shaking his head, looking alarmed. "Ah, I don't think that's a good idea—" He hated formal

House affairs with a passion, particularly where the nobility were involved. Born into the second layer of aristocracy, he nevertheless regarded the Six Families the way everyone on Ivory did who was outside them: with a mixture of respect, distrust, and a basic knowledge that they were all out of their minds.

"No, it'll be a perfect chance for you to see what's going on!" Lysander's voice was enthusiastic. "Sorcerers have their ways of finding things out, don't they?"

"Don't believe everything you hear about sorcerers—"

"Oh, of course not! I'm so glad you called tonight. There's still time to get the invitations sent around!"

"Lysander—"

"I'd better get busy. Theo, I'll tell Kylla you're coming! She'll be thrilled!" He disconnected, rather with haste, I thought.

" 'Thrilled' is a strong word," I said, into the sudden silence of the office.

My husband and I looked at each other. Finally he said, "It looks like we're going to a party."

Chapter 2

I don't like Selians.

I don't know if you've ever been to the lovely world of Tellys, land (according to the brochures) of powdery beaches, flaming sunsets, and labor-saving devices of all kinds. Not to mention the only one of the four habitable planets in our sector that I hadn't set foot on—which, considering the cost of interstellar travel and the fact that I'm a private citizen, is a pretty impressive score, don't you think?

I'd never paid a great deal of attention to Tellys. I'd never planned on visiting there, and my studies were in other areas—cross-cultural myth and legend mostly, at the university on Athena, a field that involved a wide scan of the past but not much of the present. Standard culture is, well, pretty much standard; oddball, out-of-the-mainstream worlds like Ivory are rare. Tellys didn't have a lot to interest me, though I did think I might one day include it in a grand tour after a long and distinguished career as an Athenan scholar.

Of course, I hadn't actually planned on coming to Ivory originally either, and look how that turned out.

Anyway, most of Tellys is a relatively normal variant of Standard society, no great surprise, but clustered up and down the spine of mountainous islands bisecting the Eternal Sea we have the Selians—the People of the Sealed Kingdom. And I don't like them.

This is a prejudice based on personal experience—rather a contradiction in terms, but I don't know how else to phrase it. I had no opinion at all on Selians until I'd met a few of them, and gods, it's amazing how consistently unpleasant each new one is. Every one of them so absolutely secure about his superior place in the scheme of the universe. I know that this just stems from their repulsive (to me) philosophical beliefs, but it gets on my nerves anyway.

You might call this inconsistent in me, since I've always been tickled by the shameless egos of Ivorans. But the Ivoran ego seems—how can I put this—*innocent* in some essential way. Their high opinion of themselves doesn't seem to require grinding down you and me for contrast.

I'm glad the Selians are still a minority on Tellys, and it always depresses me a little to hear the occasional newscast saying how they're gaining power there. But if I hadn't learned it before, my time on Ivory had taught me that compromises sometimes have to be made with people you'd rather avoid. So I took off my jewelry and cosmetics, put on my best outer-robe for courage, and slipped out of the house one afternoon while Ran was away. Then I walked the three miles to the Selian Free Medical Wing of the Tellys Institute.

Tellys has a technological lead on the rest of us, and it extends to their medicine. Some Athenans and even Ivorans have taken medical training on Tellys, but they never stay to practice there: Non-natives are forbidden from joining the Physicians Union. Away from the drugs and devices so hard to get outside Tellys, their training doesn't count for as much as it might. But the Selian Clinic was staffed by Tellys doctors with all the latest equipment, and that's why I was there that quiet afternoon, when the rest of the capital was keeping the Day of Meditation. Tonight was Greenrose Eve, and the city would be jumping; today it was dead.

I had an agenda, of course. As far as I was able to determine, nobody had yet proven that Ivorans were a genetically different species. But they'd been separate from the rest of us long enough for it to be *possible*, and the experts I'd tried in the capital had been pretty tight-lipped about it. Ran and I had been married for a full Ivoran year, and I thought it was time to check my implant—it really should have dissolved by now—and learn what risks, if any, a pregnancy would bring. This was to be my baseline exam.

Physician Technocrat/2 Sel-Hara greeted me after a short wait. He was not much taller than I was, young, with the dyed-white hair of a pure high-caste Selian, though I noted he'd adapted to local custom sufficiently to wear a jewel in one ear. It was a large, blood-red stone and he wore it like a peacock. Not many men can carry off such drama, but clearly Physician Sel-Hara was not one to suffer self-doubts. Probably the knowledge that he was performing his two years of altruistic duty, and could soon go home secure in the fact that paradise was his, gave him a certain edge over his patients.

"Theodora of Pyrene," he said, rather neutrally, though I thought I saw a flash of passing contempt in his eyes when they moved over my Ivoran clothing. It may have been my imagination. "Far from home, are you not?"

I made a noncommittal sound.

"I've looked through the history you submitted," he said. "Over here."

I wanted to hold onto my wallet pouch—it contained certain items that as a sorcerer's partner I don't like to be away from—but he took it from me for no good reason I could ascertain and gestured me toward the examining table.

Scanners of all kinds they had in abundance, but like all doctors, Physician Sel-Hera felt that nothing could replace an eyeball inspection. For this, a Tellys-style variation of the same device used in the back hills of Ivory provinces for centuries was employed (aggressively, by Physician Sel-Hara). Unfortunately, in addition to succoring the indigent, this clinic specialized in well-paying Ivoran citizens lured in by the reputation of barbarian medicine, and the speculums were built to scale. To the scale of the average Ivoran woman, that is, not a barbarian a bit on the small side

even on her home planet. After a quarter hour of effort
Physician Sel-Hara dropped the third one into a ster-
ilization bucket and said again, "We will try a smaller
size."

For those of you who know what this means, I know
I have your sympathy and I thank you for it. For those
of you innocent of these procedures, let me sum up
the experience by saying it was painful.

"There should be discomfort, but no pain," pro-
tested Sel-Hara when I suggested that perhaps he
should skip to the smallest size right now. Or better
yet, after I'd taken a week or so off to heal. "After the
exam, I can make an appointment for you to see the
Clinic Psychologist, if you wish."

Implying that I was unbalanced for even thinking
such a thought. You see why I love dealing with Selians.

The more assertive among you are probably wondering why I didn't tell him off then and there. But you
have to bear in mind that a young woman with her legs
up in a cold draft, trying to control involuntary tears
of pain, is not in a good psychological position to take
the offensive. Besides, he had information I wanted.

He tossed a fourth speculum into the sterilizer. Ever
since that day I've regarded those things the way ancient criminals must have regarded thumbscrews.

"I need to know . . . ." I got out, working to keep
the tremor from my voice, "if . . . there's any reason
. . . gods! . . . I can't have . . . a healthy child."

"You will wait for the final report," stated
Discomfort-But-No-Pain Sel-Hara.

"But I mean . . . do you know of any reason . . .
why an Ivoran and an outworlder . . . ." I gasped and
lost control of my grammar.

Sel-Hara was apparently annoyed by the fact that I
was not working harder to collude with him in the
unreality that he was not causing me pain. He interrupted, in the flat accents of an implanted language,
"This is not the time for talking. This is the time for
listening." Then he added, as an afterthought, "How

can I tell in any case? You say your husband will not come in to be examined.''

I really did not feel up to discussing the complications of my marriage at that moment. I thought, if only I were a follower of na'telleth philosophy, and could rise above this kind of thing, concentrate on something else. Ivoran nursery rhymes? My mind was a blank. Out of nowhere I remembered my first class on Athena, a new-made scholar fresh off the ship, and started to chant mentally from Socrates on doctors and lawyers: ''Is it not disgraceful, and a great sign of want of good breeding, that a man must go abroad for his law and physic because he has none of his own at home, and put himself in the hands of other men whom he makes lords and judges over him?'' A message from the past straight to me, not that I had sense enough to take its advice. It did give me heart to go on, as Sel-Hara showed every sign of covering old and tender ground again.

I must have been muttering.

''You are distracting me,'' said Sel-Hara, in tones of annoyance.

'' 'Of all things,' '' I finished—not aloud—'' 'the most disgraceful.' ''

He glanced thoughtfully at his instruments. ''I will use the smallest,'' he announced, as though it were his own idea.

So I shut up and endured, figuring that questions about pregnancy were probably pointless anyway. After an exam like this, I wouldn't want anyone to touch my body for the rest of my life.

At the Selian Clinic, you take the doctor you're assigned. That's the way the Selians are.

Have I mentioned I don't like them?

Four hours later I was at the Poraths' house party. My body still felt as though someone had tried to ram an interstellar liner through it earlier that day, but I ignored it.

Ran and I had hired a carriage so we could arrive

in appropriate style with Lysander and Kylla, both of whom were uncomfortably silent during the ride over. When we stopped at the gate, Lysander reached out a hand to help Kylla down and she gestured it impatiently away. Ran and I pretended not to notice.

A security guard in white and slate gray bowed, and inquired whether it was our gracious party's pleasure to have our carriage driver directed to a proper location for the evening. He spoke the words by rote, clearly not impressed in the slightest by our matched pair of fashionably designed six-legged drivebeasts, decked out in crimson and bells. Looking down the road toward the parking area, I could see why. I considered the Cormallons wealthy, and we were, but tonight we were poor relations. There was even—

"Ran, look! The seal of the Athenan embassy on that carriage!"

He looked politely where I was pointing, then turned back toward the gate.

I said, "Why are the Poraths inviting outplanet visitors?"

He shrugged, his mind obviously on other things. It had gotten my attention, though. I still retained a dual citizenship from Athena; who was here tonight? Anyone I knew? Anyone I'd heard of? If it was one of the eighth-floor people from the embassy, would they ask why I hadn't been around to report over the last year?

Ran touched my arm, and we followed the security guide through the gate in the outer wall.

The Poraths lived in the old section, north of the canal, in a huge, rambling U-shaped villa that was badly in need of repair. The gate we entered led to the middle of the U, the Poraths' garden, a place of night-blooming roses and blue pools lined with white stones; around the garden, bordering the house itself, were three low, covered porches with wooden pillars of red and green lacquer. The lacquer paint was suspiciously fresh looking. The livery of the security staff was suspiciously fresh and neat, as well, and there were at least a dozen. No doubt hired for the evening from a bonded firm here in the capital, though they were discreet enough to wear Porath House colors.

A shadow flowed out of the evening shadows on the porch wing nearest us, and something glittered jewellike in its midst. A scaled snout emerged, small bandy legs . . . a lizard the size of a small child dragged itself to the edge of the porch. The body was dark green, but the flash from its eyes was emerald bright. A long tongue showed itself briefly, then retracted, as it tried to leave the porch and go exploring. A leash circled its neck, I was glad to see. The leash was garlanded with flowers, but seemed to be doing its job, for in its restlessness the lizard had pulled it fully taut.

"What the hell is that?" I asked.

"It's an emerald lizard," said Ran, in an uninterested voice.

"Is it Ivoran?"

"Of course. You don't see them much around here, they have to be imported from the western islands. It's been a fad of the families to have them as pets."

"What's wrong with a nice puppy?"

He smiled. "Emerald lizards are fairly tame. And they don't spray poison unless they're provoked. Supposedly."

"Poison?"

He pointed to the translucent sac in the crook behind the lizard's neck, just above the collar of the leash. "See, it's been emptied. Perfectly safe."

"I'm sure," I said. Just then a servant girl of about nine, robed in three shades of red, her hair set with jewels, stooped to pick up an empty glass from the floor of the porch. She patted the lizard on the head as she did so, then set the glass on a tray and continued on her way. The lizard tongue went in and out, in and out, and a sound not unlike purring reached me where we were standing.

"Just the same, I don't want one in our house," I said.

"Not likely, at the price." He took my hand and

turned me back toward the main party. We made our way into the throng.

The garden was clogged with guests. Grass was trampled right and left, food and drink servers maneuvered their way around the rim of the blue pools, and I saw a square of ripped silk outerrobe snagged on a thorn near the gate. Flute players were somewhere—somewhere high? I looked up and saw a treehouse filled with musicians. The Poraths were putting a lot on this roll of the dice. If their treasury was near empty tonight, they'd be in debt tomorrow.

"Ky—" I turned to address my sister-in-law and saw her standing at the garden entrance, nostrils flaring, scanning east and west like a hunting falcon with only one prey on its mind: the infamous Eliana Porath.

I said, "Do you know what she looks like?"

"No."

Neither did I, beyond the fact that Lysander'd said she had a face like a mud pudding. "You know, Kylla, this wasn't her idea."

"I know that." Kylla's expression did not change. Eliana Porath was about to start a new Trojan War.

Lysander stopped and tapped Ran. "Kade," he said. "Oldest son." He was looking toward a strapping, broad-shouldered young man with hair so short he could have been in the army. His face was brown and his muscles seemed to put him out of place in this array of peacock robes. His own blue silk outerrobe was open over an undertunic of plain, respectable white that might have been a work outfit; an inappropriate touch. Kade was laughing at some joke made by one of a knot of well-dressed people around him. As I watched, he stopped one of the servers, snagged a drink, and offered it to one of the other men.

Lysander said, "As soon as he spots me, he'll be over here. He's really pushing the marriage." On cue, Kade's glance passed over the crowd and Lysander twirled toward Ran, presenting the first son of Porath with a view of his back and a finely embroidered silk panel.

"You'll have to speak with him eventually," said Kylla coldly.

"Ran, help me," he said. "It's going to be a very long evening."

Ran drew him away. "Show us some of the other players," he said kindly. Kylla and I followed.

I drew a breath to say, *You're a little hard on him, aren't you?*—then thought the better of it and let it out again. "Do you know any of these people?" I asked her.

She glanced around indifferently. "Edra Simmeroneth—I went to school with her. Some of the provincial Sakris."

We passed the Athenan ambassador. He and I looked at each other. I've never been introduced to this one, but he might well have heard of me—I'd made enough of a pest of myself to his predecessor. Most likely he was only wondering what a fellow barbarian was doing in full Ivoran dress, attending a party of one of the Six Families. Occasionally I wonder things like that myself.

"Think anyone will get killed here tonight?" I asked Kylla. The nobility play some strange games among themselves.

She got hold of a glass of something pink off a passing tray and took a sip. "It would be rude, at a party," she said.

She turned then, and the contents of the glass went over the front of a young man trying to cross between her and the edge of one of the pools. "I'm so sorry! I beg your forgiveness, gracious—uh, noble sir." With a party like this one, it was better not to take any chances with your honorifics. "My clumsiness calls for a thousand years of penance—"

Sometimes these apologies can take days. The young man—I saw now that he was no more than a boy, really, slender and light-haired for an Ivoran—bowed and raised a hand to cut her short. His mouth had quirked very slightly with irritation, more at the apology, I think, than the spill, which had only seemed to surprise him.

"It's nothing," he said.

"I'm afraid I've ruined your suit," said Kylla.

"Ishin na'telleth," he said, *I'm not about to care.* Not with a shrug verging on rudeness, the way you hear it said every day in the streets, but a calm statement of fact. Then he bowed again, with great self-possession for one his age, I thought, and went off into the crowd.

We watched him go. "Well!" said Kylla. Then she looked around, and her eyes narrowed. "Where's Lysander?"

We'd lost Lysander and Ran.

If they were anywhere near Eliana Porath, we were in big trouble. Kylla and I wandered through the garden for an hour, cadging drinks and eavesdropping, but they were nowhere to be found. I spotted another barbarian across one of the larger pools, a fair-skinned blond woman talking animatedly to two men who had "important" written all over them. One of them had to be somebody very high up in government, because although he wasn't gauche enough to wear the Blue Hat of Imperial Favor to a social occasion, he wore a large pin on his robe in the shape of a hat, just to let us know.

They seemed to be arguing. Her hair was pulled back in a long Tellys-style braid, and underneath her open robe she wore snug-fitting Tellys pants. Although the Blue Hat held up his end of the argument, I saw that his eyes kept straying down toward those pants as though he couldn't believe what he was seeing. The woman was edging past middle-age, but with an undeniably trim figure. She looked away for a moment in pointed disgust with what someone was saying, and her eyes met mine.

She frowned, put her hand on the Blue Hat's arm, and asked him something. He turned and looked across the pool toward me. He shrugged. I heard the word "Cormallon" drift over the water.

Well, I suppose a lot of people had heard how Ran Cormallon had married a barbarian. It was nothing to get nervous about. Was it?

"Kylla, who is that woman?"

"What woman?"

Just then the flute players stopped playing and three clear horn notes split the summer evening. The guests fell silent. In the center wing of the house, the door to the porch opened and six stout security guards appeared carrying a sedan chair of ornate black wood. Atop the chair was an old woman in a shiny robe of royal purple. She looked pudgy but small, nearly as small as I am, dwarfed by the massive chair. Grandmother Porath, no doubt. The six sedan carriers, all in matched costume, carried her easily down the two porch steps into the garden. They let the chair to the grass with perfect coordination, where it sat like a throne in the clearing. In grandmother's wake came a girl of about eighteen, in a white robe with white satin slippers, her straight dark hair falling down her back. Two white puppies followed at her heels.

I turned to see how Kylla was taking this. She was absorbed, too intent on the scene to notice me. Then I looked around the garden for Lysander's reaction, but he was still missing.

The old woman gestured impatiently and Eliana—if that's who she was—came forward at once and handed her a blackwood cane carved at the top to match the sedan chair. Grandmother glanced down once, to make sure she would miss the puppies, then stamped the cane several times for our attention. It didn't make much noise on the ground, but she certainly did have our attention.

"Dear friends," she said. "You give us joy by coming to share our Greenrose Eve. Our house has been quiet too long. We trust it may always be filled with the sounds of visitors, like you, who will ever be welcome." She spat in the direction of a flowerbush. Then

she said, "As a token of our regard for you, further
entertainment has been provided. Eliana!"

The girl hesitated, looking genuinely uncomfortable. I supposed all hundred people jammed into the
garden were staring at her.

"Eliana!" said her grandmother again, in the voice
of one who brooks no nonsense.

Eliana stepped forward. Her cheeks were pink. It
wasn't cosmetic; they'd been pale before. She raised
her arms straight to the sky, her white robes falling
around her. She was certainly graceful, no doubt about
it.

"I ask," she began.

"Louder," snapped Grandmother.

"I ask the blessing of good fortune on this gathering," she said, more loudly. "Wine for the thirsty,
conversation for the wise, and entertainment for all."

Grandmother thumped her cane again. And snow-
flakes started to fall from the sky! It took a moment
to register with the guests, who probably, like me,
thought it was confetti. Until the points of cold landed
on our hands and faces and disappeared, melting.
There was a stunned silence and then a roll of ap-
plause that filled the garden; snow had fallen on the
capital maybe twice in the winters of the past century,
and now it was high summer. Obviously the Poraths
had hired a sorcerer and promised him a fortune. You
didn't see conspicuous display like this every day; it
was the kind of thing the Six Families used to do forty
or fifty years ago, before it went out of fashion.

Grandmother looked smug. Eliana had retreated to
the safety of the area behind the sedan chair. The old
woman peered around and called, "Jusik! My son!
Where's Jusik?"

There was a ripple of activity among the people on
the porch, and a few minutes later a man in his fifties
rushed out, puffing, and presented himself to her. The
First of Porath bowed over her hand, still out of breath.

She said, annoyed, "Where have you been?"

"Arranging the caterers, Mother."

"You've been sampling the goodies while I'm out here working?"

"I'm sorry, Mother. They had to be told where to stow the wine."

"Hmm, I'm sure they did. Never around when I need you, Jusik. I want you to tell the musicians to play some real music. "Trampling the Moons," or "Cousins Greeting," not this silliness they play today. I want to see some dancing."

Jusik Porath—shrewd businessman and tyrant to the rest of the family, or so I'd heard—looked around the garden uncertainly. "I don't think there's a lot of room for dancing, Mother."

Not unless we all shrank to the size of mushrooms. Grandmother Porath said, "You told me there would be dancing!"

Jusik's voice was lowered. "That's *tomorrow*, Mother. On the boat."

Ah. Not everyone was invited on the boat, apparently. But Lysander, of course, had gotten us aboard. If he could have arranged it, I think Lysander would have had us accompany him to the privy, he was that nervous about dealing with "the marriage thing," as he called it.

"Well, have them play something anyway." At once Jusik Porath raised his arm and made a motion in the air, and the flute players started up again. If I hadn't been standing relatively nearby, I wouldn't have heard the rest. "And Eliana, I want you to mix. Let people see you. You've got nothing to be ashamed of."

"Grandmother, I—"

"Oh, pooh, child, I know you're nervous, but you'll get over it. You can make too big a thing of modesty, you know."

"But you've always said—"

"I know what I've always said, but listen to me now. See if you can find this Lysander Shikron and walk by him a few times. You're a beautiful girl, Eliana. Mind you don't approach him, now! That'd be too easy. You must never look like you want the same thing your husband wants, girl, that's the key to success in a marriage.''

Eliana mumbled, ''We're not married yet, Grandmother.''

''No, and if we left it in the hands of your brother you might never be. Money's not enough to seal a wedding match, and he's a blockhead if he doesn't see it. For favorable terms, they've got to want what you've got. Where's Auntie Jace? She'll see you do it right.'' The old lady looked around, then jabbed her son with one elbow. ''Get Auntie out here. She can go 'round with Eliana and keep her out of trouble.''

Jusik bowed and spoke to one of the servants, who ran inside. I turned to see if Kylla was anywhere near critical mass, but she seemed under control. As far as I could tell.

A minute later a little, middle-aged, black-haired woman ran out. She wore a scarlet outerrobe and practically prostrated herself in the gathering snow at granny's feet. Going a touch far, I thought, but Grandmother didn't seem offended.

The woman extended her arms straight out; she was holding something. ''I've brought an umbrella for you, Grandmother,'' she said breathlessly.

The old lady made a motion, and one of the sedan bearers took up the umbrella, opened it, and held it above Grandmother's head. It was a huge scarlet thing, and the man held it as though he were personally unaware of any snow.

Fortunately it wasn't falling very heavily; but the garden was definitely colder, and what had fallen was sticking in patches on the grass. Like Eliana, I was wearing thin satin slippers, and I wondered if the Poraths had really thought through the consequences of their excursion into climate control.

Grandmother said, ''Auntie, take little Eli around to meet some of the guests, would you? I know I can count on you to see she makes the right impression.''

If Auntie bowed any further, her head would be in the snow. ''Your confidence honors me,'' she said.

Then she stood straight and added, in an entirely different voice, "Come along, Eli."

"Auntie Jace, I—my feet are cold. Can I get a pair of boots first?"

"What nonsense! Your feet would look enormous in boots. Is that the way you want people to remember you? Don't forget, 'It takes the endurance of a warrior on the inside—' "

" 'To make a delicate flower on the outside.' I know. But—"

"Then come along at once." She held out her hand like a young mother on the way to the park with her five-year-old.

As they moved off into the crowd, Kylla turned to me with a look of disgust on her face. "She's still in the charge of a nurse."

Dangerous though it might be to defend Eliana Porath, I felt obligated to say, "Ky, you know she's expected to have a chaperone."

"But a *defensive* chaperone. Not a nurse-chaperone, at her age."

I watched Auntie Jace and Eliana disappear among the guests, and saw a tall woman detach herself from the knot of people by the porch and follow them. The woman wore a robe tied back behind a pair of trousers that would have seemed provincial if they weren't embroidered silk, and there was a suspicious bulge on one side of her hips. "I think she's got one of those, too," I said to Kylla.

A voice said, "There they are!" and Lysander and Ran made their way to us.

"And where have you been?" Kylla inquired, as her husband meekly kissed her cheek.

Ran said, "We were talking to Kade first—didn't you see him catch up to us? And then we had to see the steward about the overnight arrangements. I sent back to the carriage for our cases, Theodora, and they're already stored in our room."

Kylla said, "How many of the guests are sleeping over at this house party, anyway? The house is big, but I think they'll have trouble tucking everybody away in a manner they'd be accustomed to.''

There was a reason for her asking. Lysander glanced at Ran, who gave him no help, then hemmed and said, ''Well, actually, just us four are actually staying for the whole night. But there'll be plenty of people on the boat ride tomorrow.''

''I see,'' said Kylla.

''I thought there would be more houseguests,'' said Lysander. ''But it wouldn't be polite to refuse at this point.''

''I said that I see.''

Ran put in, ''We do have something of a problem, though.'' He turned to me and said, apologetically, ''The Poraths keep cats.''

''Oh, gods.'' This put an entirely new complexion on the matter. ''Cats, in the plural?''

''Three,'' he said, with sympathy. ''Scythian yellow toms. I made inquiries, and I think they're mostly confined to the kitchen and downstairs.''

Kylla looked bewildered. Ran explained, ''Theodora is allergic to cats.'' He used the Standard word ''allergic,'' which has no Ivoran equivalent.

''I never met anyone who was allergic to cats,'' she said, with interest. ''What do you do, go into fits?''

''Everything but,'' I muttered. It always turns into a big deal when I find myself required to visit people with cats. The hosts invariably offer to move the cat to another room while I'm there, proud of their sacrifice, and they look at me disapprovingly when my thanks aren't effusive enough. Moving the cat accomplishes nothing—it's the little invisible bits from the cat hair that drive me to thoughts of suicide, and they're all over the house.

''You want to go home?'' asked Ran.

Kylla and Lysander looked at me, waiting. I had the feeling that both of them would kill me, for different reasons, if I said yes.

I said slowly, ''It *might* possibly be manageable, if they've never been in the upstairs rooms—''

"Wonderful!" Kylla beamed. "Darling—" this to Lysander—"do you know if we'll be staying next to Ran and Theo?"

"Uh, we'll be on the same floor," began Lysander. We all knew Kylla was wondering if somehow Eliana would be packaged and delivered to Lysander in the middle of the night, an unlikely event, but our Kylla was not her usual practical self.

"I think we'd better check on the cats' territory," said Ran. "The steward said they belonged to some odd person with the name Auntie Jace. Some maiden relative, I guess."

"A hired nurse," Kylla corrected flatly.

"Oh, you know her. Can you point her out?"

Kylla didn't move. "She's small, with curly hair, and wearing a scarlet robe."

Lysander said helpfully, "I'll go search for her—"

"The hell you will," said Kylla, grasping his sleeve and pulling him back. "Theo and I will locate this person. You two can go see that our things are left properly in our rooms."

I gave Ran a look that said, Trust me, it's a good idea. He touched Lysander's shoulder and said mildly, "Why don't we do that?"

Still slightly bewildered, Lysander was led away toward the house.

Kylla turned and began stalking through the party like a lioness on the prowl. She spotted Auntie Jace and cut her out of the herd with the practiced gesture of one accustomed to being noticed and obeyed. Eliana, standing miserably behind her, was ignored.

Auntie Jace took a step forward in response to Kylla's signal. "Yes?"

I jumped in, wary of how Kylla might handle this. My only current aim, after all, was to avoid a night of allergic suffering. "Your pardon, gracious lady, but we were told you own three excellent cats in the Porath household?"

". . . Yes," she answered, confused.

I smiled. "We're in the Shikron-Cormallon party.

We'll be staying the night. Perhaps you've heard?''
She nodded. "Forgive my weakness, gracious lady,
but I'm afraid I suffer from an unusual ailment—an
aversion to cats.'' I used the Ivoran word, which covers both allergies and emotional antipathies.

"I don't understand,'' she said.

"I sneeze, my nose runs, my eyes get red, I have
difficulty breathing . . .''

"Ah. Yes, I've heard of it. You're the first I ever
met with the sickness . . . gracious lady.'' She openly
observed my barbarian coloring, and threw in the gracious lady as though she wasn't quite sure whether I
deserved it or was trying to con her.

"I was wondering whether you could tell me if the
cats tend to go in the upstairs chambers.''

"I don't understand,'' she said again.

A long explanation followed. Finally she said, with
a hint of triumph, "I can solve this easily enough, my
lady. I'll just lock the cats in the kitchen for the night.''

I took a deep breath. "Ah, yes, that's very kind of
you—''

"They won't be happy about it, you know.'' She
fixed me with a severe look.

"No, yes, thank you, that's very thoughtful, but—''

"They'll probably wail all night long, they're used
to the freedom of the house. They don't do any harm,
you know.''

"I'm sure they don't. But what I really need to know is
whether they ever go in the upstairs bedrooms. . . .''

A quarter of an hour later, I gave up. I was never
going to know whether they went in the upstairs bedrooms. For all I could get out of Auntie Jace, they
might spend their afternoons there wenching and chas-
ing mice through the lace bedclothes. At last I said,
"Thank you, we'd better go now.''

I nudged Kylla. Actually I had to nudge her twice,
as I found she was staring at Eliana Porath. "We
should leave, Ky.''

Auntie Jace said, "Good evening to you both, then.

And the cats will be in the kitchen, so everything will be just fine, won't it, gracious lady?''

"Just fine," I agreed. I pulled Kylla away.

We walked toward the porch. I kept hearing a strange sound. Finally I said, "That isn't you gnashing your teeth, is it?"

". . . stupid idea . . ." I heard in a stream of muttering. ". . . council full of old men . . . if he thinks I'm going to stand by . . ." She stopped, looked up at the stars, took a deep breath and let it out. "So!" she turned to me brightly. "The offending cats will be locked up, and everything will be fine." She patted me on the shoulder and went off toward the porch steps.

"Oh, everything will be just perfect," I agreed. I followed her into the house.

Chapter 3

The party broke up rather earlier than it might have, probably due to soggy shoe syndrome. But don't think the Poraths' display was a failure; they'd impressed the hell out of everybody, and were more than pleased with themselves. The room we were shown to on the second floor had a glassed window facing the garden, well over my eye level. When the servant had left, I climbed up on the chest of bedclothes beneath it and screwed it open to get rid of the musty smell that pervaded the entire house, and to dissipate any residual cat allergens.

I climbed down again and said to Ran, "I am not happy."

He said, "They're doing their best. You're annoyed because Kylla's annoyed." He hung his best outerrobe on a peg by the door.

"And the room's chilly."

"You just opened the window."

"And I'm not closing it, either."

He smiled. I sighed and pulled back the quilts. If he wasn't going to fight back, it was hardly worth my being righteously indignant.

Ran got in next to me. "It's kind of nice being chilly under the covers. Reminds me of last summer, in the Northwest Sector."

"You can get nostalgic about that? At the time you didn't impress me with your cheerful outlook."

"But Theodora, we were 'courting the moon.'" This is a little bit like a honeymoon, but before the wedding party. Take my word for it, getting married on Ivory can be a complicated business. "It made being kidnapped by outlaws bearable." He kissed me. Oh, well, the hell with the cats. I helped him out of his party tunic. "What a day. I hate dealing on a social level with the Six Families."

"I can tell." His neck was like cordwood. "Let me make you more comfortable . . ."

"Why, Theodora, what a surprise."

"Oh, shush." Ran's so controlled as a rule, so damned intense when he has something to be intent about, that I like breaking him up. About twenty minutes later he said in a mellow voice, "You know, you're really getting good at this."

I looked up, shifting mood immediately. "What do you mean, I'm *getting* good? We've been married for a year. What was I like before?"

"Not again." He sighed. "That barbarian self-consciousness is your biggest enemy."

"I am *not* self-conscious." I felt myself getting red. "No more than anybody else, anyway." I turned my face into the pillow so he couldn't see my fair outlander cheeks catching fire.

A second later I felt a cool finger touch the edge of my face. "I guess I didn't say the right thing. —Theodora? Are you coming out of there?"

"No," I said, muffled, into the pillow. Not until the evidence was gone.

"You know, you shouldn't take the idea that you've improved as an insult. Whatever you were like before, I was more than happy. You barbarians take this whole subject so seriously—"

"You're digging yourself in deeper," I said, to an air pocket in the pillow.

"Ah." He fell silent. After a few seconds he said, "Do I take it we're finished for the time being?"

"Good night, Ran."

He pulled back the edge of my tunic, kissed my shoulder, and prudently turned over and settled down for the night.

* * *

Looking back, I tend to think of that day as the Evening of Snow, followed by the Night of Cats. I had good reason to look back on it later, but we'll get to that. As I lay there in the dark hour after hour, perfectly awake, it became more and more clear to me that the Porath house felines had the run of the upper bedrooms. In fact, as my nose turned into a geyser, it became clear that they spent substantial amounts of time there.

I got up in the dark and felt around in my case till I found my handkerchief. About an hour later I got up and felt around till I found Ran's handkerchief, a thing of pure dazzling linen that I hated to use for its necessary purpose. I made the mistake of rubbing my eyes, and one of them started to itch fiendishly.

Ran, of course, slept the sleep of the innocent through all this. A base part of me longed to wake him up so that he could suffer too, but I managed to ignore it. It wasn't his fault, after all. (Base Part of Theodora: "No, but he's put it out of his mind easily enough, hasn't he? It would serve this household right if you died under their roof, then maybe they would have listened to you!" Under the pressure of prolonged discomfort, I was rapidly reverting to a five-year-old mentality.)

Eventually I found myself lying there listening to the sound of my breathing—an audible, wheezing sound, like a steel whistle. My windpipe felt as though it had closed up to the size of a straw.

This wasn't working. And perhaps more seriously, I only had about a third of a handkerchief left. A dark future loomed before me.

I got out of bed, padded across the carpet, and took the Andulsine quilt off the chest by the window and a bound copy of Kesey's *Poems* from my case. I stole a look at Ran, draped over the majority of the mattress, dribbling into the silk pillow sheet. The man was dead to the world. Not that he wasn't a fine-looking corpse. I thumbed my unhappy nose at his sprawled figure, and taking my stiff, damp silk shoes, I left the room.

It was verging on dawn—still very early, as it was summer—and the house was quiet. I went downstairs, threaded my way along the halls, passed through the darkened kitchen, and emerged onto the long wooden porch that faced the garden.

There I found a new world. Past the steps of the porch, snow covered everything. The fountain, the rocks, the discreet lights of the garden, all transformed by a white, alien weight. The party might as well never have happened. The silence had a quality one never heard in the capital. Possibly I was the only one who had ever seen this sight: That new-morning-of-the-world freshness that marks a virgin snowfall, but laid over the rich, verdant, never quiet, neverending summer of a capital formal garden. I may have been the only human, at any rate; a robber-finch sat in a wet tree bough near the porch, its yellow chest puffed for warmth, surveying the view with a look that I could only have called dazed if I'd seen it in my own species. Over on the east wing porch, the emerald lizard lay stuporous in the chill, a scarlet blanket thrown over him, the leash in a flowery pile on the floor. By now, of course, the garden should have been full of birdsong and insect hum, and the rustle of a housecat or two on the prowl.

The cats wouldn't want to go out and play today, I thought with some vindictive satisfaction. I settled down onto the chaise at the side of the porch and pulled the quilt around me. I felt better than I had all night. After about half an hour my nose stopped running, and I fell asleep to the constant throb of my right eye.

A couple of hours later, it felt like, I heard sounds. Opening my eyes from my cozy nest in the chaise, I saw three servants out in the garden, brushing snow from the paths with great straw brooms. An old, bent woman in a gray outerrobe opened the two wooden doors on the east side of the courtyard that probably led to the pantries. I heard a jingle of keys as she passed the porch. She saw that I was awake and smiled at me, a gap-toothed smile. I smiled back and went to sleep.

Something woke me again, not long after. I lay there and started to think about all the chores that had to be done before breakfast: Ran's outerrobe ought to be handed over for pressing, he always forgot when he slept late, and I should do something to make myself look presentable—I stopped. What would I accomplish in life that was better than what I had now? Lying here under the purple and blue rectangles of the quilt, with a copy of Kesey's *Poems* by my feet and the wet branches and clear false-winter sky in front of me. The muted sounds of pots and pans came from the kitchen, letting me know that someone else was up and there would be society when I wanted it—soon enough, in fact. I looked out at a speckled black bird sitting on the railing about two feet from my face. Oh, it was good to be human, and have consciousness, and be on the receiving end of ten thousand years of my ancestors' effort, that gave me this quilt and this sheltering porch and the muted sounds that came from inside.

Yes, I felt pretty satisfied with myself as I burrowed down into the quilt. It was one of those moments that come once or twice a year, the kind that give such spiritual sustenance you can deceive yourself into thinking you can handle the rest of your existence. "While I enjoy the friendship of the seasons, I trust nothing can make my life a burden to me." That's from one of the ancients, who made a great deal about living by a pond. I spent the chief part of my life on Athena reading through the old records, and I must say they do add texture to one's adventures.

Musing sleepily on one level, while on another I enjoyed, animal-like, the warmth of the quilt and the cold of the air on my face, I became aware that one of the pairs of distant footsteps was coming closer. I opened an eye.

The redoubtable Auntie Jace. She was glaring at me in disbelief.

"Uh, hello." I straightened the blanket. Absurd to

feel so guilty suddenly, as though I'd been caught
stealing from my hosts. The look on her face would
have been appropriate if I'd had.

"What do you think you're doing?" Suppressed
outrage was in her voice. She was wearing a rainbow
nightrobe that she pulled more tightly around herself,
her knuckles white.

"I couldn't sleep in my room, so I came down
here." What time was it, anyway? The kitchen staff
was still mostly asleep, from the sound of it.

"Not sleep? In the fine room the Poraths have given
you? I saw the bed linens changed only yesterday, saw
it myself!"

"Yes, I'm sure—"

"And saw the room was swept out, too!"

Didn't do a very good job, though, I thought. "Yes,
well, I told you I'm allergic to cats—"

"Made me lock up my dear friends, and here you
are downstairs anyway! Insulting our hospitality!"

I'm not at my best when I'm half-asleep, to begin
with; and social crises often throw me completely off-
stride. A lot of thoughts came to me: That she hadn't
locked up her dear friends, because I'd seen them
roaming the halls on the way down; that the open air
here was more friendly to my allergies than any room
inside, upstairs or down—though I couldn't see me
making that clear to this tiny madwoman.

My mind was a blank. Frantically I thought, What
would Ran or Kylla do?

And an answer came. I sat straight up, took the
apology out of my voice, and said, "Forgive me, but
is this the way to address a guest?"

She actually took a step back. I remembered that
she was only a retainer here, and I was not her guest
in any case. Still hearing Ran's coldest tones in my
mind, I echoed, "If the Poraths have some objection
to my behavior, I trust they will honor me with it. I
would not want to cause them any offense after their
generosity of yesterday."

My most formal capital accent: It's amazing how the

words will come sometimes when you pretend you're somebody else. Auntie Jace looked shocked.

She stood there frozen, so I added, "Should I go and inquire of them if they have some complaint to lodge?"

At this she took several more steps back, then turned and went down the porch steps, off through the garden. She was wearing ankle boots under her rainbow robe. I heard her muttering as she squished through the snow: "No consideration for other people . . . barbarians making themselves at home . . . never thought I'd live to see it. . . ."

I closed my eyes again. Maybe I should have stayed upstairs. But no, I'd've been a complete wreck by morning, and they still expected me to go on that damned boat ride today. And it would have caused quite the little brouhaha if my throat had closed up completely during the night.

I fell asleep imagining the tomb marker: She Died Polite.

When I woke an hour later, A Scythian yellow tom was sitting on the edge of the chaise watching me. Lethally long-haired, champion shedders that they are, I had not perhaps picked the best house to stay overnight in. Out here in the open air, though, I felt confident enough to actually consider stroking him before common sense reasserted itself.

The house was up and stirring, so I returned to our room for a quick wash and dress, then took a plate of hard market bread and Iychan apples out to the porch again for breakfast. This morning was the boat ride on the old capital canal. As it turned out, our carriages didn't leave till almost noon, and I spent a boring few hours in the nasal safety of the garden, where the winterspell was breaking up and the ground was turning muddy. I left the social niceties to Ran, who claimed I was laid up (in my room, he allowed them to infer) with some malady of my delicate barbarian constitution. The Poraths expressed proper sympathy and promptly forgot about me, to my relief.

I wandered the length of the garden, down to the guardhouse by the gate, and back again. Two of the Scythian yellows followed me as I went, in instant and touching loyalty. This is typical of my experience with cats.

At noon, when Ran emerged to accompany me to our carriage, he observed my new followers. He shook his head. "Why do you let them rub against your ankles? This always happens, Theodora. You know that they know you're allergic."

"Yeah, but they also know I'm not going to kick them away." Increasing my speed to avoid one of the toms, I began shaking the hem of my robe, careful not to touch any gold hairs. "I thought this was a *morning* boat ride."

"Try to get the nobility out of bed before noon. Eliana was dead to the world—wouldn't even answer till an hour ago, and came out still yawning. Just as well, I guess. I wouldn't want to have to watch her and Kylla stare at each other over the marmalade. Grandmother and Jusik are the only punctual souls in the house."

We came to the gate, and one of the security guards stepped over to open it for us. He was young, with curly brown hair cut short, and he wore his uniform with a faintly uncomfortable air. "Noble sir and lady, may I ask you if the family looks ready to leave yet?"

He must have been preoccupied; no "forgive my presumption," or any of the usual superfluous layers of politeness. Ran looked at him speculatively. "They were getting their cloaks when I left. If you're to accompany them on the boat, I'd suggest you prepare to go now."

He nodded. "Thank you, sir. Thank you, my lady." His eyes met mine briefly, and I couldn't help but be struck by the fact that they were a remarkably deep, fine shade of brown. I also couldn't help noticing there were black circles in the sun-gold skin beneath them.

And that both eyes had a reddish cast that usually comes from a recent abuse of drugs or alcohol. Not that there was any need to be judgmental: One of my eyes had no doubt had a similar appearance just last night, from quite a different cause. He hauled open the gate, waited till we were through, closed it, and started walking back through the garden toward the house.

"Where are Kylla and Lysander?" I asked Ran.

"They're riding with the Poraths in the family carriage."

We looked at each other. I said, "I hope Grandmother Porath has some discretion in the seating arrangements."

"You know," he said, "I rather doubt that she does."

The boat was big for a canaler. There were two levels for passengers, an enclosed one on the main deck and an upper level open to the air. The musicians, I saw, had been brought back for the day, and their ranks had swollen to include more horn and string players.

About two dozen of last night's partygoers had been asked back for the ride. I saw the blond Tellys woman, again talking animatedly, this time to a knot of three new people. She spotted me across the room as I came in and I saw her react. She made a motion to her listeners as though she were going to leave them, but one, a woman, put a hand on her arm and said something. And then the blond woman was off again, gesturing authoritatively as she spoke. She was a naturally strong talker, it seemed.

The boat loaded up and cast off into the canal. I pressed my face against the glass as we pulled out, and saw a carriage drive up madly to the pier, stop short, and discharge a red-faced man in multicolored robes who threw something down in disgust and waved his arms angrily before whirling around and getting back in his carriage. Apparently some people are too tardy even for the nobility.

I turned back to the big salon on the main deck. Here all was happiness and light. Grandmother's chair had been brought in, and when the musicians struck up, a look of serene joy came over her—you wouldn't have known it was the same woman. Kade took his sister Eliana out onto the floor and led six other couples in a pattern dance, one of the stately things I hear they do at court. They "bowed to the sun," "bowed to the moons," "laced the boot," "kissed the stranger," "circled their partners," and did any number of complicated figures before the tune was over. Lacing the boot was particularly complex. One young woman flubbed it and had to be drawn back into place by the person next to her, several beats too late.

The second the music stopped, Grandmother Porath stood up—it seemed there was no pressing constitutional reason for her to use her sedan chair—and walked to the head of the couples. "Kade!" she snapped. She held out her hand. He bowed, took it obediently, and Eliana withdrew from the dance. I noticed that her defensive chaperone, the tall skinny woman, followed her as she moved away.

And this time there was none of that slow, stately stuff. Grandmother led them in a wild country pattern dance, and if you've never seen one I can only say it's a lot like the previous dance, only about a hundred times more enthusiastic. Speed and the ability to jump are essentials.

Ran had wandered to the front of the salon to watch the jabith player, and I found I was standing next to somebody familiar. Sixteen or seventeen, light brown hair, nicely dressed . . . He was watching me, too. "Excuse me," I said. "Have we met, noble sir?" The "noble sir" prompted my memory; this was the young man Kylla had spilled a drink on last night.

"We were nearly introduced," he said, with a dry look that told me he had not forgotten. "I'm Coalis." He gave it to me in three syllables: Co-al-is.

I must have looked blank. He wasn't offended by it; apparently he expected people not to know who he was. "Kade is my brother," he explained. Apparently he did expect people to know Kade.

And he was right. "Ah," I said.

"You're the barbarian that Cormallon sorcerer married," he remarked. Usually they don't come right out and say it.

"Yes. I'm Athenan."

"Oh? What's your field of interest?"

Now, that was an unusual thing for an Ivoran to say. "Cross-cultural myths and legends. I haven't done a lot of work in it lately, though."

"No, I'm the same way. Other things interfere."

I raised an eyebrow. "What's *your* field of study, noble sir?"

"Coalis, please. It's na'telleth philosophy."

"You're—" I stopped.

"What?"

"I was going to say, you're a little young for na'telleth philosophy, aren't you? I tend to associate it with the old and jaded."

He said without emotion, "No point in not getting a head start."

I supposed not. I wondered what the Poraths thought about their second son opting out of the game. Well, he seemed like a frank sort of boy—"Are you planning on going into a monastery? Or is this just a personal study?"

"I've been accepted at Teshin. I go on the winter solstice." He took a glass from a table and sipped at it; I saw it was water. "My family wants to give me the summer to change my mind. Prediction is fruitless—" This is a na'telleth saying—"but I see nothing so far that would change it."

I've always been fascinated by this sort of conversation with strangers. Completely ignoring etiquette, I said, "I suppose they've been throwing you at nice young girls for months."

"They have. It's a pointless exercise. Sex isn't prohibited to monks, you know, only passion. And marriage."

What's wrong with passion and marriage? I decided not to say it; it seemed like the kind of answer that would take up the rest of the day.

"What do you think of this wedding thing?" "Wedding thing"—I was starting to sound like Lysander.

He understood what I meant. "Not the best idea Kade's ever had. But Grandmother's supporting it, so I guess it will happen." He might have been talking about the rain.

I was saying, "So this was Kade's idea—" when Ran approached and took both my hands. He nodded his head toward the dance floor.

I stood fast. "Coalis, this is my husband, Ran Cormallon."

"Honored by this meeting," Coalis said agreeably. "We passed at breakfast, I think."

"The honor is mine. Come on, Theodora, dance with me."

"My leg's broken."

"I know the jabith player, he used to live with one of my aunts. He's going to play 'The Other Side of the Mirror' next for us. I know you can do that one, I saw you do it at our wedding."

"The other side of the mirror" is an Ivoran term that implies the meeting of life, love, and death; that sunny mornings are followed by rainy afternoons, and that we'll all come to dust in the end. The other side of the mirror is a skull. Unless you understand that it's a wildly cheerful dance, you'll miss the point.

I said, "Coalis here is a na'telleth. He'd probably love to dance this one."

Coalis smiled austerely. Ran pulled me out onto the floor.

I found that we were standing, alarmingly, at the far right of the double row of dancers. "We're lead couple!" I said.

"I know."

The musicians looked ready to start up any moment. I hissed and pulled his sleeve to make Ran face me.

We'll have to go first, and everyone will be watching us! I don't know this dance that well!''

"Nonsense. You'll do perfectly well, you always do."

Ran's often overinflated views of my capabilities can be soothing, but there are times when reality must be injected into a situation. I turned to the woman on my left and smiled politely. "Would you mind being lead couple? My partner and I are going to the bottom."

Ran said, "Theodora—" but I ignored him, grasped his hand, and pulled him to the end of the row. "That wasn't necessary, was it?" he said, as we took up our facing positions.

Ran's ego rarely admits other viewpoints—actually, it's one of his more endearing qualities. Mind you, he'll yield to my wishes often enough, he just makes it clear that he thinks I'm crazy.

At that moment Grandmother Porath announced, from the chair she'd retired to, "We'll begin this dance from the left side! Musicians!"

The row of dancers all turned to us. I felt the blood leave my face.

"Barbarian self-consciousness," murmured Ran. "Don't panic. We can do this."

My mind had gone completely blank.

"Left-right palm touch," said Ran, as the music started up. "Then place, advance, place. And *turn*—no, to your left—"

Moments of terror followed by moments of enjoyment. I've always gotten a kick out of that backward-skipping thing during the jig, and did this time too, until I skipped right into the two people behind me. However, we all seemed to survive it.

When it was over, we all bowed and I said to Ran, "I need to go somewhere and sit down." I felt as if I'd been digging ditches for a day and a half.

"Kylla and Lysander must be on the top deck. I hear there are benches up there."

"Terrific."

We made our way across the salon to three doors

behind the musicians' seats. Two of the doors had
stairs going up. Ran said, "One of them's probably to
the watch. —You look tired. I'll see which one goes to
the upper deck." He started up one of the staircases.
I leaned against the doorjamb, turning to face the salon, and found my sleeve tugged—by Grandmother
Porath, who'd come by to harangue the musicians.

"I know," she said, sympathetically. "Sometimes
it's so hard to know where to go."

I wasn't sure whether she meant directionally, or if
it was a reference to my nearly sending four people
keeling over in "The Other Side of the Mirror."

I said, "Do you mean in the dance or in life?"

She cackled. "The dance. I've *done* life."

"Theodora?" Ran's voice floated down. "This is
it."

I bowed to Grandmother Porath and went up the
stairs. At the top it was all sunlight and soft winds,
and the buildings of the capital passing slowly on either
side of the canal. About a half dozen people had come
up here for the relative silence and the relaxed atmo-
sphere; Kylla and Lysander were sitting on a bench
near the railing. Ran and I joined them. A striped aw-
ning had been set up to shade this side of the boat.

"Nice," I said tentatively, wondering how things
were between them.

We were passing under Kyme Bridge. Lysander said,
"You can see the roof of our house if you stand in
front."

"We'll probably be passing it in another ten minutes," added Kylla, calmly enough. At least they didn't
seem to be throwing things.

Unfortunately, one of the Poraths chose that moment to invade the upper deck: Kade, architect of "the
marriage thing," and probably the person Kylla least
wanted to see, next to Eliana, emerged from the stairs.
He peered around the deck, then started angrily toward the opposite rail. The security guard who'd let
us out the gate that morning was leaning there weakly,
looking none too well.

You could hear Kade's voice clear across the deck.
"Aren't you supposed to be watching my sister?"

The guard's voice was harder to catch. ". . . fine,
on the boat . . . nothing's going to happen . . ."

"That's not your job to say! Your job is to watch
her!"

". . . job is to watch everybody . . . defensive
chaperone all the time . . . better protection than the
Emperor . . ."

Kade glanced around at the rest of us—I must honestly say that our group had fallen silent and was
eavesdropping openly—and realized he was creating a
spectacle. He grabbed the guard and hauled him over
behind the stairway entrance, where their voices became unintelligible.

"Oh, well," I said, with some disappointment. A
minute or so later, the guard, looking rather subdued,
preceded Kade down the stairs.

Kylla turned to her husband. "Even their security
guard doesn't want to spend his life with Eliana Porath."

"Oh, gods, Kylla—"

Ran caught my eye and we withdrew a few feet to
the railing. He said seriously, "You know, I don't see
any good way out of this. The Poraths have put their
House on the line so obviously, it'd be a slap in the
face if Lysander tries to squeeze away."

"That's *why* they're being so open."

"Trap or not, it'll still be an insult. And you know
how the Six Families are. Murder's a game to them.
They do it all the time without reason, and when they
do have a reason—" Ran's face expressed his disap-
proval of killing for impractical motives; it was a judgment he shared with all the commoner classes of Ivory,
right down to the market square beggar.

"So what are you saying? That Kylla's going to have
to grin and bear it? She won't, you know."

"I—" He broke off, looking surprised. "Did you
feel that?"

"Feel what?" Something in his voice made me nervous. I put a hand on his arm for reassurance, and just then there was a kind of shimmering, a faint tremor. There'd been an earthquake in the capital about sixty years ago, but there was no reason to think we were due for another. Except that something different and uncontrollable was definitely happening—

I took a step back and looked around, but everything was all right: The buildings, the canal, the passengers still intent on their conversations. Whatever it was seemed to have stopped.

I looked at Ran. He was leaning against the rail. "We're getting closer to it," he said thickly. His face was white.

The only thing we were getting closer to was Catmeral Bridge, near Kylla and Lysander's villa. I went back to Ran. "What is it? Do you want me to get help?"

There was a commotion on the level beneath us. Somebody yelled. A voice tried to answer reassuringly, there was another yell, and running footsteps. The window just below us was open and we could hear it all. There was a woman's scream.

I looked over the side of the boat. Someone was in the canal; a blue and gold silk robe floated, bobbing and then disappearing as the wearer sank, dragging it into the gray water. A few seconds later there was the flutter of an arm, and a dark head appeared and vanished.

Splashes directly under us marked two security guards diving out the same window. The boat was slowing down. Everyone on the upper deck had joined us at the railing to stare. "Who is it?" I heard someone ask. There was no answer. The guards cut their way through the water, diving and reappearing where the head and arm had made their last appearance. They must have spent a good twenty minutes swimming back and forth to the boat and then diving again and again. I was impressed with their training: Swimming is not a widespread art on Ivory.

Kylla, Lysander, Ran and I all watched silently, along with the rest of the boat, until the two guards returned. There was no sign of a body.

We looked at each other. Blue and gold silk: Kade.

Chapter 4

We missed most of the confusion downstairs. I was told later that that scream we'd heard was Grandmother Porath, who'd fainted immediately and had to be laid on some pillows the crew brought out. Between dealing with her and watching the security guards dive for his son, Jusik must have been in a state.

When Ran and I went downstairs, we found Eliana being clutched by the old lady, who was lying propped against a set of red cushions, looking about a hundred years old. The two security guards were standing dripping by the bar. And Jusik was in an argument with the steersman about turning this damned boat around, *now!* so they could return home at once. A typical Ivoran of the great families, nothing was more important than returning to safe, familiar territory in times of stress. I could see Eliana agreed with him. The steersman kept trying to explain that the canal wasn't wide enough here to turn in.

Finally Jusik bowed to physical law and announced to his guests that it would be another hour before they would come around to the pier again. Please make yourselves as comfortable as possible, etc.

I found myself drifting over toward the bar and thought maybe a drink wouldn't be a bad idea. I'd never even spoken to Kade, he meant nothing to me, but it was impossible to avoid the shock of his death in the faces of the people he *had* known. And in conjunction with whatever Ran and I had experienced upstairs, it threw me off balance.

The bartender had wandered away, so I poured my-

self a pink ringer and offered one to Ran. He shook
his head. The security guard who'd argued with Kade
and then dived for him in the canal sat down heavily
on a bench next to the bar, creating a puddle of water
beneath it. He pulled off his wet jacket and dropped it
in a ball at his feet. He glanced over toward the old
woman, where Eliana sat rubbing her hands, and his
face was as drawn and pale as hers.

No wonder. This wasn't going to look any too good
on his record. Coalis had already taken the other place
on the bench; he was staring at nothing, in a state of
shock. I had the rare experience of seeing a professed
na'telleth completely and obviously at a loss.

I suddenly grasped that, whatever his relationship
with Kade had been, the Poraths no longer had an heir
and a spare. Coalis was now first son of the House.
He must have realized by now that he could forget
about being a monk.

It was funny, but I could empathize a lot more
quickly with the destruction of a dream, selfish though
that may be, than with any sorrow over Kade, whom
I'd only known as an irritant. I poured a new ringer
into a large glass, walked over to Coalis, and held it
out.

"Medicinal purposes," I said. "It won't do any
harm."

He accepted it and started drinking. Poor kid. He'd
lost that self-possession that made him seem ageless
last night, and looked like what he was: A boy in his
late teens, who'd just taken a major blow.

I realized that the still-wet guard next to him was
shivering. "I'm sorry," I said belatedly. "I can get
you one, too. And they ought to have brought you
some towels." Typical insular House reaction, to take
care of themselves and forget everybody else.

"Thanks," he said. He wiped his nose with his arm
in a distracted sort of way.

I turned to go, when a voice said to Coalis, in pure
provincial argot, "Tough break, kid."

A voice I knew very well. A voice that could not

possibly be here. I turned back, shocked, to see the
Imperial Minister for Provincial Affairs holding out a
towel to the shivering guard. "You look like you could
use this." Then he smiled at me. "Hello, Theodora."

A height between medium and tall, dark hair shot
with premature gray, the calm certainty in his face of
a very heavy falling rock. He wasn't wearing his
glasses. Stereth Tar'krim, one of the few outlaw lead-
ers to ever successfully get out of the Northwest Sector
and into the Imperial power structure . . . and the only
one who kept his old name.

I became aware that my mouth was open, and I
closed it. "What are you doing here? Where were you?
I didn't see you with the guests before." Not the most
polite, or even most coherent greeting, but it was out
before I could think about it.

"I was downstairs, chatting with friends." There's
a kind of phoniness, when Stereth uses words like
chatting, that he enjoys and likes his listeners to enjoy.

Coalis looked up dully. "You two know each
other?"

I might have asked the same thing. What was Stereth doing on an intimate conversational basis with the
younger son of Porath? Or rather, the first son, now. I
looked at him speculatively.

He said, "I suppose this means Ran's aboard, too.
I should have come upstairs earlier. Where is he?"

"Right here." Ran appeared behind him, looking,
I am glad to say, nowhere near as shocked as I felt.

Stereth turned happily. "Sokol," he said. Quietly,
thank the gods.

Ran's eyes went wide, and he took Stereth by the
arm and pulled him behind the bar. I followed. In a
fierce whisper he said, "Do *not* call me Sokol."

"Your past is nothing to be ashamed of."

"I'm not ashamed, and *don't do it.*" Ran was morally entitled to give orders on this subject, as it was
Stereth's fault that we'd once used aliases to begin
with. "What's going on here?" Without waiting for

an answer, he added, "Look, I don't want my family name pulled into some new affair of yours."

"I beg your pardon, old friend, but you'll have to tell me what you're talking about." There was a slight edge of coldness in his voice now.

"Kade Porath. He was killed by sorcery."

I said, "He was?"

"That's interesting," said Stereth. He said it thoughtfully, not with sarcasm. "I was downstairs when it happened, but from what I heard it did sound strange."

"Are you seriously telling me you had nothing to do with this? You seem to know the new heir pretty well, Stereth. And I know how you like to make alliances."

He did not appear offended. "I'm seriously telling you I had nothing to do with it. I never lie to my crew, remember."

"You don't tell them the whole story, either. And anyway, we're not in your crew anymore." He took a deep breath. Stereth was the one person who could sometimes put Ran at a loss. "We were *never* in your crew."

This was debatable. We'd spent the previous summer as involuntary guests and co-conspirators in Stereth's outlaw band. Fortunately, the Imperial prosecuters were still unaware of this. The penalty for the use of sorcery as a weapon against the Empire is decapitation for every member of the family. Technically, that would mean every Cormallon on the planet, down to the last newborn child. I didn't want to test the law to see if they'd go through with it.

I said, "So, Stereth—did you buy new eyes from the barbarians?"

"I beg your pardon?"

"You're not wearing your glasses."

"Ah." The Legend of the Northwest Sector felt vaguely around an inside robe pocket. "I left them in my other robe."

Ran was giving me this look that said, *Must* we speak to him socially?

I went on, "And how's your wife?"

From his seat by the wall, Coalis was watching us all with great interest.

"You know Cantry, she never changes. Ah, Theodora, Ran, I believe you've met my secretary."

I turned and got another in the series of small electric shocks I'd been receiving all day. A member of the old outlaw band I'd never expected to see again—"Clintris?" I said disbelievingly. A stocky woman, born to disapprove, her hair pulled back severely; wearing a set of robes she never could have afforded in the old days, that nevertheless managed to seem unbecoming.

Clintris . . . Ran groaned. "Oh, gods, are they all here?"

I said, "Clintris, how are you?" There was warmth in my voice; we'd actually gotten to the point where we were getting along, by the time our adventure ended. She glowered back. What had I—

Oh. I'd called her by her road name, that we never used to her face. "Tight-Ass" would be the nearest translation.

Stereth corrected us. "The lady Nossa Kombriline."

"Oh, right. Of course." I bowed to her and she inclined her head a fraction of a millimeter. Clintris was not a forgiving sort.

She turned at once to Stereth. "Sir, I've been talking to the captain." Nobody avoids talking to Clintris if she's set on reaching them. "We'll be at the pier in about forty minutes. You have an early dinner tonight with the undersecretary from the department of power, and I believe in any case we should distance ourselves from . . . the events of the day."

"In other words, you'd like me to bundle us both into a closed carriage and go straight home."

"It's my recommendation."

Clintris—that is, the lady Nossa—was in her element as a governmental secretary, though her accent was still tinged with the provinces and the scarlet outerrobe she wore looked as though it had been hastily wrapped around a tree stump with a face. I glanced down at my own clothing involuntarily; was that how I looked in Ivoran robes?

I looked up to find Stereth meeting Ran's eyes. "I'd recommend the same course to you, old friend."

Ran looked away toward the rows of liquor bottles, as though they were the most interesting objects on the boat. "We're here with some relatives. We'll have to see what they want to do."

"Oh, yes, the Shikrons. I suppose they may feel the family has some claim on them. What with the engagement, I mean."

Typical Stereth. But I suppose Coalis had told him. Ran said, "Nobody's engaged yet." It came out more firmly, I think, than he meant it to.

Stereth raised an eyebrow. "And nobody will be, if you have your way. I see. I guess you have more reason than I do to be glad Kade had an urge to go swimming."

He smiled. Ran turned a blazing look on him, and I grasped my husband's sleeve. "Shouldn't we find Kylla and Lysander and see what they want to do?"

I could see him banking the fires. Ran does not approve of losing one's temper in public; he thinks it's common. Stereth is one of the only people in the world who can bring him so near to it.

"If there's anything I can do," said Stereth, as Ran turned away. "And let me know if you need a ride."

Ran strode off toward the stairwell, making a sound very like a growl.

We took Kylla and Lysander home in our carriage. They were both very quiet. Ran was sitting beside Lysander, and I held Kylla's hand.

Ran nudged Lysander and spoke quietly. "Did you know the Minister for Provincial Affairs was on board?"

Lysander blinked. "Stereth Tar'krim? Was he? I didn't see him."

"Do you know of any reason the Poraths would be associating with him?"

"The notorious Rice Thief? Maybe they thought his reputation would add to the party. I don't know, it's the first I heard of it. Why? Is it important?"

Ran slid the steel shutter open an inch; we were approaching the Shikron villa. He let it down again. "What will this do to the marriage proposal?"

Lysander sighed. "I doubt if they'll let it go. On the other hand, it was Kade's idea, and he kept pushing it. It'll be easier to kill, now that he's gone."

"Easier to kill," Ran muttered, to himself. The carriage rolled to a stop and Lysander climbed out. He helped Kylla down, and slid shut the door without a word.

We rode back to our house in silence. When we reached there, I gave Ran a five-tabal coin to tip the driver and we climbed the two steps to the door.

Ran said, "Do you think Stereth had anything to do with this?"

"The gods only know," I said, tiredly. "Let's get some sleep."

Between Scythian gold cats, murder, and old blackmailing friends, it had been a long night and day. Ran said, "The parcel light's blinking on the security station."

"Fine. You handle it—gracious sir, First of Cormallon."

He just looked at me. "You'll be better," he said, "when you've had a nap."

I was better when I'd had a nap. As a matter of fact, I was better when I'd had a full night's sleep with unobstructed breathing. As a collector of tales and an Athenan scholar, I loved to read about knights and princesses and quests, and imagine myself bumming from one perilous castle to the next; but the fact is, physical exhaustion just makes me cranky. It's not very flattering, and really, I do try—I just don't get very far in graciousness until I'm fed and rested.

I woke up next morning, got some hermitmeat and rice from the larder, cracked open a pellfruit, and padded into the downstairs parlor balancing plates. Ran was sprawled on the divan, staring at the ceiling. I'd downed half the pellfruit while still in the pantry, and therefore looked kindly on him. He was, after all, my dearest friend and the light of my heart. I said, "Last night you said there was a parcel?"

He turned his head. "Already took care of it. It was just the last three copies of the Capital News. They got sent to Cormallon and Jad sent them on here."

A pile of nondescript pamphlets lay on the floor. "I see we've got today's, too. Jad must've notified them to change the address."

The Capital News is not on the Net because it is not a very respectable publication. It has an insert called the "Gossip Gazette," and various highly placed persons try from time to time to halt its publication. But it's just too damned entertaining. Ivorans love to read about stuff like that. I understood that the Emperor got a copy every morning.

I snagged one of the Newses, opened it on a pillow, sat on another pillow, and started to eat and read. I skipped over the trade articles and went straight to the insert. "Oh, *kanz*," I said.

Ran looked up. "What?"

"Today's date. Listen: 'What branch of the tree of six is offering its youngest blossom to a merchant house? The lovely lady E., still fresh from school, met her potential suitor at a garden party yesterday evening. We understand the gentleman in question already has one bride, but who could refuse such a rose in springtime? And here at Gossip Gazette, we've always heard that a pair beats one of a kind."

Ran put a hand over his eyes. "They don't actually name the Poraths . . . what am I saying? Of course everyone will know it's the Poraths."

"In case they're in any doubt, there's a description

of the snowfall at the party. Where do they get this information?''

"Paid off one of the guests.''

I scanned the other articles for mention of Shikrons or Poraths. "You'd think the guests at a Six Families party would be too wealthy to be tempted by whatever the Gossip Gazette can pay.''

"Huh. For all we know, some of them are on the staff.''

I closed the sheet. "This is going to make it difficult for the Poraths to back out, isn't it?''

Ran sat up suddenly. "It may have been the Poraths who planted that item. They were already going out on a limb to commit themselves, true? Imagine the effect on poor Lysander, picking up this paper in the morning, knowing he'd never be able to argue now that Eliana wasn't publicly compromised. That's if events had gone as planned, I mean. If Kade hadn't died.''

I gave him my attention. "You think that was sorcerously caused?''

"I know it. The entire field of balance changed. And anyway, common sense will tell you that a man who doesn't know how to swim won't suddenly dive off a boat. Not when he's in his right mind.''

In his right mind. I thought back over what I'd studied of the field. Sorcery cannot really affect the mind directly, but it can deceive the mind through physical changes. Giving a person the physical symptoms of fear can convince him he's afraid of something; the symptoms of lust or hunger were likewise easy to stimulate. "A fire spell? Raise his body temperature, convince him he's burning up?''

"It's how I would do it,'' said Ran. Then he added, "If I were going to do it publicly, which I never would.''

"I don't know, it seems so unlikely. Wouldn't he just call for help? I mean, diving into the canal! He *knew* he couldn't swim, odds were good he'd die anyway—''

"Sweetheart, I see you've had the good fortune never to be near a major fire disaster. People dive off twelve-story buildings with nothing but stone underneath when their rooms catch fire. There's no force more persuasive." I had been in a fire, once, but it had been a small one, and thankfully I'd lost consciousness early on. Ran continued, "Actually, using a fire spell to kill by water is really a charming conceit, sorcerously speaking."

"And which of the guests do you think did it?"

It was indeed the question. Ran considered it, as I knew he'd been considering since it happened; then he said, regretfully, "We don't have sufficient data."

"We could make wild guesses."

"So could the Gossip Gazette. Though I doubt that they will, it's too close to real news." He walked over to join me, and I gave him a slice of fruit. "I'll have to make a condolence call this morning on Jusik Porath. It's my duty as the First of Cormallon, and having had the bad luck to be on the scene when it happened, I suppose I can't get out of it."

"Do I have to go?" I was willing to foist this one off on others if I could; rather the way Ran was somehow never around on major housecleaning days. I suppose it all evened out.

He shook his head. "If you were close to Grandmother Porath or Eliana, they'd expect you to call on them; but you'd still be under no obligation."

Ran had shed his outerrobe when he came in. Now he opened his underrobe, stretched his legs out on the carpet, swallowed a piece of fruit, and sighed in pleased physicality.

"Nice legs, stranger," I said in Standard. "You new in town?"

He laughed, nearly choking on the fruit. He slid an arm around my waist and said, "A man not married to a barbarian doesn't know what he's missing." He kissed the back of my neck. "Moon of my heart," he said in Ivoran.

Just then the doorbells jangled. We froze, like two

children caught playing doctor in the back garden. I said, "If we wait, they'll go away."

He pulled his underrobe together. I said, "Ignore it."

But I knew better than that. The First of Cormallon never ignores doorbells. Or Net messages, or parcel signals, or mail of any kind. There's always a chance it might be something his duty requires of him. He pulled himself to his feet and slipped on a respectable pair of embroidered house slippers.

I waited for him to come back. Several minutes passed. I heard a heavy tread of feet in the passage; two pairs of feet, by the sound of it. The slippered pair was clearly Ran's, but his footfall was silent by nature—he was warning me that company was on its way. His voice came from the passage, overly loud: "This way, if you don't mind, noble sir; my wife is within."

I jumped up and kicked the cushions out of the way and ran a hand through my hair and checked to see my robe was done up correctly. It's not always easy to go from being freewheeling Theodora of Pyrene to a respectable Cormallon matron. Was there time to grab the plates? I dived for them, heard footsteps just outside the doorway, and straightened up again. Close enough. The noble sir, whoever he was, should have sent word he was coming, and would have to deal with life as it was rather than the more courteous fiction it could be.

The divider from the passage is just a thick cotton tapestry, half open; Ran flung it the rest of the way and bowed like a proper host.

And in walked Jusik Porath. He hadn't even changed his clothes.

Chapter 5

Ran threw me a baffled look and said, "Apparently the noble sir has anticipated my call, Theodora."

Jusik, who was striding into the room like an army on the march, stopped short. "Your call?"

"Of condolence," said Ran. "I was just remarking to my wife that I should go and present my family's regret at this tragedy to your House."

"Condolence call," repeated Jusik. "Yes. Of course. Might I sit down?"

Ran gestured to a tasseled cushion far from my plates, and Jusik seated himself with the air of one making a conscious effort of control. Up close he looked both tired and restless, the lines in his face more pronounced. I'd watched him at the garden party and on the boat, and—when not placating his mother—he'd struck me as a man used to getting his own way, as the First of Porath no doubt would be. He hardly seemed separable from his family, when you thought of him: Father, son, first of his House, representative of one of the six noble branches; it was what he *was*. As he probably would tell you if you were presumptuous enough to ask.

So why at this moment, as he sat on the cushion in our parlor, did I have the sense that he was here all alone? He seemed . . . so much an *individual*. So un-Ivoran.

I didn't even know the man, but suddenly I felt very sorry for him. On impulse I knelt on the carpet, met his eyes, and said, "We mean it, you know. This must

be terrible for you. If there's anything we can
do. . . .''

He seemed slightly taken aback. The barbarian
breaks ritual again. Probably there was a set of statement and reply we were supposed to follow here, and
probably Ran was supposed to do it in any case. My
sincerity must have been plain, however, as he was
not offended. He even broke ritual himself long enough
to lean over and touch my hand, before he gave up
trying to deal with the outlander, took a deep breath,
and turned back to Ran.

"Well, here I am," he said.

"I beg your pardon?" said Ran.

"Here I am. Surely you expected me."

Ran and I looked at each other.

You have any idea?

Not a clue. I rolled my eyes toward Jusik briefly as
though to add, What can you expect? Maybe he's unbalanced by grief.

Ran said, "Uh, perhaps the noble sir could be more
explicit?"

Jusik glanced at me. "I wonder if your gracious wife
should remain."

The man deserved a lot of slack, of course, but this
vagueness could get just a little irritating. Ran said,
"I wonder if you could give me some idea of what
we're talking about."

This was treading a bit toward direct speech early
in a social call; but clearly Jusik had something on his
mind . . . and the truth, I may as well tell you now,
is that Ran really didn't care much about Jusik, Kade,
or the whole lot of Poraths wherever they may be. He
had people of his own that he spent his worry on. Not
that he would dream of being discourteous.

Jusik coughed. "I've been very polite, I think, gracious sir. I've come alone—no security, no retainers
of any kind, check the street outside. I come here in
all good faith, and I really don't think that I deserve
to be passed over like this—"

"Sir!" Ran had dropped the "noble." "We realize

that you've had a terrible shock. That you're under enormous strain. I hate to be crude at such a time, but let me put this as simply as I can: *I have no idea what you're talking about.*"

Jusik blinked. "Then you refuse to answer my questions."

"Sir, it is you who refuse to ask them."

I touched his sleeve to get Jusik's attention. "Noble sir, I'm a barbarian, remember? Be as simple and clear as you can be, and tell *me* why you've come."

He was deciding whether or not to be insulted. I added, "Please?"

Ran was about to say something else. Hidden by our robes, I jabbed him in the thigh. I didn't want to distract Jusik's attention from me, or it might take hours to get him to talk sensibly. As soon as he went back to Ran, he'd expect to be understood. Not being understood by a barbarian is normal.

"Lady Theodora, I'm here on a business matter, relating to some work of your husband's. That's all."

I jabbed Ran again and smiled at Jusik. "You refer to the sorcery business?"

"Of course. The House of Cormallon is unequaled in its practice."

"The noble sir is too kind. Such compliments are no less treasures than the gold of our House." Spend a year or two on Ivory and you'll be able to toss this stuff off, too. "Now, are you saying that you want to hire my husband to perform some sorcerous assignment for your House?"

"Gracious lady . . . not exactly. Rather, I wish to consult with him on his present assignment."

"Really. His present assignment. And which assignment would that be?"

Jusik shifted uncomfortably. "Umm, the assignment of yesterday. That is . . . the assignment . . . of yesterday."

The First of Porath, known for firmness to the point of tyranny, was near to stuttering. Ran leaned over then, and I sat back on my heels. "Is the noble sir under the impression that I killed his son?"

The adjectives are flowery on Ivory, but they don't mince their verbs. Jusik Porath looked even more uncomfortable. A lifetime of training was holding him back: The Six Families, who so often practice murder as an art form, regard straight business assassination as the lowest of taste. It was sometimes unavoidable, but one never talked about it.

Jusik met Ran's eyes with dignity. "I come as is my responsibility, as the First of my House. I come to ascertain what danger we may be in. To see what it is your employer wants of us. So public an . . . incident, surely can be nothing but a warning. I should be at home, sir, seeing to my family, but I am here in fulfillment of my duty. I dared not wait. I trust that you will respect the . . . restraint . . . I have shown."

Ran was momentarily speechless. Jusik said, impatiently, "Is it war? Whom has my House offended? You could not expect me not to ask you, not when your work was done in full view of the world!"

"Sir, do you think I'd assassinate a member of your family while I was your guest?"

"Isn't that what sorcerers do?"

The gulf between the first and second tiers of aristocracy had never seemed so wide. The scary thing was that Jusik could *be* so controlled about it—he could be that way because his pain and anger weren't directed at Ran. I don't think he thought any more of Ran than he thought of a gun or a knife, or a soup ladle.

Gods! Did *Ran* ever think of himself purely in terms of functionality? I needed to give this some thought, when time presented.

Ran said, "It's not what *I* do. And it's not what Cormallon does. I don't speak for the rest of the world." Or give a damn about it, either, said his voice. "To target your son would be discourteous and stupid both. There are far more subtle ways of killing people than a long run off the side of a boat. This whole action has the stamp of the amateur on it, and amateur sorcerers are fools of the worst stripe.''

That all came from the heart. Jusik listened in silence. I said, "It's true, noble sir. I handle the bookings for my husband; if he were on any assignment, I would know about it.''

Jusik glanced at me. Come on, I thought, look at me: A barbarian. An idiot child. Wouldn't know how to lie. Barely can get my shoes on—

He let out his breath. "Possibly," he said.

Ran said, "Sir, believe me, the House of Cormallon would never get involved in such an obvious project. It's only a matter of time before the sorcerer's run to ground—"

"Is it?" cut in Jusik.

"How not? The sorcerer was either on the boat itself, or his spell was grounded on some person or thing on board. There's only a finite set of possibilities, and I assume Porath will spare no effort in following each one up.''

Jusik said, slowly, "I've heard that the employment of magic leaves an 'echo' that can be traced. I suppose the first step would be to hire a sorcerer of our own to do the trace. . . .''

Ran was shaking his head. "There are reasons why that probably won't work—"

"Don't tell me them." Jusik put up his hand. "I see that I need an expert for this. Would you be willing to take it up?''

Ran's eyes widened. "Sir, just a minute ago you suggested—" He stopped, glanced around the room as though the proper phrases might be somewhere under one of the dirty dishes, then started again. "Noble sir, you've just had a shock. It's not for me to suggest a course of action for your House. I entered your property on a social basis; I would prefer to keep it that way.''

"I'll be very busy for the next few days," said Jusik, straightening his robe as he spoke. He sat up straighter, seeming to put on the House of Porath again with every gesture. "It would be a great favor to me personally, if you would take up this task for us."

"With all respect—"

"And it would give us an opportunity to talk over this marriage idea."

Another silence while we assimilated this.

Jusik added, "Although it would be a favor, I don't mean to suggest there would be no fee involved—"

Ran shook his head—not in negation, more as though he'd been hit by a few too many sandbags. "I'm sure your fee would be . . . would you mind if I discussed this with my wife?"

"Not at all! I have to leave in any case." He rose to his feet with that born Ivoran grace I'll never match if I live to be two hundred. "There's no need for any delay, if the proposal finds your favor. You would have the run of my house, my grounds, the boat. Simply send a message, and I'll notify everyone to give you full cooperation." He smiled at us both and bowed. Then he turned to Ran and added, "I would prefer a swift solution."

"I don't doubt it." Ran accompanied him to the door.

He was back a few seconds later. "Well?" he asked.

I said, "Ran, I've been on Ivory for several years now, and I've sat in on any number of unusual conversations. But I have to say that this was the weirdest."

He smiled, not a happy smile. "He's still more than half convinced I'm guilty. That's why he wants to hire me. So I can let my principals know that he's looking for a meeting. Or if the price is right, so I can tell him my principals' names."

"He didn't say that."

"Yes, he did."

I found myself staring at the dirty dishes. "So you'll have to turn him down."

"That would be an admission of guilt, too. Protecting my client's identity, the first duty of a good sorcerer.''

"Well, you can't take him up on it, not if you don't have a client to hand over."

"And then there's Kylla and the marriage."

I sighed. "I thought this was going to be a simple social problem."

He stooped and picked up the plates. "Theodora, why do people always think I'm guilty of something? Is it my face?"

"Has this been happening all your life, or only since you met me?"

"Good point." He balanced my cup atop the pile. "I'm glad you're finally starting to take some responsibility for this constant disruption of my life."

"Huh! If we're going to start talking about disrupting people's lives—"

"I didn't force you to come back to Ivory, that was your fate."

Yeah, fate operating under a Cormallon pseudonym. I followed him into the pantry. "So what are we going to do? Want to talk to Kylla before we get any deeper in this? We'll wake her if we call now."

"Kanz, no. Kylla would grab me by the throat and tell me to do anything it takes, *now,* to get Jusik in our debt."

"You want me to run the cards? I don't know how helpful they'll be in a situation like this. I mean, they're your cards, they don't care about Kylla or Kade. I can do a regular business configuration . . . although, technically, you haven't accepted this as a business offer."

Ran stopped short. "A *business* offer. Why was Jusik so quick to assume Kade was killed for business reasons? It's the normal assumption for most of our clients, but the Six Families practice murder as an art form. Why shouldn't Kade have been the loser in one of their damned games?"

"That's easy." I took the dishes from him and set them down. "Kade was killed by a sorcerer. You were the only known sorcerer on board, and you're not a gameplayer, you're a businessman.''

"*We* can't assume that, though. There may very well have been an amateur sorcerer on board.'' He leaned on the sideboard unhappily. "This is a mess, sweetheart. Assassinations among the aristocracy are none of our business.''

"So turn him down.'' I smiled, knowing he wouldn't.

Another sigh. "And you know what else,'' he said. "Now we have Stereth Tar'krim to worry about.''

At that point I wasn't really worried about Stereth, because I trusted that as an old friend he would find some way of warning us off the case if he were involved. I wasn't even worried about Kylla and Lysander's marriage, because somehow in the end Kylla always get things the way she wants them in life. Although I hated to see her unhappy meanwhile.

I was worried about an entirely different subject. That night in bed, I said to Ran, "I want to talk to you about us.''

He shifted uncomfortably. Ran does not like to talk about important topics; talk implies uncertainty, and as Cormallon heir he seems to feel the path of his life should not admit uncertainty in any area. He's known since childhood what his duty was and his life should be, so why talk?

I said, "About children.''

He looked unhappy. "You don't talk about children, they're something that happens.''

"They're something that doesn't happen, too. There's good reason to think that Ivorans might be different genetically from the rest of Standard society. Maybe even a different species. I've looked and looked, but I can't find any hard evidence anywhere—maybe somebody knows, somewhere in the Tellys medical complex, but they're not telling if they do—''

"You went to the Tellys medical complex?''

"Just for research. On the Net.''

"Oh."

"Listen to me. There's always a chance that you and I won't be able to have children. Or if I do get pregnant we have no idea what'll happen. On the other hand, if you went to the Selian Clinic, we could get a good genetic scenario, with percentage probabilities—"

"No."

"They need both parents to run a scenario."

"What do you mean, both? Have you been?"

"Why would I go without you? Anyway, I've been examined plenty of times back on Athena, so nobody's getting any novel data from me."

He was silent. I got tired of listening to the dark, so I said, "Ran?"

He said, "Look. I will not turn over any informational property of Cormallon, including my body, for study."

"Come on, Ran, we're talking about an outworlder medical clinic. It's not a rival House."

He sat up, throwing back the light summer coverlet. He switched on the light. There was no anger in his face, but I had the feeling he was upset. "Times are changing. With every generation it gets worse. We only reestablished contact with Standard society a hundred years ago, did you know that?" He didn't wait for an answer. "It's not going to end now. Every time a new piece of technology is imported, we change a little more. Someday our rivals will *be* on Tellys and Pyrene, not down the road and over the hill. That's what our grandson will have to worry about; I'd be a fool to make it harder for him."

"Well." I stared at him. "I never thought to hear this from you."

He smiled wryly. "Because I spend all my time focused on whatever the current sorcery assignment is? Because I only seem to worry about this fiscal year?"

"Yes."

The smile was painful. "I'm the First; it's my job to consider the future of the House. Which will not be enhanced by handing goodies to potential enemies."

I didn't try to argue that; to an Ivoran, anyone not in his family is a potential enemy. I said, "Even if the Tellys doctors could isolate a gene in your body for sorcery—if it exists, and if they care enough to try, which I doubt—what good would it do them without the genes themselves, without any practical means of expressing them?"

"Understanding something is the first step to controlling it."

"Without the rest of the steps, the first one doesn't count for much."

"I'm not going." He switched off the light.

I waited till he settled back, then said, "If I can't get pregnant, this hypothetical grandson will never exist. Have you thought about that?"

Silence. My eyes readjusted to the dark. I looked around the small bedroom, at the dressertop with its vials and bottles and containers, at the chest, at the stool in the corner. I gave him plenty of time, then I said, "If I can't get pregnant, will the Cormallon council pressure you to marry somebody else? Take a second wife, the way Lysander's being pressured?"

He said, "I would resist that most strenuously."

He sounded like a politician holding the line against taxes. And we all know how long that lasts. I said, "You should run for one of the democratic offices." Then I slapped my pillow a couple of times to plump it up, and settled down to go to sleep.

Chapter 6

I entered the Porath house again with mixed feelings. We were intruding on a private grief, yet we'd been invited. Add to that the fact that I didn't really know what we were going to do. The role of a sorcerer is generally to *cause* trouble, not to work out how the trouble came about. When Ran needed investigating done, he generally paid people to do it for him . . . but then, the investigating was usually nonsorcerous in nature. And strictly business.

I'd run the cards, to be on the safe side, as with any client assignment; they'd suggested a good chance of success and no great danger to Ran, so I'd given my stamp of approval. I hoped I wouldn't regret it.

I touched Ran's arm as we passed the lacquered pillars of the central porch. He looked at me.

"I won't be able to stay long," I said, tapping my nose. Cats.

"Twenty minutes. We'll talk to Grandmother Porath if we can, and then Coalis."

I nodded. The lizard, at least, was gone from the immediate vicinity. Maybe there was a shed or something on the property where he was kept. On the other hand, this could mean we'd come upon a heavy reptilian shape dragging itself toward us in any dark corridor.

The doors around the porch had been hung with bolts of silver cloth, and silver paper lanterns dangled from the roof. A smell of incense came from a doorway at the right wing of the house. Kade's body would be laid out there before it was burnt.

I said, "If this were Athena, someone would have to examine the corpse."

Ran nodded. "We will."

"What do you mean, we will? We're not doctors."

"What good would a doctor be?" He used the Standard word, as I had. "We know the physical cause of death. Drowning. And if there are any traces of sorcery to be found, a doctor would hardly be helpful."

"Look, I really don't think I'm up to—"

The house steward met us at the door, and we all bowed. He was a tall, gray-haired man on the verge of retirement, as stewards often seem to be—it must be a job you work up to—and he said, "The orders of the House are to lend you every assistance." He had a kind, rather quiet voice; his whole style was that of one whom it would be difficult to shock. "I hope you'll forgive my not meeting you at the gate, but things have been quite turned around today."

"Of course," said Ran. "One of the reasons I came was to offer the sympathy of my House."

"It is much appreciated. Please come in. The guard at the gate said you'd inquired whether Coalis was at home?"

"Yes," said Ran, as we exchanged looks. Neither of us had suspected the gatehouse had a Net terminal, or even that the Poraths were on the Net; they looked dirt-poor, and the subscription fees were stiff. But there was no other way our question could have reached the steward so quickly. "We'd like to speak with him, if we may. Although we'd prefer to speak to his grandmother first."

The steward led us in through the main hall, passing the arch that opened into the kitchen. "I'm afraid Grandmother's asleep at the moment, gracious sir. Actually, I wouldn't expect to see her till tomorrow at the earliest. She was, well, given medication. She hasn't taken this well."

"I see." Ran cleared his throat. "In that case, I suppose we could see Co—"

"Sir Cormallon!" The tall woman who'd shadowed

Eliana Porath through the garden party and onto the canal boat strode down the flight of stairs at the corridor's end. "Your pardon—you *are* Ran Cormallon, the sorcerer?"

Ran admitted that he was. She bowed. "Leel Canarol, defensive chaperone to Eliana Porath. My lady asked me to come down and see if it was you who were our visitors. She'd like to speak with you, if you don't mind." She wore black provincial trousers, worked in silver thread, and had a quilted silk vest above them that was also silver: half-mourning clothes, out of respect to the Poraths. I noted there was still a pistol-sized bulge beneath the vest, even here in the family compound.

The steward turned to us, awaiting our reply. Well, nothing had gone as planned so far; we might as well see what Eliana wanted. I conveyed this to Ran with a shrug, and he spoke to Leel Canarol. "We are, of course, honored by the summons. We'll follow you."

As she led us upstairs, she said, "I'm afraid Grandmother won't be able to see you today in any case." As in the couple of other great houses I'd visited (and married into) I saw that even the staff called the old lady "Grandmother." I'd bet they called Jusik "Lord Porath," though.

"Yes, the steward told us." Ran did not confirm that we were here to see her, or specify any other names. I smiled to myself. If Leel Canerol—or Eliana Porath—wanted to find out anything about what we were doing here, they would have a hard time of it. Ran gripped information like a miser.

Past a hanging of fringed purple, Eliana's room was laid out in the morning sun. It faced the garden; the branches of the coyu tree near the porch brushed her window. The room was white and yellow, clean and old. An alcove for her nurse's bed, a low sleeping platform in the center for herself, with a place for her defensive chaperone built into the foot. (One room, three people; odds were that at least one of them snored. I was glad I wasn't a Six-Families girl.) The sleeping platform was draped in a thick bolt of soft gold cloth, with the mattress and a small lamp atop it.

Some printed books near the window, no doubt with topics appropriate for young ladies. Flowers near the alcove. Two wardrobes. And this was it; this was, pretty much, Eliana's life. A city girl of good family, particularly without money, would not get out very much. The necessary supervision would be too expensive, even given the limited number of places she would be allowed to go.

It occurred to me suddenly that she might well be looking forward to a marriage with anybody, to let her into the ranks of married women and their extra freedoms.

Poor kid. She stood up from the bench by the window and waited, like a well-trained child, for our greeting. She wore plain house robes of light green, no silver anywhere. Her black hair was pulled back through a velvet band, and hung to her waist.

"Honored by this meeting," said Ran. "Please accept the sympathy of our House."

She nodded. "I hope you'll overlook my clothes. They only just realized that I have no mourning dress." Her voice, high and clear, reported it as a fact, not an assignment of blame. "Auntie Jace, do you think you could get us some tah?"

The temperamental Auntie Jace, I now saw, had been sitting mouselike in the corner; now she jumped up and scurried for the door.

I said quickly, "That won't be necessary. We can't stay long." Besides the cat factor, we were here on business. I didn't want to open up any hospitality debts with Eliana. Besides, I'd gotten as nervous as a born Ivoran about eating untested food—we'd done all right here yesterday, but then yesterday Kade had been alive, and Ran hadn't been a suspect in his death.

Ran said, "I hope you'll forgive our haste. The lady Theodora and I are pressed for time today."

She bit her lip. Then she sat again, smoothing the green robes. "Please sit down," she said, so we seated ourselves on the edge of the sleeping platform. She cleared her throat, then started again. "This is very difficult. I suppose I should just— They tell me you've agreed to investigate my brother's death. Is that true?"

It's always interesting to watch Ran field other people's questions. He said, "If that's what you've been told, I won't deny it."

"Because, you see, if it is true, I have to speak with you."

Ran waited.

Finally she said, "I'm sorry at how self-centered this sounds. But don't you see how this will affect me? A prolonged inquiry, turning over all the rocks in the family garden, just when I'm—well, practically engaged? And you're his brother-in-law! He'll hear all kinds of things!"

"Will he?" asked Ran coolly.

"Every family has its quirks, gracious sir, and I'd prefer that those of mine be left decently at rest."

"Is the lady telling me she believes I'll pass any interesting gossip I may hear along the way to Lysander Shikron?"

"Won't you?"

I would have smiled if I could have gotten away with it without being rude. If she thought Ran would commit himself either way, she'd have a long wait. In the pause that followed, she turned to me. "Gracious lady, I appeal to you. Speak to your husband for me, I have no one to take my part. Don't I have a right to a good marriage?"

Kid, if I can't get him to cooperate on more important issues, I don't think you're going to get very far. I tried to think of some temporizing remark, but Ran spared me.

"Why 'prolonged'?" he said.

"I beg your pardon?" said Eliana.

"You said 'a prolonged inquiry.' Why 'prolonged'?"

"Well, obviously, the scope would have to be pretty wide—I don't see what this has to do—"

"Why would it have to be wide?"

"There's the gameplayers, of course, and Kade's business associates, and the gods only know—"

"Kade was a player?" She and Ran were referring to the game of controlled murder, popular among the Six Families. There were complicated rules that governed it, or so I gathered, anyway; as long as I stayed out of their way, I really didn't care what they did among themselves. I should add that when I say it was popular, I don't mean they all played it. It was really only a small minority, but that makes it a lot more popular than it is in any other population, true?

She sighed. "Father didn't want him playing. He's first son, and it's not like our House has branches to spare. He said that he'd stopped, but I know he didn't."

"I see. You mentioned business associates, too."

So she had. I'd lost track of that in the tangle of other possibilities.

"Yes." That seemed to be the end of the topic as far as Eliana was concerned.

Ran said, "I was unaware that the House of Porath was involved in any form of business."

She said, with a trace of anger, "If you'd let me marry into Shikron, we'd be involved in business enough."

"But Kade was involved already."

We waited. Leel Canerol lounged in false relaxation at the other end of the sleeping platform, her short boots resting on a stool. Auntie Jace made an exasperated sound, got up, and made a show of going to the window ledge to pick up a bowl of sewing materials.

Eliana finally spoke. "It was a personal matter for him. None of the rest of the House had anything to do with it."

Lee Canerol said, "Eliana, I wouldn't advise—"

"Oh, shush, Lely. He's going to find out anyway, isn't he?"

The more sensible of her two chaperones shrugged.

Eliana said, "Kade started a moneylending association."

This is a respectable enough activity on Ivory, though perhaps a bit déclassé for one of the Six Families. Ran said, ". . . Yes?"

She seemed surprised. "That's it."

Ran and I looked at each other. I said, "Where did he get the money? Was he partners with one of the marketplace banks?" I knew a little bit about the less official banking methods in the capital, due to some money troubles I'd gotten into earlier in my life.

"Oh, no, he borrowed the initial capital on the strength of his name."

"He borrowed it," said Ran slowly. "For this to turn a profit, he'd have to lend it out at a rather high rate of interest."

Leel Canerol chuckled. "He certainly did." Eliana glared at her.

Well, well. If I understood correctly, the first son and heir to Porath had been carving out a reputation as a loanshark.

"Sorry I missed knowing him," I said softly.

Eliana looked up. "Don't tell Father. Whatever you do."

Ran stood. "We'll do what we can," he said, keeping it vague. "I'm afraid we'll have to move on, now—"

"But Lysander? Are you going to tell him about this?"

"At the moment," he said, "I consider the marriage a separate issue from the matter of your brother."

She smiled. We left her to her keepers, both aware that no promises had been made.

Coalis was a very different sort of fish. We found him lying on his stomach in the tiny courtyard attached to the west wing, reading a book of poetry. He was stretched on a patch of very carefully cultivated lawn grass of soft yellow-green, facing a miniature fountain. He sat up when we came.

"Room for three," he said, speaking of the patch

of grass. "Hello, Theodora. My greetings, sir Cormallon."

He wore an undertunic of silver and a silver outer-robe. Death of his hopes and dreams, possibly. "Hello, Coalis," I said in the same direct way, not waiting for Ran to speak. "My husband offers the sympathy of our House."

Coalis smiled lazily, pleased in a gentle fashion with the way we'd just run over tradition. Na'telleths were often amused by that sort of thing. "It's appreciated. I heard you were coming, you know. Heard Eliana cornered you when you got in."

"She did," said Ran. "She seemed concerned about your family's reputation."

"Well, she probably has her reasons."

"What are you reading?" I asked.

He held up the book. "Kesey's *Erotic Poems*."

"Really, I was flipping through his general collection just yesterday." Kesey had been dead about six hundred years, but his work enjoyed a certain vogue among classicists. The edition I had was a translation to modern Ivoran, but Coalis's looked like the real thing. "What do you think of them?"

He pursed his lips thoughtfully. Finally he said, "I suppose I'm not the best person to ask." He put down the volume. "Perhaps I should have gotten the illustrated version." He looked toward Ran, then back to me. "You have questions for me," he said.

"We do," agreed Ran.

I said, "Your father thinks—or thought—that we might have had something to do with Kade's death."

Ran gave me one of his unreadable looks, but it's not as though everyone else wouldn't have thought of it.

Coalis lifted a fistful of grass. "Well, he would, wouldn't he?"

"We didn't."

"And you'd like to know where else the blame might be spread?"

Ran said, "Briefly put—yes."

"Well, it's nothing to me one way or the other. I have to deal with the fact he's no longer here; how he got that way is irrelevant."

"Not to us," said Ran.

I said, "Eliana told us he was a gameplayer."

"She said that? How odd."

"He wasn't a gameplayer?"

"When he was fourteen, fifteen. I was that way myself at that age," added Coalis, from the height of his sixteen years. "He swore off when he reached majority, and if he ever dabbled, I never heard of it."

"She also said that he lent money at high rates of interest." I could see that Ran disapproved of my method of questioning, but he kept quiet.

"Well, now, *that* I'd heard of. I suppose I'll have to take over the business for a while, or sell it to somebody—the House could use the money, and somebody's got to bring it in now that the marriage thing is drying up. —Don't tell Father, though."

Ran frowned. "Kade brought you into the business? I wouldn't think it would hold much appeal for a na'telleth."

"Oh, I didn't learn about it from Kade."

"Then who?"

"The Provincial Minister," said Coalis. "Stereth Tar'krim."

Tripping over Stereth's name always throws me— and, I suspect, Ran—a little off balance. Particularly at a time like this, when the connection seemed so remote. Ran sat back slightly, looking as though a small, impossible-to-swat insect was buzzing in his ears. He said, "Stereth Tar'krim discussed your brother's business with you?"

"Yes, he's a friend of mine. We met at a na'telleth retreat day."

Now that was a setup if I'd ever heard one. Stereth Tar'krim was about as na'telleth as . . . or was he? I remembered a fateful hour several lifetimes ago, when I'd talked about blood and death and failure with Stereth. "If it happens, it happens," he'd said, though he knew then how likely it was; a na'telleth answer if there ever was one. Stereth . . . rebel, killer, gangster . . . monk? I shook my head as though to clear it.

"Wait," I said. "How did Stereth know about Kade's moneylending?"

"He wanted to be partners with Kade," said Coalis. "He wanted an alliance with our House, an official alliance—he asked to be listed as an acknowledged House-friend. Father couldn't know about the business, of course, but once he was gone—"

"So he was a friend of Kade's," said Ran, trying to get this straight.

"No, Kade would have nothing to do with it. Why split it, when he could keep it all?"

"And Kade told you this."

"No. Stereth told me. Kade never knew I knew anything about what he was doing."

Ran looked irritated. "You knew Stereth, you knew he wanted to ally with your House, Kade was in the way—and you didn't warn him?"

"Why would I do that?"

Before Ran became more annoyed I said, "For one thing, to avoid the situation you're in now. Heir to Porath, good-bye to the monastery."

"Oh! Kade's death. Oh, I'm sure Stereth had nothing to do with that."

After a moment of blankness, Ran and I mutually decided to leave that statement where it lay. I said, "I don't suppose you'd know where we could get a list of Kade's vict— clients?"

"I'm sorry. I'm sure he had a list somewhere, but I've no idea where it is."

Ran let out a breath and rose to his feet, extending a hand to me. "We won't interrupt you any further, then." Clearly we were going to postpone a discussion of the hopelessness of this entire situation till we were out of earshot of the family.

Coalis didn't bother to get up. He dipped his head to acknowledge our bows and smiled politely. As we left the courtyard I saw he'd opened the book again. His feet were propped on the rim of the fountain.

We made our way through the hall that led to the garden. None too soon, I'd been digging out my handkerchief rather frequently there toward the end of the conversation. I gave a good blow, tucked the white linen square into the sleeve of my robe where I could get at it again quickly, and said, "I don't like all this talk of Stereth."

"Can you believe he'd get into loansharking in the capital, now that he's a minister of the empire?"

"All too willingly. Ministers need money like everybody else."

"But he must have negotiated a big payoff from the Emperor when he quit being an outlaw."

I shrugged. "I don't know how big. And who knows what he might want the money for? Maybe he has other projects in mind."

"Great bumbling gods." We reached the main door. It would be polite to wait for the steward to let us out, but I wanted to get into the open air. "Do you see a pattern of repetition here? With Stereth, I mean?"

"I'm not sure. What do you mean?" I reminded myself not to rub my eyes or they'd become infected.

"Remember our summer with his outlaw crew? He wanted to combine forces with the Deathwell bands, but Dramonta Sol opposed it. Tarniss Cord was willing."

I nodded. "And suddenly Dramonta Sol was dead and Tarniss Cord was in charge of all the Deathwell outlaws. I know. It's not a day I'm likely to forget. But what are we supposed to do now? We don't know he's behind Kade's murder, but what if he is? I mean, he *is* sort of a friend of ours."

Ran was silent, the way he'd been with Eliana, neither confirming nor denying. I started to push against the heavy wooden door.

"Besides," I went on, "even if he weren't, I don't think I'd like to make an enemy of him."

Ran looked at me. I said, "Come on, you know it's true. If it comes down to alienating the Poraths or alienating Stereth Tar'krim—"

"Somebody mention my name?"

Stereth stood in the doorway, smiling in the midday sun.

"It's good to be remembered," he said. "I hope you were saying nice things."

Ran took a step backward that he probably wasn't even aware of, leaving me to say, "Hello, Stereth."

"Hello, Tymon." He called me by my old road name, and now that there was nobody to see, he bent and kissed me on the cheek. Then he glanced past me. "Ran. It was good to see you both yesterday." He reached behind to close the door, but I put a hand on his arm.

"Don't, please. I'd rather get some fresh air. I'm allergic to this place." I used the Ivoran word "aversion."

"Tymon, really? All the silver crepe getting you down?" His voice was not without sympathy. He was scary that way sometimes.

"Cats. I get stuffed up."

"My poor barbarian." He opened the heavy door easily, with one arm. He doesn't look that strong until you get to know him. Sunlight streamed in, with the musty smell of old wood from the porch and a faint perfumey scent from the garden.

I ducked under his arm and stepped outside, taking a long draught of uncontaminated air. Ran followed me out. Then Stereth joined us, shutting the door behind him. "I ought to wait for the house steward anyway. I hate to be rude. We can talk here."

Ran's feelings toward Stereth I can only describe as mixed, but certainly he'd always regarded Stereth's "talks" with unadulterated suspicion. He said quietly, "I suppose you're another one who wants to question us about the investigation."

"What investigation? I came to pay a condolence call."

We looked at him.

He said, "There has been a death, you know."

"Yes." Ran took a deep breath. "Jusik Porath asked us to look into it." Everyone did seem to know that fact anyway.

"Oh? Well, best of luck to you." His tone was uninterested. "Actually, I was wondering if I might speak to Tymon here alone."

There's nobody like Stereth for surprising the hell out of you. I had no idea what to say to that, and left it to Ran. He groped for a response. "I really don't see what—"

"Oh, come on, Sokol, humor me and wait under that coyu tree there. We all know she'll just stroll over to you shortly and repeat everything I've said."

Back in control, Ran said coolly, "Then why ask me to leave?"

"Because I'll feel less inhibited in my conversation. Now, please? For an old companion-of-the-road?"

The trouble with Stereth is that he's like a force of nature. He can say "please" all he wants, but you still have the feeling that if you disagree with him on something like this, a giant hand will reach out of heaven and move you over to the coyu tree anyway.

Still, he did say "please." And asked as a friend. Ran sighed and walked down the path to the tree. When he reached it, he turned and raised his hands as though to say, Well? What more do you want?

Stereth watched him with a look of affectionate familiarity. "He's not happy. He wasn't very happy in the Northwest Sector, either. I swear, Tymon, sometimes I wonder what you see in him."

"He's happy enough when you're not around, Stereth."

He chuckled. "Because you let him have things his own way, no doubt."

"Well, you would know about needing to have things your own way."

"Touché." Stereth spoke of Ran as one would of a

troublesome younger brother. "But what I want to talk to you about is doing me a favor."

"Oh?"

"What a noncommittal sound after all we've been through together. What about 'Yes, Stereth, nothing you want can be too great?' "

"What did you have in mind?"

"Do you remember Keleen Van Gelder?"

I was disoriented for a moment, thinking he meant someone who'd been in the outlaw band, though it wasn't an Ivoran name. "I don't think I know the person."

"She's junior ambassador from Tellys. You saw her at the garden party and again on the boat." I frowned. He said, "A blond woman, handsome, in her forties or fifties. A bit taller than the average barbarian. She said she tried to speak to you but couldn't get your attention in the press of the crowd."

I flashed back to the woman with the blonde braid who'd stopped her conversation and stared at me. "Yes, I think I remember. I didn't know she was the Tellys ambassador."

"She wants to talk to you."

Another surprise. "Whatever for?"

"I have no idea. But I'm trying to make some Tellysian friends and I told her I'd get you to visit her."

Couldn't he tell her he'd *ask* me to visit her? Not and be Stereth, he couldn't. "Why do you want Tellysian friends?"

"I'm a friendly person. What about it, Theodora?"

"And you really don't know what she wants."

"I really don't. I'm just collecting a favor."

I considered it. An idea occurred. I said, "Listen here, companion-of-the-road. It's not customary to exchange favors within the same family, because it's assumed that all family members are working toward the same goals anyway."

"We're not in the same family."

"I'm not talking about you and me. I'll go see the junior ambassador—"

"Thank you."

"You'll owe me a favor. Hold onto it. Should you ever, in the future, be in a position where *Ran* owes you a favor, I want you to ask him to go visit the medical clinic of his wife's choosing, and take what tests she decrees."

For once I'd thrown Stereth off-stride. He repeated, "Medical clinic." Then he said, "Forgive my pointing this out, but as his wife you seem in a unique position to make this request yourself."

"I'll forgive you," I said. "Now do we have a deal?"

"We do." We clasped hands. Ran, down at the coyu tree, dug one foot in the ground impatiently.

I said, "I'll have to tell him about Van Gelder."

"I thought you would. I only wanted you alone because you'd be more likely to agree."

"No mention of our deal, though," I said warningly.

"No, I didn't think so."

I waved to Ran from the porch and he walked up the path, looking far from pleased.

Chapter 7

When the house steward had led Stereth away, Ran simply said, "If you've taken in enough lungfuls, we'd better get to the west wing."

I'd been so expecting him to launch into a cross-examination that it left me at a momentary loss, as no doubt he'd intended. Besides— "You mean the body? Now?"

"No better time. He'll be burnt by tomorrow."

Ugh. I followed him over the path to the west porch and up the step. The aroma of bitter incense was strong here, to drive away the evil spirits. (If you've never seen Ivoran death customs, I should mention that nobody on the entire planet takes these evil spirits seriously. Well, not entirely, anyway. Nobody omits the incense either. I suppose if you offered a bereaved family member a thousand tabals to dump the incense, they'd take the cash. But I don't think they'd be entirely comfortable about it.)

Silver streamers hung over the doorway. Having already been admitted to the house proper, there was no reason we couldn't step right in, but I hesitated. "Will there be people in there?" I asked.

"Possibly. Beloved family members are supposed to keep watch over the body."

And Coalis was reading a book, Eliana was working through her options, and Grandmother was sedated. "Maybe Jusik will be in there. He might not be thrilled at our monkeying around with the corpse. Especially since he's not sure you didn't kill him, anyway."

"Jusik will be too busy at a time like this," said

Ran, and he pushed aside the streamers and opened the door.

The room was empty. I hoped for his sake that Kade's popularity in death didn't match that of life but I was beginning to get the impression that it did. Except for Grandmother, of course, but they'd probably only wake her up for the funeral ceremony.

There was no coffin. Instead there was a flat board, like a wooden stretcher, set atop a heavy table. It being Kade Porath, first son of his House, the wood was a dark, carved mahogany, and the shallow silver incense bowls set on the floor at each of the four corners had the look of heirlooms. Kade's body was laid out on the board, wearing a suit of robes in gray, burgundy, and snow white. His head rested on a white satin pillow. Appearances had been maintained, I saw; somebody had been in to touch up his face with cosmetics and brush his hair. There is no embalming on Ivory, except for the occasional emperor. They consider it a repulsive custom, and about what one could expect of barbarians; the one or two people I'd asked about it had made disgusted faces, looked away, and changed the subject.

So much the better for us, anyway; aside from a little rouge and face powder, Kade was much the way he'd been when they fished him out of the canal. Ran went over at once and lifted the body's head, touching his thumbs to the base of Kade's chin. I found that I'd backed up as far as the ceremonial candlesticks lined against the wall.

"Come here, Theodora, give me a hand with this."

"Right." I walked over to the table, working for some normalcy in my stride. *Theodora of Pyrene, I had no idea you were so squeamish.*

—What did you expect? How many dead people have I seen? And I never had to touch any of them.

—*You're seriously disappointing me. This is disgraceful. You're just not living up to my image of you.*

—Time you found out the truth, then.

I get schizoid sometimes in moments of stress. Bear with it, you'll probably see it happen again.

I ignored the sense of repulsion and put my hands where Ran indicated, turning Kade's head to one side while Ran rubbed Kade's earlobe between his fingers, as though testing a lettuce leaf.

"The doorways of the senses," said Ran softly. "This is where traces of tampering can usually be found."

I grunted. Something about the situation made conversation difficult for me. And what did he mean by "usually?" Were there forensic sorcerers on this planet who made a career of this sort of thing? There are definitely gaps in my education, but I'm never aware of what they are till I trip over them.

He ran his little finger over Kade's lips. The finger came away red.

I said, "Does that mean anything?"

"Lip rouge," he said.

He pulled the corners of Kade's eyes back and peered into each one.

"So," he said, "What did Stereth want?"

"What?"

"What did the Minister for Provincial Affairs want with you, tymon?"

"Oh. He wanted me to meet somebody. Keleen Van Gelder, the junior ambassador from Tellys."

Ran's glance flicked to my face, then returned to the corpse at hand. "Let the head down, sweetheart. Now pull up the sleeve of the outerrobe. Why does he want you to see the ambassador?"

"I'm not sure. He wants the Tellysians to like him, and Van Gelder asked to meet me. He said he'd arrange it as a courtesy."

"No, hold it all the way back. I want to see the complete arm. What about Van Gelder? Why does he want to meet you?"

"She. Keleen's a female name. And Stereth says he doesn't know."

The glance flicked upward again. "Do you believe him?"

I shrugged. "Who knows?" He sounds sincere. And I can't see any harm in a simple meeting."

"You mean you already agreed?"

"Well, yes."

Ran sighed. "I knew he wanted me to stand under that tree for some reason."

I was relieved. Ran thought he'd found the secret at the heart of the conversation, which meant he wouldn't keep pressing.

He said, "Was that the whole matter?"

"Pretty much."

"Pretty much?"

"Yes, that was whole matter. You get a little touchy around Stereth, you know."

"Sorry." He held Kade's right hand with one hand of his own, and pulled Kade's thumb with the other. I know a tinaje massage-healing type move that's exactly the same, but Kade was in no shape to appreciate it. I shifted my grip on the corpse, let a handkerchief drop out of my sleeve, caught it with the same hand, blew my nose, returned the handkerchief, and grabbed Kade again.

I said, "Are we going to have to cut him open?"

"Possibly. A little bit. We may need to take some samples."

Suddenly he threw down the hand. "Ow!"

"What, what's the matter?"

"Kanz!" He reached out slowly toward the hand, and very tentatively touched the massive ring on Kade's third finger. "Yow!" He drew back again as though he'd taken an electric shock. He stepped backward from the corpse and met my eyes. "It's the ring."

"What about the ring?"

"It's cursed."

I blinked. That was interesting. I'd traveled up and down the coast for weeks once carrying a cursed deck of cards and I'd never gotten any electric shocks from it. I reached toward the ring.

"Don't touch it." Suddenly Ran's fingers were circling my wrist.

"Come on, what am I going to do, vanish in a puff of smoke? Go swimming in the fountain outside?"

His face was stubborn. "We make no assumptions till I've had a chance to study it."

He was serious. I put my hand down. Instead I bent over the table and examined the ring visually: A large blue stone set in silver, etched with vine leaves around the setting. There were more designs etched in the band, but I couldn't see them properly because Kade's fingers were in the way. Probably there were characters inside, too; it looked like some kind of family-crest sort of thing. I'd have to pull the ring off to really tell. But apparently that was a no-no.

"If we can't touch it, how do we get it off?"

He said, "Did you bring extra handkerchiefs?"

"In this House of Hell? Of course." I went through the pouch on my belt, pulled out a clean one and gave it to him.

He grasped the ring with the handkerchief and pulled it off Kade's finger. Then he let the ring's weight settle in the center of the cloth like the contents of a small jewelry bag and tied a knot with the corners. He hefted the small package. "There. Most likely it only affects the one who wears it, but no harm in being careful." He smiled. "This is unexpected good fortune. The curse is still operational; we can trace it back to the sorcerer who placed it. Someone's been careless."

I said, slowly, "*Too* careless?"

He was silent for a moment. "One would think that a murder-curse would be constructed to discharge itself and dissipate, not stay tied to an object like any normal spell. That's how I would do it. But who can say what's 'too careless,' with all the incompetence that's loose in the world?" He added, "When I say that's how I'd do it, I mean of course if I performed the assassination as some public spectacle, which I would never do." Ran's personal curse, his sense of

professional pride, required him to point this out any
number of times in the course of the investigation.

I realized I was still holding Kade's arm. I laid it
down. "Do we still have to cut him up?"

"What? Oh. No, we've got what we need." He
slipped the tiny bundle into his pocket. "Let's see if
the house steward can identify Kade's ring."

"Ran, for heaven's sake, we can't just leave."

"Why not?" He seemed genuinely puzzled.

I waved toward the table. It looked as though some
necrophiliac had been having a go at the body. "The
family, Ran. Do you want them to walk in on this?"

"Oh." He came over and helped me tidy Kade's
robes.

I said, "Damn, you smeared the lip paint when you
were touching his face."

"I don't know what I can do about that at this
point." He wiped some of the smear with a corner of
his sleeve. The lip paint was half on and half off, giving Kade a vampiric look. Appropriate to his profession, perhaps, but nothing his family would appreciate.

"Wait a sec." I opened my pouch, pulled out the
tiny brush and pot Kylla'd given me and started applying rouge to his lips.

"What in the name of all the gods are you doing?"

"I'm being polite, damn it." Kylla'd chosen the
shade carefully for my barbarian coloring; it didn't go
with Kade, but he'd have to live with it. So to speak.
"There." I looked at the tiny pot and brush before
tucking them away. "I never want to use these again."

Ran sighed. "Your constant acquisition of new skills
amazes me. May we go search out the steward now?"

I glanced over the table, the body, the incense holders, the candlesticks. Everything seemed appropriate.
I blew my nose a final time. "Of course."

On being summoned, the steward met us at the front
door again, not fazed in the least by our reappearance.
Ran untied the knot in his handkerchief and displayed
the ring. "Is this familiar to you?"

The steward studied it for a second, then said, "No."

It took us both aback. Ran said, "It was on Kade's body."

"Ah. I was told he'd been found wearing a ring. The servants who took care of the matter said that his fingers were somewhat bloated at the time; we thought it best to leave the ring where it was." He paused an impeccable pause that said *Is there some problem?*

Ran said, "But you've never seen it before."

"Not to my knowledge, gracious sir."

"If this belonged to Kade, would you necessarily know?"

"If he were in the habit of wearing it, I would. I'm also familiar with the contents of his jewelry box upstairs, and this was never in it."

That was a little unsettling. Did the servants at Cormallon know what was in *my* jewelry box?

The steward went on, "I can't answer for whether he might not have kept it elsewhere, or only just bought it." Ran was retying the knot in the handkerchief, and the steward said, "Excuse me, gracious sir, but are you planning to take the ring away with you?"

"Actually, I was."

The steward coughed. "I'm afraid I'll have to ask for a receipt, sir."

"Oh. Of course." And then we all stood around for a few minutes while paper was obtained and the steward wrote out a description: "One ring, blue cadite, silver setting, etched with vine leaves on the outer band and the words 'Daring and Prudent' on the inner."

It was the first I'd heard about words on the inside of the band. They sounded like a motto. A rather contradictory motto, in fact.

Ran was handed back the handkerchief, and we thanked the steward and left the Poraths'. My allergy-pummeled body was glad to leave, but my mind had more ambiguous feelings. Having told Lord Jusik Porath that we were innocent of any involvement in the death of his son, we'd just wound up our first foray into the investigation by pocketing the main piece of evidence and taking it away with us.

Perhaps it wasn't wise, but at the time I really don't know what else we could have done.

I called ahead to the Tellysian Embassy for an appointment that afternoon. I was fairly curious, actually, perhaps more so than I was about Kade. People get murdered all the time on Ivory, but extraplanetary junior ambassadors had never gone out of their way to look me up before.

I was passed directly from a functionary to Van Gelder. "I'm so glad you called," she said. The visual circuit was open and I could see that she was in fact the woman from the party. A closer view showed her as older looking, but deserving of Stereth's "handsome," with strong, clean-cut features. She wore elegant modified Tellysian clothes, a silky one-piece suit whose pants were tailored a little on the full side, making them resemble an Ivoran robe. "I haven't had lunch yet. Have you? It's been a terrible day and I'm longing to get out of here for a bit. There's a terrace in the Imperial park where they serve some Standard dishes; would you be my guest?"

It was a little like being hit by a small cyclone. "I hadn't planned on—"

"Oh, please come; if you're not hungry, you can order one of those sherbet things and a fizz."

Well, it was a good restaurant—I'd eaten there a couple of times with Kylla and Shez. And I was still curious. "All right, but I don't think I can stay very long. Couldn't you give me some idea of what you—"

"Damn! Another call. They haven't stopped all day. I'm really very sorry to be so scatterbrained over the Net. Shall we make it in forty minutes?"

I gave in. "Fine."

"Excellent, I'm looking forward to seeing you. Oh,

if you need a lift after, don't worry about it—I have
the use of a carriage and driver!'' And she signed off.

Well. That hadn't told me a lot. And the Imperial
Park was a half hour's walk from where I was, in the
full midday heat. It was a good thing I'd brought along
a straw hat.

Somehow I always end up carrying things. My hat,
my extra handkerchiefs, my money, a deck of cards,
a list of Net numbers for vehicle rentals that had been
folded so many times it was approaching unreadable,
any number of hairpins—I was going to have to get
this mop cut pretty soon—a copy of Kesey's *Poems*
that I hadn't gotten very far in reading. . . . Fortunately my robes have lots of pockets.

I was a little disappointed, actually; I'd been looking forward to seeing what the inside of the Tellysian
embassy was like. The facade was pure, sculpted,
classic Ivoran style, but the gods only knew what they'd
done indoors. Athenans and Pryenese are minimalists;
Ivorans tend to the baroque; I had no idea what Tellysians approved of. Except that their own government
limited them technologically in what they could bring
on-planet, they might have anything there. Solid gold
drinking fountains. Grav lifts with Old Master paint-
ings on the walls. Ask an Ivoran, and he'd tell you
they could afford it, with what they squeezed out of
other planets for their tech designs. But I wondered.
How many things had Ivory, for example, actually
bought from Tellys? Not very many that I knew about.

The Imperial Park is cool and green, as cool as you
can get in the capital in the summertime, with trees,
paths, fountains, statues, artificial wading streams, and
a contingent of Imperial Security whose efficiency is
matched only by their extraordinary politeness. A set
of terraces leads down to the river, and on the final
terrace, just above the water, you will find a fairly
small restaurant surrounded by a flagstoned area with
white tables and chairs. I highly recommend it. The

chairs, considered a pointless luxury, have seats more
than half a meter off the ground—something an outworlder can appreciate—with intricate backs and arms.
An overhang of crisscrossed wood provides a sun
shield while creating a dappled effect. Just across the
river you can see the striped dome of the First Wife's
Palace through the trees.

And the food's not bad, either. I was hot and tired
when I got there so I immediately ordered a cherry
fizz and snow sherbet. Then I waved the brim of my
hat at myself until I'd gotten back into a cheerful
mood. Midway between lunch and dinner, the place
was empty, so I tucked one foot under my knee on the
chair in a most unladylike position and watched the
white birds flying among the trees across the way, trying to remember details of a legend I'd heard about
how the First Wife's Palace got built. The sherbet was
delicious.

"Theodora of Pyrene?"

I squinted up toward a patch of sunlight and eased my
foot surreptitiously down to the flagstones. "Yes." The
woman from the Net call was there, her long blond
braid falling past the shoulders of her sky-blue suit.

"Keleen Van Gelder, junior ambassador from Tellys." She extended a hand, the first hand I'd shaken
in a long time. I took it. "This is my colleague, Jack
Lykon," she continued. The man beside her was
younger, perhaps in his early thirties, brown hair thin-
ning on top and darker brown eyes with a friendly look
to them. I shook his hand, too.

"It's a lovely place, isn't it?" she asked, pulling out
a chair. Jack Lykon took the third.

"Yes, I've been here before. They've got some Pyrenese beer stocked, but it costs a fortune."

Lykon said, "They do?"—looking interested. "How
much is it?"

Van Gelder turned to him with a slight smile, slant-
ing her eyes. "Imagine paying someone to carry the
mug to you personally from the south coast, Jack.
That's about how much it costs."

He seemed disappointed.

Van Gelder said to me, "I see you've ordered sherbet. I may myself. Where's the waiter?"

I reached over and pushed the bell in the center of the table. The lone waiter, an old fellow who covered about an inch a minute, tottered out. Van Gelder, interestingly, ordered tah with her meal. Lykon settled for beer from the Northwest Sector.

"We're the only ones here," said Lykon, looking around uncomfortably. "I wouldn't have known the place was even open."

It occurred to me suddenly that I might have been uncomfortable once myself, sitting alone on a terrace being served by a thousand-year-old waiter. All those social doubts: Should I be here? Are passersby watching me? What do the restaurant people think? But I'd been hanging around Ran too long. Wherever you were is where you were supposed to be, by definition; Cormallons are never treated below-status, except by the confused; and waiters and cooks can think what they like, as long as they provide the excellent service you are paying them to give. End of story.

Or perhaps it was just that I was getting old.

Van Gelder shrugged. "If we're alone, so much the better."

Enough of comparative social philosophy, too. I said, "The Minister for Provincial Affairs made your invitation intriguing. May I ask how you know him?"

She grinned. "A good diplomat never claims greater acquaintance than a local figure may wish to allow. You'll have to tell me what Minister Tar'krim said about our relationship, before I can confirm or deny."

So, she could be inoffensively discreet, too. I said, "Is it asking too much to inquire about why you wanted to see me?"

"Not at all, Theodora.—I hope I don't offend in calling you Theodora. I know Pyrene custom only provides one name for its people, and I understand that you're Pyrenese."

I looked down at my empty sherbet bowl. "I was born on Pyrene, but at the moment I've actually got joint Athenan/Ivoran citizenship."

"That must make you virtually unique."

"I wouldn't know. I don't have any statistics on the matter."

She seemed to be flipping through an invisible folder. "Pyrene, Athena, Ivory. Out of the four habitable planets in this sector, Tellys is the only one you've never seen. Or have you?"

"Well, it's nothing personal. You know what interstellar travel costs, ambassador, it's not something many private citizens can afford. Other people picked up my tab—well, except for one trip, and I had a little help on that—and I had to go wherever the ticket was stamped. I was on a government scholarship to Athena, you know."

"I'd heard that. I also heard that you paid your own fare from here to Athena a couple of years ago. A remarkable achievement, at your age."

I blinked and said, "I had no idea I was such a topic of conversation in embassy hallways."

She cracked a smile. "Perhaps we don't get out enough," she acknowledged.

Our waiter began his snail-like progress from the pavilion of the restaurant proper. We were speaking Standard, but none of us made any attempt to continue the conversation until he'd deposited his load of three large plates, tah cup, and beer mug, and returned inside. You wouldn't think he could carry a sheet of paper successfully, but he negotiated the load with a flawless execution. This was a man with experience in his field.

"He must have been waiting tables while our ancestors were still working to go multicellular." I'd said it aloud. Lykon broke up. I looked at him, surprised.

"I was just thinking the same thing," he said. Then he went into another fit of chuckles.

Van Gelder raised a perfectly groomed eyebrow and

said to me, "Jack gets set off by things sometimes." She took a sip of pink tah. "Anyway, he takes an interest in biological references. But we'll get to that."

Would we? This would be an unusual lunch.

Chapter 8

The junior ambassador from Tellys wiped grease from her fingers. She was talking about sorcery, a subject I have more than a passing interest in. "There've been two Standard papers on Ivoran 'sorcery'—only two, in the hundred years we've been in contact. Both by eccentrics, both paid little attention to by the Athenan University Committee. The latter one was slightly more exhaustive. Written by a kinsman of mine, a Tellysian, named Branusci."

I leaned forward, already interested. Following my first stay on Ivory I'd hunted the Athenan libraries obsessively for any work on Ivoran sorcery, and found a single paper. The second, if it existed, must have been indexed under some other subject.

"It was indexed under 'Stage Magic,' " she said, veering into telepathy. "Not an appropriate category, really, but that was the approach the article took. Branusci studied eight marketplace sorcerers—not perhaps the best pool, to begin with—and decided, in the end, that any of their effects could be duplicated in some 'rational' fashion. If there was no visible and outward evidence—as in a luckspell, where the results could so easily be ascribed to random chance—then what did it prove? If there was visible evidence—say, with a visual illusion—then a holographic projector could do as well. Or any number of other methods, to achieve other effects."

"There are no holographic projectors on Ivory."

"Branusci points out they might have been smuggled in."

"You don't sound impressed with your kinsman."

She shrugged. "If a man can levitate an elephant, saying that you can do the same thing with strings and pulleys is hardly the point, is it?" She put down her tah cup. "The Athenans like to think of themselves as rationalists, but I suspect they're just afraid of looking silly."

I'd had the same thought myself more than once.

She went on, "Otherwise, why wouldn't they put the same rigorous, thorough study into it that they put into dissecting the dozen variants of a legend?"

"Interesting you should choose that metaphor. My field of study was cross-cultural myths and legends."

She smiled austerely. "What an amazing coincidence."

I laughed.

She leaned forward. "Let's hypothesize for a moment that 'Magic is real.' Or to put it another way, the more respectable sorcerers of Ivory are tapping into something we have not previously had experience with. They've learned rules for using this . . . whatever it is . . . that seem to work for them. Whether they want to call them spells or something more acceptable to Standard culture is irrelevant to our purpose, for the moment."

It was nice to hear somebody talking about Ivoran magic in the language I'd grown up in. I don't mean Standard.

She wiped her lips with the green linen napkin our ancient waiter had provided. "Even given the extraordinary lack of interest on this planet in strictly academic matters, there must be theories about magic. Where it comes from, why it can be accessed by some people and not others. . . ." She let her voice trail off.

I said, "I've heard the three most respectable theories and about twenty more oddball ones. But nobody really knows—knows in a good Athenan sense, I mean. Nobody has any evidence." This is the simple truth, and I saw no reason not to share it.

She nodded. "It doesn't surprise me. But one can hardly help zeroing in on some genetic relationship."

I was silent.

"This is speculation, of course. But I understand your present husband accompanied you to Athena a couple of years ago. He's a top-ranked sorcerer here in the capital, they tell me. One can't help wondering if he was able to continue using his abilities away from this planet. You would think that he *would* be able to, if sorcery is more linked with genetics then geography. But the whole subject is so out of the usual ken, I'd hesitate even to guess."

I was becoming uncomfortable. My Athenan past taught me to revere the free sharing of information, and on one level I would have been pleased if a serious inquiry into the messy category of magic had been taken up by the Standard community. After all, they might make some breakthrough on the subject, bringing it into a neat line with the laws of the universe as I had once known them, and they might do it before my death. That bothered me, you know. That I'd gotten involved in a subculture based on a force that even the people who used it didn't understand; and that someday, people would figure it all out—too late to tell Theodora.

On the other hand, this was veering close to House secrets. Ran had indeed tried to use sorcery during his foray into culture shock on Athena, and I knew what the results were.

As a Cormallon, I did not feel at liberty to tell anyone.

I said, "Life is complicated, isn't it?"

"More so every year," she agreed. "When I was twelve, I understood the universe thoroughly."

"Me, too."

Jack Lykon spoke up suddenly. I'd nearly forgotten he was there. "Keleen," he said, "tell Theodora who I am."

She touched his hand. "Jack is a very talented genalycist."

"Is he?" I looked at him with new interest.

"He'd be just delighted, intellectually, if he could meet your husband."

"Yes, I'm beginning to understand that." I took a deep breath, knowing I ought to head them off before they made the mistake of offering a fee. "Look, it's nothing against you or Tellys. I know that someday people are going to have Ivoran sorcery down pat, quantified, boxed up in little boxes with ribbons. And good for them. They'll probably call it something other than sorcery when that day comes. But they're going to have to do it without my help." Damn, they looked so understanding. I hate it when people do that. "You seem to know a lot about sorcery, for an outworlder. But I don't know how much you know about the Houses of Ivory. They're all paranoid, all selfish, and their loyalty is only to themselves."

Van Gelder quirked a smile. I said, "I know. I'm making them sound so attractive. They do have one great virtue, though: They won't go out of their way to hurt you if you don't present an obstacle."

Van Gelder's smile had vanished. She said, "Not something that can be said of all human cultures."

I didn't pick up on it at the time, I was too busy going for my point. "What I'm trying to say here is, I'm a Cormallon. Sorcery is a Cormallon specialty, and I can't share information on our House business with anybody. It would be considered as working against our best interests—even if you offered to pay us."

She said, "A minute ago you spoke of the Houses in the third person; now you speak in the first."

"Blame it on my schizoid history. I'm not Pyrenese, and I'm not really Ivoran; all I really know I am, at this moment, is Cormallon. And if the universe takes five centuries to get around to cracking the sorcery game, then that's how long they'll have to wait."

They stared at me, and the pause lengthened. I felt myself getting red. It was probably as close to a patriotic speech as I'd ever been qualified to make. The silence became more awkward, and I groped to fill it. "Look, the bottom line is, my House will never agree to share any secrets with the Tellysian government."

They looked at each other. Van Gelder leaned back in her chair and tapped her silver spoon once against her empty sherbet bowl. She said, "But Theodora, my friend, we do not speak for the Tellysian government."

I hoped my jaw wasn't touching the floor. *"What?"*

Lykon said, "Keleen—"

She rode over him. "No, we speak neither for the Tellys Unity nor the Sealed Kingdom. We speak for a much smaller, more controllable group. Your families here make House allies, don't they? I think we'd like to be regarded in that light."

"We?"

She crossed her arms, still leaning back, and smiled. Lykon looked unhappy. "Tell me, have you heard much about the Tolla?"

I sat up, shocked. "Great gods of scholars."

She nodded. "That's right."

I'm going to have to stop here and tell you about the Tolla. If you already know about them, you can skip ahead, but I don't want to leave anybody behind.

I think you already know I don't like Selians. What you may not be aware of is that the Selians are a historically recent development, only germinating after the destruction of Gate 53 cut off our sector. Unlike Tolla propagandists, I can't tell you that they were involved in blowing up the gate, because they didn't exist at the time, but I have to admit that that's about the only obnoxious act that can't be laid at their door. As a group, I mean. As individuals they may be perfectly fine. I'm sure someday I'll meet a Selian I can like. . . . The nice ones probably stay home and don't go out in public.

Anyway. About sixty years ago the other worlds started hearing discomforting news events coming out of Tellys. The Sealed Kingdom declared independence around then and somehow got away with it—I don't know the ins and outs of Tellysian politics—and after stewing in their own self-congratulation for a while, started to become more and more militant.

(I know. This is all my own view of the matter. I can't give you somebody else's view, can I?)

Selians seek to perfect the universe until it reaches a state that matches the ideal; at that time the Perfect Kingdom will exist in reality as well as an abstraction. "The Perfect Kingdom Is At Hand" is a prime Selian credo. Understand, this has nothing to do with temples or supreme beings—on the contrary, they feel perfection is attainable with their own hot little hands. Selian houses are spotlessly clean. If Selian children don't match the physical ideal, they are dieted, exercised, and surgically altered, or else constantly humiliated for the rest of their lives.

Their definition of perfection, and their mechanism for attaining it, are based on two things: The worship of Fate (under the leadership of the Selian Central Committee), and a sense of differentiation. Differentiation means in the aggregate sense that the Selians are superior to other people. Fate means that their destiny is to one day have that superiority acknowledged. In the most peaceful way, mind you; their object is not to kill or torture. They only want to help others to understand that their ordained place is in service to the Kingdom. Once this understanding is reached, the universe will start to operate on the level it should be at.

As you may guess, any group this hierarchical is pretty rigid within its own ranks, as well. From what I understand, there are at least twenty separate levels, from the top three classes, who dye their hair silver-white to *differentiate* themselves—it would be a pity if their fellow citizens failed to recognize their natural superiority—down to the dregs at the bottom of the ladder, who are nevertheless a rung above anybody not Selian.

Women are placed just beneath the bottom rank. This is where the Tolla come in.

I must have been about thirteen, still living on Pyrene, when I saw the first news spot out of Tellys. It was a clip from a Unity talk show, with a regular Tellysian host, interviewing a Selian man. He wasn't silver-haired, so he couldn't have even been highly placed in the SK, but he was amused and contemptuous of the non-Selian interviewer. The interviewee was considered news because he'd just been acquitted of killing his wife. He'd been accused of setting her on fire because she was a bad cook. They showed a picture of her remains, a brief interview with the woman's sister—who had very little to say—and then cut back to the husband.

They cut back, and he smiled widely, showing a set of straight white teeth. It was the smile of somebody who has gotten away with something.

Since that first interview I heard the occasional stories of dowry murders, of a rise in female emigration from the Sealed Kingdom to the Tellys Unity—until there was a swift law passed forbidding women to carry identity papers themselves, or to travel when not under the supervision of an authorized male.

I know that none of this is historically new, but that's my point—this is a modern, industrialized, technologically advanced world I'm talking about. One that had seemed relatively sane before the destruction of Gate 53.

The rest of Tellys seems to consider the Kingdom a temporary aberration, and lack the ability or will to do much about it. After all, they were only about fifteen percent of the world population. And they were only preying on their own people. And in case you haven't dealt with any Selians, I ought to point out that they are not crazed lunatics who run around foaming at the mouth. Even for them, wife murderers are not on every corner, and except for the dye job, most of them look pretty normal. They have trades and families like any other society, and some of them do a lot of good. Altruism is built into their philosophical structure—kind of a noblesse oblige attitude; the upper ranks are expected to devote several years to collective good works. That's how the Selian Medical Clinic came to Ivory. It's amazing what a sincere case some of them make for their way of life.

Not that I, personally, like them. But I feel obliged to point this out.

But where slavery exists, you get abolitionists, and where the Selians exist—you get the Tolla.

They appeared one day, leaving a note famous for its brevity on the body of the gentleman interviewed by the talk show. "Shot by the Tolla." No manifesto, no explanations—for murderers, you had to like them. And then there was their choice of label, *Tolla*, "The Wrath of the Goddess." The word came from an old legend, a selection not without historical charm. They were, as much as we could tell from so far away—I was still on Pyrene at the time—a group of hitwomen. Soon they didn't bother to leave even brief notes; everyone knew who they were.

On Pyrene they were considered an interesting footnote, an eccentric example of life away from civilization. On Athena, I found, they were strongly disapproved of as a terrorist group. "One acts to change unjust laws; two wrongs don't make a right; if they weren't ashamed of what they were doing, they'd stand trial openly." Their anonymity seemed rather practical-minded to me, but I did not express this view at the time. Public opinion is a powerful force on Athena.

So now here I was, shocked—and I have to admit, a trifle delighted—to be facing someone who claimed involvement in the Tolla.

The life of a plain sorcerer's apprentice had been getting monotonous. It would be nice to talk to someone who did exciting things.

I said, glancing at Lykon, "I didn't know they let men in the Tolla."

"What a narrow way of doing things that would

be,'' said Van Gelder. "Not that I said that either of us were in the Tolla. I speak hypothetically.''

I was completely fascinated. "Your government doesn't even like the Tolla. They're always trying to capture them. Or is that an act?''

She shook her head. " 'The Tolla are a terrorist organization. We do not condone their actions.' And we're perfectly serious, Theodora—I speak now as a representative of the Tellys Unity. When a government lends itself to acts of terrorism, it loses its moral center.''

She seemed to mean it. I said, "Then you're not Tolla yourself?''

"On the other hand, what a private individual may feel impelled to do should not have repercussions beyond his own conscience. One may disobey a law, and nevertheless believe that law to be necessary.''

"That's not what they teach on Athena.''

Her long, sunburnt fingers tapped her plate. "They can afford to be finicky on Athena. The most that happens to anyone there is getting tossed off a committee.''

I'd once heard of a man who'd committed suicide after getting tossed off a committee. However, I suppose that would seem an unjustified response to someone involved in an organization whose purpose was so openly lethal.

I suddenly became aware that the sun was past the striped dome across the river, and that afternoon was practically evening. Two other tables had somehow become occupied, and I hadn't even been aware of it.

"This is fascinating,'' I said honestly, "but I'm not sure how it affects me or my House.''

She hesitated. "From your records, I thought you might lean toward a sympathy with our cause. You're not the usual Athenan scholar. Was I only reading into it what I wanted to believe?''

"No . . .'' I said slowly. "If you want the truth, I have mixed feelings about the subject. But I've seen people killed for less reason than the Tolla has. And if you were shooting somebody today, I'd step out of range of fire and go on my way."

Lykon made one of his rare remarks. "That's all we really expected."

I turned to him. "You look too gentle to be in the Tolla."

He smiled. It was a gentle smile. "It evens out," he said. "Keleen looks like a very general, doesn't she?"

I had to admit that she did. Everything about her, from her well-chosen semi-but-not-quite-Ivoran wardrobe to the knowledgeably applied cosmetics, spoke of planning. The few items that seemed to have escaped her control, like the ray of lines around her eyes, only gave weight and character to her looks. It was a good thing, really, that she had a slightly burnt complexion; otherwise one could be put off by her inhumanly precise elegance. Strength was in every bone and angle; but strength in the service of what?

Lykon, on the other hand, with his quiet, good-humored face, might as well have a sign around his neck saying "Trustworthy." If you ran into Jack Lykon while your city was falling, you'd give him your child to hold while you hammered your fists against the seal of the last departing ship. It *seemed* like the sort of face that is well-attached to the soul behind it, but until we knew this for sure I resolved to hang onto my wallet and my skepticism.

He sighed, looking at his empty mug, and said, "Do you think I could get another beer? I hesitate to ring for the waiter. . . ."

"Yes, he might not make it out till autumn." I squeezed the button on my airtight jar of cherry fizz and watched a stream pour into my glass. "If you're just thirsty, this might hold you till you get the real thing." I offered him my glass.

How much did they really understand about Ivory? Would they pass the test? He took the glass and drained it, getting a head of fizz around his mouth. Silly, but endearing, particularly in a balding terrorist. He said, in Ivoran, "My thanks."

Van Gelder seemed quietly amused. Points for their team. If Cormallon did make some kind of arrangement with them, they wouldn't disgrace us.

A sudden breeze blew up from the river, ruffling the table napkins. Here I was, naive, apolitical Theodora of Pyrene, sitting with two enemies of the Tellysian government, and I just didn't feel in any great danger. I suppose the Tolla has to recruit somehow; there must be some way, even if it's not the most reliable, of feeling out when to tell, and when not to tell. And perhaps it wasn't a great leap of faith at that—I wasn't a citizen of the Tellys Unity, I had no stake in what their world did. My very disinterest was a shield. Nor are Ivorans in the habit of mixing in governmental matters at all, if they can avoid them.

However they'd come to their conclusion, it was a correct one. I had no intention of telling any Tellysian officials about them. Even if I had, all the Tellysian officials were at the embassy, and it was more than possible Van Gelder had some system in place there for dealing with civilians who tried to bring embarrassing things to their attention.

It occurred to me that it must be useful for the Tolla, having a junior ambassador in their pocket. Maybe their influence went even further than that; I'd never been to Tellys and had no feel for their pattern of views in general, but it was no secret that the Kingdom was not well-liked there, to say the least. Quite apart from their politics, Unity citizens couldn't help but feel that the Selians had had a lot of nerve, seceding the way they did. There must be a good amount of underground support for the Tolla there—surely there was sympathy for their aims, if not their methods.

If they really were a power at home, allying with the Tolla might not be a bad idea for Cormallon. As long as it was a secret alliance. And a group like the Tolla must be pretty used to the concept of secrets.

She said, "Will you at least take the proposal to your husband? He is the First of his House, is he not?"

"Ambassador Van Gelder, I'm still at sea as to what your proposal *is*."

"Keleen, please."

"Keleen." Always glad to address a member of a dangerous terrorist group by their first name.

"The Tolla face certain problems currently," she said, in a brisk, businesslike tone. That reference to "our cause" a minute ago was the closest she tended to come to speaking of the group in the first person; it was always third-person, always an official distance. "First, Unity nationals are searched before entering the Kingdom. And in the last planetary year, the Kingdom has begun searching people who are traveling internally from territory to territory. Even long-range weapons that are already on Kingdom soil need transport, obviously; and then there's the matter of getting recharges to those weapons."

"I see." Nobody had ever spoken to me before on the subject of weapons running. I may have given up my opportunity for a degree on Athena, but living on Ivory is an education in itself.

"It's not like this planet; the officials are very chancy when it comes to bribery. There are always old-fashioned items like knives and clubs that can't really be controlled, but I'm sure you see at once that the proximity required for application makes capture much more likely."

"Oh, definitely. First thing I thought of."

She took me seriously. "Well, it goes without saying. So some people have been looking into the matter of weapons transport in general. The majority have been approaching this from the angle of transport; but it occurred to . . . others . . . that it might be rewarding to approach from the angle of the weapons themselves."

"You just said that knives and clubs . . ."

She smiled faintly. "Living on this world cannot

help but give one a more creative attitude as to what constitutes a weapon.''

''. . . Oh.''

''I understand the tragedy of young Kade Porath has been traced to sorcery.''

''Yeah, I'd heard that, too.''

''A vivid demonstration of its capabilities, I must admit—''

I sat up straight. ''What do you mean, demonstration? *Was* Kade's death some kind of demo for you people? Are you already negotiating with some other House?''

She seemed honestly surprised. ''Good lord, no. When we get to the demo stage I'm sure we can find someone less visible than a first son of the nobility. What do you take us for?''

''Honestly, I have no idea what to take you for. You'll have to tell me.''

Jack Lykon said, ''The Tolla had nothing to do with Kade Porath. It's true. I mean, for god's sake, Theodora—that would be murder.''

I let that line lie.

Van Gelder said, ''My principals' only wish is to enter into a long and profitable relationship with your House. I understand the penalties for using sorcery in an organized way here—against the government, that sort of thing—can be quite severe. But let me point out, there are no such laws on Tellys. Sorcery is not even recognized there. This would seem to open up a whole new area of expansion for Cormallon, Theodora. Surely it would be your duty to communicate my offer.''

''I'll think it over.''

''Good plain Ivoran tabals would be placed in your House account—no nasty, suspicious foreign money, I promise. In return, a consultant relationship would be opened, regarding how best to handle the weapons problem I described earlier.'' She reeled it off as though from a business contract. ''No actual sorcerer would have to travel to Tellys to do the executions, not

unless it proves absolutely necessary. Some form of
weapon that can be used by any knowledgeable person
will do the trick nicely.''

I raised my hands. ''You've made it all very clear,
ambassador.'' Suddenly I'd had enough of murder for
the day. I found myself wishing I could lie down and
sleep for twenty hours, like Kade's grandmother.

Van Gelder seemed to sense my withdrawal. ''I hope
I haven't offended in any way, Theodora. I was under
the impression that your husband took on assassinations from time to time himself, so it hardly seemed—''

''Yes, I know. All right.'' I stood up. ''I'll consider
passing the matter on.''

Jack Lykon rose at once and shook my hand. I still
couldn't see him as Tolla. It would be easier to imagine him as a country veterinarian, rising to a spot of
mild indignation only over the occasional mistreat-
ment of puppies. I said, ''I may want something from
you, though.''

''Me?'' He looked surprised.

''I'll let you know,'' I said. Reflex almost made me
bow, but I caught it in time and confined myself to a
polite smile in the ambassador's direction.

She said, ''I have a carriage at the Lin Entrance.''

''Thank you, I'd prefer to walk. I have some thinking to do.''

She inclined her head. ''A very great pleasure, Theodora, whatever you decide.''

Well, that's why she was an ambassador. I left the
terrace, made my way to the upper level of the
grounds, and took the Walk of Plum Trees down its
ruler-straight course to the Kyl Entrance. From there
it's about a half hour to our house.

I like to walk in the early evening, when a cool hand
finally lays itself on the feverish skin of a capital summer day. Of course, by then any passing breath of air
is considered cool, not to mention blessed. The shops
next to the Kyl Entrance of the Imperial Park are
known for their ridiculous prices; it's fun to look in
the windows, guess the tag amount, then peer closer

and have the shock of seeing how thoroughly your imagination has underestimated.

So, while playing this innocent game I considered the less innocent ones being proffered by these two Tellysians. What should I do? Probably I ought to disapprove of the Tolla, but the truth was that I didn't. At the same time, I had no wish to get personally involved; by nature I'm neither a martyr nor a soldier, and had my hands full just trying to lead an honorable life where I was. As for Ran—I tried to imagine Ran agreeing to share House secrets with any ally of less than five hundred years, and failed miserably.

This seemed to get us nowhere. At the same time, Jack Lykon was a genalycist, and a genalycist would be a useful person to have in my life this particular year. If only—

I passed a shop with an antique book on display; a gold-encrusted cover, opened with a key, and the words "Stories of the Third Empire" in gold and crimson letters of ancient calligraphy.

I collect stories, you know. At one time I thought it was a vocation, but lately I've come to wonder whether it's a hobby. Whatever the stories of the Third Empire were, I could probably track them down more cheaply elsewhere—

Stories. I'd collected stories from Ran's family, too. Tall stories, legends, anecdotes, recollections—not all of them believable, but all of them interesting, and none, unfortunately, released for public consumption. They were in a notebook back in my room in Cormallon, tucked under a pile of things on a table by the window. I hadn't taken them out in months; hadn't been back at Cormallon in weeks.

Damn, I couldn't remember the details, but hadn't there been one about a similar alliance? One of Ran's legions of aunts had told me, when she was passing through the estate on her way to some kind of appointment in the capital . . . her dressmaker's, that was it. Come on, Theodora, you can remember the dressmaker, what about the plot of the story?

There had been a House of brewers, on the edge of the Northwest Sector, who'd been having some kind of trouble with deliberately contaminated beer—Jack Lykon's choice of beverage must have reminded me. A pair of reps had requested a House alliance with Cormallon to track down the saboteurs, but there was some reason the alliance couldn't go through—something about offending our long-time allies, the Ducorts (though I didn't see why; the Ducorts handle wine and tah, and consider themselves above honest beer). So what had happened?

The First at that time had figured a method of weeding out any contaminated tubs, and tracing back any sorcerous damage to the beer to its source. Nonsorcerers could use the method, but only by a quick education in Cormallon techniques and the use of House materials. I couldn't recall the sorcery involved, but I remembered the political answer: Three brewery employees had been adopted into the House of Cormallon and then loaned back to their birth house to supervise the beermaking.

This was the crux: The adoption gave Cormallon House-justice rights over the lives of the brewers. They'd all had spells placed on them that prevented their spilling any House secrets to outsiders. Gagspells, they're called, and they're the kind of thing that can be very dangerous, very complicated, and only done with the person's consent. The brewers accepted it out of self-interest, being well-paid for their cooperation. When the crisis was over, Cormallon released them back to their birth house—with gags intact, and if I know the Cormallons, probably some memory impairment. (The latter was never admitted. Removing memory is easy; what's hard is to be *selective.*)

So no alliance, Cormallon pockets its fee, the brewers get their reputation for good beer returned . . . I never found out what happened to the three shifted employees. Spells that fool around with memory and volition are risky things; if the three ended up committing suicide somewhere down the road, I would not be surprised.

On the other hand, the Tolla was by definition composed of high risk-taking individuals.

Given a choice between a lengthy gene search for hypothetical magic abilities and a workable weapons program, Van Gelder would go for the weapons. Pure research was not her aim. And if we could work out a trade, perhaps she would lend me Jack Lykon for a day or two . . . because research *was* my aim.

The next question would be, was Jack Lykon a high risk-taking individual?

And what in the world was I going to tell Ran?

Chapter 9

As it turned out, I had time to think about it, as Kylla and Lysander were in the parlor when I got home. They were both holding drinks, which I thought was a good idea on Ran's part, and since nobody seemed to be throwing anything at anybody, I walked right in.

Lysander was seated on the red-fringed cushion by the table. He raised his glass an inch when I entered, and nodded. "Theodora." Kylla, who was half-sitting, half-lying on the divan, now sat up straight and patted the space beside her. "Theo, sit by me. Ran's telling us about your day. It sounds wonderfully gruesome."

I loosened my outerrobe and sat down. Nobody asked me where I'd been, which made things simpler, so I took a sip of Ky's proffered drink—a Soldier's Delight, apparently; Lysander must have stopped somewhere on the way here and bought a flask to go. It was not the custom for old aristocratic families to keep the ingredients for mixed drinks in the house, and it never occurred to Ran that we might stock up. Most of the time I didn't feel the lack, but there were occasional nights when Ran was off putting in an appearance for one of the Cormallon branches and I was stuck in the capital; when the Net seemed supremely uninteresting, and I'd sung all the old Pyrenese songs I could think of in the bathroom, and I found myself wishing for a nudge to get to sleep. No point in opening up the expensive Ducort for that.

Gods, I hoped Ran wasn't going to get himself killed in his profession any time soon. The mortality rate for the upper-rank males of Ivory is relatively high, and that thought did tend to surface from time to time, presenting itself in all its bleak surfaces. I'd been alone most of my life, but I was rapidly losing the knack for it, if it wasn't gone already. It's probably like languages—you've got to keep in practice to handle it with any confidence.

"Theo?" inquired Kylla. She was holding the glass. So was I. I let go, and she said, "Something on your mind?"

"The usual mess. Ran tell you I used up your lip rouge?"

"That was the pot I gave you? Ugh! Theo, that was Cachine Cosmetics, it cost a fortune. What were you thinking?"

Good old practical Kylla. For one paranoid second I wondered if we should be sharing all this data with her and Lysander, considering they were, technically, suspects; but I stamped "unworthy" on that thought and put it back in the closet. Of course, we'd never gotten to know Lysander as well as we might. . . .

Lysander said, "You were about to show us the ring."

Ran did his handkerchief trick once again and made the silver and cadite lump appear in the center. Lysander whistled. "I never saw anything with a curse on it before. That I knew of."

Kylla, an old hand from a house of sorcerers, shrugged. Her long gold earrings tinkled gently. "It's not a thing of beauty," she said. "Kade's taste must have run to the obvious . . . I can't say I'm surprised, having met the sister."

Lysander said, quickly, "Can you use this to identify the sorcerer?"

Ran covered the ring again. "Yes and no. I've been examining it all afternoon—it seems to be safe enough as long as you don't put it on your finger—and the curse is still operational. So by the Rule of Connectivity, we ought to be able to stand wherever the sorcerer stood when he ignited the spell, and follow the spoor back to trace him.''

"If only we knew where he was standing," I said.

"Yes," agreed Ran.

"I suppose you could request the use of the boat," said Lysander. "Take it out toward Catmeral Bridge, and move randomly around on the decks till—"

Kylla interrupted. "Does it have to be on the boat?"

Her husband looked puzzled, but Ran said, "No, I was going to mention that little problem. As long as he knew Kade had the ring on, the sorcerer could have been anywhere in line-of-sight—and the lounge deck had big windows, remember—to set the curse loose. That means it could have been somebody on the roof of a warehouse, or on the garden wall of one of your neighbors' houses, Ky.''

Lysander groaned. "Anybody in the city, that means.''

"Or on Catmeral Bridge," said Kylla.

We all looked at her. I said, "Why the bridge?"

She set her drink on the floor. "There was a man there. I noticed him because he was leaning over the rail, staring at us. It annoyed me." True, at the time Kylla had been in no mood to be stared at, or to be anything else, actually. "It was mid-afternoon, and the Catmeral isn't a covered bridge, right? And it was hot and sunny—the place was practically deserted, and the one or two people crossing over were racing their little fannies across and darting back into the shade. But not this man. He had his arms on the rail and was just leaning there, glaring down. I thought, Who does he think he's looking at, anyway? Then I thought, This one is strange.''

Ran said, "Lysander, did you—"

"No, I didn't see him. It's the first I heard of it. But then, my back was to the bridge most of the time. I was facing Kylla.''

Ran turned to his sister. "You didn't mention this before.''

"Well, if I'd known he was going to drown a Porath, I would have paid more attention! Anyway, then there was that splash down below, and I forgot all about it. Till now."

Ran glanced at me. We'd been on deck at the same time. I said, "I wasn't facing the bridge either." He looked unhappy. I added, "That security guard was up there with us for a while. The one Kade chewed out about not covering Eliana? But I don't remember if we were near the bridge then, or not."

Ran brightened. "Even if he wasn't, he could help us physically place who was where on the boat. Security guards are always making visual sweeps. We could call the Poraths and find out what service they used, and make an appointment to see him before we take the boat out again."

Lysander said, "Could you call them tonight?"

Poor man, Kylla must really be putting the screws to him at home. He definitely wanted the murder, the wedding, and the Poraths taken care of and far away.

Ran glanced down for a second at the bunched handkerchief, then slipped it in the inner pocket of his robe and gave Lysander his full attention. "How are things going, by the way, with your own problem? Has Jusik been in touch since the boat ride?"

Kylla swung her own gaze full on him as well, waiting with that patient, without-mercy born Cormallon expression on her face. Lysander grabbed hold of his glass and downed a long swallow. "He did call," he admitted. "He suggested I might attend the funeral tomorrow. I told him I had to be out of town. He didn't insist."

"Well," said Ran after a moment, "perhaps he won't insist on the marriage, either."

"He might be all the more in need of the money, though, now that Kade's gone," I contributed. The look Lysander shot me was not a kind one.

He said, "I'm sure they all want Eliana to marry money, but there's no reason I have to be the money.

I think if I struggle enough, they'll let me escape. After all, it was Kade's pet idea, and he's gone.''

Conveniently. Ran's eyes met my own, and I thought, Tsk, tsk. What unbrotherly suspicion. If Lysander's surname had been Cormallon, Ran would have no doubts about his character; if he'd killed Kade, he'd report that fact to Ran so we could all deal with it more intelligently. Despite past experiences, Ran still believed Cormallons could do no wrong.

"We'd better get back," said Kylla, standing up. "I promised Shez I'd kiss her goodnight. It's bedtime now, and she'll torture her nurse till I get there." She gave me a peck on the cheek, then whispered, "How are things going? Missed any periods yet?"

"For the love of heaven, Ky!" I glanced over toward Ran and Lysander, who were continuing the conversation by themselves.

She smiled unrepentently. "You know, I never thought of you as having any nurturing instincts whatsoever. Or not till that afternoon my robe got stuck in the door at the jewelry shop and you spent the hour shaking keys over Shez's carriage to stop her wailing."

"It had to be done."

"And making noises like a ship taking off—"

"All right, Ky."

"Somehow I'd just never pictured you having such a good time with the next generation."

"I know." Kylla saw me as the kind of person who'd mix up the pram with the grocery bags and send the baby off for delivery because I was too busy thinking of which third-person form to use in a translation.

She kissed me again, then went to the low table by the wall and picked up a wrapped bouquet of flowers that I hadn't noticed before. She grabbed and swung them without respect for their delicacy, as though they were a frying pan.

"What are they?" I asked. "I've never seen them before."

She brought the bouquet over for me to inspect. "I

don't know their name," she said, "but they're in season now. Lysander bought them for me on the way here."

They were a violet blue, made up of masses of perfect, tiny petals that fooled the eye into thinking they were a single entity from a distance. A rich scent rose in a cloud from the wrappings. "They're wonderful! There must be hundreds of petals. Ran, what are they called?"

"No idea," said Ran.

Kylla bent over and patted my hand with friendly patronization. "We're all glad you like them, Theo. Ran, buy this woman more gifts. If a few flowers get her this excited, she must be deprived. When's the last time you gave her jewelry?"

Ran stopped and thought. "I don't think I ever have."

"Great gods," said Lysander, revealing volumes about his own relationship. After a moment he said, "What do you do when she's mad at you?"

"If she's been angry with me, she hasn't told me. Theodora, have you been angry with me?"

I said, "Not since that time in the Sector last summer. And neither of us had any opportunity to go shopping then."

Kylla said, "Brother, rectify this matter. I speak as one with your interests at heart. Come along, Lysander."

Her husband followed her to the door. "Ran, you'll let me know—"

"I'll keep you up to date," Ran assured him.

They left. Ran said to me, "If we want to interview the security guard, we'll probably have to get to his office early tomorrow, before his shift starts. That means rising at dawn."

"Kanz, komo, and the destruction of profit." He was unsurprised at my immediate profanity; Ran knows I hate to get up early. Mentally I revised my schedule: I'd discuss the Tolla's offer with him tomorrow night—otherwise we'd be up till dawn debating it, and I'd be a wreck in the morning.

"Want to hear about my tests on the ring?" he asked.

"Tomorrow," I said.

"Want to tell me about your meeting with the Tellysian ambassador?"

"Tomorrow."

He walked over, knelt by the chaise, and put his head on my thigh. My hand went out to his hair, thick and soft. He lifted his face. "Don't tell me you're tired already. The night is young."

The night wasn't all that was young. He slid his hands up to the drawstring that held my underpants, removing them without disturbing the silk of my outerrobe, a rewarding but complicated movement that required my cooperation. For a moment the memory of what he'd said the other night flashed through my mind, about my sexual performance: Just the sort of thing a self-conscious barbarian doesn't need to remember. At once he said, "What is it?"

"Nothing. Please don't let me interrupt you."

He chuckled and completed the maneuver. When he was finished, I said, "Ghost Eve before last, you gave me a necklace of caneblood with a jade pendant."

He'd stood up as I spoke. Now he bent over. Just before his lips came down on mine he said, "I wish you'd thought of that while Kylla was in the room."

Loden Broca Mercia, security guard with the Mercia firm, was on the day shift of his current assignment. He reported into the Mercia office on the corner of Gold Street and Luster at two hours after dawn— and dawn comes early in the summer. I was not at my keenest edge of awareness, to make my point more plain.

The offices were small and bare, only to be expected, I suppose, of a place where people were mostly sent out to work in other locations. No windows, only some vents and a ceiling fan to redistribute the heat.

The building was old, modified for power packs in the visitor's area but with the smell of oil lamps coming from the other rooms.

I sat on a bench, nodding, while Ran established the following facts with the Mercia branch head: That the Poraths had hired a full dozen guards, spread over two shifts, with livery modified for the occasion. Five of these guards had been on the boat when Kade went swimming. (Between five guards and Eliana's personal fighting chaperone, Loden Broca had probably been right when he'd told Kade his sister was in no great danger.)

Loden Broca, as his name implies, was of the House but not the family of Mercia—a firm of good reputation, small, but listed on the registry of fine Houses in the Golden Virtue Administration Building in the Capital Triangle. Still, what did that prove? Go into the Capital Triangle with enough coinage, and you can get anything listed anywhere. The Beggar Monopoly, the House of Helad, was top of the registry, from what I'd heard; they threw enough money at government officials that they were supporting the entire city police force. Anyway, that was the rumor. But the Mercia Guard Firm had a good reputation by word of mouth as well, and that was more to be relied upon than any official writings.

Loden Broca had joined the House of Mercia two years ago, after paying for and receiving their course of education in Mercia security techniques. He was about twenty standard years old. The average age of the guards on duty at the Poraths' had been thirty-one; the average length of service, eight years. (Ran always likes to go for the numbers. Sometimes they come in handy.) Loden Broca was apparently just starting his career. As his branch supervisor made plain, losing the first son of the family one is protecting was not a good way to begin.

"He's on probation," said Supervisor Ben Mercia, a trim, gray-haired man somewhere near his fifties.

(Of House and family both, my reflexes pointed out at once; how far could you advance in this particular organization without snagging an adoption? Maybe Loden Broca should look into another line of work.) "I can assure you we're dealing with the matter appropriately, gracious sir. Every man on duty that day is undergoing a performance review. If Lord Porath wants to initiate disciplinary action—"

"That's not why we've come," said Ran.

"We've already returned our fee—our entire fee, not just that day's. But in plain fact, not every contingency can be anticipated. We offer no guarantees. If Lord Porath wants a face-price, I can only point out that first, we would never be able to pay the equivalent of a first son, and second, that this act would not make him popular with other security agencies or indeed other Houses—firms would be reluctant to sell their protection if they were to be held responsible for every . . . odd circumstance . . . that arose—"

The words were rolling out like an opened bag of marbles. Ran gave up trying to find an opening and simply overrode him. "We're not here for that purpose, sir. We only wanted to ask a few questions—of you, Loden Broca, and possibly some of the other guards on duty that day. That's it. Any reference to monetary arrangements will have to be gone into with the House of Porath itself."

Ben Mercia stared at Ran suspiciously. "You said you represented the Poraths."

"Not monetarily."

The suspicious look remained. "Grant me your indulgence, gracious sir. I'll return in a moment." The supervisor turned and went into another room, closing the door behind him.

Ran sat down beside me on the bench.

"He's checking us out," I said.

"I thought you were fast asleep," he replied. "The sound of your snores was making conversation difficult."

"What lies you tell. No wonder the man doesn't trust you." I closed my eyes again, my head leaning against the old plaster wall. "Anyway, I wasn't asleep; I was just—"

"Resting your eyes, I know." Suddenly he jabbed me in the side.

I didn't respond. "Ran, I can't keep you entertained every single moment."

"No, look, open your eyes."

I did so. Loden Broca had just entered the anteroom to our left. Another man was with him, slightly older, and familiar-looking. I said quietly, "The other one— was he on duty, too?"

Ran frowned, remembering. "He directed our carriage driver the night of the garden party. And I think he was on the boat."

"Let's talk to them both, as long as we've got them."

He nodded. "The supervisor better finish his checking before they leave for their assignments."

Loden Broca had curly, wind-tousled brown hair, a jaunty step, and a quirky half-smile that he bestowed on the dispatcher as he was handed his schedule for the day. It was the sort of half-smile that suggests all this paperwork is a joke, but he'll be tolerant enough to go along with it. A few short encounters don't make a secure base to speculate, but I had the strong impression that Loden Broca was one of those men who do not like authority as it applies to themselves.

I recalled that when we were first entering the pleasure boat, Kylla had made some remarks about his being extraordinarily good looking. I watched him closely as he touched his companion on the shoulder, making a joke. He was handsome, certainly, and I remembered that his eyes were particularly fine, but her comments seemed far beyond his desserts—more appropriate to a young god than a nice-looking boy on a planet that was overrun with vibrant and beautiful people. Ran put him in the shade.

Ben Mercia's door opened. He nodded to us, then called, "Loden! Trey! Come in here!" He turned to Ran and said, "Trey Lesseret was on the Porath detail as well; I thought you might want to speak with him."

It's nice to be anticipated. "Thank you," said Ran, as though it were no more than his due, and he added, "I trust I do not keep you from your duties." It would be easier to question them away from their supervisor.

"Not at all," said Ben Mercia, sinking down on the bench by the window with what was almost a smirk. "I'm happy to stay and be of help."

"Commendable." Ran rose to exchange polite bows with the two men entering the room. I got to my feet as well and made that incline of the head appropriate in the wife of a first of Cormallon, rather than the smile and matching bow I sometimes made in the course of easier social encounters. I'm not really sure why; but I didn't feel at home in the Mercia Guard Service building, and wanted all the formal status I could get. I saw from a brief look that Ran took notice of my choice of greeting. "Loden Broca Mercia, Trey Lesseret Mercia, we've met briefly before. I'm Ran Cormallon, here on behalf of Lord Jusik Porath. This is my—" Wife? Assistant? "—colleague, Theodora Cormallon." And let them make what they will of the last name.

"Honored by this meeting," said Trey Lesseret, and Loden Broca mumbled the same after him. Lesseret had at least a half-dozen years on his friend; he looked to be brushing thirty, a little shorter and stockier than Loden Broca, who was muscled, but on the slender side. Lesseret was paler, too, and his hazel eyes squinted toward us as though we were standing in the sun instead of with our backs against the wall of a windowless room in a cheaper quarter of the capital. He put one foot up on the boot-polisher stool by the bench. "Take it you're here about Lord Porath's boy."

"Boy" was debatable, coming from him. Kade and he were probably of an age, though Lesseret looked as though he'd packed more experience into the time than the ex-first-son of Porath had.

"Yes," said Ran, "a terrible tragedy."

"Terrible," agreed Lesseret, adding briskly, "so how can I help you, gracious sir?"

"My colleague and I are trying to get a better idea of what happened. Physically, I mean, in terms of placement. Who was where. Anything anybody saw."

"I was in the lounge most of the time," Lesseret said at once. "My house-brother here was above-deck for a bit, having a smoke—" he gestured toward Loden Broca—"but I stayed by the musicians for the whole trip. Get a better view of the salon that way, you know."

I said, "So you would more or less remember where people were?"

He turned to me. "More, rather than less, gracious lady. It's the kind of thing I pay attention to."

"What about you?" Ran addressed Loden Broca. "You could do the same for the upper deck?"

The guard smiled. "You, this gracious lady, and another man and woman were the only people on the front side. There were three others looking down the canal by the railing in back."

"Not including Kade."

His smile vanished. "No. But he only came up for a moment."

I thought Ran would ask Loden Broca now if he'd seen Kylla's mysterious stranger on Catmeral Bridge. Instead he pulled a familiar handkerchief from an inner pocket and untied the knot. "Both of you had a good view of Kade Porath," he said. "Can you tell me if he was wearing this the entire time he was on board?" He pulled out the last of the knot and extended the massive cadite ring.

Lesseret was making a shrugging gesture, but Loden Broca's expression was one of surprise, followed by blank incomprehension. His gaze went up to Ran's, a furrow cutting the golden skin of his brow.

"What are you doing with my ring?" he asked.

* * *

He got everyone's attention in the room, no doubt about that. Neither Trey Lesseret nor Ben Mercia knew what significance the ring had, but they wanted to hear more. Ben Mercia *insisted* on hearing more, to Broca's acute and obvious discomfort. Ran solved the problem by buying the guard's services for the morning for a rather inflated fee, and a quarter hour later found the three of us wandering somewhat aimlessly down Luster Street, looking in vain for a place to sit and talk. The Mercia agency, when it came down to it, was happy to put another guard in Loden's place for the day if it could get an extra fee from us, and postpone its natural curiosity (in the form of Ben Mercia) in the higher cause of House profit. Ben Mercia knew his duty.

"Your ring?" repeated Ran, as he scanned the scruffy shopfronts at this end of Luster.

"A family inheritance," said Loden Broca. "The only one I've got, really. Boldness and prudence, the Broca mottoes." He smiled that twisty grin. "My father left it to me, and enough to put a down payment on security school. Though we don't know how that'll turn out, at the moment. I'm on probation."

Ran said, carefully, "Would you have any guesses as to where we found the ring?"

"You said Kade Porath was wearing it. That wouldn't surprise me. I gave it to him."

I looked at his face as we turned the corner of Luster and Tin. He didn't seem to find anything unusual in the statement.

"Pure charity?" prompted Ran.

In this part of town people who ran small-scale, miserable businesses out of their homes sat on doorsteps, by windows, even in the gutter, trying to catch a breeze as they weaved and sharpened knives and made paper animals for the tourists over in Trade Square. There wasn't enough room here for courtyards in the back, so they took relief where they could, heedless of danger. But then, they were in more danger from each other than from any violent, game-playing nobility, who probably wouldn't be caught dead in this neighborhood. I'd stayed in the equivalent of this sort of place when I first came to Ivory, but we'd had a bit more space—my inn had had a court-yard. That practically made me a merchant prince by comparison.

Loden's face wore a wincing, sheepish look; he seemed to be picking through a pile in search of the proper words, and not finding any. "It wasn't," he began, and stopped again. We passed a massive, elderly woman in a faded orange robe, sitting on a stool by the curb, sharpening kitchen knives on a wheel. A bolt of ragged striped cloth had been rigged for shade in the branches of the spindly tree beside her. As we passed she moved her stool back an inch, further into the shadows. "You see—" said Loden, and discarded those words, too. The old woman in orange glanced up and met my eyes; there was a crazy look there that, taken in conjunction with all these sharp objects, made me uncomfortable. I walked around to the other side of Ran.

"It's like this," said Loden. He paused one more time. I had a momentary urge to yell *spit it out, man!*—which, fortunately, I got the better of, because he finally achieved takeoff velocity. "I play cards," he said, "not, you understand, that I'm a gambler. Just as a pastime. But it happened that I lost a lot of money one night—I'd had a few drinks, you know how that is,' he said, confidingly, though in fact I had no idea how it was to get drunk and gamble my savings away. It was an alien concept. But then, other people are alien to us in so many ways I try to be careful about making any quick judgments. "So I ended up owing these fellows some money. And since I didn't have any to pay them back, I borrowed some."

"Transferring your debt to someone else," I said, puzzled. "I don't see the point."

"Well, it got these guys off my back," he said reasonably.

"This new loan was at a lower rate of interest, then?" I asked.

"Not exactly. Ah, no, it wasn't. But it was only one person to worry about."

Finally outlines were emerging from the mist. I said, "Did you by any chance borrow this money from Kade Porath?"

Ran stopped. He turned to Loden and said, "Are you trying to tell us that Kade was your creditor as well as your employer?"

"Well, yes, it's not as if—"

"Was this before or after the house party? I mean, did you meet Kade through being assigned to the Poraths, and borrow the money then?"

"Uh, no, I borrowed it back at the beginning of spring. Five months ago. Kade knew I was with the Mercia agency and he chose us when he wanted to cover his sister's party. He said he may as well make sure I kept getting a salary."

We were midway down Tin Street. Ran looked irritably around for a route out of this neighborhood. "Doesn't this hook up with Grapefruit Alley somewhere?" he said, seemingly in my direction.

"You're asking me? You've spent a lot more years in this city than I have."

"But you're the one who's map crazy."

This was true. I like to know where I am, in the larger scheme of things. Since philosophy gives no final answers, I make do with maps. I'd unofficially inherited a lot of them from Ran's grandmother—an incredible woman who'd never left the estate in all the decades since she'd married into the family, but who had closets full of starcharts, geological surveys, and plans showing the waterpipes under cities I'd never heard of. The servants were still running across them occasionally in pantries and under old sets of drawers.

Grapefruit Alley leads into Trade Square eventually, so—"It would have to be in that direction," I said, pointing crosswise over the road.

"There's a robemaker's in the way," he said, implying my contribution was less than helpful.

"That isn't my fault. I didn't build it."

Loden Broca looked from one of us to the other uncertainly.

Ran kicked a loose stone with the edge of his sandal and we continued down the street. "How much did you owe?" he said, suddenly addressing Loden again.

"About four, well, five, uh—I don't see what this has to do with anything."

"Neither do I," said my husband disarmingly. "You brought it up."

It took another few seconds for the logic of this to penetrate. Finally Loden said, unwillingly, "Five hundred and fifty tabals. But it only started out as three hundred."

"Oh." Noncommittal.

"The thing is, I'd missed a payment. And Kade kept giving me a hard time about it. He wanted something, and I don't *own* anything, except this ring, so . . . he said to give him that. So I did."

"When?"

"On the boat. You saw when he came up to get me. He was mad, because I hadn't paid him, and he saw my ring when I had my hand on the railing on the stairway."

Ran and I looked at each other. I said, "You were wearing it openly when you got on the boat?"

"I had it on my hand, if that's what you mean by openly."

"And this was a spur-of-the-moment thing?" asked Ran. "Nobody had any reason to believe you'd take the ring off? Kade never demanded it before?"

"No, it was the first time he'd mentioned it. I wore my ring all the time, you don't expect somebody to ask you for a family heirloom. But, look, I didn't think I was in any position to say no, especially with my house-brothers all over the ship. You aren't going to mention this to them, are you?"

He said it so wistfully, like a little kid. Well—more like a little kid trying to get away with something.

Still. If this was true, maybe we should give him whatever slack we could. After all, somebody was trying to murder him.

Chapter 10

Loden Broca couldn't confirm Kylla's story about the sinister watcher on Catmeral Bridge. "I went down below before we were close enough to the bridge to see," he said. "Why, do you think that might have been the sorcerer? It *was* sorcery, wasn't it? Kade didn't just have some kind of weird fit? I mean, he never struck me as entirely normal."

Ran stopped by a wide, unpaved opening between two buildings. "Grapefruit Alley," he said to me, pleased, bowing slightly as though he were presenting me with it as a gift. "It's a good half-kilometer from the robemaker's," he had to point out.

"It probably curves around behind it when you get further in," I said. (It did.)

Loden said, "Gracious sir?"

Ran turned a courteously meaningless smile on him. "Thank you so much for your help, sir. Please take the rest of the morning off, with our compliments to your supervisor."

Loden stood there a moment, looking bewildered. I felt a little sorry for him. "Do you have any enemies?" I inquired.

"Well, uh, not really . . . there are a few people who've gotten mad at me sometimes . . . ah, why do you ask?"

Ran took hold of my elbow and pulled me a couple of steps into the alley. "No reason," I said hastily. "Just wondered." Apparently we were not telling Loden Broca Mercia that he was a potential murder target. This did not seem quite right. But Ran always has his reasons for acting the way he does. I don't always agree with him, but he does have them.

"Gracious lady?" asked Loden, still with that confused expression, like a just-born puppy trying to come to terms with its suddenly colorful lifestyle. Oh, it was a shame not to at least warn him.

"Sorry, can't chat," I said, as Ran set a walking pace that took us deep into the alley and around the corner of a building with remarkable speed.

"Why aren't we telling him?" I asked, when he'd slowed down enough for me to get sufficient breath.

"We're doing this for Jusik Porath," Ran said, "whatever he may think. He gets our first report, not somebody in the Mercia agency."

"But in a situation like this—"

"A situation like what? We still have no hard evidence, only suspicions."

"But if Loden's telling the truth—"

Ran finally slowed down a little. He glanced back along the curve of the alley. "Then we'll visit him later and suggest that he take care."

I considered that as we walked. Within a few minutes we reached the beginning of the market stalls that line Grapefruit Alley all the way up to Trade Square. Every other cart was a food cart, and the smells would detour a truckload of monks on their way to the Court of Contemplation. Heavily spiced meat of every description, cut into cubes and stuck on sticks; cut into slices and added to hot rice; shredded into a dusting of protein and sprinkled over yellow and white vegetables. Raw vegetables and fruits in the cart next door, and eight sorts of flavored water in the cart beyond that. There were stationers, too, and dollmakers, and all the usual mishmosh of Ivoran businesses, but Grapefruit Alley was—contrary to all appearances—the gourmand's heart of the world. Not even the bustling cookshops around the Square itself could match these dirty-looking vendors, who'd handed down their three meters of turf from parent to child since as far back as anyone's ever heard. One of the refrigerated

carts we passed was stocked full of Pyrenese beer;
how the beggarly seeming gentleman behind it managed that, when the most exclusive restaurants in the
city were often out, was a mystery.

A mystery. I glanced over at Ran. "What are you
going to tell Jusik?"

"Nothing, maybe, for the moment. We don't know
anything for certain yet."

"Maybe, but I don't feel right leaving Loden twisting in the wind while we get our thoughts together."

So we walked along in more silence, getting our
thoughts together. I said, "Let's try Kylla's theory."

"The mysterious stranger on the bridge?"

I saw it had occurred to him, too. "Why not? We
don't need a boat to test that one. You just need to
stand where the sorcerer stood, to start a backward
trace—so let's go to the south railing of Catmeral
Bridge, Ran, and see what we can see."

The alley turned into a straightaway around that
point, cutting diagonally across the streets in the center of town. A long way off in the distance I could see
the opening into the bright sunlight of Trade Square.
You could almost hear the noise from there. Ran said,
thoughtfully, "We do seem to be going in the right
direction for it, don't we." The section of the canal
crossed by Catmeral Bridge is half a mile north of the
Square.

I grinned. I had to admit that Loden Broca or no, I
was curious about this thing with Kade, and hanging
about on open bridges in the midday sun seemed a
small price to pay, at least at that moment. Just then
my gaze fell on a cart-stall piled to overflowing with
blossoms of red, white, violet, blue, and burnt gold—
and the violet ones were versions of the unidentified
bouquet Kylla had carried so jauntily away with her
last night.

The fat face of an old woman was framed beyond
the heaps of flowers; her head just topped the mer-
chandise. "Oh, Ran! Look! Could you—"

He trudged over toward the cart. "I know," he said mournfully. "The little purple ones."

He handed over a coin—I didn't even have to advance it to him—and all the way up to Catmeral Bridge I carried a huge bunch of lavender bells in my sweaty hands.

Midway over the bridge we stopped and looked southeast, down the canal. The waters were dark and still. Not many folks used the canal these days; farther up, the neighborhood watch had had to institute stiff rules about garbage dumping. That was ten (Ivoran) years ago, before my time. "The Year of the Big Stink," they called it. Kylla was just entering her teens then, staying with friends in the capital, and she told me she'd gone the whole summer drenched in perfume, like every other person who could afford it. The street vendors had all had little shelves set underneath their carts, covered with cologne bottles for passersby to purchase if they ran out of supply.

I watched a ragged boy play in the dirt near the edge, ignoring the glare of noon sun. He looked down at the water, then went back to his play—it wasn't the sort of water you felt tempted to swim in, regardless of the summer heat.

I glanced over at Ran's left hand, where the cadite ring sparkled. He'd scared me when he put it on, but he'd said shortly that (a) it was necessary and (b) he could handle it. His mood hadn't exactly been upbeat, so I didn't press my concerns.

"So far, nothing," said Ran. He said it grimly. His tone went beyond the temperature and a walk through the less glamorous parts of the capital. He hadn't been at his best since we stepped into Grapefruit Alley, in fact, so I turned to him and touched his arm to get his attention.

"What's the matter?"

He sighed, and said gently, "I suppose you mean beyond the fact that Kylla's unhappy and I've been taken for the assassin of a first son of the Six Families.

And beyond the fact that Stereth Tar'krim is another possible suspect. And beyond the discomfort of this entire morning.''

"Yes, beyond all that.'' Those were all things I had every faith he could handle.

"All right,'' he said, "I'm angry. I've been thinking about this ever since Loden Broca told us about his ring, and getting angrier with every step.''

"Angry?'' It took me completely by surprise. "What is it, what are you angry about? You've always taken this kind of thing in stride!'' Whatever I meant by "this kind of thing'' . . . sorcery, assassination, the general distrust of humankind.

"Whatever sorcerer did this—'' He took a deep breath and let it out. "Whatever incompetent fool—'' Another breath. "It wasn't enough that he acted in public; he targeted the wrong man, too. And not because it was one of those accidents that 'happen because we are in this world.' Because he was careless and stupid and didn't give the same thought to this you or I would give to planning a dinner menu—''

"But he couldn't have known Loden would lose the ring. Loden said it himself: Who would have the nerve to ask for a family heirloom?''

"What difference does it make?'' His face was slightly flushed; he really was angry. "Using an object like a ring is brainless to begin with, when you're dealing with something as permanent as death. I've been training to be a sorcerer since I was eight years old, and seeing negligence like this—something I would have avoided *when* I was eight—'' His fists came down on the railing, and he let the rest of the sentence go. Finally he said, "What's he doing being a sorcerer? Throwing mud on all our reputations, leading clients to distrust us. And beside that—besides that, it tramples over the field itself. The beauty of sorcery is based on symbol and function being allied, on everything having its proper aspect, on dancing the dance so carefully— Theodora, sweetheart, it's so beautiful when it's all done the way it should be done. I know you're

not a practitioner, but you've studied it now; you must
see that.''

I saw that not agreeing at this moment would be
tantamount to a divorce. And truly, I did *almost* see.
I nodded.

"And this fool thought he could do it as crudely as
pointing a gun at someone. Even *that* takes experience
and training."

I didn't know what to say, so I took the safer route
and said nothing. A moment later Ran took hold of
my arm and said, hoarsely, "Let's finish the sweep of
the bridge and find this *kanz.*" We started down the
midpoint of the arc.

Dancing the dance, he'd said; like ''The Other Side
of the Mirror,'' that I'd danced (granted, with several
errors) on the afternoon that Kade died. Dances on
Ivory are complex and never spontaneous, unless
you're a trained and acknowledged artist; great sor-
ceries, too, I supposed.

He stopped suddenly a few meters away, with the
look of someone who'd been punched in the stomach.
The fact that he wore the ring still bothered me; I ran
over to him and grabbed one arm, in case he had a
sudden desire to dive in the canal. "I've got it," he
said. "Gods! I didn't think we'd get a trace this
quickly. I figured he was probably just some stranger
Kylla saw." He looked over at where my hands still
gripped him. "What are you doing?"

I let go. "You made me nervous."

He blinked and shook his head slowly. "My dear
tymon. Really."

"Be that way, then, but don't expect me to dive in
after you if you end up in the canal."

He smiled. "This way." He pointed southwest, back
in the direction we'd come.

We walked down the bridge, with me still watching
him narrowly. No point in not being careful. For some
reason my suspicious nature seemed to cheer him up,
because he slipped one hand around my waist, beneath
my outerrobe (so no one would notice and be scan-

dalized), and said, "I haven't asked you to recite the hundred and ten laws of magic in a long time."

"Don't tell me we're going to have a review quiz now."

"Just a hypothetical problem, Theodora. If you were going to assassinate Kade, would you have used a ring?"

"Considering your strong views on the matter, as you've only just expressed them, I'm not likely to say yes, am I?"

"Humor me, and give me your best answer."

We were off the bridge and getting farther from the dark waters of the canal, so I put my mind to the problem. "No. I would treat it as a variant of the search hierarchy, using inside and outside traits. I would place the spell on the person himself, and tie him to it by definition."

"The definition being?"

"Well, I'd have to research who Kade was. Rings, clothing, and general appearance would be outside traits; I'd leave them for the icing on the spell. The heart I would base on inside traits, where you're less likely to go wrong. In Kade's case, I don't know— greed for money is an inside trait, and he seemed to have that, though probably half the people on the boat that day did, too—"

He interrupted. "Never mind, tymon, you've made my point. You're already ten times the sorcerer this idiot is, even just in theory. It's a pity you don't have the gift."

"I read your cards for you well enough."

"Because the virtue is in the deck. You'd be a top-rung professional if you were gifted yourself."

It was nice that he thought so, since the Cormallons lived and died by sorcery; it was their vocation and avocation, they followed it like an art and a sporting event. But I had no desire for the gift. I got pleasure from reading the cards (for reasons too voyeuristic to do me credit), but beyond that magic held no great allure for me. Maybe I'd seen them all working too hard at it for it to keep its romance. Or maybe it was just that there were so many other horses crying to be ridden—the scholarship of folklore and storytelling, my training in tinaje, even the recordkeeping and accounting expected of me at Cormallon—for me to want to submerge myself in artistic obsession.

Still— "You think I'd approach magic with the proper flair?" I asked, pluming at the compliment.

"Well, you'd be patient and careful," he said, dwelling instead on my grayer virtues.

There you are: You can't bother my Ran with murder or sabotage, but carelessness upsets him. Ah, well, we must take our compliments where we find them in this world. We continued, following the sorcerer's trace back the exact route we'd taken, till the street we were on emptied into the noisy expanse of Trade Square. Here open tents and awnings sprouted in multicolor abundance and vendors sold rugs, pots, fruit, weapons, live fowl, themselves, challenges at gaming contests, lucky names and numbers, promises of expertise in any field wanted, tickets to the Imperial Dance Company, baths in battered old metal tubs, displays of balance and agility, feats of memory, lessons in spoken Standard, recycled car parts. . . . I'd set up daily shop here myself, back when I'd first gotten stranded on Ivory without money or work, and with no connections to supply either.

We stepped into the controlled chaos and my gaze went at once to the spot by the wall where I used to sit beside Irsa, who sold fruit from a cart. But it was the height of the day; there were too many people passing for me to see if she was there. "Irsa!" I yelled, hoping to see a face pop up from the mass of strangers. As I squinted, Ran tapped my arm and pointed to the ring. "We're getting closer," he said loudly, against the noise. I squinted at the ring instead. It didn't look any different to me than it was before.

"How can you t—" I began.

The crowd in front of us parted, and a groundcar made its way slowly through. I stopped in my tracks and stared at it. Who would be fool enough to drive a groundcar through Trade Square? Even wagon and carriage drivers took care to detour to the streets around. The unlucky car was low-slung, covered in durasteel, with no way to peer inside at the no-doubt impatient face of the driver.

Suddenly it accelerated sharply, causing the knot of people remaining to jump aside; there was cursing, and somebody gave a piercing scream, in apparent pain. I stood, rooted, for an eternal millisecond, before my fear seemed to pick me up bodily and toss me out of the way. The groundcar barreled through. I rolled on the ground, not the only person down there, and the noise of the marketplace dwindled to a distant hum backing the main sound of my beating heart. I put my hands against the ground to push myself up, and felt how shaky and weak they seemed. Hands on either side of me helped me to my feet. Long-taught reflexes reminded me that nobody in Trade Square takes hold of you unless it's to distract you from their pocketpicking, and without thinking about it I tried to shake them off.

They wouldn't shake. I looked left and right, at two men in faded robes who were pulling me away. I opened my mouth, and a length of white cloth was dropped over my head, pulled tight between my lips, and tied in back. I felt the fingers behind my head, tying it, ruffling my hair—an unpleasant feeling, even aside from the fear. So there were more than two of them. My legs were still free, and I kicked out at the men on either side, but unfortunately I was not at a good angle to do much damage. I aimed a vicious one behind me, but that unseen gentleman had prudently dropped back a pace.

We were only a few steps from a small, jury-rigged tent by the wall of a building on the edge of the square. I was hustled toward the opening. One of the few fully covered tents in the marketplace; once inside, nobody would know I was there. I could be within a few inches of Ran and he'd have no way of knowing. Assuming he wasn't going to be dumped inside next to me. I half-hoped that he would be.

It had all happened in seconds. I was pushed inside, where I stumbled in the sudden gloom. Hands shoved me down onto the ground; at least there were some cushions scattered there. I turned, awkwardly, to look up.

A knifeblade glinted in the dim light. As he dropped to one knee, one of the men pulled it from a sheath on his belt and drew back to—there was no mistaking this—get a good angle when he shoved it into my body. There had been no hesitation, no stop to rest, no attempt to talk to me. I'd been walking in the square thirty seconds ago, chatting with Ran. I was paralyzed with terror and disbelief.

The knife was drawn back to strike. The world turned a sharp, sickening corner and shrank to this few meters of space, the dirty tent, and the man with me. I wasn't thinking about Ran, or anything else. If you'd asked me my husband's name, I doubt I could have told you. I doubt I could have told you my own name.

Then the blade paused. By whatever incomprehensible rules the universe used, that had got me to this tent, the weapon hesitated. I no more expected to understand a reason for it than I expected to understand why I was there. The man turned. I followed his glance to the tent flap, where the other two were waiting outside. Except that one of them seemed to be lying on the ground, taking a nap in the sunlight. The man with the knife—the only important person here, from my point of view—twisted around, launched himself to his feet and out through the opening. I lay there, pretty much at my limit in handling simple breathing, and picked up scuffles and yells from the world outside as my ability to hear turned itself back on.

A fat, gray-haired woman with a mountainous chest appeared in the tent flap. In her hand she held a heavy brass lamp with blood and hair on one end. She peered in and grinned a wide grin that showed teeth were a minority population in her head. "Theo, love," she said. "I thought it was you."

Irsa, my old mate from the days of no money, who sold pellfruit and red pears to support her innumerable children. I mumbled something. She came farther in and knelt beside me. "Are you all right, child?"

I nodded. But logical speech felt a long way beyond me, as did getting up. She puckered her lips in sympathy. "I yelled for the protective association, and last I saw your friend was being chased over Kymul's Table of Pleasurable Devices. He won't be coming back, you know." She put a hand on my forehead, like a young mother testing for fever. "I hope you didn't want to question the one lying out front; I don't think he'll be rising from where he is."

"Uhh. Irsa. . . ."

"He didn't hit you, did he, sweetheart?"

I shook my head. "I'm sorry . . . I don't know what's wrong with me . . . I just can't seem to. . . ."

"Had the life frightened out of you, I 'spect. We shouldn't be surprised; that groundcar nearly did the job, too; did you realize it was coming straight at you in particular? Jumping two skulls in a row is more than anybody ought to have to put up with, at least in the same five minutes. The body's not made for that sort of thing, you've got to rest up in between. Do you think you can sit? I can get you water from the bottle on my cart."

She helped me sit, and a shadow crossed the opening of the tent. Ran. Irsa turned; she knew him, and satisfied herself with a mere disapproving look. "You could keep a better eye on her, you know," she said. "You're the one who got her to leave the market, where she was safe."

His clothes were covered with dirt. "Safe," he repeated. He made a sound that could have been a laugh, but wasn't.

"Safe I said and safe I meant," said Irsa. "Nobody tried to kill her in all the time *I* knew her."

Ran knelt down, more as if he didn't have the strength to stand than as a convenience in talking to me. "You're all right," he said. He seemed to be telling me.

I nodded. "He had a knife," I said. My voice embarrassed me by suddenly coming out like a child's.

"Mine probably had one too, but they got separated from me when a couple of angry people tried to run after the groundcar. Pure luck."

Pure luck. Three minutes ago we were walking across the market like a pair of innocents.

I made out a mound of pillows in the dim light behind me; they weren't much help in trying to get to my feet. Not that it would have been so comfortable to stand up anyway. Ran and Irsa were both stooping under the low roof.

"What are you doing?" asked Ran.

"Trying to get up."

"You're the color of new paper. Stay where you are for a while. We're not late for anything."

It was a bit embarrassing how my body had just switched off. I'd been in tight spots before—you can't really hang around professionally with the Cormallons and *not* be in tight spots—but the wall of eternity had never thudded down so forcefully in front of me. So quickly. While I was alert and conscious, and yet without any time to prepare for it.

The other side of the mirror is a skull.

I admitted, "Maybe a couple of minutes' rest isn't a bad idea."

He put his arms around my shoulders, and since there was nobody but Irsa to see me snuffle on his robe I let him do it. As a matter of fact I was quite glad about it.

After a moment, Irsa said, "Children, who's the fellow back there?"

At once I tensed. My alarm systems were apparently

still quivering. But her voice had been casual, and Irsa was no fool. "What fellow?"

"Behind you there."

I stopped snuffling and turned to the mound of pillows between me and the wall. In the gray light I could just make out some sort of non-pillow shape on the far cushiony slope. Irsa got up and held open the flap of the tent a little farther.

The pillows were wet, I now realized. "The fellow's" throat had been cut.

Without speaking, Ran and I pulled the top cushions off and tossed them aside for a better view. I think we each had the same idea.

The bar of dim sunlight showed a man of middle age, completely bald, still wearing a green felt cap to protect his skin. He was pale for an Ivoran, but not sunburnt; he'd probably taken good care of himself, didn't go out much in daytime, stayed in his tent when he plied his trade. Assuming this was his tent. Well, he'd escaped sunburn. The bloody crescent under his chin was dark and already starting to cake. I couldn't swear as to what color his robes had been originally. The pillows beneath him were soaked.

Ran extended his hand toward the other side of the pile. He still wore the cadite ring. There was a bruise on the fingers on either side of the stone, probably from when he'd thrown himself away from the car. His hand stopped a few centimeters from the man's face. He turned to me.

"Our sorcerer," I said.

He nodded.

It was a pretty gruesome sight, and added to it was a fecal kind of scent I'd only just become aware of; but I found there was no more space left in me to be shocked, or even surprised. And in terms of luck it was all of a piece with a miserable day that had gone before it.

I glanced around the tent and saw a torn sign tacked to one canvas wall:

LUCKSPELLS . . . . .   5t.–15t.
LOVE FILTERS . . .   10t.–25t.
CURSES . . . .   2t.–8t.
DELIGHTFUL ILLUSIONS . . . 17t.–30t.

YOUR PAST AND FUTURE,
WONDERS OF ALL KINDS, PLEASE INQUIRE

That certainly seemed to nail down his professional identity. I guess we could have skipped the ring after all.

I said, "I think I'd rather rest someplace else," and Ran extended a hand to help me up.

I turned to Irsa. "What about the protective association? Will they report this to anybody, will they want to question us?"

"I don't see why, sweet. It's nobody's business. This fellow probably paid his dues like everybody else, but I'll tell them you two had nothing to do with it, and who cares about the rest?"

Ran said, "Thank you."

"Ah, it's nothing. The cops like to stick their noses into every silly thing, like they'll find a payoff somewhere if they keep looking—but we'll just roll the gentleman up in one of Ton's old rugs and carry him away tonight, when the market breaks up."

Ran understood at once. He said, "Theodora, do you still have your moneypouch?"

My hands went under my robe, to my belt. "Yes." I opened it and counted out tabals until Ran waved me to stop. He collected the coins and gave them to Irsa.

He said, "Please thank them for their kindness."

She smiled, displaying that lovely, half-toothless mouth again. " 'The gratitude of a virtuous man is worth more than gold.' "

"True, but 'the excellence of friendship is a coin no emperor can mint.' "

They might have exchanged a few more anti-money aphorisms just for the heck of it, but Irsa was busy dropping the coins into a bag inside her outerrobe, counting them as she went. We waited courteously for her to finish, then we all three left that tent forever, stepping out into the brightness of a normal market day in high summer.

Irsa's first victim had been dragged away, perhaps in the name of neatness; I saw his legs protruding from behind a cart of sugar ices. Belatedly, I said, "There was a third man."

Her face creased. "Was there, child? I didn't see him. He must've dropped out before the other two went for the kill."

I nodded reasonably. I was functional, but behind it my mind was still playing back the last ten minutes over and over. The aim of today's excitement became clear. There would have been three bodies found in the tent, throats cut. I gagged involuntarily.

A skinny young man in a brown robe walked up to Irsa. He wiped sweat from his forehead. "No luck, Mother. We tracked him as far as Brindle Road, but he must have climbed atop a carriage or some such thing. He vanished."

I don't *think* this was one of Irsa's surfeit of children; I think he just called her mother out of respect and familiarity; but in the two years of our market association I'd never laid eyes on any of her family. Though she complained about them enough.

The young man's glance passed on to Ran and me. "I'm very sorry," he said, sketching a bow.

Ran bowed himself, then shrugged. "It happens. We appreciate your effort."

It must have been a wild chase; Brindle Road was well over a kilometer away. Whatever were we going to do now?

Around the three of us, Trade Square bustled with its usual enthusiasm. Nobody could say these people didn't have energy. "Six tabals?" I heard someone cry nearby. "*Six tabals? Are* you out of your mind? Don't our children play together like brothers and sisters? *Six?*"

Whoever slashed our sorcerer had gone into that tent

recently. Probably it was the same knife-wielder I'd been introduced to so abruptly; he and his friends could have waited with their draining corpse till Ran and I came in sight. We could question the nearby vendors, offer a reward. . . .

Why bother? I knew the system here as well as anyone.

Five hundred people in Trade Square, and I'll bet none of them had seen a thing.

Chapter 11

As Irsa had said, the car was coming straight at us. It's hard not to take a thing like that personally. Meanwhile, tired and wrung-out as I was (and no doubt as Ran was, though he never admits to such), self-preservation gets the wheels of the mind to turning. In order to wait for someone, you have to know that they're coming; that much seemed obvious even in my state of rapidly descending IQ. Who knew we were tracking the sorcerer?

Well, practically everybody who had anything to do with the Poraths knew that we were looking into the matter. And the Poraths knew an amazing lot of people. Assuming for a moment that Loden was the real target here, why pick the boating party to aim for him? Maybe that public display was no accident. Maybe they wanted it to be seen, and a scandal to start?

Really? said that annoying schizoid voice in my head. *How much of a scandal starts from drowning a journeyman guard? Who of any importance would ever care?*

All right, but the point is that the Poraths and their hangers-on are not definitely out of the picture, regardless of who the intended victim was. Now, Ran pulled the ring off Kade's finger yesterday. Any number of people could have heard about it by now, and if they assumed the logical next step, that we could somehow trace the sorcerer by it . . . apparently a hired sorcerer, who might be willing to drop his ethics and name names—

A hired sorcerer, just doing his job. The same way Ran does his job.

—Shut up. Anyway, the point is that . . . is that . . . we don't seem to really be any closer, do we? Almost ended up on the floor of that ratty tent, soaking the rest of *that fellow's* pillows, and we still don't have the faintest idea of who's responsible.

Perhaps a holiday and a good book would be in order.

Ran agreed that any further action could wait till tomorrow. We both went home and I sat in the downstairs study with its specially imported chair—a desk chair, but a marvel of soft upholstery—and I tilted it back and put my feet on the desktop, while Ran went out to the cookshop for our dinner.

I noticed that we had messages waiting on the Net, and I exerted myself so far as to reach over and push a button.

One of them was the House secretary's notice of the revised agenda for the yearly meeting of the Cormallon council. It was marked with a family seal, and the notation PRIVATE. The meeting was scheduled for later in the week, so Ran would probably want to get a look at this when he came in. I hadn't seen the last agenda list, so I used my privilege code to open it.

It read:

2nd of Kace

6th Hour	Breakfast/Welcome
7th	Financial Review
9th	Branch Reporting
10th	Midday Meal Served at Central Pond
12th	Particulars and Problems:
	. Mira-Stoden
	. Theodora
	. Andulsine alliance
15th	Recess
1st/eve.	Supper, Wine, Entertainment

Does my name leap out at you there from the middle? It leapt out at me.

Notice there's no explanation listed for Mira-Stoden; everyone knows our branch in that city has been having problems. No explanation necessary for the Andulsine alliance either—people have been talking about it, off and on, for years.

And no explanation necessary for Theodora.

Damn, I didn't need an explanation either. When I asked Ran a while back about how our House would handle my not producing any heirs, I had the Cormallon council meeting in the back of my mind. It might seem, to non-Ivorans, a little early in the marriage for anybody to be concerned on that topic, but the unfortunate tendency of males of the great families to get themselves knocked off has made the Houses prudent about succession rights. They like to have it all clear as soon as possible. I'd already seen what happened from one disagreement over succession, and I could understand wanting to avoid anything similar.

I did want children, but left to my own devices I'd probably have waited a couple of years. When the hints I'd picked up led me to conclude that I didn't have a couple of years, I'd made that check-in with the Selian Free Clinic. The big news was that my implant had indeed dissolved, months ago, and there was nothing standing between me and kids but random chance. And the unknown factors of our separate genetic heritage.

Not that I'd considered this anybody's business. But if you think the Cormallons won't jump right in and inquire about all kinds of personal particulars in regard to child-production, you don't know them. I noticed they'd left a lot of time for it, too; the whole long afternoon was reserved for their "particulars and problems."

Did they have the potential junior wives lined up already? I'd bet my House share that somebody, somewhere, had a written list. A nice neat one, like this agenda here.

Maybe with ratings next to each name. Gee, maybe

when the branch reps showed up for the meeting they'd each get a copy.

I had only just reached that thought when the door opened, and Ran came in carrying a large bag. He put down the issue of that day's Capital News, and walked over to set the bag on the desk. "Be careful, it's hot," he said. He pulled the bag open so I could get to the bowls of food more easily, then he turned and went back toward the door to get the News again.

I let fly with the top bowl. It hit the wall just over his head, as he bent down to pick up the News. Chunks of red groundhermit slid down the wall and most of the rice fell in a lump on his sandals. He jumped.

"What the—" I sent the vegetables after them. He dove out the door.

"Theodora?" came his voice, tentatively, from the hallway.

I sat there, bubbling like a pot on a stove. You should understand that I am not, by nature, a thrower. That was more Kylla's speed. Perhaps nearly getting killed this afternoon had had an effect on my personality.

"Theodora?" he said again.

I said—good heavens, it was amazing how steady and cold my voice sounded—"Go upstairs and ask the Net for a copy of the council agenda."

There was a pause.

"Are you going?" I asked.

"Uh, Theodora . . ."

"You've seen it, haven't you?"

"Sweetheart, there's no need to take this personall—"

"How long has my name been on the list?"

"Listen to me," he said, still from around the corner of the hall. "I knew you'd be upset—"

"How long?"

"Um, it was on the first draft, but I had it taken off. But then so many people brought it up, I had to let them put it on again. It's not as though it *means* anything, Theodora."

I tested the pot again; it was still bubbling.

"Theodora?" came the voice from the hall, when I

didn't answer. The left half of his face appeared in the doorway. "Are you going to throw any more bowls?"

I checked, but there was no immediate impulse. "Not at the moment."

He slipped into the room. "It's just a meaningless agenda item, you know. Nobody can make us take any action on it."

I said, "You don't want to talk about children with me, but you'll spend an hour on it in a full council meeting?"

"That's not fair. I don't want to talk about it with them, either. And if I can get the discussion of Mira-Stoden spun out long enough, I may not have to talk about it at all. They'll all have their minds on the wine and the gold-coin girls, they won't want to let the meeting run over. It's the only time a lot of them have in the capital all year."

Not forgetting the written schedule, I said, "You won't be able to cover the Andulsine alliance question then, either."

"What of it? It'll keep for another ten years. It's not like anything really gets done at these meetings, anyway; I've already seen all the branch reports, and so have you. If there were a real problem, we'd fly out to the people involved and go over it with them. Which we'll have to do in Mira-Stoden anyway, pretty soon. You can't settle anything in an hour, one day of the year."

I said, "But the others care enough about this to have it put on the agenda."

He sighed and pulled over a stool. He sank onto it, and I realized I'd managed to get hold of the real problem, right there; the simple fact that they'd gotten it on the agenda was a message to Ran.

And of course to me. What got said at the discussion was superfluous.

Ran was the First of the House. No doubt my body was a topic of discussion in Cormallon homes around the planet. "There is no privacy inside the House," the old saying has it, and it isn't said cheerfully. But for the first time it occurred to me that Ran's capabilities were probably debated just as freely. Did they check up on whether there were any bastards left around? Or would they simply insist on handing him another wife, like a sports player handed a new ball and told not to mess up on this round?

I looked at my husband sitting on the stool and said, "I begin to see why you never give any information to anybody. It's the only way you can keep any privacy."

He seemed reassured by this remark, and we sat there glumly. Red sauce dripped on the wall, which I would have to clean later. No wonder I'd never gotten into the habit of throwing things.

I said, "Ran, face it, our . . . mating . . . is an unknown quantity. Maybe Ivoran and barbarian have had children before, but I've never heard of it. There's no record of it. I can't get a straight answer from anybody on whether we're still one species. And what about sorcerers? Magic runs in families, you've got to believe there's something physical in that. Are you different even from the run-of-the-mill Ivoran? How different? Do you know? The gods know I don't."

He was silent.

"We might try for the next twenty years and not get pregnant. Or it might happen next week . . . and then what? What kind of a child would we produce? Don't you see that I need some kind of answer to that, some hint, some clue?"

He said, finally, "I'm not as worried as you—"

"Thanks, you won't be bearing it!" I said, unable to stop myself from giving the age-old answer.

"Listen to me. You remember Grandmother left a message for me—"

I sat up straight, startled. Ran's grandmother had been a woman of surprises, formidable, a little scary, and impossible not to respect. For some reason she'd taken a liking to me, and I'd walked carefully the few times I'd met her. As everyone else did, I suspect.

He went on, "She was a great sorcerer. But I think

we both know there were things she had in mind she wasn't telling us.''

"I know.'' Grandmother was one who wrote her own agendas, which she didn't always share.

"I spent time in the library with her bluestone after she died. The psychic impressions were still strong . . . knowing Grandmother, they'd probably be readable if I picked it up today. When she wanted to leave a message, she made it crystal clear. She was fond of you, Theodora.''

"I kind of liked her, myself.''

"She told me—well, I guess you can imagine, she told me to stop fooling around and get married to you. She said you might take ship for home, but a good hunter doesn't quit when the sun goes down.''

"Gods! You never told me this.''

"I told you she'd said for me to stop being a fool.''

"But not in these exact words. And how did she know I'd decided on shipping out? Her message to me didn't. . . .''

Ran looked thoughtful. "What was her message to you, anyway?''

"Hmm, she told me to stop being a fool, too.''

Ran waited for more, then said, "Well. Anyway, she said I was an idiot if I didn't follow through, since you were just the sort of woman I ne— The point is, she said you were good for the family. She said relations among the Four Planets would be shifting, and you'd bring new blood and better awareness of barbarian thinking. I mention the new blood because she seemed to have great hopes for our offspring.''

That made me drop the question I'd been hanging onto and pick up another one. "What did she say about these offspring?''

"Nothing specific, but she was always an extraordinary card-reader. She would never have worked so hard to get you safely into Cormallon if she hadn't thought you'd be valuable. That you, and me, together, would be valuable.''

I sat there for a minute taking this in. The vague

suggestions of an elderly relative, now deceased, would not generally have an effect for me on such a personal issue—except that if you'd known Ran's grandmother, you'd take her very seriously, too.

"You never mentioned any of this," I said again.

"Well, it was a personal message. Didn't anyone ever tell you it's not nice to look into other people's private correspondence? Like council agendas with PRIVATE stamped on them?"

I waved that away. "You toss the House business mail at me to open half the time anyway. Besides, my privilege codes exceed yours." This was true. I handled family expenses, like most wives, and had access to the House financial records. "They should have stamped EYES ONLY if they didn't want me to see it. Or BORING."

He shrugged. I said, "About your grandmother, though, I'm glad you told me. It's very reassuring." If also rather alarming in its suggestion that I had a mission.

"Good."

"But I'd still like to have us both looked over by a genalycist."

Now he looked disgusted. "First of all, I'm familiar with some outplanet history, and there haven't been any real, trained genalycists around for over a hundred and fifty years. Just cooks following recipes."

"Tellys claims to be making strides."

"Where did you hear that?"

"Around."

"Well, it makes no difference to us, anyway. We don't know any Tellysian genalycists."

Jack Lykon, I thought. Just call the embassy. All we have to do is do them a favor.

I was silent.

He said, "So we may as well consider the issue closed. Trust Grandmother, Theodora; she's a lot more reliable than some barbarian with a good line of talk."

I stood up. "I'd better get a rag and clean off the wall before it stains."

"I'd better get us some more food," he said, joining me.

"What are you going to say at the meeting, if the discussion comes around to me?"

"I'll think of something."

I considered that as we walked down the hallway. "Tell them that I had an implant when I was on Athena last, and it's only just wearing off. They need to give us another year."

He stopped, surprised. "Is that true?"

"Ran, I'm telling you what to tell them I said. Do you really need to know whether it's true?"

"No," he said thoughtfully. "Perhaps I don't.— Would you like me to pick up groundhermit again?"

"Please. Extra sauce."

He left for the cookshop, and I went to hunt up a rag and do some thinking.

We made our report to Jusik the next day. He was sitting in the garden beside the pond, a small table beside him with a pot of tah on a warmer and an empty cup. He was wearing a silver outerrobe covered with tassels—funeral clothes.

Ran sat on a boulder to the left of the table, and I sat on one to the right. Jusik didn't acknowledge our presence; I'm not certain whether he knew we were there or not. He may just not have cared. After at least five full minutes, Ran said, "Our sorrow dwells with yours on this day."

He glanced up. "Thank you."

The funeral had finished an hour ago. Firebowls were still set around the garden, and an arc of silver metal rose from a black pedestal nearby. The arc was just a remembrance, left out for half a year after a death, to bring the thought of the dead person back to mind. Silver streamers hung from it, from today's ceremony, but they'd soon crumble or blow away. There are no cemeteries on Ivory, and no monuments, except for emperors.

Lord Porath showed no inclination to pursue the

conversation. My husband, however, is not one to allow the exigencies of real life to get in the way of business. After what he considered a decent interval, he said, "Noble sir, we must speak with you regarding our investigation."

Jusik raised his eyes to Ran's like one performing a rote task. "You have arranged a meeting with your employer?"

Ran's right hand, half-hidden in his robes beside the low table, clenched, and by that I knew his temper had been scratched. His voice was nothing but courteous when he said, "Noble sir, I'm afraid you yourself are my only employer. It's for that reason we've come to you to present such findings as we have, rather than to one more closely concerned with them."

Mild interest flickered in Jusik's black eyes. "Who is more closely concerned with them than I?"

"The true target of the sorcerer who caused your son's death." Jusik sat up straight and fixed his gaze on us both. Now that he was assured of an audience, Ran hauled out his facts as though Lord Porath were any other client who'd asked advice on a matter of magic. "We know that the sorcerer who killed your son was a hired market mountebank with a stall in Trade Square. He was using the name Moros when last heard from. He initiated his attack from Catmeral Bridge, where he waited till the boat was within range and his victim in line-of-sight."

"And you allege this victim was?" Jusik rapped out the words.

"We haven't completed our investigation, but at the moment the likeliest victim seems to be one of your security guards—Loden Broca Mercia."

I broke in here. "We'd like your permission to warn him, noble sir."

Jusik glanced at me briefly, then said, "And how did you come by this farfetched theory?"

Ran said, "Are you familiar with a blue ring Kade was laid out still wearing? Your steward will confirm it if you're not."

Jusik looked startled. He nodded, and Ran told him the rest of the story, leaving out one or two details of minor interest. Jusik said eagerly, "So you traced this sorcerer to his lair! What did he say? Who hired him?"

Ran and I looked at each other. Ran said, "We didn't actually finish the trace. Moros seems to have left town."

"But you can follow him, can't you, now that you've got the ring?"

"I really don't think he's likely to ever turn up," Ran said firmly.

Jusik sat back. "I see." He looked at me. "You agree, I suppose, that this witness won't be back."

"I would be very surprised," I said.

Jusik had returned once again to being the First of Porath. He picked up the tah pot and poured a new cup, his eyes far away. Ran looked at me and shook his head. I really don't know how he knew I was going to ask about warning Loden again.

After a moment Jusik said, "Are you willing to stake your reputation on this? That Kade's death was accidental?"

Ran said, choosing his words slowly, "I would stake my reputation on what I've just told you."

Jusik put down his cup and smiled, as though a silver arc no longer hung behind his head. "Then there's no reason to believe my family is involved with this at all."

"One might say that the use of your boating party as a murder location was an insult to you," said Ran, tentatively.

The smile grew slightly broader. "An insult if I choose to regard it as such. I choose to be tolerant."

Behind Jusik, I saw the short form of Auntie Jace make its way across the garden. She approached the silver arc, folded her knees, and sat beneath it in an attitude of respectful meditation. I wasn't sure if she was scoring points with the family or just wanted to hear what we were saying.

Lord Porath leaned forward. "May I speak frankly to you, my brother First?"

"Please do," said Ran, in an absolutely toneless voice.

"My House is . . . distracted," said Jusik, spreading his hands. "We have our attention in other places right now. Coalis needs seasoning, experience; and then there's the matter of Eliana, and your brother-in-law."

"Yes," said Ran.

"If you had come to me with some other scenario—hypothetically, if you had come to me with some news of a House enemy, who had killed Kade deliberately—I would have met with this enemy and tried to accommodate him. I don't want our name involved in this anymore. I don't want our attention on it, or our money poured into it. I want to cut free of it altogether."

"I see."

Jusik stood up, and manners required that we stand up too. He extended his hand. "You bring me good news," he pronounced, more loudly. Ran allowed his hand to be grasped for a moment in fellowship, then slid it away. Jusik bowed to me, and I inclined my head. "We will discuss some fair recompense in a few days, when the initial mourning is over."

It was a dismissal, but I lingered. "Noble sir."

"Ah—yes, gracious lady?"

"You haven't officially given us your permission to notify Loden Broca of the danger he's in."

He appeared mildly surprised. "Your task is over, is it not?"

"But he could be killed at any moment. And he's never done anything to you."

"I never said he had," he said, bewilderedly.

Ran took my arm. "My wife takes a different attitude to these things."

Jusik wore a look I'd seen before, a look of one at a loss before barbarian ways.

Ran smiled. "I hope you'll indulge us by granting permission."

"Well . . . of course. It's nothing to me. But make it clear to anyone who's interested that my House wants to stay out of this."

"Naturally," agreed Ran. He started steering me around the pond before I could say something else.

I threw a glance behind me as we left and saw Jusik standing, looking across the garden toward the distance, the tah service beside his feet. Behind him, I saw that Auntie Jace had finally gotten off her knees.

"He seemed thrilled to pieces to get rid of us," I said. We were standing by the door, waiting for the steward to accompany us down the path and out to the front gate. Our official leavetaking, and hopefully the last time we (or I) would have to step foot on these cat-consecrated grounds.

"Understandable," said Ran. "We're useless baggage tying him to an incident he wants put behind him."

"I'm surprised he even believed us, considering how set he seemed to have your guilt in his mind."

He made a face. "I'm sure he'll check up on his own to confirm." He sighed, ran a hand over the top of his head, and said, "But he'll get confirmation. The case is over."

I stopped. "What do you mean, over? Who killed Kade?"

"Do we care?" he asked, in honest puzzlement.

"You care! You spent a quarter of an hour telling me what a useless excuse for a sorcerer he was."

"Well, and so Moros was. And now he's dead. Good for the profession."

"But who hired him?"

Ran paused with the look of one who is trying to translate each word into some obscure dialect. He said, "Jusik is satisfied. We've exchanged favors. He'll give us a break with this marriage business. I'm sure the question of who killed Kade is an interesting intellectual exercise—"

"This intellectual exercise nearly had us both knifed in Trade Square!"

"That wasn't anything personal, Theodora."

I'd taken it damned personally. I still have occasional nightmares about it. "What if they try again?"

"Why should they? Once word is out that the case is closed and we're no longer interested. It's really none of our business, sweetheart."

The last sentence came out in a slightly reproving tone. He sounded as though, if one weren't being paid for it, looking into a homicide was an invasion of the murderer's privacy. As though it would be *rude* to pursue it.

All right, this is an Ivoran, I told myself. Give him a reason that means something to him. "Won't it look bad for our reputation if people still think you're the one who knocked off the first son of Porath? While a guest in their house?"

He bit his lip. "Jusik won't support that rumor."

"Some people will still believe it."

He said, "Look, Theodora—"

The door opened. Eliana, Coalis, and Leel Canarol piled out. I took a step or two back.

Coalis's eyes went at once to mine. "Theodora! Is it true? You found Kade's murderer?"

Eliana, meanwhile, had zeroed in on Ran. But still affecting modesty (or maybe it was real), she didn't want to leap on him and shout for his attention, so she tugged urgently at her chaperone's sleeve. Leel Canarol stepped forward and addressed Ran (she was, I saw, slightly taller than he was): "Is it true, gracious sir? Kade wasn't the victim at all, it was meant to be that nice-looking guard on the boat?"

Ran winced slightly at the latest woman in his path to comment on Loden's looks. Kylla had had more than a few things to say on that subject in his hearing.

"Fast work," I murmured. We'd only left their father and Auntie Jace about four minutes ago. She must have raced inside and flew upstairs to pass the word.

"You'll have to speak with Lord Porath about it," said Ran firmly. "I would not presume to comment on the affairs of your family—"

"Oh, come!" said Coalis. "He never tells us anything. And if it's not really anything to do with our family, shouldn't we know that we're not involved?"

Ran began, "I'm sorry—"

Coalis sniffed through his thin, aristocratic nose. He did that very well, I thought. "*Stereth* will tell me," he said.

"You're at liberty to ask him," said Ran, "if you think he knows."

Coalis said, "I think if he doesn't know, you'll have to tell *him* when he asks."

Looking as though he'd just swallowed something bad, Ran turned and went down the steps without waiting any longer for the house steward or giving his farewells. It was verging on bad manners, in which he almost never indulged; and saved from that only by the fact it was deliberate. A reply to what he considered presumption.

Eliana and her defensive chaperone seemed taken aback. I shrugged hurriedly, said "Sorry, noble lady; bad day," and clattered over the porch and down the steps after him.

There was a Net message from Stereth Tar'krim waiting for us when we got home. Ran put it on permanent hold, unread, with a privacy code beside it. Yes, I was *very* curious. But considering my recent adventure with privacy codes and Net messages, I thought it best to stay away from it.

Chapter 12

We duly warned Loden Broca that evening. His lodgings, in a cheap inn in a nasty part of town, were not on the Net, and this being the kind of message one doesn't like to give to a courier, we were compelled to visit him at home.

Climbing the dark and dirty stairs to his room, Ran said, "Theodora, whenever you get me involved in one of these affairs—"

Catch that?

"—no matter how high the birth of our client, we always seem to end up rattling around with the dregs of society."

I stepped up the steep stairs behind him, noting how airless the place was. "This time we have a nice house to go home to at night, and you're not wandering around penniless."

"Mmm, there is that." On the fourth floor the stairs ran out and we emerged into a hallway every bit as brilliantly lit. He counted off the doorways. "One, two, three, four—five." He hit the flat of his hand against the door.

We waited. He pounded again. I said, "He's probably not home. If I lived in this place, I'd spend as much time away as I could, myself."

"I refuse to come back here again," said Ran, making yet more noise, as though he would conjure Loden Broca home and available through force of will alone.

The door to number four opened. A woman in a nightshirt appeared, her black hair caught back in a long fall. She looked in her thirties, and she appeared unaware that her legs were on display from the knees down. Perhaps she didn't own a nightrobe. "Do you mind?" she said. "I'm trying to get a few hours' sleep."

It was still early evening, but Ran said politely, "I beg your pardon, gracious lady."

She blinked and peered at him in the dimly lit hall. I don't know if I've mentioned it, but my husband is one of the better looking creations in the universe. She said, "Oh," as though in reply to something. Then she said, "He's not home. And if he were home, he wouldn't answer. Nobody comes but creditors."

"You saw him go out?" asked Ran. I could tell he was trying to keep his gaze up around face-level. You don't often see legs on Ivory, except on performers in a few dance shows.

"Heard him. A couple of hours ago. He's probably at a tith-parlor, that's where he spends his time."

"Do you know which one?" I asked.

Her eyes went to me, then shifted back to Ran. "No, sorry, could be any of 'em," she said, as though he'd asked the question.

Ran said, "When does he usually come back?"

She shrugged and slowly wiped one hand against her thigh as though it had jam on it. "Depends on how much money his friends have on 'em. Or if he got paid today. Or if he meets somebody and goes to her place—that means he won't be back at all." She paused. "If the money runs out, he could show up any time. If you want, you can wait at my place—"

"Thanks for your help," I said warmly. "We'll carry on from here. Please don't let us interrupt you."

"No trouble," she assured Ran, still not looking my way.

It would be undignified to check and see where *he* was looking, so I confined myself to surreptitiously jabbing him in the ribs. I heard the intake of breath, but he gave no other sign. Then he smiled at our informant, bowed, and echoed, "We'll carry on from here. Please don't let us interrupt you."

She sighed, shrugged again, and went back into her room. Ran turned and looked at me. "What?" I said.

"I'll be black and blue in a couple of hours."

"I have no idea what you're talking about."

He took my hand. "You're not usually this hair-trigger. Does the council agenda have you that nervous?"

I was going to deny that, but he pulled my hand, and the next thing I know I had my head against his chest and we were holding each other in Loden's ratty hallway, and I was having trouble talking. *"Kanz,"* I said, finally, "I don't know. I don't know. It's just that—I don't have any place to go. I *left* Pyrene, and I *left* Athena, and I don't regret it . . . but this business with the council, somehow that's not what I envisioned when I took on your family."

"You're not leaving Ivory."

"I know."

Reassured as to my sanity—nobody leaves Cormallon, you get thrown out or you're in for life—he pushed back my hair and said, "Listen, this custom of multiple wives isn't the horror you seem to think it is."

"Kylla doesn't seem to be looking forward to it!"

"I wonder if it's the marriage she minds or the fact that she'd be junior wife. That's not the point, though, the point is that of course if it bothers you so much, we won't do it. Nobody can marry into a pair unless the senior wife accepts her in full ritual during the ceremony."

"People have consented to wedding ceremonies before, who didn't want to. Because of pressure."

He smiled. "I'd like to see them pressure you, foreign-barbarian-without-manners."

"They'd pressure *you,* that's the problem."

He was silent. I said, "Should I wait while they figure out sneaky Ivory ways to make your life as difficult as possible? And while all the time you know yourself that any confusion over succession rights is not a good idea for the House."

Finally he said, "The marriage is young. The council is overconcerned. We have plenty of time."

"We only have the time they're willing to give us—"

Footsteps on the stairs made us step apart. We faded into the shadows at the edge of the hall, aware that if Loden Broca had creditors his first reflex upon seeing anybody would be to fly down the stairs again. And if it weren't Loden, who knew how friendly this particular tenant would be?

That second one wasn't a problem. Loden appeared at the head of the stairs, walking easily but not quite as steadily as he had yesterday morning on duty. The smell of bredesmoke accompanied him.

We waited till he had his door open and then Ran stepped forward on one side of him, and I took the other. He started to bolt inside—a bad move if we'd really been after him—but Ran got a foot in the door and grabbed hold of the shirt beneath his short outer-robe. A minute of undignified back-and-forthing gave Loden time to see who we were. He stopped, looking confused. "Sir Cormallon," he said. He peered my way. "Gracious lady. Uh, what are you doing here?"

"May we come in for a moment?" asked Ran.

Loden hesitated. Then he said, "Of course, gracious sir, but it's kind of a mess." He held open the door.

It wasn't kind of a mess, it was a total mess. Rolled-up piles of robes, shirts, and trousers were sitting in mounds over the floor. You'd almost think he was a university student back on Athena, except if he'd been Athenan books would have been mixed up with the clothes. A flute was on the tiny windowsill, beside a glass with something old and encrusted in it. A bag of half-eaten apples lay open on the floor beneath, the apples spilling out over the dusty floorboards. There was a bed and a stool, standard issue from the inn-keeper; no other furniture or pictures.

Loden was fortunate in his choice of inn. It was the kind of housekeeping that asked for vermin, but there didn't seem to be any at the moment. I watched Ran to see where he was going to sit, but like me he apparently decided standing was the better part of valor. "Sir Broca Mercia," he began.

Loden made a sound like an unhappy laugh. "Maybe not Mercia for much longer," he said.

"Oh?" asked Ran, derailed from his path.

Loden sat down on the bed. "My supervisor isn't pleased with me. He isn't pleased with any of us who were there when Kade Porath died, but he's particularly not pleased with me. I wish you hadn't come to the agency, gracious sir. People get the idea that you wouldn't have paid so much attention to me unless I were involved in some way."

I said, "We think you *are* involved."

He glanced up at me. "I swear, I didn't even know Kade Porath that well—"

"No, you misunderstand. We think you might have been the intended target."

He opened his mouth, closed it, and opened it again, but nothing came out. Apparently the idea was so new he needed time to comprehend it. Then he said, "I think you must be mistaken—"

"Possibly," said Ran, "but listen to our evidence." He told Loden Broca the story of his ring. "Clearly it was the focus for the murder," he finished. "And you've already told us nobody knew you were going to give it to Kade."

You could practically see an invisible iron anvil settling on Loden's shoulders.

I said, "Have there been any other attempts on your life?"

He made some fishlike motions with his lips, then said, "No. And they know where to find me, it's no secret I live here . . . although I . . . generally don't answer the door. I like privacy."

The grave's a fine and private place, said the scholar's voice in my head. I didn't have a lot of respect for Loden Broca as a human being, but suddenly I felt sorry for him. His life, such as it was, was rapidly going down the chute. Maybe he was a bad gambler and hung out in tith-parlors, but did that mean he deserved to die? This dingy room was the best he'd done for himself, and now he was going to lose that, and possibly his job, and possibly a lot more.

Once I'd lived in a cheap inn, and gone hungry when I couldn't work.

I gave Ran a look which he met with alarm. "We've done what we can," he said quickly, walking toward the door. "We felt we should warn you. Come along, Theodora, we've got a lot to do."

"Wait a minute," I said, irritated. I groped for the moneypouch on the belt beneath my outerrobe, and pulled out two ten-tabal coins by feel. I stepped over to the bed and said, "Here." Loden put out a hand, still looking rather blank, and I dropped them into it. "Maybe you should leave the capital for a while. Do the Mercians have any branches elsewhere?"

"In Timial," said Loden. "But my supervisor would be more suspicious than ever if I asked for a transfer."

"Theodora," said Ran, from the doorway, with a trace of grimness.

"All right, all right," I muttered, and joined him.

"Best of luck, sir Broca Mercia," said Ran politely.

Loden nodded, sitting in the dark, that blank look still on his face. We left him there.

That night I woke up a few hours before dawn, and decided to go downstairs to get a drink of water. I stumbled down, half-awake, got the drink, and was making my way along the hall to the stairs to go back up, when I saw a shape in the dimness by the front door that shouldn't have been there. A large, bulky shape. A man-sized shape, lying on the floor.

My heart started going like a power drill. How could someone possibly have gotten in? Ran had the house spell-protected. Not that they couldn't get past that if they wanted to, but only a fool would deliberately bring down a curse on his head. Not to mention there were the locks and bolts to contend with. But there he was. My brain tried to figure out some other shape that could legitimately be hulking there in the darkness, but nothing came to mind. What the hell was he doing on the floor? Did he break in, get tired, and take a nap? Nerves of steel, or just stupid? Gods, what if this was another corpse? Which would suggest somebody else was likely in the house at this very moment. . . .

These thoughts stampeded through my head, one after the other, like a crowd that's just heard ''Fire!'' It was only about three seconds since I'd first seen his shape there in the shadows. It was too dark to make out his face; were his eyes open or closed? Well, we were going to have to assume they were closed because otherwise we were in the deep kanz. I kept moving forward, very gently, till I reached the stairs. Then I started backward up the first couple of steps.

The shape heaved itself up, shoving my heartrate into the stratosphere. I'd half-convinced myself he was dead. I flew up the stairs yelling, ''RAN!''

With a yell like that—and let me tell you, I put my heart and soul into it—you'd think he'd get the pistol from its compartment in the headboard before he did anything else. And you'd be right.

In nonemergencies he's hard to get up, but he was already standing in the doorway to the bedroom, armed, by the time I got there. ''There's somebody here,'' I panted. Probably right behind me, in fact. I threw a look over my shoulder, saw a moving shape on the stairs, ducked past Ran and went for the knife hanging from yesterday's belt on the corner of the bed. Then I turned around.

Lights snapped on. We all blinked. Ran said, ''Sim? There's not anybody else here, is there?''

A rumbly voice said, ''No, none I saw. I think I startled the lady.''

I'd reached the doorway. At the end of the hall, looking slightly embarrassed, was a man of about forty, wearing a conservative street tunic with a nightrobe over it. There was a holster showing beneath the nightrobe, but his hands were empty. I looked at him, then back at my husband. I said, ''Ran?''

He turned and laid the pistol on the sleeping platform. He said, ''Theodora, this is my cousin Sim, from Mira-Stoden.''

One of Ran's innumerable cousins? I decided it would be better for my marriage if I put down my knife also. I opened my mouth to say something telling to Ran, then closed it and turned to Sim. ''Honored by this meeting.'' I turned back to Ran. ''What's he doing here in the middle of the night?''

''You went to sleep early,'' said Ran. ''He got in after you went to bed. I was going to tell you in the morning—I didn't know you'd go downstairs. Or if you did, I thought I'd wake up when you left the bed.''

''I don't know why. You never wake up when I leave the bed. I do it every night.''

''You do?—Anyway, breakfast would have been plenty of time to reintroduce you properly.''

''*Re*-introduce?''

''You must remember Sim. He was at our wedding party.''

''Everyone in the known universe was at our wedding party.'' I glanced toward Sim, who looked silently uncomfortable. ''Hello, Sim. Sorry if I startled you.''

''Quite all right, lady Theodora. Sorry I gave you such a shock.''

Fortunately he was too embarrassed by the whole incident to call attention to himself by opening up the long exchange of complimentary apologies we might have gotten trapped in. ''Please drop the 'lady,' since we're definitely introduced. Ah, may I ask why you were lying by the door? It seems an eccentric place to choose to sleep. Not that you aren't welcome to bed down anywhere you like, of course.''

I felt Ran's fingers on my arm as he stepped in to relieve Sim of further explanation. ''It's the traditional place for bodyguards to sleep, Theodora. I asked Sim to come stay with us for a while. After what happened in Trade Square, it seemed prudent. My cousin's worked in security before.''

''I . . . see.'' I scanned Ran's face, which as usual was giving little away. ''You left me with the impression that you didn't consider us as still in danger. Now that the case is closed.''

''It's possible that not everyone has heard yet that the case is closed. You know I like to be careful, Theodora.''

''Yes, I do know that.'' I paused. ''Will Sim be accompanying you to the council meetings? It'll cause a little talk, won't it?''

''Well, actually I thought that when I went to the meetings he'd stay with you.''

''I see,'' I said again.

''I thought it might give you more sense of security,'' he added.

I felt my chest, which was thumping the exhausted rhythm of a mount that's been ridden hard for the day and needs wiping down. ''You thought it would give me a sense of security.'' I walked past Ran and back into the bedroom, tapping the back of his hand where it rested on the doorway. ''We'll discuss that further in the morning.'' I pulled open the coverlet and slid into bed.

I heard Ran's voice say, ''I guess we'll see you at breakfast, Sim.''

''Sorry about the excitement,'' came the reply.

''It's all right.''

''Say, do you folks have tri-grain in the larder? I always have that for breakfast.''

''I wouldn't worry about that right now, Sim.''

I heard steps going down the stairs, and pulled the coverlet over my head. ''Gods of fools and scholars.''

''Did you say something?'' asked Ran.

''I said good night.''

So four days later I was sitting in the arboretum of the Taka Hospitality Building, just down the river from the Imperial Park, with a hulking shadow named Sim waiting by the entrance. The Taka had gone up a mere ten years ago, a durasteel tower with weapon-proof glass and endless suites of rooms, providing conference facilities for all persuasions—polished mahogany tables, seating twenty at a time, with full Net facilities, for the more democratic meetings; polished marble bowls with a raised podium in the center for more arenalike get-togethers; polished stone group baths, with or without pleasant Taka personnel to scrub your back while you discuss business. There were also group beds, for when the intellectual and physical aspects of discussion became blurrily entwined. I know all this because they had a brochure in the lobby.

I was not, you see, invited to the Cormallon council meeting, taking place at that moment on the twenty-first floor. (In a room with a table, Ran assured me.) This was a branch-heads-only meeting. I had been invited to the financial controllers' conference, that takes place in the spring; since women traditionally handle the budget, that one is heavily female. Supposedly the branch heads meeting is more policy-oriented, although as Ran pointed out, nothing can really be settled in a day. But just in case anyone was tempted to make any promises he couldn't keep, each delegate would have been primed by his sister, wife, or mother before coming, as to what he could give away and what he couldn't.

It occurred to me suddenly that I had done the same thing with Ran, when I told him to tell the council I still had an implant.

I sat in the arboretum among the sprays of flowering plants, listening to the three fountains plash in the background. Ran hadn't asked me to wait, but I had no immediate responsibilities and my thoughts were too unsettled to take on any. What was I doing on this planet, anyway? What in the name of heaven had come over me? Things would be *safe* on Athena. As long as I followed the path the university had laid out, my future would have been financially assured, though never rich. And nobody could have hurt me too much.

Nothing is for life on Athena, not like marrying into the Cormallons; when things go wrong you move to another cluster and make a half-hearted commitment there instead.

I didn't even feel competent to raise a child, and here I was fighting the council for the opportunity, swearing it would be no problem. Not that they'd require much from me in the actual bringing up; my duties ended with the actual physical production. I was free to lie in a chaise all day and dine on lemon ices, as far as the House was concerned; there were plenty of people available to watch over children and see to their education.

But the truth was that I was having more problems with the idea than I'd been able to tell Ran about. More problems than I was totally willing to look at, myself. Ever since that little event in Trade Square, every fear I'd ever had about bearing children on this crazy planet had magnified enormously. Had nearly getting killed made me more intuitive, more aware of the skull on the other side of the mirror? Or just more nervous? Was I seeing things more clearly now, things I hadn't wanted to face? Or was I reaching new levels of cowardice?

Admit it, Theodora, this *physical production* thing scares you. Somewhere in the back of your mind you suspect it might kill you. But even if we're too far apart genetically—even if the fetus wasn't compatible—surely the odds are far better that it would die rather than you would? Hire an offworld doctor to be with you day and night, if you're so nervous. This isn't the beginning of historical time, there are techniques available. . . . You took this on when you agreed to stay.

Human bodies are such complicated, pathetic bundles of apparatus. Addressing the huge pink flower in front of my arboretum bench, I said, "Why can't I just plant a seed in a pot and come back in nine months?"

"I don't know," said a voice behind me. "Why can't you?"

I whirled around. Stereth Tar'krim stood behind my bench, his spectacles making him look like an intellectually curious rabbit. He pulled them off and wiped them on his blue silk outerrobe. "The moisture here is fogging them up," he complained. "You'd think we were back in the Northwest Sector."

I saw Sim approaching from behind Stereth, and waved him back. I became suddenly aware that except for my new friend at the entrance we were all alone in this big, empty, plant-infested room. And Stereth probably knew a lot more dirty tricks than Sim ever had. Still, there was no reason Stereth should be mad at me. Was there?

"Hello," I said.

"Hello, Tymon. Can I sit next to you?"

I moved over on the bench. He settled down, smoothing his robe, and said, "You never used to talk to yourself back in the Sector."

"I was never alone there," I pointed out. "You always had people checking on me."

He smiled reminiscently. "Great days, weren't they? Remember the night you and Des rode in after ditching half the provincial militia?"

"What is it you want, Stereth?"

"Funny you should ask, Tymon, because I was just going to wonder what you wanted. You're sitting here making mournful remarks at lysus plants. I'm surprised you chose that big pink one to converse with—you never struck me as someone who went for the flashy type."

I felt my face getting red. "They keep this room too hot," I muttered.

"Yes, I noticed that," he agreed courteously. "But in regard to your happiness, my friend, is there anything I can do? All well with your love life? You're not quarreling with Ran again, are you?"

"We're doing fine, thank you. Why this interest in my personal life?"

"Can't think what brought it to mind," said Stereth, gazing out over the enormous pink blossom in front of us. It was a flamboyant junglelike flower, with a central stamen rising from the heart, flushed a deeper pink at its base, and resting its flaccid length on the jumble of petals around it. It was an embarrassingly lush piece of nature, and I had to keep checking the impulse to throw a cloth over it.

"Ran's upstairs," I said, changing the subject. "Having a meeting."

"I know. I called the Cormallon estate, identified myself as an Imperial minister, and asked if they could put me in touch with you or Ran. They said I could leave a message with the staff here if it was urgent. So I strolled over, and here we are. —You know, I left a message on the Net for you both a few days ago."

"Uh, yes. Sorry about that, we've been busy."

"We shall let it pass. More to the point, my friend Coalis tells me that you seem to have decided that one of the security guards was the real target. Is that true?"

"You take a sharp interest in this affair, Minister Tar'krim."

"I *do* take a sharp interest. That's why I'd like to be kept informed if you pursue it any further."

"Why should you care what happens to a hired guard?"

He pushed his glasses back up the bridge of his nose and let out a sigh. "Coalis and I are in partnership over some of his inherited business interests. I'd just like to know they're safe. Is that too much to ask of an old friend?"

I pulled a curling leaf off the mutant plant irritably. "You know, I can't see you and the young monk getting along on a long-term basis. Particularly in the loan-shark business."

"Coalis is a good boy at heart. He reminds me of Lex na'Valory."

I turned to stare at him. He looked innocently back at me. Lex na'Valory was one of Stereth's old outlaw band, avoided for his tendency toward psychotic violence. *"Coalis?* I *like* Coalis."

"I always liked Lex," he replied equably, "though one had to give him extra room."

"Gods." I returned my mind to the issue at hand with an effort. "Well, if you think Loden Broca Mercia is the target, I guess you might consider the Poraths out of the picture."

"Not necessarily. Broca did owe Kade a fair amount of coin, so there's an established connection with the business."

I felt my eyes widen. "You have Kade's client book!"

He smiled.

"Where did you get it?"

"I won it in a contest. Come on, Tymon, you know I don't reveal my sources. If I did, you and Ran would have been beheaded by now."

This was the closest Stereth had ever come to reminding us how much we relied on his discretion.

I said, "Maybe you can do a favor for me, old friend." He looked expectant. "A market sorcerer named Moros was involved. We can't discover much about him. If you can find out where he lived, or who his friends were. . . ."

"Lived," he repeated. "Were. Do I understand that Moros himself won't be showing up?"

"That's a safe assumption."

He grinned. "My old barbarian comrade . . . I'm impressed. How did you dispose of the body without gossip? Do you travel with a corps of private guards now?"

I nodded. "Won them in a contest."

Snorting sounds were coming through his nose. After a moment he said, in a steady voice, "I'm sorry I didn't look up you and Ran earlier."

"Frankly, I'm surprised you claimed acquaintance with us on the boat. I thought you wanted us not to acknowledge you if we met."

He appeared genuinely hurt. "Only until some time

had passed. That was for your sake, not mine, Tymon. You couldn't afford to have your sorcerer husband linked with Stereth Tar'krim's outlaw band. But now a full year's gone by, time enough that I could have met you both legitimately here in the capital.''

"Then I apologize, Stereth. That was very considerate of you.''

"Damned right it was.'' He glanced irritably around, then said, "Let's leave this pink fellow.'' He gestured toward the immense flower. "I don't feel I can compete with him for your attention.''

We moved farther into the arboretum, settling beside one of the fountains. The entrance was exactly opposite now, half-hidden by leaves though it was, and you could just make out Sim in the distance. Splashing water backed the rest of the conversation.

Stereth said, "By the way, who's the large gentleman who takes such an interest?''

"A cousin of Ran's. Here to see the capital.'' Sim came stolidly forward a few meters to keep us better in view.

"Ah.'' Stereth smiled toward him in a friendly way. "I take it he's only interested in those parts of the capital you happen to be in.'' Perhaps coincidentally, Stereth placed his hands in plain sight on his knees. Then he turned to me and said, "So tell me now, old comrade. Don't make me get you drunk, like in the old days.''

I was startled. "Honestly, you know as much as I do about Kade Porath—''

"Damn Kade Porath. He's a passing business matter. He lived long ago and in another country. Not even his family will miss him in six months.'' His glasses gleamed in the overhead light. "I want to know why you have that pinched look on your face. I don't believe it's from a case of sorcerous assassination.''

The trouble with being on your guard all the time is that when you hear a kind voice it starts to unravel you. As you may have gathered, our relations with Stereth are complex, to say the least, but I had reason to believe he was genuinely concerned about my welfare. As concerned as he ever is about anything; he's a little bit dead in some ways. But he was always true to his troops, as long as he knew they were dependable.

"Now, you see what I mean?" I heard Stereth's voice continue. "There your expression goes, screwing itself up again."

I wasn't near tears, but I was having a hard time maintaining equilibrium. "Oh, gods," I said finally. "It's nothing important to an Ivoran."

"An Ivoran? Don't try to categorize me, Tymon, it won't work for you. Just spill it."

I took a deep breath. "Ran's upstairs trying to explain to the council why we don't have any children yet."

He blinked. This was obviously nothing he'd expected to hear. Then he put a hand on my shoulder and said, "You're barren, is that it? Tymon, there are ways around this, in terms of House heirs. You can—"

"No, no, no. That is, I may be, with Ran, but we don't know yet. Look, it's a complicated issue, but the thing that really bothers me is that I'm scared of getting pregnant." A sudden thought hit me. "Cantry!"

"What does my wife have to do with this?"

"She's part-barbarian, isn't she?"

"Actually, she's full-barbarian. Both her parents were Tellysian."

I was crestfallen. "So we still don't know. But wait a minute, Stereth, what about your kids?"

I saw a surprised look come into his eyes. Stereth had had a child, but that was a long time ago, by subjective reckoning; it was dead now. I said, quickly, "I mean, what if Cantry gets pregnant?"

Anyone else would have been annoyed with me by now, but Stereth is incapable of annoyance when he's after something he wants. Even if it's only a whim to find out what's bothering his old companion of the road. He said, mildly, "That's not an issue with us. My wife can't have children."

"Oh. I'm sorry."

"It's a long story, Tymon. And isn't it time now to tell me why you're so interested?"

I started to explain the species problem to him, and he held up a hand.

"I see." He thought. "You took a chance when you decided to marry into an Ivoran house, didn't you."

"We both took a chance. But I keep having this feeling—I don't know what it is, I'm not usually that intuitive—that if I try to have Ran's child, I'll die doing it."

Intuitions like this are not dismissed on Ivory, even by my gangster friend Stereth. He sat there thoughtfully, laying his chin on one fist. "This is serious," he said finally. "What does the council say?"

"Oh, gods, I don't want to tell the council! They'll make him marry somebody else!"

Why could I tell all this to Stereth, when it was so hard to say to Ran?

Stereth lifted his chin. "Ran doesn't respect your feelings in this?"

"I haven't told him."

He shook his head. "Tymon, tymon."

"You know how he is about duty; I don't want him to think I'm a coward."

He chuckled. "Given your past history, I really don't think that's something you have to worry about."

"This is different. This is . . . more personal, more . . . immediate. Stereth, a few days ago in Trade Square somebody tried to knife me. I was closer to death, in terms of seconds, than I've ever been in my life, and that includes the Sector. It threw me."

"Normal, Tymon."

"It wouldn't have thrown you."

"I'm not normal." We both knew this to be true.

I said, "I don't know . . . I feel as though I came too close to the other side of the mirror. Maybe I'm being over-sensitive to think Ran would lose respect for me, but I'm not exactly filled with respect myself."

"You're dwelling too much on a simple physical re-action. The body wants to live. You can't help feeling it."

"So it might just be a simple case of the jitters? I've been hoping that's all it is."

"Take advice from your Uncle Stereth, sweetheart. Tell Ran about your doubts. Get drunk if you have to. Gods, he's a sorcerer; he ought to have a better idea of what's good intuition and what isn't. Why struggle along by yourself, when expert knowledge is available?"

I was quiet, and Stereth let me be for a minute. Then I said, "You know, I'm not usually the sort who gets agonizingly introspective. I guess I expect to screw up my own life to some extent, but in cases like this, where the consequences go beyond myself—it's like I'm letting the team down. That's why I hate re-sponsibility."

I thought he'd have something to say to that, but he didn't. I found myself going on. "And what if I don't die? What if I produce some kind of monster? Or a baby that'll suffer for the rest of his life because I decided to take a chance? —Do you know, when I learned to pilot an aircar, I found I could go ahead with the thought of crashing and dying, but the idea of crashing into somebody else and killing *them* totally paralyzed me?"

I was coming up with thoughts I hadn't fully ac-knowledged until now. "You're very good at this, you know?" I said, with a trace of anger.

"You're only telling me all this because you really want to tell Ran," he said mildly. "Don't blame me for it. And please don't look upset with me, or the large fellow over there will come over to see what I've done to you."

I said suddenly, "Gods, I hate the idea of every Cormallon on the planet pinning their hopes on me!"

For some reason this made him smile. Having said all he was going to say, Stereth sat there with me by the fountain, holding my hand. We must have sat for a good quarter of an hour, at least, following our own trains of thought, when he remarked out of nowhere, "The other side of the mirror . . . There's a saying in the empire; 'Sons and daughters are what we have instead of cemeteries.' The continuation of the House, affirmation of life, that kind of thing. You know, having kids could be the best thing for you; it's easier to be brave on someone else's behalf than on your own." He smiled. "Or so I've heard. We can't go by my reactions; they're too idiosyncratic."

"Huh. That's certainly the truth." I turned to him. "Stereth, what's all this business about the Tellysian embassy? Why are you building connections there? Loan-sharking to the ambassadorial staff will only get you in trouble."

He smiled, pulled off his glasses, and polished them again. Then he put them on.

I said, "And what's all this about the Tolla? Did you know they were involved?"

He got up, leaned over, and kissed me on the cheek. "The Tolla," he said, "are a figment of the imagination of barbarian newscasters." Then he bowed like a gentleman—the first time he'd ever taken leave of me in such a fashion—and turned and walked the length of the arboretum out to the main lobby.

I spent the day in the park—Sim trailed me at a discreet distance, and I did not invite him closer because I wanted to think—and returned to the arboretum in late afternoon. I left a message at the lobby desk to have Ran paged when he came down, and that's where he found me, by the fountain. "You waited here all day?" he asked. He sat down beside me on the bench where Stereth had sat.

"No, I was up the street in the park most of the time." Walking about the fine grounds and considering those topics a virtuous Ivoran woman ought to think about: Murder, loansharking, outplanet terrorism, and whether to have children. "You don't look happy."

"No," he agreed. He took a breath. "They insisted on discussing our marriage. I told them the implant story, but they said there was no harm in having a backup plan ready. One of my cousins pulled out an unofficial list of junior wives."

Well, I couldn't complain that he wasn't telling me everything. "What did you do?"

"There's a breakfast meeting tomorrow before we break up. I said I'd discuss my position then."

I'd done a lot of thinking in the park. "Here's what I want you to do. When you see them tomorrow, tell them that your wife says any further action is unnecessary. Tell them we'll have a child by next year's meeting."

He looked at me.

I said, "Tell them if I don't know, who does?"

Chapter 13

I dreamed of tombs again that night.

In the morning I slept late and heavily, and woke up disoriented. Ran had already left for the breakfast meeting, so I got up, pulled on a nightrobe and puttered around getting some fruit and a roll. Usually I wash up and dress right away, to get the morning routine over with, but today I gave myself a little slack, as though I already felt like an invalid.

At my suggestion, Sim had gone along with Ran to the Taka Building. I'd told them last night that I'd be home all morning, with no need for a bodyguard, and why waste his cousin's talents? I hoped Sim would hulk discreetly.

I brought my cup of tah over to the Net link and asked for messages. Stereth's old message still lay there with its privacy code intact, unread, like something dead. A message from Kylla saying to call her. And a message from Loden Broca Mercia.

Loden Broca Mercia? I wouldn't have thought he even had a Net code. I read:

> *Gracious lady:*
> *Your kindness was much appreciated. Something has happened that forces me to beg your help again, much as I would wish not to. Please come to my room as soon as possible. This is an emergency. I need to see you right away. Every minute counts.*
>
> *Loden Broca*

Heavens! It was timed as half an hour ago. Barbarian that I am, a direct appeal for help seemed to me to call for an answer, and I couldn't say that the message hadn't hit a desperate note. Clearly some action needed to be taken immediately. My imagination started to race. What the hell was going on at Loden Broca's? In my mind's eye I saw men trying to break down his door while he cowered inside . . . in which case, how had he gotten to a Net terminal? All right, scratch that vision.

But damn it, what was I supposed to do about his problem? Surely I'd been through enough lately. Suddenly I recalled my embarrassing flight through the house the other night, pursued by Cousin Sim. . . . Two days later, alone by the Net link, I felt my face get warm. I had not, perhaps, been comporting myself at my best these past few days.

I abandoned the remains of my breakfast, splashed water on my face, and pulled on my clothes. Enough of the invalid life.

Now . . . should I call Ran before I go? I really didn't want to interrupt his breakfast meeting when he was busy bringing the council around to where I wanted them to be. I penned a brief note saying where I was going and hurried to the door. Then I paused. All right, you don't want to act like a coward, but there's no need to act like a fool, either, is there? I went back to the trapdoor in the closet by the stairway, opened it, and took out one of the pistols and a new charge. Then I wrapped a green silk scarf around my head, tucking up my red-brown hair, and set a sun hat over it. The picture of Ivoran normalcy, if a little on the small side. The bulge under my robe would not be seen as unusual by anybody.

I arrived at Loden's inn sweaty and breathless, about twenty minutes later. There was no one out front. I slowed down, checking the doorway and the nearby buildings. Paranoia is always helpful. Maybe I shouldn't have come, it wasn't really my business what trouble Loden got into . . . but the man did appeal for help.

It was daytime, so the main door was unbolted. I was wondering whether to just cross the street and try pulling on the handle when it burst open in front of me. Loden appeared, hauling a dirty mattress. As he pulled it down the steps a skinny, gray-haired man strode up and stood in the doorway behind him. "And don't leave your *kanz* on my steps," he yelled. "Put it in the road! And you've got one more trip, and I lock the door behind you!"

I took my hand off the tip of the pistol, where it had apparently gone without my command. The gray-haired man slammed the door. Loden wrestled the mattress down to the edge of the road. He didn't appear to see me.

I walked over to him and tapped him on the shoulder. He jumped slightly. "Gracious lady!" he exclaimed. "Thank you for coming—"

"That was your landlord, wasn't it," I said.

"Uh, yes. He seems to have gotten himself excited—I didn't do anything—"

"You had me run over here because you're being evicted."

"He's throwing me out on the street! I have nowhere to go—"

I turned and started walking away. He ran after me. "Wait! Wait, noble lady, please—you haven't heard the whole story. Just give me a few seconds—you're here anyway."

I stopped and waited. He pulled out a handkerchief and wiped his brow. "Look, it's more serious than you think. I'm suspended without pay from the Mercia Agency. Len's throwing me out here because I'm a couple of weeks late. I'm not on the job any more, so I don't have guards around me; I'm not even behind shelter at night. You're the one who told me my life was in danger! What am I supposed to do?"

He did have a point. The odds on his getting killed

had gone way up. "Looks like it's time for you to leave town," I said.

"But if I do that, they'll never take me back into the Mercians. It's the only thing I'm trained for. And I owe them the rest of my journeyman duty."

I sighed. He did seem to be painted into a corner. "I don't see what you think I can do."

"I don't know either, but . . . isn't there something?"

Suddenly Loden seemed very young. In Standard reckoning, he must have been less than twenty—inexperienced, from the provinces . . . and a trouble-seeking idiot. Ran would never agree to take this kid in, and I didn't blame him. Where else could we tuck him away? Kylla's? I'd never saddle her with this. "I suppose I could lend you some money for an inn," I said reluctantly, knowing the House of Cormallon would never see that money again.

He pursed his lips. "Uh . . . if there's any other way . . . there's no security in an inn, gracious lady. Not from somebody who really wants to get you. I haven't been able to sleep a full night here since you warned me."

"Well, what is it you want?"

"I don't know."

We stood there on the edge of the dusty street. I said, "All right, what's left in your room?"

"Clothes," he said eagerly. "Robes and uniforms, boots and sandals."

"Get what you can carry into a sack. Don't get a second sack for me—I'm not carrying anything." I glanced at the dirty mattress suspiciously—heaven knew what was living in it—and said, "and throw that thing away."

He dropped it at once into the street and went back indoors.

As it turned out, when he took a long time upstairs, I went up and helped him go through his possessions. And I did end up carrying a sack, of course. You probably suspected I would.

We marched through the streets with our respective loads, and I thought, What a sucker you are, Theodora.

I had him drop off the two sacks at a street laundry, which I paid for. Then I led him to the road outside our house. He put his foot onto one of the four concrete steps that lead to our front door, and I said, "Wait a minute, sonny."

Sonny? Where had that come from? Suddenly I felt like a grandmother. He stood down again and waited.

I said, "I'm not bringing a stranger onto the territory of my husband's House. I don't know you, and you haven't impressed me with your reliability." A trifle harsh, but my real opinion of him was that the only reason I absolved him from suspicion in Kade's murder was because he struck me as having no ability whatsoever to plan ahead. Granted that Ran felt the murder was poorly executed, if Loden had been involved I strongly doubted it would have come off at all. On grounds of incompetence alone, it was far more likely he was just what he seemed—a person in deep trouble.

I circled around to the back of our steps, by the wall, and tapped a square durasteel plate about a meter and a half high. "This is our security station for receiving parcels. Nobody can see inside, and its walls are six centimeters thick, pure weapon-proof material. It's ventilated, because in olden times a Cormallon retainer used to sit in there to receive and open the mail." I grinned suddenly. "A very brave retainer, I assume. Anyway, there's room to sit up or lie down in it, and we can give you a slops bucket for your personal needs. That's no worse than some inns. It's a safe enough place to sleep."

I looked at him. "Or if you feel it offends your dignity, I can lend you that money for another inn."

He said at once, "No, this will be fine." Then he hesitated. "You are serious, right?"

"Look, I went to your place today to risk my life for you, and I'll do what I can for you otherwise, but

I'm not bringing you on Cormallon territory. So make up your mind—''

"No, no—I didn't mean—I'll be happy to stay here. Just till I figure out what to do next.''

Yeah, the Emperor will step down from the throne and start sailing paper boats in the park before you come to any intelligent decision. —Nasty, Theodora. Be fair. The boy is under a lot of pressure.

I said, reluctantly, "I'd better give you food money. Don't eat it inside there, it'll stink the place up.''

"All right.'' He took without hesitation the new ten-tabal coin I gave him.

Then he went to the cookshop, and I put up a brief note on the station to the effect that it was out of order, and all parcels should be diverted to the Shikron villa.

When Ran came home, I hoped he would be in a tolerant mood.

"I put him in the mail box,'' I said to him as Sim discreetly left the room.

"I beg your pardon?'' said Ran. *"Mail box?''*

"The one out front. I figured he could sleep there till he gets his life a little more in order.''

"Mail box?'' he repeated.

"I put a note on it,'' I said, "telling any messengers to shuttle deliveries over to Kylla's. And I cleaned out what was in it this morning.''

"Theodora, you're telling me that Loden Broca is spending his nights in our parcel receipt?''

"Well, it's not a Taka hospitality suite, but it is weapon-proof, and we've both slept in worse places—''

He sat down on the divan in our parlor. "Great bumbling gods.'' He looked up. "Do we have any tah on hand?''

I went to get him a cup of the pink kind, because that's the most soothing, and he clearly hadn't had a good morning. I spooned it in, let it boil, and took him out the square tah holder with two empty cups. After he'd drunk a little, I said, "So how was the breakfast meeting?''

"Are you going to tell me the rest of this Loden Broca story?"

"I want to hear your story first."

"Gods. All right, I told them what you'd said."

"And?"

"They're a polite bunch. They couldn't attack the word of a Cormallon lady, so they agreed to table the entire matter till next year."

"Hallelujah!"

It wasn't an Ivoran word, but he recognized it. "Theodora, what are you going to do next year?"

"Let me fill you in on Loden," I said, and I did. When I'd finished he said, "What an idiot he is."

"I know."

"I'd just as soon not even have him in our parcel receipt. But I suppose he took advantage of your soft barbarian heart."

"He did appeal to us for help, Ran."

"What of it? Let him appeal to the Mercians for help. And why didn't you have me paged at the Taka? I could've sent Sim back to you."

"More likely you'd have told me to let him appeal to the Mercians."

"Well, yes." Ran does not deny the obvious truths. "But I would have sent you Sim just the same."

"There wasn't time. Besides, why would you want me to wait for Sim when you've said we're not targets anymore? *Are* we in danger?"

He looked pained. I said, "Just what is Sim's purpose in life, anyway?"

"He's here on a holiday," Ran said. "Show him the capital."

We looked at each other. He sighed. "All right, what's done is done, I suppose. If anyone trails Loden to our house to pick him off, at least we've got Sim on hand to aid in the defense. —Mind you, that's if we look in the least degree of danger, Theodora. If the danger's only to Loden, he can deal with it himself."

"Well, naturally."

"I mean it. I don't want you taking any chances because his cute brown eyes are in jeopardy."

"Kylla said that about his eyes. I didn't."

"Yes, I recall now. You simply said they were remarkably fine."

I smiled. "Thank you for your understanding." I kissed him on the cheek.

Sim stuck his head in the door and said, "Do you have an extra pair of slippers? And did I see the Gossip Gazette somewhere this morning?"

I whispered to Ran, "He's adapting very well."

"And do we have any hard bread and jam?" asked Sim. 'I'm very fond of bread and jam. Cherry would be best. Though I don't want to put you to any trouble."

The Cormallons had all gone home (except for Sim); our assignment for Jusik was officially over; and with Loden turning out to be a quiet guest, I had to agree with Ran that our attackers from Trade Square had probably lost interest when the case was canceled. He and Sim had gone to Ran's robemaker to get new suits for the two of them, and I'd pushed them out of the house gladly, looking forward to a few hours of peaceful reading.

Naturally the doorbells began to jingle. I checked the plate, saw it was Coalis, and let him in.

"You've interrupted Kesey's *Poems*," I said. "I may never get through that damned book."

"What a welcome, gracious lady." But he smiled, and I could see my way of greeting him pleased his na'telleth heart. "We should exchange volumes before I go. I'm carrying the *Erotic Poems* in my wallet, and *I* can't get through *them*."

"Importunate strangers keep interrupting you, too?"

"No, I just don't like the poems. Though I shouldn't prejudice you against them." He stooped to pass through the hanging that separates the parlor from hall, took off his sun hat, and whirled it expertly onto a table; narrowly missing a wildly expensive vase in the process.

He plopped himself down on a cushion and grinned up at me. "I'm glad you're home. Sit down, I've come to show you something."

I dragged a cushion over and sat beside him. He said, "Stereth asked me to come."

"He did?" It did take me a little by surprise, but then, I had no other good reason for him to visit.

"He wanted me to set your mind to rest on an issue." Coalis reached into the pocket of his inner robe, and pulled out a slim, worn book held together by a piece of string tied in an untangleable schoolboy knot.

"I hope that's not your volume of Kesey," I said, sensing it wasn't.

He slipped the string off and flipped forward, then backward a few pages. "Here," he said, and handed it to me.

Loden Broca Mercia had a page to himself. I whistled. "Six hundred tabals. That's a lot of money for a journeyman guard to owe."

"He wasn't very consistent in paying it back, either," Coalis pointed out.

I read the notations in green ink, payments of twenty to thirty tabals at a time. No wonder the boy had been living on scraps and tap water in that inn. Still, Coalis had a point; Loden often skipped a week or two, letting his interest rise dangerously. Even on his salary, he ought to have made higher payments at the very beginning. The figures were clear about that, particularly the figures done in black ink by a neater hand, near the bottom of the page. I said, "Is this true? He's up to twelve hundred tabals?"

"That's what happens when you miss payments," said Coalis. "He's barely scratched the principal at all."

I closed the book and returned it to Coalis for him to re-string. This all served to confirm Loden's story. Though he'd lied about how much he owed, which was, I supposed, understandable. It's hard to admit you've been that much of a fool.

I said, "Stereth asked you to show me this?"

"He said he wanted to limit the uncertainty in your life. He didn't tell me what he meant by that."

Who ever was sure what Stereth meant? "How well do you know the minister, anyway?"

"Me?" The question seemed to surprise him. "I told you, we met on a na'telleth retreat. I was impressed with his talent for concentration. We've been spending a fair amount of time together lately because of the partnership, but I suppose once I'm settled he'll have other things to be working on."

"So he's been helpful to you in the partnership. Worth bringing him in."

"Oh, definitely! I wouldn't have had any guidance at all in this, if not for Stereth." Coalis's face shone. "He's been wonderful."

"Does he talk to you much about . . . about before, when he was an outlaw leader?"

"I wish he would. He said those days are past."

I breathed a tiny sigh of relief at that. Not that Stereth was a gossip, by any stretch of the imagination, but it was good to hear.

Coalis was going on. "He shows me all kinds of things now, though."

"Oh? What kind of things?"

"All kinds. He's got a lot of friends, and he introduced me to some of them. They were able to help me a lot in the business."

"I thought you were mainly handling the business as a one-man operation. Isn't that what Kade was doing?"

"Well, yes, but you need to know what to do . . . you need people to run the operations end of things. I'm too small to do it all myself."

Too small? Oh— "You're talking about the beating-people-up, leg-breaking end of things."

"Well, it *is* part of the business, Theodora. Otherwise no one would pay us back. They don't have regular collateral.''

"No, I understand the concept. So you . . . direct the operations now, is that it?''

"Not yet. So far I've just watched. It's very interesting.''

"I'm sure,'' I said noncommittally, thinking, *So this is why he reminds Stereth of Lex na'Valory.*

"But Stereth's promised me a chance to direct.''

"Well, that sounds . . . promising.''

"I'll be supervising everything myself, once Stereth gets us on track.''

"Really.'' I wondered how to change the subject. I said, "I guess Kade's death opened up a whole new world for you. Maybe missing the monastery wasn't the worst thing, after all. It seems more of a liberation.''

He looked slightly shocked. "How can you say that, Theodora? The field of moneylending is an interesting one, but it's only an illusion. Like any other lender, I'll be teaching that fact to my clients. Not that it takes much deliberate teaching. I can assure you, practically all of them eventually realize that the money they wanted in the first place was not that important.''

"I see. You'll be bringing na'telleth philosophy into ordinary life.''

"Of course; that's where it belongs. Naturally I'd advance further in the monastery, but I intend to follow the path as well as I can.''

"That's very, uh, admirable of you. I'm not far advanced in the na'telleth way, myself.''

"You're only a barbarian,'' he said tolerantly. "And I'm sure you've learned more than you think. One can't help getting lessons in na'telleth-ri, just by living.''

"You may have a point. I've been thinking a lot about 'the other side of the mirror' lately.''

"Excellent,'' he said happily. "That's exactly what I mean. But don't be afraid of it. Look the skull in the face. That's the na'telleth way.''

I laughed. "The barbarian way is to avoid.''

"That way the skull finds *you*."

Look the skull in the face. Easier said than done. Coalis was reaching for his sun hat, gathering his robes together as he got to his feet. "I'm afraid I must hurry," he said, apologetically. "I'm expected at home. —Oh! Let's exchange books," he added, holding out his volume of Kesey. I gave him mine and took his. We stood at the front doorway for a moment and he smiled, an innocent smile for a sixteen-year-old nobly born loanshark monk. "I'm glad this business with Kade is over," he said suddenly. He turned to go out into the sunlight. Then he turned back and said, confiding, "I couldn't make head or tail of the Kesey. If you do, you must promise to explain it to me."

"I promise."

He tied his sun hat, took our front steps jauntily, and went off down the street under the row of spindly mirandis trees.

It was a rather ordinary day, that day, the sixth of Kace. I did some chores that needed to be done, went through some records, thought about organizing the paper files and decided not to. When Ran and Sim came home, I listened to their lengthy descriptions and duly admired the sets of robes they'd ordered.

That night I lay in bed listening to one of the rare summer rainfalls. I'd been interested in what Coalis had had to say during his visit; somehow the story of Kade's dunk in the canal wasn't finished with me, whatever Ran might think. If I did pursue it, it would be on my own time, that much was clear.

Why pursue it? I couldn't presume to any claim to justice; I didn't even know Kade, and what I did know of him did not impress me. Was it just because I hated not knowing how stories come out? I had to admit that the thought that I would never know did offend my scholarly sense of neatness. Or was I just getting desperate for what Stereth called "certainty in my life"?

It would be good to have something to concentrate on, something outside myself. Lately I couldn't even concentrate on that damned book of poetry, even when I was alone and without any distractions. In fact, being alone and without any distractions was the worst of all.

What was my problem, anyway? Why couldn't I just tell Ran the idea of carrying our child scared me? But I was a product of the Athenan University. I had no evidence to offer, just nerves, and that was insufficient reason to avoid something that had to be done. (*He'll lose respect for you, Theodora.* —*Oh, shut up.*) I'd known our marriage would be complicated when I agreed to come back, but somehow I thought we could just dance around this issue.

A bad assumption for a scholar.

Ran was lying next to me, propped on one arm, looking through some papers. Minutes of the council meeting. I'd been quite interested in them till I found there was no mention of the "Theodora problem" in there; the issue had been debated "off the record." Out of respect for my privacy, no doubt, but I'd have liked to have gotten hold of a transcript so I could arm myself for the future.

I heard the papers being put down. He stretched. "You're quiet tonight. And you don't even have a book in your hand."

"I'm thinking."

"Oh?"

Perfect opportunity to bring it up— "I was thinking I'd better get my hair cut. It keeps falling in my face, unless I pin it back with ten thousand pins."

Ten Thousand Pins. The Biography of Theodora of Pyrene and Her Basic Lack of Organization. Ran rolled over a little closer. "Don't get it cut. This is the longest it's ever been."

What is this thing men have about long hair? I said, "Desire is a reflex, physical appearance an illusion."

"You've been talking to Coalis again," he said simply, making a connection that impressed me.

"He was here today. Showed me Kade's loan book, which confirmed Loden's story."

"Let's leave Loden in the mail box for tonight. Don't get your hair cut."

"It's more convenient short, I won't need to do anything with it. Have you ever noticed how in plays the hero pulls out a single pin and the heroine's hair tumbles down in a sensuous mass, just before they make passionate love? If that was me we'd be searching and pulling out pins for the next twenty minutes."

"But Theodora. I rather *like* searching for pins." He'd rolled over and was looking down me with all sincerity. "Let's count backward," he said. "Nine thousand, nine hundred, and ninety-nine." He slipped one out. "Nine thousand, nine hundred, and ninety-eight. You know, if you're going to laugh at me, we'll never get this done."

It was still raining near midnight. I lay awake, wishing for fire, flood, or earthquake; something solid and awful in the outside world that I could concentrate on. Something other than myself.

Look the skull in the face. Easy for you, Coalis.

I got out of bed and wandered into the upstairs study, bringing the leather pouch I keep behind my pillow. I sat on the carpet, opened the pouch, and took out the deck of cards Ran inherited from his grandmother.

Maybe this was a waste of time. I'd run the deck when we took on Jusik's case, and it had given straight business answers to a business question. The pack was tuned to Ran's concerns and safety; when it came to answering my personal doubts, the odds were that it would be less than helpful.

But if Coalis could look things in the face, so could I. I shuffled quickly, before I could change my mind, and started laying out cards.

The Band of Brothers. The card showed a table of six men drinking themselves into quite a happy state of inebriation. I kept my finger on the card and watched it dissolve into a room I'd never seen, a room with a huge thick glass window showing blue sky, a mahogany table, and over a dozen men wearing re-

spectable robes sitting around a curved bench with
cushions. Ran was by the window. *The Taka Hospitality Building,* I thought. Ran was answering something, giving short replies while one man after another
made excited comments. Damn, if only the deck gave
me sound as well as visual! Finally a short man with
a rainbow holiday tunic under his street robe stood up
and gestured wildly. Ran strode from the window, eyes
blazing, spitting out words, and ended by smashing
his fist on the table. The short man drew back, and
everyone stopped talking. Heavens—I'd never seen Ran
hit his fist on a table in his life.

I took my finger off the card when I shifted position,
wondering if there was any way in the world I could
get a transcript from the Net. The card turned back
into the Band of Brothers, ink and color, vine leaves
under the table.

An interesting window, in its way. Still, this wasn't
what I was looking for, it was just a slice of an old
reality. I needed better data.

A wild and grim impulse came over me. Enough of
this shilly-shallying. I shuffled the card back into the
pack, placed it on the floor, stood up, and went into
the bathroom. There I took the beveled mirror from
its hook over the sink and carried it back to the study.
I laid it on the carpet, facedown.

I was looking at the plain wooden backing with its
twist of wire stretching across. Once or twice in the
past I'd experienced a deeper and stranger kind of card-
reading; scarier, more symbolic, not just a window
into normal reality. I tried to keep away from that kind
of thing, generally . . . could I call it up now? I
crossed to Ran's desk and took out an old brush-pen,
and brought the inkstone he used as a paperweight to
the bathroom sink to grind and wet it. When the ink
seemed sufficient, I knelt down by the mirror, dipped
the brush, and drew a skull-shape over the back.

It wasn't hard. The old waterstains on the wood
seemed to suggest a skull before I even began, though
I tried not to think about that too closely. When I com-

pleted it, I carried the pen back to the sink to wash so I wouldn't get ink on Ran's desk. I left it there to dry.

All responsibilities taken care of, I sat cross-legged by the mirror. I picked up the cards and shuffled them over it, trying to disengage my mind from the circle of daily tasks that keeps us all nose-to-the-ground until we die. It was death I was looking for . . . a sighting from a distance, nothing nearer, and with luck even that might be a phantom.

I waited until I didn't care whether I put down one card or another, and so I put one down. It was The Old House, a stone place in the forest, half in sunlight and half in tree-shadow. Why in the world did that turn up? A reference to the House of Cormallon? In an ordinary configuration it might suggest regrets or nostalgia. . . . Before I could ruin the reading by analyzing it, I put my finger on the picture.

And I was standing in an old passageway, in a place half-familiar. I started walking down the passage. My footsteps made no sound. Why did I know this place?

A moldy, tattered hanging was in one doorway. I passed by and went down a staircase, feeling a terrible sense of abandonment about the building with every step I took. There was nobody living here, I was sure of that. At the end of the staircase there was a short hallway and a massive wooden door. Some kind of old moss was growing on the side of the wood. I pulled it open with an effort—and remembered suddenly how Stereth had pulled this door open once, days ago.

I was in the Poraths' house in the old quarter of town. What did this have to do with me and the other side of the mirror? I walked out onto the low wooden porch with its lacquered pillars . . . rotting now, with great gaps in the floor that I had to inch around. No sound of bird or insect came from the garden, overgrown and abandoned. I stepped off the porch in the unnatural silence.

I took the remains of the path through the garden to the place where we'd spoken with Jusik Porath. The silver arc in memory of Kade was gone, but there was a white marble statue in its place. And somebody was sitting where Jusik had sat, in a tangle of silk robes. He stood up, looking past me. It was Ran.

He turned toward the statue. I called "Ran!" and heard the sound echo in my head as though it only existed internally. It was the kind of sound you hear through ear coverings, though my ears were open. I walked toward him.

The statue was of me! That was somehow the most horrible touch of the night, and I felt shivers run up my arms. It wasn't a classical statue, there was no noble look on my face; it was me in one of my street outfits, looking as though someone had tipped a thin sheathing of white over my head and trapped me in a passing moment. Ran put a hand on the crook of the statue's elbow. A surface of red pooled up beneath it.

The statue was bleeding. I was vaguely aware that I was watching this from some other place, and was sorry that I'd come. More wounds appeared. Ran stripped off his outerrobe and his shirt, and tried to clean the statue off. But the blood was inexhaustible. It pooled at the statue's feet, soaked through the shirt, and left stains on Ran's face and hands and clothing.

I wanted to leave here. I wanted to leave here *now*. I didn't live here, right? I came from some other place. This was just a picture, I could go back if I wanted to! . . . If I could remember how.

I started yelling. It echoed in my head without disturbing the air around me. I was completely alone.

Chapter 14

I woke up in my bed. The room was light. I looked around; Kylla was dozing on a cushion by the wall, the long gold string-earring in her left ear curling on her chest where the robe fell open.

I still felt unreal. I was afraid to take a step out of bed, not knowing if the floor would open beneath me or the walls would start to bleed. Somehow I'd lost control of normalcy.

Kylla's eyes opened. "Theo," she said, not that awful silence of the symbolic world of the cards, but "Theo," like any summer afternoon. The world righted itself, as quickly as waking up from a nightmare and suddenly *knowing* what was true and what wasn't. "Are you all right?" she asked, getting up and coming over to the bed.

"I guess. What happened?"

"Wait." She walked to the door and called, "She's awake!" Then she came back to the bed. "Theo, darling, I understand you've been messing with magic that you shouldn't."

"I've done it before—" I began to protest, but she put a finger on my lips.

"Save it for Ran. I'm sure he'll have lots to say."

I supposed that he would. Ran is not one of those people who are above second-guessing you. Kylla busied herself putting the cushions back on the cedar chest, then picked up a glass of water she had ready and waiting on the side of the sleeping platform and handed it to me. I drank it to please her, though I wasn't thirsty.

Ran appeared, fully dressed. I wondered what time it was. He came over and sat on the side of the platform. He took my hand. Then he said, "What in the world did you think you were doing?"

By all means, let's not waste time on being sentimental. "Come on, Ran, it was just a normal run of the cards."

"I don't have to carry you, unconscious, out of the study after a normal run of the cards. You don't start screaming during a normal run of the cards."

"All right, I grant you, you might have a point—"

"During a normal run of the cards," he said, "you *maintain control.*"

Oh-oh. The lecture on "the most dangerous thing"—

"The most dangerous thing you can do with magic is to let it have the least bit of random freedom! You have to define and control every variable! Sorcery is not a place to have a na'telleth attitude!"

This is the one topic I never fool with Ran about. I made myself look attentive and embarrassed, and in fact it was not at all difficult.

He said, more quietly, "Theodora, I hesitate to say this, but—were you asking an open-ended question of the cards?"

"I've asked general questions before," I said, trying to recall exactly what my state of mind had been last night—death, children, memories of the assassin in the marketplace, all mixed up together. Perhaps I *had* been a little too open-ended in my worries.

"You've asked general questions before, but not when you use that na'telleth technique, that wipe-your-mind and see what happens *thing* that you do. You know I don't like it when you experiment. The cards are a perfectly reasonable source of information when you use them as a simple window. So *use* them that way, Theodora. Half the time when you use this off-the-wall method we get symbolic answers we can't even interpret!"

"I'm sorry if I worried you."

He sighed. "What where you so curious about, anyway, that you had to get up in the middle of the night and do dangerous experiments to find out?''

I was not up to opening that discussion now. I felt wrung-out, as though I'd just recovered from a long illness. "Can we go into it later?"

He hesitated. His face went expressionless. "Of course," he said stiffly. "We can discuss it some other time. I have to call Mira-Stoden anyway and arrange to postpone my trip."

"What trip?"

"We decided in council that I'd arbitrate Jula's dispute in person. It'll probably take a couple of days, it's not the sort of thing to try over the Net."

"Why are you postponing it? Did something else happen?"

"Yes, Theodora, I picked you up off the floor of the study."

"Oh." He really did not look pleased with me at all. "Look, you don't have to stick around for me, I'm fine."

"I'll stay."

"Honestly, I'd prefer it if you went."

He was silent. I said, "I'm perfectly well."

Finally he said, "You want me to leave."

"Well, why get the council any more annoyed than we have already?" And I didn't want to face all the questions I knew he'd have as soon as he got off the Net.

He stood up. "As you wish." He certainly didn't sound any happier about it or me. "I'll see that it doesn't last beyond noon tomorrow." That last came out almost like a warning. He added, "Sim will be here, and Kylla will look in on you tonight."

Belatedly, it seemed to occur to him that he might ask Kylla how she felt about that. "Ky, you won't have any problem dropping over, will you?"

Before she could answer, I said, "It's not necessary, Ky. Last night was a fluke. I'm all right now, really."

"I'll come by this evening, just the same," she said.

So Ran left, looking dissatisfied.

To give you an idea of my state of mind as we approached High Summer Week, I suppose I should mention that at least once every few days I found myself sharply reliving those seconds in the sorcerer's tent in Trade Square. I'd heard of people flashing back to traumatic moments, and I don't know if this was what was meant by it or not. I was never in any doubt as to where I really was, or what was really happening, but in the midst of walking down the street or opening up a food container, or—most often—lying in bed waiting to fall asleep—I would suddenly find myself, double-vision-like, inside an amazingly vivid memory of those few seconds. I could feel the grit under my hands when I hit the ground, see that knife looming up, and sense the horrible twisting in my stomach that had taken place at that moment.

I experienced it again, after Kylla and Ran had left and I was sitting in the larder spooning jam onto a piece of bread. *Interesting,* said a detached part of my mind, as jam dribbled onto my fingers. It didn't do a lot for the appetite, though.

"Are you finished with that jam?" asked Sim's voice.

I turned around. "Oh. Sorry, yes, here you are."

"Thank you, my lady."

"You know, you can call me Theodora. We *are* cousins."

He took a big bite of bread and jam.

As he chewed away, I said, "So you're taking a holiday. Have you been to the Lavender Palace yet?"

He shook his head.

"The Lantern Gardens? The Imperial Park?"

"No, my lady."

I didn't correct him. "Well, do you want to go out? I'm tired of being a burden on society. Go on, see the sights."

"No, thank you, my lady."

"There's a flyer race in Goldenweed Fields today."

"No, thank you."

It was clear that Ran had gotten in before me. He, on the other hand, felt free to go off to Mira-Stoden by himself, while not bothering to ask my permission before chaining this babysitter to me. I pried the jam pot away from Sim and spooned out another sliceful, thinking vengeful thoughts. It was nice to be angry at somebody else for a while.

The doorbells rattled furiously and I put down my breakfast and went to see who it was. Sim was already checking the spyplate. "Nobody I know," he said to me.

I looked for myself. It was Trey Lesseret, Loden's coworker from the Mercian agency. "We'll let him in," I said. "But stick around."

Sim nodded. He approved of paranoia. I hit all the locks and opened the door.

Trey Lesseret bowed quickly, saying, "Gracious lady. May I speak with you a moment?" He wore the trousers and tunic of his profession, and looked to be either on his way to work or on a break in midassignment. His expression was unhappy, and a little desperate.

He ignored Sim. As soon as he was inside, he turned to me and said, "Forgive my imposition, but do you know where Loden Broca is?"

"Why should I know where sir Broca is? Surely he's at work. Why don't you ask your supervisor?"

"Excuse me, but Loden already told me he was staying here." Well, Pinnacle-of-Discretion Loden. "I have good reason for asking, you see—a Net inquiry was made this morning at the agency—someone wanting to know where he is. Loden's only family is in the provinces, and none of them would use the Net."

"I see." I hesitated. "Are you aware of Loden's situation?"

"He told me someone's trying to kill him, if that's what you mean. That's why I figured I'd better find the young idi—why I'd better locate him. It's the first time, ever, that anyone's tried to reach him at work. Anyone who's not a girl, I mean." He paused and ran a hand through his sparse grayish hair. "Now, I only know about this because I overheard the secretary talking. I haven't got details. But I think he's damned lucky he was sent off till his probation's over. Otherwise he'd've been locatable within minutes—we're all supposed to be constantly locatable, it's part of our coverage strategy."

I considered this. "Did Loden tell you *exactly* where he was staying?"

"In your parcel receipt. But there's no answer when I hit the entrance with my knife butt."

"Wait." I ran and got my overrobe, tied on my belt and pouch, and slipped on a pair of sandals. "Sim, come with me."

We all filed outside and down the steps to the parcel receipt entrance. While Sim watched to make sure Lesseret was looking elsewhere—as he was, in all politeness—I keyed open the entrance. Metal slid aside and a man-sized opening formed to the right of the locked delivery tube. It struck me suddenly that this was the place, in one of those old puzzle-stories, where the second body would be found.

A strong smell of bredesmoke assailed us. I started to cough, and Lesseret looked a little embarrassed. I stooped and peered through the drug haze to the interior; empty, but for a pallet of old cloaks and half a nutcake. Getting that close made me cough some more. "You could get high just sitting in there," I said, as I stood up straight and topped the entrance. "Evidently he isn't worried about ventilation."

"Please help me," said Lesseret.

I was surprised. "What can I do? You see he's not here."

"He needs to be warned. But I can't look for him, I have to be back at my assignment in twenty minutes. I'm on probation, too, but they're letting me keep working—I can't afford any black marks."

"I'm sorry, but I don't see what it is you want me to do."

"Look, he's not at work and he's not here. He's almost certainly at a tith-parlor."

I glanced at Sim, who was expressionless. "Are you suggesting I call every tith-parlor in the capital . . . ?"

"No, of course not. They'd never tell you the truth about whether a customer was there. You'll have to go personally and look."

I would, would I? "Sir Lesseret . . . you seem like a nice person, and it's good that you're concerned about a friend, but this is getting out of hand. I don't even *know* Loden."

"He could be killed! He could *die* today! I don't know who else to go to. Look, I don't have a lot of money, but I could pay you a little a week—"

I winced, thinking of Kade and Coalis. "No, wait." I said to Sim, "Do you have any idea how many tith-parlors there are in this city?"

"I'd figure, thirty or forty," he said.

"It's not that bad," said Lesseret eagerly. "He always goes to the gambling quarter, and there are only about twenty there."

"The gambling quarter" is a five-block section of town where tith-parlors and cardhalls and things I still don't know about seem to have congregated; there are a lot of pretty colored lights there. At least it was a relatively small distance to cover.

A small distance for Loden's enemies to cover, too, if they figured out that that's where he was.

I sighed. "I take it he doesn't have a favorite place."

"Not really. He usually goes to Red Tah Street, there are five or six places there . . . but sometimes he goes somewhere else."

"Terrific." I suppose I'd accepted responsibility for him when I'd stuck him in our mailbox. I should have let him find his own way out to the provinces in the beginning. Apropos of nothing, I pointed to the half-eaten nutcake on the floor. "You know, I asked him not to bring food in there."

"The boy doesn't listen," said Lesseret worriedly, echoing my own thoughts.

"No," I sighed, "he doesn't." I looked at Sim. If you can't trust your husband's taste in bodyguards, what's the point of being married? "Are you game for this? We're not under obligation."

"It's not for me to say," he replied primly. "If you go, I go with you."

"Cousin Sim, this is the time for you to raise objections. We can go back inside and have lunch, if you want. If there's any danger in this, you'll probably get hit first, and I won't take you into something you'd just as soon avoid."

"It's up to you," he said stubbornly. The Cormallon sense of duty. I gave it up.

"Go back to your job," I said to Trey Lesseret. "We'll see if we can find Loden."

"My thanks," he said happily, going so far as to take my hand and bow over it.

"Never mind. We probably won't run across him anyway."

But he was too thrilled with having dumped his problem in someone else's lap to let me dampen his spirits. He hurried off down the street before anyone could change their mind.

Red Tah Street has closer to a dozen parlors on it, counting the cardhalls and smoke dens on both sides of the road. I'd never stopped in this little part of town before; it had no attraction. Aside from an occasional card game to pass the time, gambling has always been a closed book to me. The more random chance rules a situation, the more I tend to avoid it—probably because I lose. It's amazing, in fact, how consistently I lose. Back on Pyrene, when I was a kid, there was a little arcade off the recreation hall where we could bet study-tokens on a wheel with six numbers. I was the only child in the creche who never won even once in all the years I was there. Winners got to pick from the bakery products left over from that day's kitchen detail. It was understood that our creche-guardian would have to bring hard currency and purchase one for little Theodora, since she was incapable of winning any.

It was a good inoculation against gambling fever; all I associate it with is disappointment.

Red Tah Street was packed, even in the afternoon, so obviously others don't have the benefit of my bad luck. We were standing on the edge of the neighborhood, beside the first hall, under a painted wooden sign that showed a giant wheel with kings, princes, and beggars falling off into the mud as it turned. Clearly not an establishment that made great promises. "We could split up," I said to Sim. "Take different sides of the street."

He shook his head.

"I won't tell Ran. It's not as if these people were looking for us. It's Loden they're after."

He shook his head.

"Fine. Let's try the Wheel of Illusion first. I look forward to seeing a gambling parlor with a na'telleth name. You think maybe they don't play for money?"

He held the door patiently for me, not responding. Sim has standards when he's on duty. Inside, the place was cramped, dark, and not very well cleaned; it took about ten seconds to ascertain that Loden wasn't around. There was a numbers wheel in back and a set of card tables and benches in front, with fanatical looking men and women of all ages. A twenty-ish woman in a gold-threaded robe sat opposite a man in his sixties with a ragged tunic and no teeth. Their attention was solely on the game. I began to realize that gambling creates an equality of citizenship societies have toppled trying to achieve.

"He's not here," I said, intelligently. Sim grunted. I considered the arithmetic of our hitting each parlor on the street; it would be a shame if Loden ambled from one to the next, just missing us. I nudged Sim. "Let's see if we can find the manager."

"It's not really a tith-parlor," said Sim. "Just cards and wheel."

"No harm in asking," I said.

The manager was a middle-aged woman of great politeness and no expression. She wore a green robe and carried a pipe. "Young men come in here all the time," she said, when I asked. "Old men, too. Everyone comes here."

"He might be wearing a security guard's outfit. Trousers and tunic. And his name is Loden Broca."

She paused, then tapped her pipe against the wall. Soft gray ash fell onto the floor, where it vanished in the dirt and shadows. "Loden Broca. Yes, I know the name. I know the name of everyone on the debit side of our ledger, gracious lady. I seriously doubt if Broca will come here today. He owes us quite a sum of money."

"I thought he'd paid off all his debts," I said, remembering the loan he'd taken from Kade for that purpose.

"He paid some. Not all." She pursed her hard little lips. "Should you locate him, I hope you'll bear in mind we pay a ten-percent finder's fee for notifying us where we can find recalcitrants."

"Well, I'll certainly consider that." I started backing away. "Come on, Sim."

No one from the Wheel of Illusion made any move to follow us, and I was glad when we reached sunlight again. "What a jolly street this is. I can see why it's so popular. Let's try the Green and Gold."

The Green and Gold was better-lit than its predecessor, but not more helpful. At least Loden didn't have a tab there. We went through six more halls in the next two hours; fortunately Sim and I were well-dressed enough to receive courteous treatment from the managers.

At the Rainbow Enchantment Palace, a particularly small and no-frills place, I sat down for a moment by one of the machines. My feet hurt. Sim stood beside us, surveying the customers. A chubby girl about five years old ran up to me at once, wearing a pink ribbon; she bowed and offered me a cup of tah on a round silver tray. I was thirsty, so I thanked her and took it.

She ran off again before I could pay her. "Now you'll have to light up the machine," said Sim. "Drinks are only for players."

"You seem to know a lot about these places," I said. I stuffed a few kembits into the slot and watched the board take form, then read the instructions idly as I drained my cup. "Say, I think I know this. It's a variation on Solitaire."

Sim greeted this remark with his usual interest, so I tested my theory by using the button to move a few tiles around on the screen. My score started to climb. It wasn't quite like Solitaire, but it was similar; the strategic element had a little more influence, otherwise I probably would have experienced my usual losing streak. Instead I won two games out of three.

I was going for four when Sim tapped my shoulder. "Isn't this fellow in danger of his life, or something?"

"Oh. Yes." I swiveled the seat around and stepped off, feeling my face get hot. "I was only resting my feet for a few minutes."

"It was a quarter of an hour."

"You're joking."

I should know better than to accuse Sim of joking. He pointed out, in all seriousness, the information on his own timepiece, the clock over the machine rack, and (when we got outside) the sun in the sky. By the time we reached the doors to the Inner Courts of Heaven I was sorry I'd said anything.

Heaven was jumping. It was a big place, noisy and scrupulously clean, with the kind of lighting that tells you more about people than you wanted to know. Specifically, it was Tithball Heaven; there were a dozen ranges built against three of the walls. The fourth wall had racks of smaller machines with brightly lit tiles, like the addictive one I'd just left behind at the Rainbow. The center of the building was filled with tables and benches where people who were waiting for a range to open up could pay for food and drink. The Courts of Heaven provided everything; a customer could spend days here and never have to set foot outdoors.

There were well over a hundred people present already, and their busy time probably wasn't till evening. Sim and I made our way past the ranges, aiming for the back, where a raised platform would provide a better view of the room. Three brawny-looking gentlemen, their sleeves tied back, were too intent on their game to see they were blocking our progress. I watched as one with a jeweled bracelet clamped around his wrist threw his arm back and let the ball fly down the range. It hit the floor near the far end, bounced, and tapped the wall marked "east." The player laughed. A bronze phoenix head over the range opened its mouth ponderously, displaying a score of 450. The tithball bounced three more times on the floor, hitting a tilted slope in back. Jeweled Bracelet stared, his triumphant look changing to that of a child whose bottle is being unfairly taken away. The ball rolled down the slope and disappeared. The score in the phoenix's mouth rippled and changed to 10.

His companions laughed. "You're right," said one of them. "Your playing has really improved."

Jeweled Bracelet glared. He clapped his hands, muttered, and pointed to the crack where the ball had vanished.

It popped up again and rolled down the range to his open hands.

The score in the phoenix's mouth changed back to 450.

"Hey, that's not fair," said one of the other men.

"An act of the gods," said Jeweled Bracelet. "If a server had bumped into me while I threw, we would have counted *that*."

"This is different."

"I don't see why."

"Look, sorcery is not allowed!"

"The rules don't say anything about sorcery one way or the other."

Sim finally managed to push a route through them,

and they were far too busy arguing to take issue with it. We hadn't quite reached the platform when Sim stopped short and pointed.

Loden was sitting at one of the tables in the center. He was wearing provincial trousers, but with a stained silk robe over his shirt. Two empty winebowls were in front of him, stacked one atop the other, and a small plate of something that had had reddish sauce. A light-haired girl of about eighteen was in his lap.

"The prodigal," I murmured. Sim started his dignified progress through the crowd once again, and I sailed in his wake. When we reached Loden's table, he looked up and smiled happily.

"Theodora!" he cried. "Have a seat, gwacious—gracious lady. Let me introduce you. This is Pearl," he said, slapping his lapful's fanny gently.

She giggled. "Ruby," she corrected.

"She's a jewel, anyway. And this is Rickert." He waved an arm toward the third person at the table, a young man with his sleeves still tied back from the game. Rickert nodded sourly.

I said, "Loden, we need to talk."

"Sure, that's what I'm saying. Have a seat. Move over on the bench, Ricki, and let Theodora sit down." He grabbed the robe of a passing server, and the woman stopped. "Two more bowls here, all right? Thanks, sweet one." He winked at her.

The server's gaze met mine briefly. She rolled her eyes.

I said, "Loden, we need to talk. Privately. Right now."

Rickert stood up. "We have to go anyway. Come on, Ruby."

Ruby didn't look at him. "We've got hours yet, sweetheart. I'm fine where I am."

"No, you're not," said Rickert, in a tone that got even Ruby's attention.

She turned to him slowly and blinked. "It's still early—"

"*Now.*"

She got up from Loden's lap, taking her time, a pout forming on her face. I noticed that Loden still had a hand under her robe. I couldn't tell if Rickert could see that from his angle. She moved away slowly, her robe trailing.

Rickert took her hand and pulled her in the direction of the door.

"I don't know what you're so excited about all of a sudden," I heard her complain as the crowd swallowed them up.

I looked at Loden, who returned my gaze with happy obliviousness. Sim sat down next to me.

"It's good to get out, isn't it?" asked Loden. "I have to say, that parcel receipt can get on your nerves. Not that I'm not glad to have it to go home to."

With Loden, it was hard to tell how much was drunkeness and how much was his normal lack of discernment. I hoped he wasn't too far gone to pay attention.

"Listen," I said, "your friend Trey came to see me today."

"Trey! A great guy. Was he looking for me?" Loden's two new winebowls appeared on the table, and he reached for one. Sim, bless him, pulled it out of reach.

"Loden, Trey says that someone's been asking for you at work. You know what that means?"

He looked blank. "Who would ask for me at work?"

"I don't know, Loden, this is the point. But considering people are trying to kill you, Trey thought you ought to stay under cover."

The idea was still making its way through the outer courts of his brain. I saw it hit center.

"Ohh," he said, in simultaneous comprehension and pain.

Thank the gods for that. Now maybe we could get him out of here quietly.

Sim stood up, clearly expecting we would leave now. I don't know what it was—the effects of the crowds, the constant sense of money and danger, the impersonal desperation all around me—but suddenly I didn't believe at all that Loden didn't know who was after him.

I said, "You're involved in something, aren't you?"

He managed to look both crafty and ashamed at the same time.

"Oh, Loden." I sighed. "How can you manage to make such a mess of your life?"

I spoke at that moment from pure sadness at the waste, and he put his hand across the table over mine. "Theodora—" he began.

"Here he is," said a voice.

It was Jeweled Bracelet and his two friends. "I thought you were going to give us a rematch," said one.

"Oh, sure," said Loden, "you wait till I'm eight winebowls down—"

"You haven't had time to drink more than three. And I thought you said you could beat us playing with your feet?"

"How much did you have in mind?" asked Loden, apparently forgetting Sim and me entirely.

The men looked at each other. "Twenty tabals," said Jeweled Bracelet.

"Thirty," said Loden.

I waved a hand to get his attention. "We were leaving, weren't we?"

He blinked at me slowly. "I'll only be a few minutes."

"That's right, gracious lady," said one of the men. "It shouldn't take us that long to pound him."

They started toward the far wall of tithball ranges. Loden paused to tie back the sleeves of his robe. I stopped next to him. "What were you about to tell me, a minute ago?"

"What?"

"A minute ago. You were going to tell me something about what you're mixed up in."

"Oh, that." He seemed to be turning his mind back to something that had happened years ago, and in another country. "No, I was just going to explain why I was here. I don't usually throw back this many wine-bowls in the middle of the day, but I had a fight with my girlfriend and I guess I was upset.''

"You had a fight with Ruby?''

"Ruby?'' He frowned.

"The girl you were with, Loden.''

"Oh! Her. No, no, I had a fight with my *girl-friend.*''

How many did the boy have? Jeweled Bracelet called, ''Are you coming or not?''

"Don't get your shorts in a wad,'' said Loden cheerfully, fussing with his sleeves. He reached the edge of the range. ''If I go first, you're never going to get a shot,'' he told Bracelet.

"Right,'' said his opponent, in the voice of one who humors an idiot. He put a ball in Loden's hand. ''The phoenix has been fed.''

"For the score,'' announced Loden, and he threw straight to the north wall, hitting the ''thrower's choice'' stripe. He grinned. ''I'll go for eight hun-dred.''

There was a murmur at this. I looked around and saw that a few people had already begun to gather, scenting blood. A woman in an orange robe shook her head at what she clearly saw as foolhardiness. Sim's voice, beside me, whispered, ''If he can't make his points in three throws, he'll lose. And at two hundred a wall, he'll need a lot of luck.''

I knew nothing at all about tith stakes, but I knew that Loden and I were very different people. I would never make a bet like that, regardless of how good I thought I was.

Loden rolled the ball around in his hand, tossed it, caught it, and extended his arm experimentally. More bystanders gathered.

He threw. The ball bounced on the range floor, hit the north wall, ricocheted off the west, hitting scorable territory each time, and flew over the trap to return down the range to Loden. He smiled.

The bronze mouth of the phoenix opened, displaying a 400.

A pleased buzz came from the crowd. Someone had taken a wild chance and surprised them by pulling it off, and that was entertainment. Loden's popularity was probably hitting 400, too.

But they held back. They were an Ivoran crowd; and he still could screw it all up. Loden glanced at Jeweled Bracelet, whose face was carefully blank, and smiled again. Without preliminary, he let loose his second throw. East wall, north, bounce over the trap, and home.

The phoenix hit 800. So did the crowd. Loden was clapped on the back, congratulated, called everything good. His three betting opponents were the only unhappy looking people in the room. Jeweled Bracelet made his way through the knot of people around Loden; he put a hand in his robe to pull out his money.

The hand came out with something slim and shiny . . . I frowned. He slipped next to Loden and touched it to his wrist.

A hotpencil. I yelled, "Sim!" and tried to push through the crowd.

Jeweled Bracelet had taken hold of Loden's hand and held it in a vise grip. I saw panic rising in Loden's eyes. Then Sim took hold of Bracelet's shoulders and pulled him bodily away. Bracelet fought back with the weapon he had so conveniently handy, the hotpencil. He jabbed it in Sim's arm and kept it there while Sim's other arm reached for his neck. Sim sank to the floor.

I had once undergone training in how to fight, but unfortunately it was responsive training; I had no idea how to jump someone from behind. But I'd managed to get close to Bracelet, and I kicked him in the right knee joint. It buckled, and he lost his balance.

He let go of Sim, whose body was now splayed on the floor. He turned to me, looking angrier than I've ever seen anyone look.

Uh-oh. The crowd had withdrawn somewhat, but

there were still too many pressed around us to run. I jumped onto the tithball range.

A forfeit bell sounded. Apparently I'd crossed the boundary and would have to lose points. I ran down the middle of the range toward the back walls.

Now sirens were going off. I looked back and saw Bracelet had climbed onto the range after me. What in the name of heaven had possessed me to run into a dead end like this? North, east, and west walls enclosed me.

I knelt down, reached into the trap, and started pulling out balls lost earlier in the day. I threw one, missed. The second hit Bracelet on the side of the head. That gained me about half a second, and considering my aim it was all I was likely to get.

By now lights were flashing and hefty-looking parlor employees were approaching from all over. *This* was why I'd run into a dead-end—thank you, subconscious. An expression of uncertainty came over Bracelet's face. His companions had already fled. He turned and ran, jumping off the range into the crowd, who very quickly made way for him. Ivorans do not like to become involved in danger they feel rightly belongs to other people.

The Courts of Heaven bouncers helped me off the range, none too gently. One of them had turned Sim over and was feeling for a pulse. "Is he all right?" I asked, as they dragged me past him toward the manager.

The manager was a little man in an impeccable set of robes, about forty years old. He was nearly my height, amazing in an Ivoran male. When I reached him, he started to scream in a thick provincial accent. "What do you think you're doing! Tracking dirt all over my range, interrupting paying customers! Are you drunk? Are you crazy? Never, never do I want to see you here again! You owe us money! Money to clean the range, money to make up for lost time! We are a respectable business! Money to compensate for harm to reputation!"

I bowed deeply twice, to reassure the bouncers, then reached slowly into my belt pouch and took out a handful of ten-tabal pieces. I bowed again, held out my hands toward the manager, and started to count from one hand to another. "Ten, twenty, thirty, forty . . ." My voice was low, and his tirade drowned it initially, but by the time I reached fifty he'd trailed off and I was speaking in silence.

"Sixty," I said, holding it out to him.

He looked me over suspiciously. I said, "Though a barbarian, I, too, am from a respectable House. Please accept my apology, unworthy as I am, for the trouble I have caused. To harm the shining reputation of your business is the furthest thing from my mind."

I bowed again. The bouncers looked at a loss. The manager said, at last, "There should be a fine." But his voice had lost the conviction of righteous anger.

"Please send your bill to the House of Cormallon," I said. "If there is any disagreement at all in our compensation, we will be happy to submit the matter to any House of arbitration you like."

Sixty tabals was twice what he'd get in any arbitration. He bit his lip. "So be it," he agreed, taking all my money.

I looked toward the bouncers. "Is my companion all right?"

Sim. My responsibility.

"The player?" asked one of them. "He's all right, just a burn mark and a little shook up."

The hell with Loden. "No, the other one."

"The big fellow," said one man to the other.

"Oh. Lon's called for help to carry him across the street. There's a healer lives over the Green Rush Light."

"He's alive?" I said.

"He's alive. Had a longer exposure to hotpencil than the other one, though. Don't know how he'll do."

I turned to the manager. "Cormallon will pay for any medical aid. He's one of our House. We want the best."

"Kat's all right," he told me. "She must see six pencil burns a week, in this neighborhood. Not to mention knife and pistol wounds."

He'd calmed down considerably, and I was just starting to get upset. I could feel the adrenaline tide receding in my veins. Should I ask to have Sim taken to an outplanet clinic? But time was important with pencil burns, and if this Kat were really experienced. . . . I nodded. "Cormallon would be grateful if you'd see to his welfare." He smiled and bowed, understanding that I'd committed my House to looking kindly on his bill.

At once he said, "Kery! Jin! Make sure he gets to the healer's in one piece, and stay with him when you get there."

I dearly wanted to sit down. But if I did that, I might not get up again. I moved to where I could lean against one of the tile machines.

Loden was a few meters away, sitting on the floor, white-faced. He was holding one wrist, looking down at a red mark that traveled up his arm. If I were a better person, perhaps I might empathize; I'd felt much the same that day in Trade Square.

The manager followed my glance. "Come," he said, and motioned for me to accompany him to Loden's side. Speaking above his head, the manager said to me, "This one is not of your House?"

"Absolutely not," I said.

"Cormallon takes no responsibility for him."

"None at all."

"Then he must pay a fine, too, for his involvement."

Fairness is not an issue here, in case you haven't gotten that point. Loden seemed oblivious to us, still staring into the other side of the mirror. The manager nudged him with one foot.

"Youngster! You owe a fine to the Courts of Heaven."

I couldn't commit Cormallon to paying for him later; that would link us publicly, and whatever Loden was involved in I didn't want it leaking over onto our House. And I had no money left, myself.

In any case, he seemed deaf. The manager squatted by his ear and shouted. "Do you hear me? You owe a fine!"

His head turned slowly. "I didn't do anything."

They'd never let him leave till he paid. I squatted down on his other side. From that proximity I could smell his cheap perfume. "Loden," I said, speaking slowly and distinctly. "Pay him, or I'll kill you."

After a moment he nodded, still slowly, and took out his money pouch. His movements were those of a hundred-year-old man.

The manager grabbed it from his hand in disgust and searched through it. He snorted. "Eight tabals." He threw the empty pouch back in Loden's lap and pocketed the money.

They left us alone then, and I peered into Loden's stricken face. I bit back the angry tone I'd been going to use and said softly, "Don't you think you should tell me about it now?"

Still staring into some blank awfulness, he started to cry.

Chapter 15

He was not in any shape to communicate on the way home. I helped him as we walked back to the house, through street after street, but I couldn't help much. I was near the end of my strength myself, and wished that I'd had money for a carriage or wagon. I kept jumping at noises, staring around to see if Jeweled Bracelet and his friends would reappear; probably it was nerves that kept me going.

When we got to the front door I had a decision to make: accept him, however temporarily, in the house, or dump him back in the parcel receipt. An ethical dilemma. Bringing him in was bringing danger officially onto Cormallon territory; on the other hand, the boy was a mess.

I suppose the fact that Ran wasn't home that night decided me. I'd let him stay until tomorrow morning, and kick him out before Ran got back from Mira-Stoden. In arguing with a spouse, it's always easier to justify something that's already happened.

So I tucked him into a spare room with a cot, where he promptly went to sleep. It was early evening by then.

The doorbells startled me. I ran to check the spy-screen, and saw it was Kylla, carrying a bag of something from the corner cookshop. I'd forgotten she was coming this evening.

"Hello, Theo," she said, when I let her in. She dropped her bag on a table. "I've brought soup and rice and lots of sugar candies. We can stuff ourselves all night. Did you hear from Ran? How are you? Are you any better since this morning—'' as she whirled and got a good look at me. "Theo, darling," she said at once. "You look terrible. What happened?"

"Oh, Ky. It's been a long day since yesterday."

"Sweetheart! Sit down. I'll do everything. I'll bring you tah and candies and you can tell me all about it." And she led me to the divan, sat me down, and fussed over me in a very satisfactory way.

She brought me soup first, insisting I put my feet up as I ate. As she went to get the other containers open, she called, "I'm going to check for any messages on the Net, all right?"

"Fine," I said. Kylla'd spent half her life in this house. I always felt a little funny when she asked for permission to use the Net.

Kylla likes her soup hot and spicy, and that's what we'd gotten. I could feel my eyes start to water as I sipped it, and the sting was comforting. I was well prepared to be catered to for the rest of the evening . . . though I ought to check on Loden at some point, I thought vaguely.

Kylla returned without the rest of our supper. "What is it?" I asked, seeing the look on her face.

"The steward at home says I've just gotten a written invitation for tah and cards tomorrow morning—at Eliana Porath's."

Well, that took nerve, possibly even raw courage, on Eliana's part.

Kylla looked at me. "Did you hear what I said? It's an invitation to Eliana Porath's!!"

"I heard. You don't have to go, Kylla."

"The hell I don't. If that little pasty-cake has something on her mind, I want to know what it is. What do you think I should wear?"

I started to chuckle.

"This isn't funny, Theo!"

"No, of course not. Uh, your mint robe is very nice."

We talked clothes for about half an hour, while the food got cold, and shortly thereafter the bells sounded again and the Poraths' messenger appeared at our doorstep. She was a girl of nine or ten, with a set of robes in three shades of red. She bowed and offered Kylla a small sky-blue envelope. Kylla then vanished into the downstairs office to compose her reply, and I offered the girl sugar candies. I ate one first, as etiquette required, then gave her three extra to put in her pocket and take home.

When she'd left with the acceptance and the candies, Kylla came and sat next to me on the divan. "Want to finish our supper?" I asked.

She shook her head. "I'm not hungry."

I was starved to the marrow, so I opened a container of rice and steermod beef. The smell filled the room, and Kylla started to pick at it. "I'm sorry!" she said suddenly, putting down her fork. "You were going to tell me what happened today."

"It's a long story—" I began.

She frowned. "Do you really think the mint robe is all right? It's got a shawl collar."

"It's beautiful, and it suits you."

She looked at me, blushed, and we both started to laugh. I patted her hand. "It's all right, it's an obsession. I understand."

She fussed with the supper bowls, and her eyes fell on a copy of the *Capital News*. The delivery people hadn't wanted to trouble to send them on to Kylla's house, so when they found they couldn't get the slot open they'd been dropping them outside the parcel receipt. For the last few days Loden had been stepping blindly through them, scattering them in the gutter. This morning he'd actually thought to leave them in a pile by our door.

"I didn't know you got *Court Follies*," she said. *Court Follies* is a scurrilous, politically oriented sheet, less acceptably illegal than the *Capital News*.

"I don't," I said, looking at the address on front. "The neighbors on our left do."

"How did you get it?"

"Loden, the idiot." I spoke from the heart, without thinking.

Of course, Kylla wanted an explanation. It was a long one. Finally she turned to me, eyes shining. "You've been letting that gorgeous security guard stay with you?"

"Trust me," I said. "It's an overrated experience."

When I got up in the morning I made the same call I'd made before I went to bed the previous night: to the Inner Courts of Heaven. The healer they called Kat didn't have Net access. Both times the manager sent someone across the street, and both times he gave me the same answer: Sim was alive, and his recovery looked promising. "We'll notify you at once of any change," the manager said. "But Kat keeps saying he should be all right. The exposure wasn't long enough for permanent damage."

I thanked him and cut the connection. As far as I was concerned, Sim could have all the cherry jam he wanted, as long as he came back in one piece. Another message appeared on the Net just as I was getting up: from the Porath code, the Net said.

The Poraths again? Why would they call me?

I accepted it and found Eliana Porath's face looking out of my wall. Inexperienced at Net customs, she blatantly used the visual circuit. "Lady Theodora," she said, "I'm so glad you're home.

"Uh, lady Eliana. Nice to see you again."

"I have a favor to ask."

"Oh?"

"I've got, ah, a bit of a problem. My father seems to have asked your sister-in-law to join us today for a tah and card party. I only found out this morning, and we're racing to get everything ready."

"Oh."

"Yes. Well, this is very awkward . . . at this late hour it will seem too much like an afterthought . . . but would you consider attending as well?"

"Me? I don't really know any card games."

"That's *fine,*" she said, with fervent eagerness. "It doesn't matter. It's just that, you see, right now Kylla is the only guest, and even with Auntie Jace or Leel to make up the table, it really wouldn't be much of a game. You see my point?"

"I do indeed." There's safety in numbers. Eliana Porath was no fool.

"I would truly be most grateful if you'd come. And it will only be for a couple of hours. We can have a nice meal afterward, in the garden—our cook is a wonder—"

"It's all right, Eliana, I'll come."

"You will?" She let out her breath in relief. "Thank you so much. It's at the sixth hour, and I'll tell the gate to expect you. I'd better run now and see if we can get the table . . . thank you." And she was gone.

Well, chance in all forms was clearly to be my lot. Raucous machine-play and tithball yesterday, and genteel gambling with tah-and-cards this morning. I was about to sign off when it occurred to me, belatedly, to check for any messages.

There were two, both dated yesterday afternoon: one from Ran, the other from Stereth. I accepted them both.

> *Should arrive home by noon tomorrow. Hope you're feeling better. Where are you?*
>
> *Ran*

> *Your market sorcerer named Moros isn't named Moros. He used to be Bril Savin, but the Savins disowned him. He had a hut outside the city, on the west bank of the river. I hope this knowledge provides more certainty in your life.*
>
> *Stereth Tar'krim*

The one from Ran was characteristic. I would hear about that "where are you" when he returned. And good old Stereth and his provisions for certainty in my life. I wouldn't count on it, old friend. His message was intriguing, as messages from Stereth so often are. Presumably the hut was abandoned when Moros died. No mention of any wives or children. . . . disowned persons rarely find mates. It had been days since his death, and there was no reason to believe anybody would be there now, even assuming they knew where he lived. No harm in poking around a bit . . . Damn. I'd have to do it before Ran got home. He'd be quite capable of calling up three more cousins from out of town to keep me within the city walls till I lost interest.

I told myself there was no reason to follow up Stereth's information, except curiosity, powerful in itself, and a desire to get Loden out of trouble and out of our lives. Speaking of out of our lives— I woke the boy up, fed him, and told him I was throwing him out before my husband got home. He accepted the phrase as though it were one he'd heard before.

"I want to see you later today, though," I told him. "So start working on your story now." He nodded, looking sheepish. At least he didn't seem to be as harrowed as he'd been last night. "I mean it, Loden. The carriage stops here."

"I know," he said. He went off down the front steps and into, I thought, the gods knew what further trouble.

Good heavens! I hope Ran didn't feel that way about *me*.

It was nearly the fifth hour. I ran upstairs and awakened Kylla, where she lay sprawled over the bed in my room. She had her family's way of taking all the mattress space. "Ky, you've got to get up. We'll be late. Ky!"

She squinted at me blearily. "What time is it?"

"An hour till Eliana's party."

"Oh, gods, no." She let her chin fall back on the pillow. "It can't possibly be. I've barely slept!"

"You've been out since the reign of the last emperor—out like a light, I might add. I figured you'd want the time to paint over any circles under your eyes, before you see Eliana.''

This call to war got her attention. ''Ohhh . . . why, why, did you let me drink that whole bottle of Ducort?''

''You insisted, Ky. You told me you could handle it.''

She dragged herself out of bed, moaning as she did. ''Can't you see how I'm suffering? At least you could take the blame.''

''Yes, Ky. I'm sorry I forced you to drink all that wine last night.''

''That's better.'' She tottered to the bath and locked the door. I went to get ready myself, knowing she'd be at least half an hour.

I changed into one of my best robes, thought about it, and took the jade and caneblood necklace Ran had given me last Ghost Eve from its box underneath the bed. This was a social call, after all. I'd check with Kylla on whether it was too dressy for daytime, but with discreet earrings it might work.

I took it out of the box, remembering that Ghost Eve. I looked into the mirror as I held it up, and saw my eyes had gotten visibly misty. ''You should be taken in hand, girl,'' I said to the reflection there. Then I went to the upstairs office and left a Net message for Ran, telling him I'd probably be having lunch at the Poraths' when he got back, and pointing him toward Stereth's message for what I intended to do after. Manipulation works two ways, you know. At least I'd have companionship in ransacking the hut, since I had no doubt at all Ran would show up there to make his displeasure known.

I was reassured to see the silver arc in the Poraths' garden. The last time I'd seen this garden was two nights ago in my card-driven hallucination, and my statue had bled rivers were the arc now gleamed with such a reassuring lack of organic properties. Ran was right, I thought uncomfortably, that had been my own fault; mixing up the stories of Kade and the Poraths and my worries about the Cormallon council, leaving open-ended questions floating around in my head. Keep that up, Theodora, and you'll be almost as good with magic as the late Moros was. The Poraths' house loomed ahead of us, full of family, servants, cats, and lizard; not at all empty or abandoned. Do you good, I told myself, to spend a little time with quiet, respectable people, after the excitement of yesterday. Folks here may get murdered, by the gods, but they're always courteous.

Kylla and I were heading for the central porch, wearing our finest—including the caneblood necklace, by the way—when the tall jinevra bushes around the blue pool rustled.

A head looked out at us. "Hello, Theodora."

"Coalis! What in the world are you doing in there?"

"Ah, excuse me for not stepping out. I just wanted to mention, I was out on business with Stereth last night, and he asked me to let you know he's left a Net message for you."

"I know," I said, puzzled.

"Well, when I told him you might be visiting to-day—since your sister-in-law was coming—he said to tell you it's about your market sorcerer. He said he thinks you sometimes don't read his messages."

"It's kind of you to pass this on, Coalis. May I ask what you're doing in the jinevra bushes?"

Shouts came from the direction of the house. Coalis winced. "Please let this matter by," he said.

The shouts were louder now. It was Jusik's voice. The front door was flung open and Lord Porath emerged, in white-hot temper, hands in fists. You could practically see his veins throb from here. "Where is he?" he cried. "He's still in the compound, don't tell me he's not! The gatekeeper didn't pass him out!" He strode down the steps, followed by Leel Canerol, Auntie Jace, Eliana, the steward, and three others I didn't recognize. They poured through

the door and over the porch after him, like a scared
litter of kittens.

Coalis's voice came urgently from somewhere below
my ear: "Move away from the bushes!"

Jusik was stalking across the garden. I looked at
him, looked back at the bushes, and then hastily
stepped away.

Too late. I'd drawn his attention, and there must
have been some movement behind the leaves. "There!
Don't move, you fool, you disgrace, or I swear I'll
beat your organs out of your skin! Don't you *dare*
move!"

He was at the bushes in twenty strides, and yanking
Coalis out by the arm. There wasn't really room between the thin branches of jinevra for him to exit on
this side, but Jusik paid no attention to that. The recently created First Son of Porath emerged branch-
whipped and scratched.

He at once threw himself into the dirt at his father's
feet, the way they tell me the Six Families do when
they need to impress the emperor with their sincerity.

"You vermin!" yelled Jusik. "You river toad! Disappointment of all our hopes! Get up!"

Coalis scrambled immediately to his feet, still saying nothing.

"Out all night! Drinking and gambling, I have no
doubt! But what do you care? Why should it matter to
you if the House of Porath depends on you? Do you
think being first son confers the right of pissing away
your time and money?" He paused for half a second,
as though waiting for Coalis to convict himself further, but no one spoke. The other members of the
household had gathered around in a half-circle, with
identical appalled looks on their faces. "If only you
were more like your brother! I wish to heaven it were
you in the canal, and not him! Do you think anybody
would have missed *you?*"

Coalis continued to stare at the ground. "Enough!"
yelled his father. "Against that tree! Now!"

Coalis walked to the tree where Ran had once stood

and waited for me to finish with Stereth. He placed the palms of his hands against it. I now saw that a leather strap dangled from one of Jusik's tightly clenched fists.

"Take off that robe!" cried Jusik. "Do you think to fool with me?"

Coalis stripped off his outerrobe and pulled down his white cotton shirt.

I thought that he would make some protest—shout back, at least, since meekness was getting him no-where—but he didn't. And appalled though the rest of the family looked, no one made a move to interfere. Obviously they didn't want that temper turned on them, but even so—

The strap hit. Coalis's back arched and a sound came out of his mouth—not a scream and not quite a groan—a sound that convinced me that even though I'd never seen or felt a whipping before, it was an exquisitely painful event.

I was horrified. I was rooted to the spot, grotesquely fascinated, but mostly horrified, and not just by the pain. There is no corporal punishment of minors on Pyrene, and it is strongly disapproved of on Athena. This was stepping back into some kind of dark age, a stage-lit theater event somehow dropped into real life, but even worse, this was a thing so clearly taken for granted by my contemporaries.

The strap struck, and struck again. And nobody moved. Jusik was the First of Porath, he could beat the hell out of his son if he wanted to.

Alien. I became aware of Kylla standing uncom-fortably beside me—embarrassed at her presence at a private family moment, sympathizing with Coalis, dis-approving of Jusik—but without that extra layer of re-pulsion, of incomprehension, that I was watching through.

Eight strokes. I wasn't counting at the time, but I can still hear the slap of the strap reverberate. Eight strokes, not even cruel by some standards. He could have beaten Coalis to death and not been held legally accountable.

He raised his arm a ninth time and threw the strap past the tree, onto the ground. ''I want you in my library tomorrow morning! I want to hear you recite the Twenty Lessons of a Dutiful Son, and you'd better not have a word wrong! Studying, that's what you should be doing, not out on the street mingling with all the riffraff of the provinces—'' He choked in a couple of breaths with difficulty, trying to keep himself from working up to another crescendo of anger. He stepped back from the tree, and Coalis immediately threw himself to the ground again in dutiful fashion—more dropped than threw, this time. Jusik made a disgusted sound, turned away, and stalked back into the house.

Everyone else at once ran to Coalis and tried to help him up, murmuring comforting sounds and inspecting his back. Auntie Jace was sent to the kitchen for wet cloths, Leel Canerol had him turn around for her as she tsked-tsked and gave him advice about keeping his shirt off till tomorrow. Eliana sniffled and kissed him.

Kylla and I exchanged looks. Should we walk on into this? We were more or less being ignored anyway . . . maybe this would be a good time to slip away.

Eliana looked up and met our eyes. ''Our guests,'' she said to the others, like a hostess reminding someone to serve the canapes. Kylla and I came forward.

Coalis was facing us, so I couldn't see what the strap had done to his back. There was a fine grain of dust on his cheek from where he'd pressed it against the bark of the tree, with tear tracks cutting through the dust. His eyes were still moist and his skin was paler than usual, but his expression was no different than it had been ten minutes earlier in the jinevra bushes. I searched his face, looking for something I could get hold of, but there was nothing. He didn't, quite, look *calm* . . . he looked held-in, self-contained.

''I'm sorry,'' I said, meaning that I was sorry for calling attention to him in the bushes.

"That's all right. It's bound to happen, from time to time."

Auntie Jace ran back with her handfuls of dripping cloths. Coalis was made to sit, and she knelt behind him and helped Leel Canerol in applying them. Water ran down Coalis's back onto the dirt. He winced whenever Leel touched him.

Auntie Jace was muttering. "What's gotten into your father, anyway? He never used to beat you."

"Co, here, never used to spend his nights out," said Leel dryly.

"It's not that," said Coalis. "Ow!"

"Sorry."

"It's just that I've got to expect that with Kade gone, he'll be . . . giving me a lot more of his attention. After all, he used to beat Kade all the time. With me, he probably never thought it mattered."

"So now you're important enough to correct," said Leel. "Lucky you. I'm glad I'm a provincial commoner."

Eliana said, "It's so unfair. You weren't out spending House money—you were making it."

"Will you keep your voice down?" said Coalis, frowning. "If we're going to start letting Father in on everything we do in our spare time, I know a few things I could share with him."

His sister made a face but dropped the subject.

Kylla stirred. "We seem to have intruded at a bad time," she said. "Perhaps we should postpone our visit for another day."

Eliana straightened up. "No, please . . . if this is when Father asked you to come, we'd better stick to it. I'm sorry things are so—disorganized." She put a hand on her forehead and seemed to be trying to recall what she would be doing for an ordinary visit. "We only just got the table set up," she apologized. "Father didn't tell us he was inviting you, the messenger only mentioned it in passing this morning, so we've been running around trying to get things ready."

She considered this and seemed to feel it lacked a

certain graciousness, for she at once modified it. "Not that you aren't both very welcome. I just want to excuse our lack of preparation. Really, we're very happy you agreed to come." She sighed. "This hasn't been a good morning. Let's try to start over again."

"We're happy to be here," said Kylla, who knew what was expected of her. "Is there anything we can do to be of help?"

"I'll be all right," said Coalis. "I'm just going to lie down for a while. Don't change anything on my account."

"He'll be fine," agreed Leel, looking up from her cleansing of his wounds. "Why don't you go on upstairs, and I'll be there in a couple of minutes."

Perhaps it was a trifle over-direct of me, but I hadn't had a good morning either, so I went ahead and asked: "Did your father have any particular purpose in mind? Anything he wanted us to discuss during this party?"

Eliana took no offense. "We wondered the same," she said frankly. "But he's been upset ever since he found out Coalis was away all night, and we really didn't think this was quite the time to inquire."

I wouldn't have brought the matter up, either. We followed Eliana upstairs to her room, where a small black table had been set up with a deck of playing cards in the center. Cushions surrounded it. The mattress had been taken off the sleeping platform and leaned against the far wall, and a portable tah burner with pot and cups had been set up in its place.

We filed in and sat down, to rather an awkward silence. "Leel will be up in a moment," said Eliana, who knew as much about that as we did. I looked around the room, the first daughter of Porath's world: No different from last time; clean, small, well-tended. A flute sat on the windowsill beside a stack of notepaper.

"You play?" I asked.

"I'm learning," she said. Auntie Jace made an embarrassed movement.

Fortunately Leel arrived before the conversation

languished, and we could begin arguing about what game to start with. Sometimes I think card games and dinners just give us something to pretend to do while we all figure out how we stack up against each other in the human social web.

But as I'd said to Eliana on the Net, I don't know many Ivoran games. "I know how to play Sleeping Dog," I offered.

There was a strained silence at this; apparently it was considered a vulgar game. I'd learned it from some Sector outlaws the previous summer.

"We can play Flush," Eliana announced.

"It's *always* Flush," said Leel Canerol. "It's the most monotonous game on earth."

"We'll play Flush Thirty-Six," said her mistress, with a trace of temper. *That's* not monotonous, it's the most complicated game there is. You can keep score, Lely. Since you find it so easy."

Leel Canerol made a face, but stretched her lanky frame against the wall until we all heard something crack, then grinned and walked over to the windowsill where she retrieved pen and paper. The paper, I noticed, was a textured, pastel kind, that came in short sheets, suitable for young ladies' personal notes.

Leel pulled out a stool and threw one leg over it. "Shoot," she said.

"Would you care to deal?" Eliana asked Kylla.

"Many thanks," said Kylla. She took the deck, an old-fashioned one of red and black oval cards, shuffled them grimly and dealt out seven cards to Eliana, Auntie Jace, and me.

I said, "Uh, excuse me, but somebody's going to have to show me how to play."

Kylla and Eliana were staring at each other, expressions of determined courtesy on their faces. I don't think they heard me.

Auntie Jace threw down two cards and took two from the pile. Eliana smiled prettily at Kylla and said, "I'll stand pat with what I have, dear."

I decided my best move would be to blindly partic-
ipate, so I traded in one card.

Kylla took two without any comment. We went
around several times doing this, then Auntie Jace said,
"Flush," and put down her cards into three sets. They
made no particular order that I could discern. We all
put down our hands then and Leel Canerol walked
around examining, counting, and writing.

It went on like this for about an hour. I kept a low
profile and stayed away from the less understandable
moves, as when Eliana suddenly laid a card at right
angles across the discard pile and cried, "Block!"
Fortunately, nobody seemed to expect me to do anything. Of course my nose started to go critical about
forty minutes into play, and I kept my handkerchief in
my fist, transferring the cards from one hand to another as I sniffled and blew as quietly as I could. Auntie
Jace gave me some funny looks from time to time, but
the others were too well-bred to take official notice.

Auntie Jace turned to me after one round and said,
"Why in the world didn't you declare? You had a perfect hand!"

I shrugged, hoping I looked coolly above it all. Leel
said, "She doesn't have to declare if she doesn't want
to. Maybe she's working on a strategy."

In fact I was. Keep my head low and hit the floor if
the shots started to fly.

"Where do we stand?" asked Eliana suddenly,
pushing her long dark hair back over her shoulder.

Leel consulted her paper. "Twenty-six on this last
round for you, which puts you six under Kylla, twelve
over Auntie, and eighteen over Theodora."

"Six under Kylla?" She frowned. "Are you including my bonus points for a perfect flush?"

Leel held out her paper. Kylla, looking a trifle irritated, said, "Perhaps you'd like to check the math,
dear. I'd hate to take advantage of a schoolgirl."

Eliana took the paper, looked it over, and stated,
"This is a nine, not a six, Leel. Raise me three
points."

Kylla bent her head to peer at the scribbles. "It looks like a six to me," she said.

"Advanced age can have that effect on one's eyesight," replied Eliana. "Take my word for it, *elder* sister, it's a nine."

Leel Canerol and Auntie Jace began talking very quickly. "Would you like another hand?" asked Leel, gathering the cards without waiting for an answer.

"That would be delightful," said Auntie at once. "Or maybe we should all get some tah. Theodora, what do you—"

Kylla said, "Possibly those long sleeves of yours brushed the figure and smudged it, beloved sister. I meant to compliment you on that robe when I first walked in, by the way; it would have been very fashionable, let me see, about six years ago?"

"Look at the time!" I said. "Ky, shouldn't we—"

"I suppose you *would* be the expert on antique fashions," agreed Eliana.

Kylla's aristocratic nostrils were starting to flare, not a good sign. Eliana went on, "And it's true, these extra-long sleeves do get in the way. Perhaps you can lend me one of your lace bands to tie them back."

Ran's grandmother had worn lace sleevebands. I rose to my feet. "We *must* be going," I said.

The two of them sat without moving. I said, *"Kylla,"* through gritted teeth. Finally, finally, she stood up.

Eliana smiled at her and said, "So sorry you have to go. I did enjoy our game, and I must compliment you on your calligraphy when you accepted our messenger's invitation. So very elegant. Who wrote it for you?"

"I'm glad you enjoyed it, dear. Who read it to you?"

Kylla turned to leave just as a snarling sound erupted from Eliana's throat and she sprang to her feet. The little card table crashed over and Eliana grabbed Kylla's arms from behind. It looked as though she were trying to climb up Ky's back.

Kylla whirled around, knocking her away. Leel Canerol made a dive for her charge and missed. Eliana scrambled up and aimed an enthusiastic but poorly taught blow at Kylla, which she blocked. I threw aside the door hanging and yelled, "Assistance! Steward!"

Coalis was standing in the passage. I heard a loud slap from behind; somebody had made skin contact. Coalis strode past me and got between the two contenders just as Leel managed to imprison Eliana's arms. He raised his hands, palms up, to Kylla, looking vulnerable with his shirt off. "Our apologies. Our apologies," he got out. There was a red hand-shaped spot on Kylla's cheek and she was breathing hard. "Our apologies," he said again. "We humbly beg forgiveness."

After a moment, she nodded. Her eyes swept over the room like those of an heir who's just inherited a piece of land too poor to be impressed by. She turned and strode out.

I followed. A hand tugged at my robe in the passage to slow me down, and Coalis said, "That was something, wasn't it? I had no idea this would happen when I sent the invitation!"

I stared. *"You* sent the invitation?"

"Why not? I'm first son now, I don't have to ask permission to invite people home."

"Coalis . . . does the phrase 'asking for trouble' mean anything to you?"

"Oh, but it was splendid, wasn't it? What entertainment!"

I stopped, looked him in the eye, and said, "You are fooling with things you don't really understand."

"Come on, Theodora, I only wanted to see what would happen. What do you think they would have done if there'd been weapons at hand?"

His face wore its usual calm, but his eyes were glowing. "This family has even more problems than the Cormallons," I muttered.

"Pardon?"

"I said I have to go now. Kylla will need company home."

"Oh. Well, you're always welcome back. Kylla, too, of course."

"Our thanks," I got out, bowed my stiffest bow, and ran after my sister-in-law.

Leel Canerol caught up with me in the garden. "Please, gracious lady, I'd like to ask you not to mention this incident to Lord Porath."

I stopped short, remembering this morning's exhibition. "Would he beat her?" I kept my voice low. Kylla was ahead of us, at the gate, and I didn't want to put the idea into her head.

"He never has before, lady. But he can make things very difficult for everyone in the house when he's unhappy."

"I see."

"And—I couldn't help overhearing Coalis—if Lord Porath finds out his son is responsible for this, there could be a second lesson with the strap for him. Now, Grandmother was in her room with a headache this morning, but if she finds out Coalis got beaten, she'll make Lord Porath's life a misery. And if *his* life is a misery, we may as well all move to the provinces and change our names."

"Yes, I do see your point. Look, I see no reason to mention anything to Lord Porath, but I can't answer for Kylla."

"You might speak with her . . . when she's in a better frame of mind."

"Umm. I'll do what I can, that's all I can promise."

"My thanks," she said, and bowed, giving a wry smile when her head came up that suggested she knew very well I was wondering why she worked for the Poraths.

I shook my head. The smile became a grin. "Oh, it's not so bad," she said. "I've worked around, and they're probably the least trouble of any of the Six Families.''

"Heaven help us all,'' I said.

She threw me a casual salute and loped back to the porch.

Chapter 16

I gave Kylla my caneblood necklace for safekeeping, explaining that I needed to go somewhere right now and didn't want to wear it. I didn't trouble to be specific, since she clearly wasn't listening to me in any case; but I watched to make sure she put the necklace safely in her wallet.

Then she took the carriage we'd come in and rode away, looking abstracted, leaving me to start a long trek across the city to the remains of the northwest wall. It took a good hour and a half in the midday heat, and five minutes into the walk I was sweating freely into my party clothes and thinking about a cool bath. The North Gate, where the groundcars and wagons pass through, was several streets to the east, but I'd remembered seeing a footpath for pedestrians near here that ought to lead out a door in the wall and along the east bank of the river.

So it did. Wildflowers and garbage lined the bank. Once past the wall there were very few people around, and I was glad I'd given Ky the necklace. Still, at least I could see far enough ahead and behind me to know I wasn't being followed. The path branched into two routes here, one well above the bank, among the red and blue flowers, and one leading down to the muddy path beside the water. I took the drier and prettier way. There was a shed set back from the banks, where a sorrel dog barked and laundry flapped in the breeze off the river. The dog, working himself up to a pitch of excitement few manic psychotics could match, gave me to understand that, if it were not for the inconve-

nience of a wood-and-wire fence, he would have been
happy to lunge at me and tear off a few limbs. He
threw himself at the fence several times, in fact, and
I wondered just how sturdy it was.

Other than that, there were no human habitations,
not till one got out several kilometers into the country
and the farms began. But about a quarter of an hour
from the wall I came on a section of field and river-
bank that the city was using, whether officially or not,
as a junkyard. Old tables lay sunken halfway deep in
river mud; cracked pottery, broken glass in rainbow
colors, and metal parts covered the ground. There were
stacks of old used paper with government officialese
on the portions that could still be read. River rats
prowled, looking interested. And down by the bottom
path, a hut had been made of wood boards and junkyard metal; the hut, if Stereth were right, of Moros,
the sorcerer who'd killed Kade from Catmeral Bridge.

Well, I knew for sure that he wasn't home. That
didn't necessarily mean the hut was empty, of course.
A route had been cleared through the junk and garbage
down to the hut, and I followed it past an old solo
wagonseat, a set of broken tah-tables, three benches,
and part of a bed.

There was a tiny window near the door, shuttered
over. I pulled the door handle, then pushed, then gave
as good a kick as I could. It opened.

The hut was empty. I stepped inside and found myself in a one-room home with cluttered shelves, a stove
in the middle of the floor with an iron railing around
it, a tiny old-fashioned desk stuffed with papers (out
of place in its baroque elegance), and a small wooden
counter with covered jars of foodstuffs. Some uniden-
tiable piece of meat hung by a string from the ceiling;
it was just beginning to go bad. A sort of hammock
arrangement had been rigged in one corner with a
sleeping pallet and a pulley.

All just waiting for Moros to return. One would
think that if anyone else lived here, they would have
taken down the meat by now. I pulled off my outer

robe and pitched it onto the sleeping pallet. This would be a potentially boring task, but not dangerous, I decided; and I went through the food jars first.

No, I had no idea what I was looking for. I was following the "ask questions, gather data, and maybe something will turn up" school of investigative thought. Food jars were my first choice because they seemed logically least likely to contain anything of interest; this being Ivory, I assumed secrets were more likely to be there than anywhere else.

Moros had sugar, rice, and dried fruit. Not a man on a high budget. I opened the stove door; it was empty. I poked around beneath it for a while, then started inspecting Moros's endless collection of bottles, labeled neatly on his crowded shelves. Herbs and oddities, bits of this and that—a recipe book for sorcery, but nothing that meant anything to me.

I stripped the bedding and looked under the mat. I knocked on floors and walls. I pulled down the oil lamp from its ceiling hook.

Which left the desk. At least the padded stool in front of it would give me a place to sit.

We would start clockwise, I decided. I began opening the folded papers stuffed on the far top right.

A bill for a new robe, recent and unpaid.

A torn employment notice for a sorcerer willing to travel to the provinces.

Sorcery notes, apparently unrelated to drowning.

Interesting: A series of hand sketches of the river and the junkyard outside. A family of rats sat atop the old wagon seat, looking bright-eyed and very funny. Moros was in the wrong line of work.

Had been in the wrong line of work, anyway.

A letter. Aha, I thought, now we get to the good stuff!

> *Dearest Gernie,*
>   *Of course I haven't forgotten you. This just isn't the ~~right~~ ~~proper~~ most convenient time for you to join me. Things are all up in the air here;*

*it wouldn't surprise me if there was fighting in
the streets before long.*

It would have surprised me. So far the summer had
been pretty dull in the way of Imperial goings-on.

*So stay where you are, I implore you. Mean-
while, please accept this little help of 25   12   10
tabals. I hope it will ease things for your mother
and sister.*

*Give my best wishes to everyone. Truthfully, my
client list isn't growing quite as quickly as I'd
hoped, but I'm doing very well . . .*

I put down the letter. Gernie, whoever he or she
was, would wonder when there was no more correspondence. Maybe Gernie would come to the capital
to see what was the matter.

For Moros's sake, I hoped they never tracked him
as far as this place and saw how he'd been living.

Come on, Theodora, you're getting involved again.
You'll never get through all these papers if you stop
and speculate on every one.

—A review of the chakon theater-dance season, torn
from the Capital News.

—Three letters from Gernie, folded and unfolded so
they were brittle with usage; Gernie's sex was still un-
clear but his/her passion was not. Gernie kept pleading
to come to the capital to be with Moros. Some of the
letters were explicit; as a strait-laced Athenan I was a
bit shocked, but I must say, fascinated—

Still, it was getting late in the afternoon. I returned
the packet to its cubbyhole. A carved wooden box sat
atop a pile of papers; I opened the box and turned it
over.

A mass of ticket stubs from fortune halls in the gambling district. Points for just about any kind of game
I'd ever heard of and many I hadn't. Moros, like so
many others, hadn't been immune to dice fever, but at

least he'd accumulated a stash of tickets to be cashed in at the appropriate halls later. Of course, there was no way of telling how much of his own money he'd had to lay out to win all these. I flicked through them idly: Cloud Hill, Wheel of Illusion, Patens of Bright Gold. The man must have worked his way through every establishment on Red Tah Street. I turned over the crimson ticket from the Red Umbrella Tith Parlor.

"IOU 85 tab. L. Broca."

I froze.

I turned over another. "IOU 32 tab. L. Broca."

I started to flick them all over. Most were blank, but about half the ones from the Umbrella and the Silver Shoe had Loden's signature below an amount.

The idiot! Giving a signature to someone you were linked with in a criminal act—

That was an Ivoran reaction. My next one, which was Athenan, went: Wait a minute, what evidence do we actually have here? So Loden owed Moros money. Loden owed everybody money, apparently. What light could this shed on Moros's assignment on Catmeral Bridge?

Well, as long as Kade was around, Loden's money was pretty much spoken for. Moros really didn't have a prayer of seeing any of these IOUs cashed. Probably Loden had pointed that out in self-defense.

Would they really get together to murder Kade just to get Loden out from under? But they couldn't be sure someone else wouldn't pick up Kade's account book, as in fact someone had. Still, Stereth Tar'krim made the tossing of monkey wrenches a way of life. And given Coalis's monkish background, the odds would have seemed pretty good that once Kade was gone, the debt would vanish too.

I sat on the stool, clutching a handful of tickets, thinking.

Another possibility: Loden out-and-out hired Moros to kill Kade, and the IOUs were not gambling losses at all, but a plausible means of contracting to pay him after the deed.

The world was full of options, wasn't it?

But how did this get Moros dead, with his throat cut, that day in the market? And who were the thugs who tried to get Ran and me? And Loden was just, well, such an *idiot*. . . . Even a screwed-up sort of murder seemed beyond him, frankly.

I wished that damned dog would stop barking back at the shack down the path; I could hear him from here. I emptied the next cubbyhole of papers irritably. The prolific Gernie, with more to say on the same subject. More sketches. A hand-drawn map of the city; nicely done, I thought. I scooped up the gambling tickets and emptied them into my belt pouch, replaced the latest set of papers, and pulled out another.

That psychotic dog! Finally he seemed to be calming down. His impulse to murder was transitory, probably whoever was walking by the shack had passed out of canine sight.

I got up suddenly and went to peer out the small, dirty window. Two figures were silhouetted at the top of the bank.

Loden Broca and Trey Lesseret. There was *no reason* they should show up here and now, with all the hours and days since the murder to pick from. Oh, the unfairness of the gods! This went beyond coincidence, this was the malign nature of the universe revealed. I looked around the room as though expecting a solution to present itself, like a clown jumping out of a closet in a slapstick farce; but physical law remained physical law. One room. One exit. No place to conceal anything as large as a human being.

Behind the stove—too small. Behind the desk—too small. The counter. Wait—the bed? I heaved on Moros's pulley arrangement and lowered the pallet. Then I tossed my outerrobe up there again, put one foot on the railing around the stove, and rolled myself up after it. Would I be able to pull the bed up higher from this position? —Yes. With difficulty. I strained on the ropes until the pallet was so close to the ceiling I was practically plastered against it, then lay there in a sweaty, clinging tangle of robes. For a second I flashed back to that moment in Trade Square when I'd looked over at the knife. Probably Loden and Trey wouldn't need to bother with knives; Trey would still have his Mercian-issue pistol. I didn't feel concealed at all. You could probably market the hormone smell I was putting out then and sell it to sadists.

They took forever to get to the hut. It was several centuries before the door opened.

"Kanz," said Trey's voice. "Look what I stepped in."

Loden laughed.

"You think it's funny now," said Trey, "but I'll track it all over the floor, and you'll have to smell it."

"We're not going to be here that long," said Loden.

Footsteps on the wooden boards. Trey said, "Where should we start?" Without waiting for an answer, he went on, "You take the desk and I'll take the canisters."

The sound of jars being opened, lids tossed on the counter. Papers at the desk being thrown to the floor. Then what I assumed were the shelves of bottles being checked. Trey must have finished first and joined Loden at the desk, because I could hear both of them going through the papers.

"I don't think they're here," said Trey.

"They have to be here."

More papers scrunched and tossed. The sound of boots partially muffled by discarded letters on the floor.

"I don't think they're here," said Trey again, in the sort of voice a father uses to say: Your birthday present didn't arrive on time; be a man about it.

"He didn't live anywhere else, this is where he lived! They've got to be here somewhere, we just haven't looked hard enough."

"Could someone else have gotten here ahead of us?"

"Who?"

"I don't know. Your Cormallons, maybe. You said they'd been told the address."

"Cormallon's not working for Lord Porath anymore. And anyway—there wasn't time. Nobody even knew where Moros lived till yesterday. He kept a closed hatch, that one—didn't matter how drunk he was, never a word of personal information."

"You should've tried harder to find out. Your little girl was right, Loden, you can't just leave stuff with your name on it lying around."

"Don't lecture me. If I wanted to be lectured, I'd still be living at home. And what could I have done about it, anyway? Nobody knew where he lived!"

"Somebody knew."

"Nobody in the halls of fortune. Minister Tar'krim tracked down a whore he brought out here once, otherwise nobody would still know."

"Huh," said Trey, in a cynical tone of voice. "If nobody's investigating, how come Stereth Tar'krim bothered to track down the whore?"

Silence. Finally Loden said, "I'm not responsible for—"

"I know. You're not responsible for *anything.*"

"That's not fair! Nobody understands what I've been going through. Especially the last few days. The agency throws me out, I have to live in a kanz *mail chute,* for the love of—and what about the Courts of Heaven, huh? Two high-tones try to kill me with a hotpencil during a tithball duel! I practically died of shock on the spot. Nobody warned me that was going to happen!"

"Made your reaction all the more believable, didn't it?" said Trey, with cold humor.

"I don't need that kind of help," said Loden firmly. A second later he added, "Though the barbarian feather did seem more sympathetic, afterward."

Feather is not a term you hear much in the circles Ran moves in. It means female—in usage, generally a female of childbearing years. I'm not going to tell you the derivation. If you're ever on Ivory, don't use it.

"There you are," said Trey. "Be glad you've got Velvet-Eyes and me to look after you." He was crumpling papers as he spoke. "Kanz! They're not in the desk, Loden, face it."

"So what do we do?"

"Hope you're right. Hope they're here someplace. Because if they are, they'll go up when we set fire to the hut."

What?

Trey said, "Get the cans. I set them down outside."

Wait a damned minute here—

Loden's boots went out, returned, and there was a sound of something heavy and metal being set on the floor. Somebody unstoppered a can, maybe Trey, for he began gossiping as he worked. "So tell me," splash, "did you spend *all* your time in the mail chute?" Splash. "Or is it true what they say about barbarian women?" Splash, splat. "Ugly to look at, but wild animals on the mattress?" A chemical smell filled the room.

"I don't kiss and tell," said Loden.

"The hell you don't." A can was set back on the floor, now with an empty, hollow ring. "Your pants have seen more activity than an Imperial legion in the field."

Loden chuckled. Trey said thoughtfully, "Speaking of mattresses—"

"What?"

"That one up by the ceiling."

I froze, completely, as though that would somehow take the idea out of Trey's mind.

"What of it?" asked Loden.

"Well, we haven't looked there. Maybe Moros liked to take out his tickets in bed and gloat over 'em."

"Who cares? We're going to burn the whole place down, anyway."

"Loden. My boy. We want to *know* we burnt them, don't we? We don't want to worry about them for the rest of our lives?"

"Nobody cares about Kade anymore. By next spring they'll have forgotten he ever existed."

"Loden, people hang themselves on loose ends. Take the pulley."

With a rusty, squealing sound, the bed began to lower. I turned onto my right side and elbow and brought my left knee up. I got lower; the shelves of bottles came into view. I took my left foot off the mattress and brought my leg back. They would both be standing next to the pulley, on my left. I pivoted in the bed, hoping that the swinging my movement caused would be seen as a natural consequence of hauling the thing down.

I'd been taught a few tricks once by a dirty fighter, an ex-member of the Imperial Guard. I hadn't practiced them in a long time, not having any heavily padded partners on hand to try to maim and kill—the circumstances under which I'd been taught had been unusual. But when your options dwindle down to a precious few. . . .

Surprise, I could hear my old instructor say. *Surprise is your friend. Most fights are over in three seconds, if you're going to win them at all.* And she'd had us count the seconds to prove that it was true.

Trey and Loden were trained guardsmen with weapons. They knew what to do better than I did. But they weren't expecting Loden's barbarian feather on the pallet, and they wouldn't expect her to do much beyond cower. Time was on my side; it was the only blessed thing that was.

A hand on a rope was visible. In a second, there would be a head—

Trey's head. I kicked out my left foot with all my might, imagining there was a melon behind Trey's skull that I needed to burst. I could feel the heel of my sandal penetrate the softness of his face. He stumbled backward, without even time to look shocked.

But the swinging bed hadn't provided enough purchase. I jumped off it, ran up to Trey, as close against him as though we were lovers, pulled down the bloody face he was grasping between his two hands, and smashed his forehead against my knee.

He sank to the floor. I kicked his head one more time, being cautious. Probably about two seconds had passed. Loden was standing near the pulley, having taken a couple of steps back, looking horrified and at a loss. There was no belt-holster; he wasn't armed, at least not with a pistol—maybe he'd had to turn it in when the Mercians put him on probation.

I looked down at Trey, ready to grab his pistol and point it at Loden. No holster here, either? What was wrong with the world when security guards went around unarmed? Didn't they let them out with the ordnance when they were off-duty?

Kanz. This left hand-to-hand, and the element of surprise was draining rapidly from the situation. I might be able to beat Loden on an IQ test, but he was a good twelve centimeters taller than I was, not to mention stronger and in better condition. Did I leave out better trained?

Quickly, Theodora. Do it now, before he has time to assess the situation. He's still off-balance. I launched myself at him.

He backed away, arms out, not letting me close with him. "Theo," he said, "wait a minute."

Don't let them start a conversation, I could hear my instructor say. *Nothing they say is of any interest to you.*

He moved farther away, behind the stove. "Relax, dammit, will you? Look, I'm unarmed."

By now he should be willing enough to fight; he'd had time to get himself together and realize he could beat me to a pulp. The fact that he wasn't doing it lent him some credibility.

I was starting to shake. Oh, Kanz, if I'd missile'd right into him, I could've finished before the aftershock hit.

His gaze went to Trey on the floor. "Theo," he said, "we're here for good reason." He locked eyes with me and wiped sweat from his brow. "Could you just, please, give me a minute to tell you about it?"

"What? What is it?" My voice came out on the thin edge of endurance.

He was being awfully polite to somebody who wasn't a threat. Maybe he had a problem psychologically with doing the killing himself. Morally slippery, Loden. The responsibility drops onto the person who arranges it, not just the person who carries it out. Not a boy who thinks things through, are you?

"Well?" I said again.

"I was going to talk to you about this tonight . . . you have to believe me." He pulled a silk kerchief from a pocket and wiped his neck. I could smell his cheap perfume from here, even over the chemical scent from the spilled cans; a musky, repellent thing that reminded me of nothing so much as wet dog. The parcel receipt had reeked of it when we'd opened it up. The two smells twined together nauseously.

The possibility existed that I might faint. I put one hand on the edge of the stove and let as much weight onto that as I could without seeming obvious. "So talk."

"Look, uh, Theo, you've been really nice to me, and I appreciate it. My family's a thousand kilometers away. I didn't have anybody but Trey I could turn to."

Probably so. And bad sense in gambling and bad taste in perfume don't make you a murderer. Now let's see you explain the IOUs. I shifted a few steps back; he was still between me and the door.

"I owed money to half the halls on Red Tah Street. I just wanted to get them off my back, you know? So I put all my debts together with Kade." And used the new cash flow to hit more parlors, instead of paying his back debts. I was beginning to grasp the picture. "Don't tell me you've never done anything crazy in your life. Never took any risks? Never threw any dice?"

Shook off two planets and married into alien thinking, magic, and unreason. Apparently I didn't waste my time gambling with small painted counters.

"Come on, Theo. Cut me a little slack."

"What about Kade?"

"I told you, I didn't do anything to Kade. I'm not a sorcerer, I'm just an agency hire-out. Besides," he stepped closer, gesturing, "don't tell me you care *kanz* about him."

I didn't, to be perfectly honest, as a good Athenan should be. But that wasn't the point.

He said, "Be reasonable. I'm just trying to get along. How great can my life be, sweetheart? I'm living in a mail box."

I didn't need to be called "sweetheart" by Loden Broca. He was standing right next to me by then, his blue kerchief spilling out of his outer robe pocket. He put one hand against the wall behind me. "Am I asking so much?" His voice had gotten low and throaty.

Had Ivoran-style culture shock finally reached some cumulative level where I'd lost my senses, or was Loden making a play right here in Moros's hut, with his friend Trey sprawled on the floor? He leaned over and kissed my cheek, gently. "I'm just asking," he said, moving down toward my mouth, "for some understanding." Then he pulled back an inch and scanned my face.

I must say, I was utterly absorbed in morbid fascination. Never had I seen such unjustified nerve and ego married to such folly. It must be terrible to depend on *glamour* and have none. The situation was repulsive, yet riveting in a sick way. It seemed distant from my own life, like a scene from a melodrama, with the stage in lights and me way back in the tenth row caught up in watching somebody else's reality. I had a sudden suicidal urge to go along with him, just to see what he'd do next, and had to stop myself from returning the embrace.

But common sense broke into my wonderment, in the form of a voice, or rather the memory of a voice.

My old combat instructor: *He's standing right next to you.*

So he was. Wide open.

Well? You know what to do.

Regretfully, I did. At this point I was beginning to consider Loden as a minor child, in need of guardianship, or possibly institutionalization. But I knew what my instructor would expect me to do. And Ran. And Kylla. And every other non-Athenan soul on this planet.

I put my arms around his neck to position them better. He bent down again.

I brought up my knee sharply. As he doubled over he came out with an odd sound, something like a groundhermit whose neck has just been twisted for the pot. I took hold of his head, shoved it farther, and brought up my other knee to meet it.

He fell to the floor. His eyes were closed, but I heard a low, involuntary moan. He didn't move.

Give him a kick to make sure he's out, said my instructor's voice.

Come on—he's not armed. And he's in no shape to come after me without weapons.

It's proper procedure.

But he's an idiot. Can't I just let him go?

No answer from my internalized coach. I walked the other way around the stove, opened the door, and left.

I should have enough adrenaline to make it back to the city, I thought, climbing up the slippery bank. But I'd probably be out of commission for the rest of today and tomorrow. I passed the stack of broken tah tables, lying in muddy splendor, the green-lacquered sides cracked. They looked rather pathetic. Once somebody had placed them proudly in their house. Oh, well, we'd all die eventually, just like the flotsam here.

—Oh, for heaven's sake, Theodora. Go home and pour yourself out a bottle of Ducort—one bowl will put you out, the way you are now. Ran will be there, and tomorrow you'll be all right.

Good idea. I climbed past them. Something seemed

to glitter past the edges of my sight, some trick of sunlight; I turned and looked behind me.

Loden was standing in the doorway with a pistol in his hand. The charge must have gone over my head.

How in the name of the gods did he get that? I dived behind the broken wagonseat. He hadn't been wearing a holster. Trey hadn't been wearing a holster. Why would either of them tuck a pistol away anywhere else? The wagonseat wasn't going to make it as protection, I thought.

Loden started up the hill, awkwardly, one hand going to his head. I crawled through the mud behind the wagonseat and into a pile of old boxes. I didn't know what was in them, but they stank.

This was terrible. I was going to be killed by somebody I didn't even respect.

And it wasn't right, either! I pulled myself under an overturned carton. Not that I expected fairness from the universe, but this was like one of those tile-machine games that nearly laid itself out perfectly for you, then missed by a single tile. Theodora the barbarian had just taken out two fully grown security guards. Two! Trained. And after that . . . shot in the mud by a libidinous, egotistical fool without sense to come in out of the rain.

Loden reached the wagonseat. I don't know why it bothered me to be killed by Loden, particularly, but it did. It's not that I looked forward to being taken out by an honorable and intelligent enemy; I looked forward to dying in bed. Or better yet, not dying at all. But this was just so, well, lacking in dignity.

Told you to give 'im the extra kick.

Oh, shut up. I burrowed beneath the pile. Kanz, I couldn't see Loden from where I was any more. Risking death seemed preferable to suspense. I came out on the other side of the cartons and raised my head— very, very slightly.

The wagonseat had been cut cleanly in two, on the diagonal. The ground behind it was dry, no longer muddy. Loden was nowhere to be seen.

There was a wardrobe with a door missing standing farther up the bank, tall enough to hide a man. Unless Loden had chosen to crawl behind one of the piles of junk . . . but his present headache would probably make crawling unattractive. Still, he was so clearly enraged with me that he was working hard to scare me to death—otherwise he would just step out again openly with the pistol.

I did have a knife, but it can be more dangerous to pull that out in a fight than not. Knives can be taken away from little female barbarians and then their throats can be cut with them, which is a poor use of irony in one's life. But he was far enough from me now that I could throw it . . . though not as fast as he could use a pistol.

Kanz. Ran was never even going to know exactly what happened.

I am not a person of action! I thought desperately. I'm just a scholar! I *collect* things, I write things down. . . .

Movement on the periphery of my right eye. I whipped my head around. Far down the bank, on the path beside the water, two figures. . . . A red and white robe I recognized. A walk, a gesture, in the person beside him. *Ran and Stereth*. What were they doing here together? *Who cared?* I smothered a dangerous impulse to jump up and wave my arms.

They were still a good distance away. If Loden saw them, he'd shoot me quickly, pick them off, and get out of here. No. Keep him occupied, don't let him know the game has a time limit. Go on, Loden, torture me some more. Toy with me, scare me, remind me that you've got the pistol and I don't.

I crawled around the cartons and behind a table. If Loden saw any movement, it would take his eyes farther from the path below. Was that the edge of a sleeve hind the wardrobe?

"Lady Theodora!" His voice came over the empty air, the open silence around us, and the faint sound of the river. If I answered, he'd know for certain where I was, if he didn't know already. "Why are you doing this?"

Why am I crawling through the mud and stink? If you'd seen the look on your face, you wouldn't have asked.

"Come on out and talk to me, like a normal person," he called.

I'm sorry I can't reproduce his tone of voice here. What it was saying was: Come out so I can shoot you and get on with my life. I don't know if he had any idea how transparent he was.

I glanced down the bank: Still too far away. Shame to die now, with possibility so close, but that's the way some of those tile-games end—when you're one tile down, you lose the whole pot. I turned back. Loden had emerged from behind the wardrobe. "You know, I really have nothing against you personally," he assured me, walking forward, toward my hiding place. "I was angry at you a few minutes ago, but I realize you were scared." His voice sounded more sincere now. Possibly he meant it as an apology for shooting me.

"Trey's not dead," he added. Why he wanted to share this with me, I don't know. I let myself roll down the slope toward the garbage sacks just below.

My roll stopped and my face bumped into something hard sticking out of one of the garbage sacks. A chair leg. Hardly any chairs on the entire planet, and I bump into one while escaping a lunatic. My nose started to bleed enthusiastically.

The sack in front of me parted, cut neatly in half, the surfaces of the cut smoking faintly. Loden's voice, pleased, said, "You left a trail when you slipped down there, Theo."

So much for hiding. I jumped to my feet. He blinked, startled, at my sudden appearance. I turned quickly to check for my potential rescuers, and Loden's glance followed mine. My beloved husband and the Minister for Provincial Affairs were well within sight; Loden goggled. As I recalled from the hut, he did not react well to surprise.

But he pulled himself together. He turned to me, raising the pistol. I faced the lower bank, took in the biggest lungful of air I'd ever taken, and yelled, "STERETH!"

The two figures on the path turned. Loden's arm pointed straight at my face. Ran's pistolcut hit his shoulder—a full second after Stereth's cut cleaved his skull in half.

Feeling too shaky to stay on my feet, I sat down in the mud in my party robes and waited for them to climb the hill. Ran reached me first.

"There's blood all over your face," he said, breathing hard.

"It's just a nosebleed. I bunked into something."

He glanced briefly at what was left of Loden and then gave me a look that said we would talk later. Then suddenly he was kneeling in the mud next to me, looking shaken as he gazed at the pistolcut in Loden's shoulder. Stereth came a few seconds later, extending a steady hand to me that showed no trace of nerves whatsoever. "I'd prefer to sit for a minute," I said.

He stepped back obligingly and took a pipe from the pocket of his outerrobe. He packed it, lit it, and turned to Ran with an air of courtesy. Ran was still kneeling by Loden, his face pale. "Thank you," he said, without looking up.

Stereth smiled. "Well, sir Cormallon," he said kindly, "it would seem that you owe me a favor."

Chapter 17

Well, they debated debt, obligation, and what to do with the bodies for a good quarter of an hour, apparently forgetting me entirely. (In fairness, I must say that I encouraged them to ignore me while I angled my head back in an unbecoming fashion, waiting for the bleeding to stop.)

Then they hauled Loden's remains down to the hut, where it would have taken a while to find him, even if my two rescuers weren't discussing the merits of throwing a match on the spilled chemicals—no point in being asked any administrative questions by the city. When they returned, about forty minutes had passed, and my nose was gushing more violently than ever.

They fell to arguing again. "Ran!" I said. Oops. Raising my voice increased the flow. "Ran. Stereth." They didn't seem to hear me. I kicked out with my foot and landed one on Ran's shin.

"What are you—" he began, then frowned, looking down on me. "You're still bleeding."

"No foolig. I'b begidding to suspect I bay deed bedical help." Breathing through my mouth seemed the best option.

Stereth squatted down beside me. "I saw a lot of wounds in the Northwest Sector," he said kindly. "Try pinching the bridge of your nose."

We all hunkered around in the mud, pinching my nose and replacing one sopping handkerchief with another. Fortunately I'd laid in a good supply when I'd heard I was invited to the Poraths that morning. Damn the Poraths anyway. The insides of my nose had probably gotten weak from all that blowing.

After a while Ran said, "It doesn't seem to be stopping, does it?"

Stereth considered it thoughtfully. "It's getting *worse*. Coming out like a young river. We seem to have broken in on an artery."

I must have made a pitiful-sounding moan, because they both leaped to reassure me: "But you'll be fine!" —Sorry about the moan, but if you'll look back, I think you'll agree that this hadn't been a good day for me. It's not easy being the hero of your own story. We all do our best.

Anyway, my pathetic sound must have finally prodded them to action. "She's losing an awful lot of blood," said Stereth. "We'd better get her to a healer."

I said, through the mess of handkerchiefs, "Ad outpladet doctor." I have great respect for Ivoran native healers, but they're better at prevention than cure, in my opinion. Not that I wanted to debate the issue then.

Ran said, "A healer could handle this, Theodora."

"I wat a doctor."

He threw another couple of fresh handkerchiefs on my face and said, "Suppose we just take you to whatever is closer."

That made a lot of sense. I let them lead me down the bank to the path, and up the edge of the canal. I ran out of handkerchiefs around then, and Stereth took off his robe, removed his shirt, and gave it to me to hold over my face. I could barely see where I was going.

I mean, I'd just fought off two attackers and seen somebody who tried to kill me shot before my eyes. This would be the time when a real storybook heroine would be gracefully accepting accolades before marrying the prince. And there we were: A ragged line of three grimy people, with me being led along with my head tilted back and an old shirt over my face. And it wasn't even because I had a wound from fighting the dragon, a swordscrape taken in battle; no, it was a *nosebleed*. Life takes no notice of our wish for dignity.

We went to a healer in Dart Street. She was a cheerful-looking, intelligent woman with a sensible, motherly smile; just what you'd want in a healer. Of course, I couldn't see her at first through the cloth I was holding over my face. She very carefully stuffed my left nostril with enough cotton gauze to make curtains for all the conference rooms in the Taka Hospitality Building, packed it tight and covered my nose with a bandage. I can't say I was enthusiastic about it at the time, but the outcome was more than satisfactory. About ninety percent of the bleeding halted immediately.

What a simple solution. What excellent results. Perhaps I should stop fooling around with the more arcane legends of Ivory and study basic first aid.

She was pleased that I was pleased. "How do you feel?" she asked.

Under the circumstances, it was a question I needed to think about before answering. Finally I said, tentatively, "It's nice not to have blood running all over my face."

She burst out laughing. "Everything is relative, isn't it?" She helped me up off the table and we went to the next room to see Ran.

"Stereth said good-bye," Ran told me. "He was late for an appointment." He looked at the healer. "Will she be all right?"

"Help her to take it easy for a few days." She turned to me. "Don't do anything strenuous. Don't bend over. Try not to laugh too hard. And if you have to shit, don't strain on the pot," she added, with the complete lack of embarrassment Ivorans have about bodily functions. "And don't try to take the dressing off yourself; come back in two days for that. I want to have my cauterization equipment ready in case it starts bleeding hard again."

"Your what?" I asked.

"Have you ever had the inside of your nose cauterized?"

"Uh, no, I don't think so," I replied, vowing silently that I would go to one of the outplanet clinics to have the dressing removed. I smiled. "Thank you for your help, gracious lady."

"Not at all," she said, "it's a treat to have a barbarian to work on. Everyone in this neighborhood seems to be from the same province."

We sat on the steps outside her office and waited for the carriage Ran had sent for. After a moment he said, "Stereth told me I'm to go to the medical clinic of my wife's choosing."

"—Ah." I was glad suddenly not to have won my point about the outplanet doctor. He might consider the obligation discharged. "You know this healer here doesn't count as my choosing."

"I know that. Why did Stereth make that particular requirement?"

"Uh . . ." Such verbal ability as I had was deserting me.

"Theodora? My wife?"

"Well. You know I want us both to have a genalysis to see whether we can have a viable child—"

"I've told you it would be grossly irresponsible for me to allow the Selians to examine my genetic structure."

"I wasn't planning on going to the Selians."

He digested that. "Share this with me, then. Who were you planning on forcing me to see?"

I said quietly, "I thought we might both go to the Jack Lykon Free Clinic."

"There's no clinic by that name in the capital . . . although the name is familiar."

"He's the man I met at the meeting with the Tellysian junior ambassador. Ah, the Tolla representative."

He turned to me slowly. "Are you telling me you consider the Tolla a safer repository for secret House information?"

"Ran, I have an idea." The concept of using the

Tolla had shocked him into temporary silence, and I took advantage of it. I brought up the anecdote about the brewers, their adoption, and the enforced silence placed on them. I said, "Why can't we adopt Jack Lykon into Cormallon? There haven't been that many good genalycists around since Gate 53; the knowledge that you think makes him dangerous could make him useful to our House. The Tolla will be glad to lend him to us in return for our help with their weapons problem."

"Their weapons problem might be insoluble by sorcery."

"I have every faith in your ability to come up with something."

"And I doubt if this Jack Lykon would be willing to put himself in our power once the situation was fully explained to him."

"If he's really Tolla, he'll do his duty. And he seems like a nice guy, too."

Ran was silent, and I stopped myself from pressing the matter. Finally he said, "Let me think this through."

I said, "Of course," and congratulated myself for not bringing up the fact that his consent was required to repay the obligation to Stereth. It would work better if I didn't mention it.

Then Ran said, "Theodora?" His voice had changed.

"What?"

"When that fool was trying to shoot you . . . why did you call for Stereth, and not for me?"

Oh, gods. I'd been afraid he would ask that. I didn't have a good answer.

"You know, Ran, everything happened very quickly. I don't know why I yelled for Stereth; maybe I thought there was a better chance of his being armed."

"You know I've been carrying a pistol everywhere since that business in Trade Square."

"I . . . guess I forgot. I wasn't thinking clearly."

He fell silent, not fully satisfied, but not pursuing

it. I've given the matter a lot of thought since then,
because I didn't understand it myself. Did I trust Stereth more than Ran? Not that I was aware of. Didn't I
love Ran, didn't I know he would act to protect me if
necessary? Didn't I know very well he was carrying a
weapon? There's no higher professorial power to hand
me the answers to this quiz, but I think that in the end,
the simple fact was that when I needed a natural killer
my mind went automatically to Stereth.

I was in no shape to analyze the matter so thoroughly at the time, however. Ran looked troubled, and
I was troubled myself.

After a moment he said, "Did you know that fool
Loden"—it was always "that-fool-Loden," as if it
were one word—"was using an attraction spell? Of
course, *he* probably called it a love spell."

"You're joking."

"It was in his perfume. He was drenched with it. I
had to suffer through the stink when we dragged him
down to the hut."

It would in fact stink to Ran, if it was designed to
attract females, which I assume from Loden's reputation is what he would ask for. Except that I hadn't
much liked the smell either, though perhaps "stink"
was a little strong.

Ran said, "He must have bathed in it. You didn't
. . . notice anything?"

"I assure you I did not."

"No sudden urge to make love on the floor of the
hut?"

"Perhaps he was given a hate potion by mistake.
The only urge I felt was to knee him in the nuts, which
I did."

"Interesting," he said, shifting from the husband to
the professional sorcerer. "We'll have to analyze the
situation when we have time."

I was about to suggest that barbarian genes might
be different, but thought I'd pushed my luck enough
with that topic.

No wonder he was uncomfortable. I'd spent my time

hanging around with ne'er-do-wells armed with love potions, and then called on Stereth for rescue from the consequences of my visit. It wasn't surprising that my husband was a little miffed.

Only partly changing the subject, I said, "Stereth owed me a favor. For going to see the Tellysian ambassador."

"I see."

He was back to that stiff note, the same withdrawal I'd heard when I told him to go to Mira-Stoden.

Oh, hell. I'd just disgraced myself thoroughly, sliding around in the mud and bleeding all over my robes, from a situation I might have avoided with quicker thinking—since if I'd dumped Loden's IOUs back in the desk before I hid, they never would have bothered to haul down the bed. And it wasn't as if I'd needed the IOUs, the case was never going to court. Ran and I could have just told Lord Porath the story, and let him take it from there.

We may as well finish peeling the scab off any remnants of dignity and admit the whole thing.

"Ran, I'm scared."

He looked startled. "Loden and his friend are quite definitely out of the way, my love. Stereth and I made sure—"

"No, I'm scared of the idea of having a baby. I know I'm supposed to be some kind of rock-solid matriarch, passing the genetic torch down to the next stepful of Cormallons, but I keep—" I paused.

"Keep what?" His voice was quiet.

"I keep thinking I'm going to die. I keep having these dreams. I just find that, whenever I imagine having a child . . . I keep seeing him brought up posthumously."

"You never said anything."

"I'm supposed to be undeterred by this stuff, aren't I? Go bravely ahead and do my duty, count not the cost—"

"Theodora—"

"But fond though I am of your family, dying wasn't

on my list of things to do when I came back with you.''

"Theodora, we take intuition seriously around here. Why didn't you tell me this?''

I was silent. Finally, I said, "How do I know how much is intuition and how much is nerves?''

He sighed. Then he put an arm around my shoulder. "I suppose we could go to one of these outplanet medical clinics and inquire.''

Have you lost respect for me? Come on, Theodora, go for two tough questions in a row. "Ran?''

"What?''

"What were you and Stereth doing out at Moros's house?'' *Chicken. Buck-buck.*

"Oh! I got your message. I decided to call Stereth to see if he thought anybody else knew where Moros had lived, and how long they'd known. If the place was cleaned out, you know, there was hardly any point in going. While we were talking, I mentioned I was joining you there. It was his idea to come along.''

I grinned. "Stereth doesn't wait to be asked.''

"Lucky for us both he doesn't. At least in this case.'' Then he smiled. "So this is why you've been going around even more tymon-crazy than you usually are.''

"Perhaps you should rephrase that, my husband.''

"Sim will be relieved,'' he said, ignoring my suggestion. "I couldn't give him any indication as to what troubles you might be getting yourself into. Now I can tell him to relax and take his holiday. He's straining to go to the Lavender Palace, you know.''

"You mean he actually converses on topics other than food?''

"I've known Sim for years. It takes him a while to lose his natural reserve.''

"Ah. I'll look forward to chats with him, twenty years down the line.''

I looked forward to seeing him off to the Lavender Palace, too—after a prolonged period of bedrest on his part. I decided to wait for the opportune moment to fill Ran in on that escapade.

And so we sat there, waiting for the carriage, tucked up against each other like two winter birds. He must have had some idea what was on my mind because at one point he kissed the shoulder of my messy robe and said, "Come on. Don't worry about it."

I heard the faint sound of carriage wheels, and touched a finger to my cheek, checking for any dirt we'd missed. The healer had asked me whether I had any sensation in certain parts of my face; now the question seemed full of sinister implications. I touched my left cheek again. "Ran, I can't feel anything on my face when I touch it! The whole texture of the skin feels strange."

He said, "Theodora, you're touching the bandage."

Oh. I was glad Stereth wasn't around to have witnessed that.

"Here's the carriage," he said, and a minute later he was helping me to climb in.

Look, when it comes to adventure I do the best I can. Some people are born to dazzle rooms with panther-grace after receiving the plaudits of the crowds. Some people are born to wear sensible shoes, and I'm one of them. After this encounter, I spent a few days at home, taking it easy and being pleasantly spoiled by Ran and Kylla. I had time to consider that a clear-thinking individual might have been more on top of the Loden situation if he or she had stopped to think how quickly those hired thugs in the market had swung into action—only a couple of hours after we gave Loden a description of Moros.

I also had time to think about Loden's, well, impotent perfume; probably he'd gotten it from Moros. Ran had seemed to feel it was the genuine article. Why then had I looked upon it with such justifiable contempt? Here are some of the mitigating factors I came up with:

(1) I'm a barbarian; what the effects of this heritage

may be in terms of magic has never been thoroughly studied, but at its most physically mundane I don't believe my sense of smell is equal to a native Ivoran's; (2) my nose had been operating at a deficit ever since the Night of Cats; and (3) Loden, like many people, was ignorant of how an attraction spell works. It's a cheat, a bit of pure deceit that produces an array of physical symptoms which, in the right circumstances, convince the victim he (or she) is in the grip of sexual fever. When what they're really in the grip of is a list of medically determined effects, checked off coldly by the sorcerer-chef: Raised heartbeat (check one); dry mouth (check one); sweaty palms. . . . Statistically, a good attraction spell will work about eighty-five percent of the time. The other fifteen percent are people who through circumstance or sheer eccentricity can divorce their symptoms from what they've been led to believe is happening to them.

Just as a hypothetical example, I might point out that somebody who considers herself in danger of immediate murder has reason enough for a raised heartbeat and sweaty palms without ascribing them to any other source. True, there are a few symptoms caused by an attraction spell that are not on the list of, say, a fear spell—but again, somebody in immediate danger of death is going to have their mind on other things.

Loden was an idiot to have tried it. But then, as I think we've all agreed by now, Loden was an idiot.

Several days later found me waiting nervously in the courtyard of Cormallon itself. I paced the length of the pool, past the columns, turned and paced again. For the sake of his sanity, Ran had left me alone and gone into the study.

Jack Lykon was upstairs, running his genetic scenarios on a locked Net terminal. Jack Lykon Cormallon, if you want to be technical about it; his adoption had taken place the day before yesterday. Papers were filed with the Tellysian embassy detailing his voluntary agreement to place himself under House authority, and absolving the embassy and any Tellysian group or organization from any responsibility in the event of his death or disappearance.

Jack had been very nice about it, actually. "Don't be silly," he'd said, when I apologized for what we were putting him through. "I can't wait to get my hands on you, Theodora. That is to say, on your data."

"You won't be able to share it with anyone," I pointed out.

Jack grinned. He seemed none the worse for being the focus of an eight-hour, three-sorcerer spell that observers had been barred from, but which had left a very strange odor all through the top floor corridor. "Knowing the facts myself comes first; sharing is a distant second, I'm afraid."

"Hmm. No wonder you don't mind being a Cormallon."

He'd been running Net scenarios all day and night. By now he must have hundreds. He hadn't said it would take this long.

I'd been pacing, dinnerless, straight into the evening, when he appeared at the door to the dining room. "Theo?"

I went straight to him. "What? Tell me."

He ran a hand through his sparse brown hair. His eyes were deeply lined, his casually tasteful Tellysian jacket long since discarded, his shirt rumpled and stained. "I asked— God, I'm thirsty." His voice had come out as a croak. He stared around at the dining room as though at a foreign land, then picked up a carafe of water from a sideboard and drank directly from it. He wiped his mouth with the back of his hand. "I asked your husband to join us," he said, more firmly.

"I can't wait. Tell me now."

"It's not the kind of thing you can boil down to a sentence—"

Ran entered the other end of the hall. He glanced at a bottle of Ducort on a rack by the entrance, evidently wondering if fortification would shortly be necessary.

Then he walked down the length of the sideboard, took
in my state at a glance, turned to Lykon and said,
"Jack?"

"Can we sit?" asked Jack.

Ran motioned toward some scattered pillows by a
corner of the dining table. We sat.

Jack said, "First you have to understand that we're
dealing with a lot of unknowns here. One specimen
does not a statistic make. I had to tag a lot of variables
with question marks, so I'm not speaking with a high
level of confidence in anything I say."

He looked at Ran as though wondering how a sorcerer would take this kind of talk. The funny thing is,
that's exactly how-sorcerers do talk. He peered uncertainly into Ran's eyes. "Do you see the point I'm trying to make?"

"I do indeed, Mr. Lykon. You're being very clear.
Please continue."

"Uh, yeah. Anyway, I ran all kinds of simulations,
using different guesses in different phases. They're ed-
ucated guesses, based on what we know already, but
they're still guesses. I haven't found anything that looks
like a 'gene for sorcery,' by the way. I assume it's
genetically based, but it's obviously more subtle than
that. We'll have to dig harder."

"Why do you assume it's genetically based?" asked
Ran calmly, while I tried not to bite through my
tongue.

"Well, everything's genetically based, in the final
sense," said Jack. The genalycist's version of the hand
of destiny. "Anyway, that's not the question you two
are interested in. It gets complicated here—"

"Are Ran and I the same species?" I cut in.

He looked pained. "Theodora, for your own sake,
try to let me tell this my own way, or you'll only get
half the story—"

"Can't you give me a yes/no? I'll listen to the whole
story afterward, I promise."

"Nothing is ever that simple. The category of species is imposed by man—by our attempt to cut up the

universe into pieces to better understand it. The categories were never really that hard and fast, though. We want yes/no, either/or, yin/yang, but it's all really a continuum—even gender is a continuum. There are plenty of babies born each year whose sex isn't clear to the attending physician. They have to make something up on the spot, or the parents get upset, then all hell breaks loose twelve years down the road—''

"Jack, this is fascinating, but I need to know about my own kids here—''

"Theo, I'm trying to tell you why I'm not the oracle with the final answers.''

"And I'm grasping for straws, Jack. Throw me a couple of uncertain hypotheses. Please.''

He sighed heavily. "All right. The signs seem to indicate that you two can conceive.''

Score one! I would have smiled, but I was waiting for the other shoes to drop. I say 'shoes,' because Jack was showing centipedelike tendencies.

He said, "As far as I can tell, my highest-probability guess is that the child would be a functional, viable being, with a strong chance of being sterile.''

"What odds?'' I said.

"Functional and viable? Seventy-two percent. Sterile, ninety-three percent. And I'm saying it with a confidence level of eighty-five, plus or minus five.''

I turned to Ran, whose dark eyes had the slightly dazed look of someone who's been slapped but is trying to continue in proper social fashion. *The Cormallon council must never hear about this.* He took my hand.

"The functional and viable rating is based on outplanet medical care being available at all times, as well as access to a proper environment for premature births. The odds drop substantially without those two factors.''

I asked, "You think it'll be premature?''

He shifted uncomfortably on his pillow. "Not exactly. Well, yes, it probably would be. It gets complicated here because Theodora isn't a normal Pyrenese—''

"Whoa! Where did you get that idea?"

"Your genes say so, Theo. You've got a higher portion of tagged unknowns than is usual for a Standard citizen. Not that that makes you a freak or anything; there are always a proportion of unknowns showing up in the general population. It keeps us boiling. You've got plenty of company, statistically, but it makes our job that much harder."

He wiped his face again and glanced around for the carafe. It was still on top of the sideboard. He shrugged, giving it up for lost, and said, "I had to run a lot of extra scenarios. That's what took me so long. I was hoping to get a better run of luck somewhere along the way, but it didn't happen. The vast majority of combinations ended in death."

I said, slowly, "You said the fetus was viable . . ."

"Yeah. The fetus lives. You die. Eighty-nine percent of the time."

Ran's hand had frozen into something metallic. I said, *"Why?"*

"Incompatibilities between you and any offspring you would have with Ran. They're quite survival-oriented little packages, though; whenever the scenario ended in death, it was usually yours."

"Huh." I felt a slight tremor of hysteria somewhere down on the ocean floor. "It's good to know I'd be producing high-caliber individuals."

Ran said, with no emotion whatsoever, "You're not sure about this."

"I'm not sure of any of it. That's what I'm telling you. You wanted an expert opinion, and that's what you've got—an opinion." Jack let his professional facade crack by a millimeter. "I'm sorry, Theo. This isn't what I wanted to tell you."

I saw that his insistence on keeping this on a theoretical level, his clinging to the role of detached expert, was born of his own discomfort with making me unhappy. I said, "It's all right. We wanted the facts, as well as you could discern them."

"I'm sorry," he said again. He looked at a loss, as though any words beyond those two had deserted him.

I turned to my husband. "Ran?"

He still had that slapped look. His eyes focused on me slowly. I'd wanted a child, for what I thought of as the usual reasons; but Ran defined his identity around his family. I don't think it had really, seriously occurred to him that he wouldn't live the same traditional life everyone else in his family took for granted. That this particular branch of Cormallon would come to an abrupt breaking-off because he'd married me.

"Ran?" I asked, uncertainly.

We'd been speaking with Jack in Standard. Ran looked down at my hand, still in his own. He raised it and covered it with both his palms. "Beloved," he said, in Ivoran, "we will think of something."

Maybe we would. But I couldn't see any good answers anywhere on the horizon.

Chapter 18

No answers presented themselves over the next couple of weeks, either. Ran retired to his Net terminal to work on some scenarios of his own, based on the weapons requirements of the Tolla. He estimated it as a four-month project, and said somebody would have to go to Tellys at some point to do preliminary testing. Meanwhile, Jack Lykon's gag-spell was tested within an inch of his life before he was released from Cormallon territory. And our Sim was discharged from the care of the Red Tah Street healer and given a nice bonus to play with in the capital before he returned home.

And what was I doing? I wasn't studying tinaje healing; I didn't need to read the cards on new clients, as we weren't taking any new clients; I wasn't required to accomplish much of anything, at the moment, so I had plenty of time to brood. The day after Jack's talk I returned to the Dart Street healer and came out fitted with a thing she called a "cap," a gadget to prevent fertilization. Not that Ran and I had been showing any great talent in that area, but I decided not to take any chances. At the same time, you'll notice I didn't go to an outplanet clinic and pay the much higher price for an implant. Implants last for a couple of years, a length of time I felt unable to deal with at that point, despite Jack's warning. I'm not saying this made sense, I'm only telling you what I did.

Having accomplished this one errand, the days stretched before me, an open invitation to depression. So I decided to return to scholarship, the one thing in life that could be counted on not to rise up and bite you in the neck. Or not often, anyway. One day when Kylla was taking refuge in our parlor after an argument with Lysander, I sat down in the shade of the courtyard and cracked open Coalis's copy of Kesey's *Erotic Poems*.

I'd been swimming in and out of gloomy thoughts ever since our talk with Jack. Before this I would never in a million years have thought of myself as someone who found any part of their self-definition in fertility— the very idea was primitive and insulting. This mis- conception was rudely adjusted. I felt a failure as a Cormallon member, as a wife, possibly as a woman. Coming on top of all this, that remark of Jack's about my "unknowns" must have rankled more than I re- alized. I started to feel abnormal, out-of-place . . . the most distorted view of "barbarian" seemed to fit me, when I thought of who I was. Whoever I was. The word freak, in fact, was bobbing somewhere near the surface.

So it turned out I was really not in the proper state of mind to take on Kesey's view of the world.

Maybe you're familiar with the work. Kesey's *Erotic Poems* are about six centuries old, and there's been considerable language drift, but they're still under- standable, and the book is supposed to be a classic. But despite an introduction full of lavish praise from all sorts of people, I became more and more disap- pointed. It mostly seemed to be about his trouble get- ting dates.

One of the poems was written from the viewpoint of a woman making love with him—he was supposed to be a veritable wonder at getting the woman's an- gle—and as I read it I found myself wincing.

I closed the book, marking the page with a finger, and stared into space. Maybe I really wasn't normal. Jack had seemed to imply it, Kylla often found my reactions to daily life amusingly odd, and Ran's oc- casional comments on the barbarian attitude toward sexual practices made me wonder. Maybe there was something wrong with me, after all. Maybe—

I walked into the parlor, still carrying the book. Kylla was looking out the tiny slit window that faced the street. "Kylla? Do you like the idea of a man pinching your nipples? I mean, do you find it erotic?"

Kylla, bless her, showed no surprise at the question coming out of the blue like that. She shivered in an involuntary response that reminded me of my own reaction. "Good heavens, no. You enjoy that, Theo? What's your chest made of, cast iron?"

"No, no, I find the idea exquisitely painful, myself. But in this book a fellow does it and the woman thinks it's terrific stuff. They both seem to take it as a normal part of lovemaking."

She smiled. "I'll bet a man wrote that book."

"He did, actually. . . . So you don't think I'm abnormal?"

"Certainly not."

I considered it. "Then where do men get the idea we enjoy it? This isn't the first time I've read about it, and I was starting to get paranoid."

She looked a bit sheepish. "Well, I suppose we have to take part of the blame. It's happened to me once or twice, and in the heat of the moment—well, I didn't want to hurt his feelings, so I pretended I liked it."

"Are you ever going to set him straight?"

She looked puzzled. "Who?"

"Lysander."

"Oh! Um, it wasn't Lysander who did it."

I stared at her. "Kylla! When was *this*—"

There was a sound of footsteps in the hall, and Ran walked in. He kissed us both. "Talking about anything interesting?"

"We were discussing literature," said Kylla, smoothing her outerrobe as she retook her seat by the window.

"Theodora, do we still have that seed-cake from yesterday? . . . Theodora?"

"Kylla," I began, as soon as he left.

"What book are you reading?" she said.

"What? Oh—it's Kesey's *Erotic Poems*. Ky, when did you—"

"Well, no wonder, then. My brother used to call it 'superbly humorless.' He said it was the most overrated piece of literature ever perpetrated on an innocent public, but at least you could use it to separate the pretentious from the true lovers of poetry."

I blinked. "I didn't even know Ran had read it. He didn't mention it."

"Actually . . . I was referring to Eln."

References to Ran's older brother were taboo, and came rarely, even from Kylla. "Superbly humorless." That sounded like Eln, all right. Maybe recalling the lover(s) of her younger days had brought him back to mind for her. I said, "Kylla, when did all this happen?"

"There's no seed-cake," Ran announced, reentering the room.

Kylla and I exchanged a glance, and let the topic drop. I'm willing to share most things with Ran—frankly, anything but openness gets far too complicated for me to handle in the long run—but Kylla's personal scandals don't belong to me. And he wouldn't want to hear about Eln.

My husband looked hungry. "Let's go out to dinner," he said. "How does the Lantern Gardens sound? Ky?"

She shrugged. I said, "I don't think I'm up to the naked floorshow tonight."

"We can take a table in the outside garden, by the pond. Listen to the music, watch the paper boats sail. I made a breakthrough today on the weapons project, I want to relax and let my mind empty out. Indulge me, Tymon."

I grinned suddenly. Maybe I owed him something for never trying to pinch vulnerable areas of my body.

"What's so funny, my barbarian?"

"Nothing. All right, let's go to the Lantern Gardens. But, Kylla, what happens when Lysander tries to call here and beg for forgiveness?'' For this was how all her fights with Lysander ended. She had early set a precedent in their marriage that giving in would be based not on logic but on gender.

She smiled wickedly. ''Let him call and be frustrated. Maybe he'll come by and sit on your doorstep. Let's stay out *late*, Ran.''

He gave her a formal bow.

The outdoor section of the Lantern Gardens is huge. A shallow pond is on one side, and slender manmade rivers on high clay aquaducts extend out from it to curve around the tables. In the daytime, the trellises overhead are hung with cages, each containing a songbird. At night, the pond and its farflung tributaries bear an armada of colored paper boats, each carrying a candle. If you haven't gotten the idea by now, the Lantern Gardens is an expensive place to eat. It was Ran's favorite restaurant.

Kylla paid ten kembits and folded a small paper wish into a red boat, then dropped it on the pond.

''What did you wish?'' I asked.

She smiled a smile that said she wasn't going to tell me. ''For wisdom and discretion,'' she murmured, as we made our way to the table, ''as every proper woman of good family wishes.''

I looked around at the crowd: Wild tourists, showing bare legs and arms shamelessly, drinking down Ducort red as though it were fruit juice; sedate matrons, overdressed to the limit and beyond, dripping with gems; young men escorting conservatively robed young ladies and their chaperones . . . other young men escorting hard-eyed young professionals with no chaperones. One of them inched by us on the way to the lavatory, her belt of feathers brushing past me as she went—her illusionless eyes brushing over me as well. *Oh, yes,* I thought, *wisdom and discretion. I'm sure it's the wish on every boat here tonight.*

* * *

The Lantern Gardens makes what it claims is Pyrenese cheeseburger. I never saw a cheeseburger before with unidentified white sauce running down it, and hard toast instead of buns; but if it wasn't Pyrenese cheeseburger, whatever it was tasted good. I've ordered it there before. Midway through the meal, Kylla glanced toward the line of paper boats sailing on the miniature river just beyond us. "Here comes my wish," she announced, smiling.

The smile froze on her lips, even as it drained from her eyes. I turned my head to see what she was looking at. Three tables away, across the line of boats, sat Eliana Porath. Leel Canerol was on her right, a light meal in front of her and a glass of water. On Eliana's left was a young man in a robe of exquisite tailoring, edged in gold thread. He was chatting away happily . . . chatting quite a bit, in fact, apparently expounding-for-the-benefit-of-the-lady in the long-winded way some young men will, and some old men who never grew up. He had two forks set some distance apart on the table, and a knife at right-angles, and kept gesturing as he spoke, explaining . . . the mechanics of an aircar? His conception of government politics? A new addition to his house? At least he had a good-natured face, though, and there are worse things in the world than a tendency to be pompous. Eliana and her chaperone were clearly not required to do much beyond listen and make admiring sounds.

I turned back to our table and saw Ran watching them as well. "Well, life goes on," I said coolly. "I see her father's lending her out on a trial basis already."

"What did you expect?" asked Ran, taking a bite of Tellysian-style casserole. "The creditors won't wait."

I met Kylla's eyes. She shrugged and said, "It's over now. Why dwell on it?"

Why indeed? It was over and Kylla had won. Her life was safeguarded for the time being, and after all, how many times did a man outside the nobility, even one in Lysander's position, get asked to a marriage-alliance with the Six Families? I felt that my sister-in-law was quite up to handling any future approaches from commoner Houses.

I was drawn back to focus on Eliana, now turning to smile at her escort . . . a little tiredly? Did she have the illusion she was free and happy, or was she all too well aware of her cage? I could hear her grandmother's voice: *It takes the endurance of a warrior on the inside to make a fragile flower on the outside.*

Gods! I turned back to see Kylla contentedly digging into a sweet and sour ko-pocket. The same society, stirred only slightly differently—how can some people make a good and satisfied life within the confines of their cultural boundaries, and others end up smashed against the walls?

Of course, Eliana had a tyrannical father, while Kylla's father was safely dead . . . to the relief of his dependents, I sometimes suspected. But even if Lord Porath died tonight, it would only mean her custody would transfer to Coalis. And what alliances would her twisty brother have in mind? Stereth would no doubt have input into that. Everybody would but her, if she weren't extremely careful.

"A disappointing end to a disappointing summer," I said, cutting my soggy other-than-cheeseburger into neat squares.

"In what way disappointing?" asked Ran.

"This business with Kade. When I heard about foreign involvement from the ambassador, I guess I was half-hoping for some kind of political motivation—intrigue, scandal . . . ideals. And now to find that it's only money. . . ."

"Only money?" asked Ran, as Kylla's boat, now on the river to our left, finally caught fire. "Is this a Cormallon talking?"

I laughed and he covered my hand where it rested on the tablecloth. "I guess I don't know what I was expecting," I said.

Kylla's boat capsized, dousing the flames, and the other boats streamed on in a prism of colors. We fin-

ished the meal, leaving Eliana and her problems behind. When we got home, much later, we found
Lysander asleep on our doorstep, his head propped
against the front door. Kylla chuckled, knelt and kissed
him tenderly, and took him away with her.

It was after midnight when I awoke. I lay there in
bed, straining my ears; there was only silence, the
deep, vibrating silence of the darkest part of the night.
The very house seemed to be in coma, and what had
brought me up through the waves? Sim was finishing
his holiday at an inn closer to the center of town—the
more freely to play and carouse, without the inhibiting
presence of the First of Cormallon to observe him.
The only other person here was in bed on my left.
What had awakened me?

Had anything awakened me? I'd been having some
kind of confused dream, some oddball thing about
waiting in line for a manicurist in a body salon on
Athena. Kylla had been sitting in the waiting room
with me, but I knew that the people who went into the
nail salon came out changed in some awful way—
brainwashed or zombie'd or with some indefinable horror perpetrated on them. I tried to warn Ky, but she
said, "Really, Theo, it's just a nail salon." Then I
thought, maybe I should leave her here and save myself. But no, that would be wrong—I'd just have to try
harder. I ended up hauling Ky down a set of stairs and
out to the street, while she stared a look at me that
said, Theo, you should be institutionalized, but if it
means that much to you I'll come along, all right?

I lay there in bed, trying to review my little paranoic
nightmare even as it faded. I frowned. Had that been
Kylla in the dream or Eliana Porath? What was my
subconscious trying to tell me? Did I believe Eliana
was in some kind of danger?

Really, I wished if my subconscious had messages
to send it would just use the Net terminal—

I froze. How had Loden known that Stereth sent me
a Net message about Moros's hut?

Coalis had known. He'd told me about it, while he was hiding in the jinevra bushes.

I got out of bed and, taking my pack of cards, padded out to the upstairs office.

Three minutes later Ran's voice said, "I thought you weren't going to do this anymore."

I looked up to see him standing in the doorway.

"I wasn't going to try anything experimental. Just a straight card-reading."

"Is there some reason we need a straight card-reading?"

Aside from my curiosity? I sought around for an answer. "Well, do you want to still be held responsible for Kade's death?"

"Jusik's let the matter drop. He's satisfied of Loden's guilt."

"Is he really satisfied of Loden's guilt, or does he just want to close the book and get on with his other problems? An open matter of blood would be a great disincentive to any other potential bridegrooms they try to rope into the family."

He walked over and sat down, cross-legged, above the deck. "All right, granted, he probably still thinks I did it and that I gave him Loden the way people on a lifeboat toss over somebody to satisfy the predators. We will live down the reputation eventually, you know. And meanwhile, my beloved tymon, if you end up sprawled on the floor due to your nighttime rambles—in a most unbecoming position, I might add—"

"I said I wasn't going to do anything risky!"

"Then you won't mind if I stay and watch."

I hesitated. "You're not going to try and stop me?"

"You and the weather, tymon, I leave alone."

I dealt out a simple business configuration. "The Man of Substance"—satisfied, fat, and well-dressed—had to be Jusik Porath. There was no card to denote membership in the Six Families, and this was as close as we were likely to get. Beneath him, in a legitimate blood relationship, was The Daredevil, walking a tightrope between two poles as he balanced his way with a stick. And to the right of that, The Fool. I stared down at the Fool and back at Ran. "Guess who," I said.

"It's on the *right* side of the configuration."

Meaning a legitimate relationship of some kind. I hesitated. "You don't mind if I check," I said. "I'll keep it to the normal paths."

He made a half-bow, as though to say, after you.

I touched my index finger to The Daredevil and waited.

Then I grinned at Ran. "Bingo," I said, in Standard.

The emerald lizard stuck its skinny tongue out at me as I climbed up the step to the porch. I was feeling brave, and was about to stoop to scratch it behind the ears when I noticed its meter was a little high.

"They ought to milk that thing," I said to Ran.

He glanced at the half-filled poison sac. "It's very tame," he pointed out.

"Yeah, that's what they always tell the neighbors the morning after the bodies are found."

Ran tapped the hilt of his dress-knife against the front door. It was pulled open almost immediately; the steward must have been told to expect us.

"Sir Cormallon," he bowed. "Gracious lady. Lord Porath has asked if you will accompany me to the library."

And so we did. The steward took us to a cheerful room, not really what I'd expected of Jusik, full of books and papers, overlooking the back courtyard for privacy, and decorated with pictures that reflected a personal taste not at all subordinate to the current rules of aesthetics. There was an actual wooden door, not just a hanging, to enforce his voluntary solitude. When we entered, Jusik was sitting on an old pillow of royal blue, evidently a favorite, beside a low writing table with an ornate brush-pen that gave every appearance of being an heirloom. Eliana, Coalis, and Leel Ca-

nerol sat a short distance away. They all looked up
when we came in.

Ran's stride faltered. "I thought this was to be a
private meeting," he said, addressing Lord Porath.

Jusik touched the edge of his heirloom pen and said,
"I would prefer it this way."

Ran looked at me. I gave him my best right-back-
at-you look; he would know better than I would if
pursuing the matter would be politically correct in
these circumstances.

He sighed, took a few steps forward, bowed, and
spoke firmly. "Lord Porath, your judgment is of
course the only proper one. At the same time, I feel
obligated to point out that what is not said in front of
witnesses, may be later agreed upon not to have been
said. I mention this only to give you the option that
rightfully belongs to you."

Jusik rolled the pen back and forth on the table. As
he switched from his right hand to his left, I saw that
the new hand was shaking. His voice was clear and
direct, though; he said, "We may consider you've
given me that option, like a gentleman, sir; now let's
sit and talk, all of us."

I was already sorry we'd come. At the same time I
had a conflicting desire to see everything out in the
open, to see what people would say about it; an Athenan desire.

An Athenan desire with Ivoran consequences. Next
time think about it a little longer, Theodora.

We sat. There was a knock at the door.

"Enter," said Jusik.

It wasn't the steward. It was Auntie Jace, white-
faced, and she scurried in as though she feared someone would stop her. She knelt and bowed to Jusik with
an alacrity I could envy even at my age. "Lord Porath,
I hope my service has been satisfactory—I've been
with your family for sixteen years now—I've never
thought of anyone else, never lived for anything else—"

"Yes, yes." He softened his tone slightly. "Nobody

has any complaint about you, Auntie. This matter doesn't concern you at all.''

''No, yes, I know—that is to say, I beg to be allowed to stay. Please, noble sir. I've never asked any personal favors before.''

Lord Porath looked as though he might debate that, but after a slight hesitation, he said, ''Why not? Everyone else is here. Why pretend you can get the wine back in the bottle after it's been spilled? Sit down, Auntie, find yourself a seat.''

She took a place at once, at the far perimeter of the cushions, as though if she weren't noticed she couldn't be thrown out. Her bright, birdlike eyes went back and forth, taking us all in.

''And now, gracious sir,'' said Jusik, turning to my husband, ''perhaps you will enlarge on that topic we discussed during your Net call. The topic of my family's involvement in the death of my son.''

Eliana, Coalis, Leel Canerol and Auntie Jace—four heads swiveled as one to stare at Ran.

He cleared his throat. ''Loden Broca, the actual agent who paid a hired sorcerer to dispose of Kade, is dead. But before he died, he went through the sorcerer's house in a search for incriminating evidence. Now, not many people knew where the sorcerer lived, or knew that the Cormallons had just been informed of the address. But Loden knew.'' He hesitated. ''Coalis also knew.''

Coalis froze. But his father did not rise up, grab a whip, and beat him to death. Jusik merely raised an eyebrow. ''Is this an accusation? A case of treason within my House is a serious charge, far more serious than murder.''

''Uh, not quite. You see, Eliana would also have known. At least, your two children seem fairly well informed of each other's activities.'' *Those activities you are so carefully not included in, Lord Porath.*

Eliana went as white as her robe. ''Father,'' she began, horrified.

''Shush, Eli. Let's allow the gentleman to finish.''

Ran inclined his head to acknowledge this courtesy. "The lady Eliana could very well have overheard Coalis's talk with . . . whoever informed him about the address."

Jusik's gaze went to spear Coalis. His son said, "Stereth Tar'krim mentioned it to me."

"I thought I told you not to keep company with that lowlife—" began his father. Jusik cut himself off. "But we'll discuss that later. I hope it will not be eclipsed by any worse matters you may be involved in."

Coalis swallowed hard, but said nothing.

I'd have felt a lot better if these things were being presented to a court of law on Athena rather than to the tender mercies of their natural parent.

Ran said, "Theodora, perhaps you should take over here. You noted the relevant points for us."

No, no, no . . . that's your job, Ran. The gazes all swung to me.

"Uh," I said. My mind went totally blank.

I felt Ran's hand touch mine beneath the folds of our outerrobes. "The IOUs," he prompted.

"Yes. The IOUs." I swallowed. "I overheard Loden and his friend say that it was Loden's girlfriend who sent him to sweep up the evidence. Loden told me straight-out earlier that he'd had a fight with his girlfriend—at the time I thought he meant the tootsie in his lap, but—uh, in any case, from the timing, the argument could have been on that very matter. The IOUs. She was probably having trouble getting him to do the intelligent thing. Uh, she's probably somewhat brighter than Loden was." Like the majority of people in the capital. "But as soon as she got the address, she called him and told him to get out to the hut and burn the IOUs. And then she called and invited me to tah and cards so I'd be occupied for most of the day." The invitation didn't come till that morning, after Stereth's message.

"*Father,*" said Eliana.

He held up his hand. "Continue, gracious lady."

"Well, we don't have any hard evidence." And this isn't a court of law.

He said, "Are you saying my daughter would profit by her brother's death? Frankly, I can't even see how Broca would come out ahead."

I looked at Coalis, who went blank. What a family. Evidently Jusik still didn't know about Kade's profession. I said, slowly, "I believe Kade was good enough to lend Loden some money."

Jusik snorted. "I fail to see where he got it from, if he did. Look around you; you see how we live."

Coalis spoke up, in self-defense. "Father, Kade did mention something to me about loaning some money to a security guard."

Jusik looked at him in surprise. He didn't ask why Kade had shared this information with his brother, and not his father; apparently he was used to being left out of his family's information loop. He scared them too much. "Very well, son, I take your word for it. But this still doesn't give Eliana any motive." He smiled at his daughter. "Her life is as pleasant as those who love her can make it. She would not profit by alteration."

Right. I said nothing. Jusik waited, then said, "Gracious lady? You see my point. I prefer to believe that you and your husband have simply not thought this through logically, rather than that you harbor some grudge against my House. Although there are those who might feel that, after half-destroying my family through one death, you seek to put the survivors in disarray—"

"We think they were lovers," I said.

He pulled up short. "I beg your pardon?"

"Loden and Eliana. In bed. Lovers." —*What word didn't you understand?* —*Shut up.* Jusik was turning a fascinating shade of violet.

"First of all," he began, forcing the words past some obstruction in his throat, "my daughter is constantly chaperoned, by not one but two respectable women. She would have no opportunity for the kind of behavior you describe. Though considering the sort of society you must be accustomed to, I suppose it's understandable you would not grasp that.''

''Noble sir . . . it's been brought forcefully home to me, very recently, that elegant young ladies with constant chaperones can find opportunities for gaining worldly experience should they wish to. At least, the intelligent and discreet among them can; and I think Eliana is fairly intelligent, and fairly discreet.'' Her dark eyes were fastened on me. I forced myself to look at Jusik, so I could continue talking normally. ''In the case of your daughter, the connivance of at least one of her chaperones is all that would be necessary. All we really need is the opportunity for the two to meet and get to know each other. Loden was here often enough, your House employed the Mercia group before—and I have reason to believe that Loden was very . . . well-equipped when it came to attracting women. I'm sure the options presented by an alliance with a young lady of the Six Families wouldn't escape even him. He would have gone out of his way with your daughter.''

He would have, too. The more I thought about it, the more I couldn't imagine him *not* going out of his way. It seemed so obvious, in hindsight. Self-interest was the only thing that got Loden's intellect racing.

Jusik's neck was still the color of a summer sunset. He growled, ''Meeting and exchanging a few words, as youngsters will, is hardly the same thing as being lovers. The only door in this house is on the entrance to this very room; the opportunity simply did not exist.''

''Oh, I'm sure there were a number of chances. The very night I had the honor of staying with you in this house,'' I'd almost called it ''The Night of Cats,'' ''I spent the early morning hours asleep on the chaise on your central porch. Auntie Jace was very unhappy to see me there. At the time, I thought she was overly touchy, but I realize now that she didn't want me to be so close to the entrance when she returned from having collected Eliana from the gatehouse. Where she had most likely spent the night with Loden Broca.''

Auntie cried, ''A disgusting lie! And only what one could expect from a barbarian! Lord Porath, you're too generous with these people, letting them into your house—''

''Auntie, please. I take it you deny these charges.''

''I certainly do! I wasn't even near the gatehouse!''

I said, ''I saw you well down the length of the garden, heading that way. What else is in that direction?''

''I don't recall going there, but if I did it was only to offer a cup of tah to whoever was on duty!''

''You weren't carrying any tah with you.''

''I would have sent a kitchenmaid! Lord Porath, won't you protect me from this slander?''

He looked thoughtful. Her sudden change of course in mid-story had not been to her benefit. But he merely said, ''Lady Theodora, you saw my daughter return to the house that morning?''

''No. I was asleep by then.''

''Then you have no proof of this fantasy.''

''Perhaps not. But it would be interesting to use your influence to get a look at the Mercian group's log for that night. I'll bet Loden Broca was in the gatehouse.''

A silence descended on the group with that suggestion. Finally Lord Porath said, ''I will do so. Eliana, have you anything to say?''

Her face lifted, paler than the creamy color young ladies who aspire to fragile flowerdom generally paint there. ''I rely on your protection, Father.''

He glanced at Leel Canerol, who said slowly, ''While your daughter was with me, she did nothing that you would find inappropriate.''

A careful choice of words. How much did the lanky fighter know?

Jusik glanced at Auntie Jace again, causing her to actually flinch. He was about to speak when he stopped and shook his head. An indulgent smile forced its way over his lips. ''No. This is simply out of character.

My child is sheltered, young, exposed to only the best and most proper things. It's simply inconceivable that she could be involved in anything of this sort. I'm sorry. For one thing, she wouldn't have the vaguest idea what to do—even if the thought of murder could enter her head, which I can't believe.''

Ran said, ''She's fairly experienced for her age.'' I turned to him in surprise. Ran had spent a couple of hours on the Net just before we came over, and I'd had no chance to ask him about it, but I hadn't been expecting any great surprises.

He went on, ''My gracious wife informed me that a couple of confederates, whom Loden didn't recognize, were asked to make an apparent attempt on his life in a gambling hall. A show for our benefit, to drive home his role as victim. Not a bad idea, in fact; I don't doubt it was his lover's, and she showed the good sense not to warn Loden in advance.'' He actually smiled. ''She couldn't know we would have a bodyguard, or that he would involve himself so enthusiastically.'' The smile disappeared. ''The confederates were well-dressed and wore jewelry beyond what most people in the capital could afford to own. The lady Theodora has a scholarly mind; her description of a bracelet was quite exact.'' He paused for emphasis. ''It belongs to Kas Sakri, a well-known player of the game of murder within the Six Families. No doubt they were doing a favor for—an ally? An opponent? A fellow player, at any rate.''

Jusik had the appearance of a man who's dodged too many flying missiles. He said, ''My son Coalis was briefly involved in that nonsense when he was younger. I put a stop to it. Son, have you been—''

''I haven't, Father, I swear!''

''He hasn't,'' agreed Ran. ''I made inquiries. But Eliana is a well-known novice player.''

''Females simply do not play!'' Jusik thundered.

''She's acted as an accomplice in the murder scenarios of at least two friends. It's true, I haven't yet discovered a game where she was the chief player. But heaven knows she must have observed enough.''

Jusik was silent. Ran said, ''All this can be easily checked.''

Coalis spoke up. ''Father, even if it's true, it doesn't mean—''

The paternal glare swiveled toward him. ''How much do you know about this?''

''Me?'' The voice was a squeak. ''Nothing, sir! Nothing at all.''

''I doubt he knew about the murder, anyway,'' put in Ran helpfully.

Jusik turned to Auntie Jace, who looked as though an anxiety attack was not far away. He said, ''Auntie, I've relied on your discretion for years. You haven't failed me. I must warn you, if you've been involved in any twilight dealings now, you'd best say so; for I promise you, if I find out later the tiniest part of this is true, there'll be no mercy for you.''

His tone of voice was scary even to me. It must have been much worse for someone dependent on his good will. She looked horrified.

''No mercy whatsoever,'' he added.

She began to make a wheezing sound, as though she were trying to get air. She started to rock back and forth, gasping.

''Auntie's not well,'' said Eliana, accusingly. ''These two have made her ill, Father.'' She crossed to Auntie Jace's pillow and put her arms around her chaperone's shoulders. ''Let me get her to her room—''

''Stand away, Eliana,'' said her father.

Looking startled, she let go. ''Get hold of yourself, Auntie,'' said Jusik sternly. ''Breathe slowly. Slowly. In and out. There now, just calm down, and if you have anything to say—say it now.''

She gasped some more, then cried, ''It wasn't my fault, Lord Porath! I tried to talk her out of it!'' Gasp, gasp. ''But she's all grown up now, she won't listen to me!'' Gasp, gasp. ''No, she has a *defensive* chaperone now! What can I do to make her behave? I have no authority! I'm just, I'm just a retainer!'' She burst into tears, her gasps becoming louder. "I brought her up, and now I'm *nobody!*'' She buried her face in her hands. "You can't blame me. It's not *fair!*''

Eliana's lips were pursed, and a disgusted look was on her face; her neck was angled back, as though to put more distance between her and Auntie. She gazed at her chaperone with a kind of fascinated repulsion. Finally she turned toward her father.

Jusik's face had lost all expression. "Speak, daughter. Speak now. If the Mercian log confirms that Broca was in the gatehouse—''

"No doubt it will,'' she said. "But this one—'' She cocked a head toward Auntie Jace—"is showing her usual backbone. She pushed and prodded and encouraged all the way. If I believed the sordid version these people tell, I'd think Loden bribed her to introduce us, that's how enthusiastic she was. Full of stories about court ladies and secret lovers—''

Auntie Jace started to wail. Clearly she would've denied it if she were still capable of speech.

"You admit to treason against your House,'' Jusik said tiredly.

"What treason?'' she inquired with scorn. "Loden and I were *married.*''

Ran and I looked at each other, startled.

She said, "I acted for the House of Broca. We all know that legally, when a woman marries, her obligation passes to her new family.''

Jusik seemed just as surprised. He addressed Auntie: "Is this true?''

She nodded vigorously, her head still buried, her shoulders shaking.

"Great bumbling gods! When did you have time to exchange the marriage cakes? How long did you know this piece of garbage, anyway?''

"I won't listen to you talk about my husband that way.''

"House of Broca, indeed! Who ever heard of the Brocas? A two-kembit guard, who had to borrow money from—wait a minute! Did Kade know you two were married?''

"Of course not. Why would he have wanted me to marry Shikron if he knew?''

Jusik paid no attention to this flippant contradiction on the part of his daughter. He said, "Did Coalis know?''

Coalis looked up, guilty knowledge blazoned across his face. "Certainly not!''

She said, quietly, "I never told Coalis. I never told anybody.''

I could imagine Leel Canerol breathing a sigh of relief at that. It's not only his offspring that a First Ranked of the Six Families has the right to kill.

Jusik said, grasping for understanding, "I can't believe you would help to kill your own brother to settle a debt for this guardsman trash—''

"I had to stop the marriage arrangements," she said defiantly. Under her breath, I heard her add, "and Kade was no great piece of work, either.''

Truthfully, I liked her for that addition. Naked honesty has always excited my admiration, apparently even in owning up to hatred and murder. What splendid self-possession for an eighteen-year-old, I thought. And what a pathetic view of her unworthy husband, what eighteen-year-old dreams of romance. Court ladies. Oh, gods protect us.

In a way I envied her, though. I'd had no romantic illusions at all at eighteen; the ones I had now had bloomed late, and took constant watering. If I'd never met Ran, I doubted I would have had them at all.

Jusik said, heavily, "So be it.''

Coalis leaned forward, looking alarmed. "Just a minute, Father. We probably don't have the whole story—''

"Be silent." Coalis subsided, his eyes scared. So much for our na'telleth monk, removed from caring. Jusik said, "For the death of your brother, the First Son of our House—''

He hesitated. Eliana still knelt in the center, not far

from Auntie Jace, with her back straight and her head raised. A Guinevere at the tribunal. And not an Arthur or Lancelot in sight.

"—You say you are no longer of Porath. So be it. Leave here now, never come back. Don't stop in your room for clothes or jewelry—"

"Father, *please*," said Coalis. "She can't live! She can't possibly live! How will she survive?"

"She's of the 'House of Broca,' " he said coldly. "Let the Brocas care for her. If they choose to. And if she can find them."

Eliana stood up, trembling slightly, from fear or anger or both. She still displayed that self-possession drilled into her from childhood: The discipline of a warrior on the inside, to make a fragile flower. . . .

She touched the silver bracelet on her arm and for a moment I thought she was going to pull it off and throw it to the floor, in keeping with the level of high tragedy. But this was the woman who told Loden Broca to go back and burn the IOUs. She pulled the cuff of her sleeve down over it, turned, and bowed to her father for the last time.

Let the Brocas care for her.

Self-willed or not, there are damned few jobs in the capital for someone without family pull. I know this very well. And what was she trained in, but being a cultured and elegant young lady of the Six Families? A position no longer open.

So the cage was opening, now that there was no place to fly. She would never again have to placate Jusik, satisfy her chaperones, wear satin slippers in the snow and laugh delicately at the witticisms of wealthy suitors.

She turned, smoothed the wrinkles from her outer-robe with a gesture, and—quietly, carefully, gracefully—she left the room.

It felt as though a hurricane had passed. I looked at the others; they seemed as wrung-out as I felt. We all sat there for what must have been a good five minutes, like people dazed, before Jusik blinked and said, "Sir

Cormallon. Gracious lady. We may consider this incident closed, I think. I would thank you to discuss it no further.''

Ran bowed.

My mind still followed Eliana mentally, out into the garden, past that gatehouse for the last time. She must be well aware that that silver bracelet wouldn't last her very long.

So she'd taken her dignity and her dream of independence and turned to the nice-smelling security guard, Loden Broca Mercia, screwing up her life beyond any hope of redemption. What irony. She'd have been happier marrying whatever wedding card her family slapped down before her, regardless of age or temperament. She'd have had her brideprice rights, her divorce rights, her children with their duty to obey and defend her—she could have carved out a bearable, compromised life for herself. It's what I would have done. I mean, there are always books.

And plays. And sunsets. The way the capital looks from an aircar early in the morning when you're approaching from the west. I'd have taken the chips I had and banked them, and not risked all that on a question mark.

But I'm a prudent little soul, born to buy insurance. My own wild chances were always forced on me; Eliana was made of more splendid stuff. She'd have been happy as a man in this culture, or as a woman on, say, the sane part of Tellys. She chose Destiny with a capital D, chose the madness (an Ivoran phrasing) of sexual love over self-interest, recognized her enemies for who they were, regardless of family name. I admired and disliked and pitied her all at once.

I think I was the only one in Jusik's library who felt that first emotion, though.

Ran stood and helped me up. "Thank you for your time, noble sir," he said, and nudged me into an awareness of my manners. We both bowed.

There was a scream, loud and piercing, from the other side of the house. The garden side.

Everyone got to their feet. Ran looked at me. "The lizard," I said.

I must not have been the only one who thought so. Ran and I turned and started running, down the hall, down the stairs . . . behind Coalis. With Leel Canerol gaining on us, and Jusik just beyond.

We tumbled out onto the porch. At the far end, a shining patch of blue and green. . . . We raced over.

The emerald lizard stuck his narrow tongue out at us all, his calm eyes gazing at this sudden invasion of madmen. His poison sac was still half-full.

"That's as full as it was when we came in," said Ran, puzzled.

I said, "I know. And where—"

Another scream, from beyond the jinevra bushes. We ran through the garden, Leel easily outdistancing us all.

An old woman in tattered servant's dress stood at the edge of the blue pool. Eliana floated in the center, surrounded by a pink halo. Beyond the long waving curtain of her black hair, you could just make out her knife on the bottom.

Chapter 19

Eliana had kept a flute on her windowsill. I'd seen one exactly like it in Loden's room at the inn. From such little things are suicides made.

Twelve days later I got an unexpected invitation from Coalis, and on an unseasonably cool late afternoon, almost early evening, I went to the Poraths for the last time.

The garden was crowded. A closed wagon was parked near the east wing porch, crushing the flowerbed, and as I watched I saw Jusik's writing table being carried out and placed inside. Were they so hard up they were selling off the furniture? A thick hose ran from the blue pool to a groundtruck nearby. The truck was vibrating, making a woompah-woompah sound, and a workman stood beside it peering down into the pool. I peered, too.

It was nearly empty. Old leaves and dirt eddied in the shallow remains. The bushes around the edge looked mournful and precarious of life. Maybe they'd always looked that way and the pool just took your attention from it. Or maybe all the truck activity had upset their growth.

Coalis waited by the front step, one of the Scythian yellow toms in his lap. He stroked it absently. He glanced up at me as I approached.

"They're draining the pond," he said.

"So I see."

"The ferocity of feeling in violent suicide must be expunged. The emotion would leave its shade behind, fouling the pool. It has to be drained."

"Ah."

He ran his hand gently from the tom's forehead to the tip of its golden tail. "They tell me you barbarians don't believe in that kind of thing."

"You're a na'telleth. What do you believe?"

He smiled humorlessly. "Maintaining a distance from violent emotion is always wise. Besides, the pool would be a shame to my father. People would point to it and say, 'There's where Eliana Porath slashed her own throat, when she was rejected by her family.' Probably what she had in mind when she did it. She should have known Father would have the spot drained."

"Can he avoid the social shame that way?"

"Oh, no. The shame will last for years. Eliana's last gift." He smiled again. There was no blame in his tone, only a light affection. "That's why we're leaving the capital."

"You are?" He'd taken me by surprise.

"Father has a gentleman's farm, out in Syssha Province. It's one of the last pieces of property my family managed to hang onto. That's where we're going." He nodded toward the wagon. "Father's sending the heirloom pieces on ahead with the servants."

Father this, Father that. "What about you, Coalis? Are you going, too? Your tutors are here in the capital, aren't they?"

"Oh, yes, I'm going, too. Father made that very clear. That's why I invited you over today, Theodora, to say good-bye. You're one of the few people in this town I wanted to say it to formally."

Thank you, I think. "But what about your studies? Couldn't you stay with one of the other Six Families?"

"I am no longer to be exposed to the corruption of the city," he said. "We are to return to a simpler, more moral time, learning the lessons of the harvest and the seasons among good-hearted country folk."

"I see."

"Father blames the capital for what happened. He believes his children have lost touch with the true virtues. He's dropped his hobbies to concentrate on the important aspects of life. *I* am to be his sole focus now; me, the cats, and any farm stock.''

''I'm very sorry.''

''Yes.'' He grimaced. ''He fired Leel Canerol for suggesting his concern was a bit late. He invited her along with us at first, you know. To protect the goods on the way, and to help on the farm.''

''Not her speed, I would think.''

''Well, you never know who harbors these unsuspected rural longings. Perfectly innocent looking people, sometimes.'' *Not you, though, apparently.* ''Anyway, Leel was wrong to have mentioned it, even if she was upset. Besides, if Father had piled the weight of his full attention on Eli before this—''

She might have suicided that much sooner, I filled in. Coalis closed his mouth firmly. There were limits even a na'telleth did not pass in speaking of one's parents; at least, not on Ivory.

I steered back the subject. ''She's all right, then? He just fired her, nothing else?''

He rubbed the cat under its chin and a low purring sound began to gain strength. ''You think he might have blackballed her in the capital? Beaten her before throwing her past the gate, without any clothes?''

''Well . . .''

''The fire's gone out of him, Theodora. Except for this farm scheme. You don't dare say a word against that for your life. Not even Grandmother.'' He sighed. *''She's* taking it better than we all thought. After her breakdown when Kade died, we assumed she'd lose control entirely. Father was even afraid it would kill her. But she's handling it better than he is. And she was closer to Eli, too—figure that out.''

I sat down beside him, keeping a distance from the cat. ''And what about Auntie?''

''Fighting a guerrilla campaign.'' He chuckled. ''Holding on for dear life. I don't think she has any family left, and she doesn't dare ask for references. So she keeps to the corners and doesn't say a word.

Father hasn't officially asked her to accompany us to Syssha. I'm betting she'll slip into the wagon and come anyway.''

What a life. What a family. Jusik appeared at the other end of the east porch; he directed a workman to load a small cabinet of inlaid marble into the wagon. He glanced over at me where I sat and then turned back to his chore, as though dealing with anyone unnecessarily was more than could be expected of him. What in the world was Coalis going to do way out in Syssha Province? Loan-shark the sheep and cows? Collect three or four kembits a day from the peasantry?

The choice was not his, any more than the choice was Eliana's, though she'd tried to make it so. Possibly in the back of his mind Coalis was hoping for an early paternal heart attack and an early return to the capital; what was love and what was duty in his attitude toward his father, I certainly couldn't determine.

''I thought you'd like a souvenir,'' said Coalis, drawing my attention back.

I could not possibly conceive why he would think so. But he reached into a pocket and drew out a tiny bluestone globe trisected by a silver triangle. He put it in my palm. I'd seen the symbol before, over the entrance to a na'telleth monastery. No doubt I had more chance of seeing that monastery again than Coalis did. Even if Jusik died, no decent Ivoran boy would go into a monastery when he was the last of his family.

The woompah-woompah sound stopped and I saw the workman by the truck disengage his hose. He started hauling it back from the dry pond. In my mind I saw Kade, bully and loanshark; Eliana, going over the line in her plan to escape her father's house; Coalis . . . I wasn't sure exactly what Coalis's problems were, but he wasn't the boy next door. Just a typical Ivoran family, I thought, a little hysterically. Save this planet, people. Start a creche, ban family names, the way we did on Pyrene.

. . . And Jusik, tyrannizing over the rest. Except he didn't look like much of a tyrant right now.

I said to Coalis, "Does this mean you've given up monkhood forever?"

"It's not a profession, Theodora, it's a state of mind."

One you would do well to emulate, I heard unspoken. He was probably right.

I stood up. "Farewell, and good fortune. Your acquaintance has been . . . unforgettable."

"Oh, Theodora." He stood and bowed over my hand. "Believe me, *your* acquaintance has made quite an impact."

Indeed, and it was courteous of him not to kill me because of it.

I walked past the dry pond, the crushed flowers, and the still-tall jinevra bushes. It would be good not to come back here.

Behind me, the bones of a dying family stirred themselves for the move.

I thought of Coalis sometimes and his quest for achieving the true state of "na'telleth-ri"; a quest whose cold arm reached into the most normal, taken-for-granted moments of life. The last line of a disagreement with one's husband, for instance: "What do you want me to do?"

An interesting word, *want.* Close enough to *care* to make the na'telleths nervous. What do you *want?* A chair, a bed, the salt passed? I ask to be polite; I'm human myself, I know how we are. Any desires hanging on your back, pinching your toes, stirring your drink for you so it no longer tastes good? Justice, vengeance, sexual satisfaction? Feel free to speak up, we're all siblings here.

It's how we deal with each other, the basic web of civilization. We start with barter, move on to a system; we're no fools. Here, have some money, you can buy what you *want.* Should we go to the play tonight? If that's what you want. Me, I only want you to be happy.

Jack Lykon had returned to Tellys, but his specter remained. And as I snapped at Ran, "What do you want me to do?"

Not that he had asked me to do anything.

At the end of the month we went to the fair in the Imperial Park.

Twice a year the lowest level of the park, beside the river, is given over to craftspeople and farmers from the provinces who bring in every old piece of crockery and wagonload of fruit they think they can unload on city folk. Mixed in with them are acres of riches: Unexpected delights in the way of painted bowls showing mythological creatures drawn out in fiery symmetry; handblown goblets; finely patterned paper to use for decoration; and all manner of dishes, pipes, tahburners, ceramic flowerpots. . . . The park, needless to say, is crowded on such days. Stuff that would be auctioned off at a fine arts house on Athena can be picked up for a smile and a handful of old coins.

We'd wandered around for half the day to our artistic and monetary satisfaction, and toward late afternoon we started to aim for the food and spice wagons, to bring things home for supper. Today countrypeople were free of the spice monopoly's prices and could bring their whitemint and pepperfall direct to the consumer—and the consumers were lined up, happy to wait for bargains.

I stopped to look at a row of candlestick holders. A man went by in a yellow brocade robe, a little girl on his shoulders, giggling. Two others followed behind him, sucking lemon ices. Lately it seemed that everywhere I went there was a high tide of children. And the families all looked so happy. What happened to the harassed mothers, screaming red-faced at their kids, smacking them as they wailed and making passersby feel uncomfortable?

"Excuse me," said a voice. I turned to see a young woman in very plain Standard dress, a fellow barbarian. She looked about twenty, verging on pretty, and out of place. "I'm sorry to bother you," she said, uncertainty in her voice, "but you look like you know your way around here. Do you think these—" and she extended her hands, each holding a cheap brass candlestick, "look all right?"

"Well . . ." I said, not sure how to respond; actually, I've always found brass candlesticks quite ugly, and the pair she had chosen had to top the list in that department.

"You see, I'm having a guest for dinner, and I want it all to look nice," she said.

"I've never been fond of brass," I said.

"They're about all I can afford," she said frankly. She gazed at them with dissatisfaction.

They were the cheapest pair in the row, I saw. I picked up one of the less expensive looking crystal holders and glanced at the vendor. He raised four fingers. My fellow barbarian followed the exchange and her face fell.

"Is your guest Pyrenese?" I asked hopefully. A Pyrenese would hardly notice or care about the artistic merits of his dinnertable. In fact, it would be considered morally beneath him to take note of such things.

"He's Ivoran," she said.

"Oh, dear." And you don't know what you're letting yourself in for, my child.

Ran appeared then; he'd been lingering over a set of marble paperweights two wagonloads back. A true Ivoran, an aesthetic question engaged his interest at once.

"Why don't you buy one of those bowls with the phoenix-griffin design? —You remember them, Theodora. They're down by the water's edge—the craftsman was packing to leave, and selling them for almost nothing. Then you can fill it with scented water and put a few of those floating candles in."

"I never heard of floating candles," she said doubtfully.

"It would look splendid," he insisted. "Come on, I'll point you in the right direction. —You'd best get a spot for us in line, Theodora. I'll be back in five minutes."

An appeal for aesthetic judgment will get Ran's attention where an appeal for mercy may leave him cold. He pulled his victim/charitable object after him, and I filled up a string bag with fruit and pastries, and went to stand in line at the spice wagon.

Several people had brought their own carts, now piled high with loot from the day. Good gods, there were eight—no, nine—children in line in front of me, and a tired woman with the voice of a drill sergeant watching over them. Wasn't she young to have— One of the older children's robes rustled as she moved, and I saw the character for "property of." I watched till she turned around, and read, "Kenris Training School."

Trocha children: Orphans and "superfluous offspring" brought up to be sold into trade apprenticeships. Even they didn't look unhappy. They demanded attention of their guardian freely, constantly tugging on her sleeves, and she gave it to them as their due.

All a facade, I thought, standing there, remembering the Poraths and wondering about what had gone wrong in my own past.

I remember once talking to one of the therapists on Athena about the strangeness of "family" to a Pyrenese creche-graduate like me. I'd been saying nice things about the Cormallons, thinking of the relationship between Kylla and Ran, and the therapist had grinned and remarked that the older he got the more he felt the phrase "dysfunctional family" was redundant.

He had a point. But is it just families? Is the Pyrenese system really better? It didn't give me a happier childhood. And would I have found the same painful rubbing-together, one wound against another, in any group that had to live with each other, even nonrelatives on Pyrene? I never gave it a chance, so I suppose I'll never know.

I have my suspicions, though. What is it about us human beings, anyway? How can we possibly hurt each other as much as we do and still feel so put-upon while we're doing it? I sometimes feel we would all benefit greatly from having our lives recorded and played back, so we could see every wrong move we make from a spectator seat; every harmful remark and then a close-up on the eyes of the person we're talking to.

So far Ran hasn't blossomed into any super-neurosis, and the quirks he has are ones I'm prepared to live with. His distorted view of family, distorted in its way as mine, is like an anchor; he's unreasonably prejudiced in my favor, just because I had the good sense to marry him. So he's willing to put up with a great deal, too, and just assume that my intentions are good.

That's an attitude worth gold. It's not why I married him, but I'm beginning to see that people get married for reasons that are different from the reasons they don't get divorced.

All right, Theodora; you don't want anybody to take these treasures away from you. But what are you going to tell the Cormallon council next year?

Not to mention the ghost of Ran's grandmother. I wished she'd been as forthcoming in her message to me; I wished I knew her exact words. I'd heard this "new blood" phrase before, but how I could be responsible for it was beyond me. Was I supposed to trust Grandmother, unstopper the healer's cap (I felt like a bottle of old wine in someone's cellar), and go for the marginal odds as Jack Lykon had laid them out? Grandmother must have been crazy. Because if there's anything to this heredity business at all, this hypothetical offspring wouldn't be getting any terrific genes for the manipulation of magic, not from me. And yet I was the item she wanted factored into the plan. Did this make sense?

All right, assume I reported in to the council next year as barren. I'd chiseled the information out of Ran as to what would follow:

"We'd adopt," he said.

"Then what's all this about a second wife?"

"Well . . . that's who we'd adopt from. It can be done on an entirely friendly basis, Theodora. You could even help pick her out—probably one of the Ducorts or the Cymins. Then when she, uh, produces, we write her a bank order, get a divorce—"

"Forget that idea."

"It's a purely businesslike arrangement, Theodora—"

I'd given him a look that must have had more power than I'd realized because he shut up.

I reexamined that exchange from a scholar's point of view: I didn't see how a child of Ran and one of Cormallon's usual allies would satisfy Grandmother's requirements for a new genetic infusion.

I wished the old lady were alive. I wished I'd known her a little longer. I wished the Cormallons weren't so damned secretive.

The cart belonging to the Kenris Training School was piled high with goodies, and with live cargo, too; a very small member of the school sat atop, facing backward, staring directly into my face. He looked to be about two or three years old, wearing a short quilted jacket of royal blue that somebody had buttoned for him right up to the neck.

When he saw me focus on him, his dark eyes came alert. He zeroed in on my string bag, resting on the edge of the wagon.

"What's that?" he said, pointing to my rose nectarine.

"That's a rose nectarine," I replied.

"What's that?" he said, pointing to a bundle of handwoven napkins.

"They're dinner napkins," I replied.

"What's that?" he rapped out, pointing to my pellfruit—then to my phoenix-griffin dish—then to my colored papers.

Each time I answered him he moved on to the next

item. Is this kid making fun of me? I wondered, uncertainly. He can't even know what half these things are, but he keeps asking for more.

Finally his exhausted looking guardian started to pull the cart away. The boy turned to me quickly and the words tumbled out. He jabbed his finger toward each item to illustrate his fact-checking. "That's a rose nectarine. That's dinnernapkins. That's a pellfruit. That's feenixgrif'n-dish. That's festival paper. That's red oranges. That's a pen-holder."

"Yes!" I said, delighted.

He didn't smile, but the solemn eyes looked pleased at his success.

The cart moved away, past the spice line, out onto the path toward the park exit. I stared at it.

"Gracious lady?" asked the spice vendor. "You're next."

"I'll be right back."

I left the string bag on the wagon like any fool tourist and galloped after the shaky cart of the Kenris School troop.

"Excuse me! Excuse me, gracious lady." The young woman stopped, with a facial expression that suggested she was too tired to even try to understand why I was bothering her.

"Yes? Can I help you?"

"I was just wondering. Are these children . . ." I searched frantically for the right word. What we usually translate into Standard as "adoption" refers to a series of ways people are taken into Houses, usually with a task in mind; I had no task in mind here. "Uh, are these kids available?"

She said, politely, "If you require any sort of trade experience, we can probably supply it. For short-term assignments, we have contracts of even a day at a time. You have only to call on our registrar's office—"

"No, no. Are they . . . for sale?"

This phrasing she grasped. "Of course," she said. And they call us barbarians. "I'll have to get back to you on this," I said, "but meanwhile, can you tell me the name of the kid on top of the cart?"

"Tirjon. We don't have any last names, of course, but there's an ID number: 428791."

Numbers instead of surnames, just like my birthplace. I was practically nostalgic. "Four-two-eight-seven-nine-one," I said. "Many thanks. Four-two-eight-seven-nine-one." I walked away from the Kenris guardian and back toward the spice wagons. Four-two-eight-seven-nine-one. I needed a pen.

Ran was waiting, having rescued my string bag. "Did I miss something?" he asked.

"Ran, I've been thinking." As we spoke we started cleaning out the last three jars of maneroot from the vendor's display before they disappeared. "We ought to consider adoption. Regular adoption, I mean, none of this extra-wives stuff."

He seemed puzzled. "Take in a cousin for fostering? It's done all the time, but I didn't know you were interested."

"No, no. I mean bringing up a kid from scratch. Scratch from the Cormallon point of view, that is— didn't your grandmother used to talk about needing new blood?"

"I don't think that's what she—"

"There was a possible candidate here not two minutes ago. From the Kenris School."

"A *training* school? Sweetheart—look, there are a lot of reasons why that would never work. First, the council would have a fit— What are you doing?"

"I'm borrowing your pen." I slipped it out of his outerrobe pocket.

"Theodora, you were born off-planet, you have no real grasp of how sensitive some issues—"

He broke off, watching me flip open a corner of the decorator paper and write numbers on it. "Are you listening to me?" he asked.

"Of course I am!" I said, offended. "You know I always do what you say."

* * *

Not long after, autumn found us in Cormallon.

I had passed the Poraths' house a few days earlier and peered in through the empty gate. A gold cat peered back at me from some long grass and another raised a sleepy head from the porch. Hadn't Jusik taken them along? Perhaps he'd tried and they'd chosen to take the first rest stop and return to familiar territory. Well, there were other pools here beside the dry one, and the Poraths still owned the property; I hoped sufficient mice and such could be found to keep them going.

I supposed that we owed a debt of gratitude to the Poraths' Scythian yellow toms. If it weren't for them I never would have slept out on the porch, and never would have wondered what Auntie Jace was doing heading out through the garden at dawn. And who knows, without the whipping my sinuses took whenever we visited the household, my nose might have been more susceptible to Loden's perfume.

So a few days later I was sitting in our own garden, in Cormallon, beside a small red pavilion open to the air. Kursek, one of the goldbands, had just brought us out tah, grinned, and left, taking the rocks over the stream instead of the bridge as his route back. It was a gorgeous day, with scudding clouds and cool breezes. In the privacy of the estate I'd thrown off my outer-robes and slipped into wide blue trousers and a tunic. Ran doesn't like trousers, on men or women, because he thinks they're provincial; so I compromised by not wearing them as often as I liked and he compromised by not commenting when I did.

Ran sighed happily from the boulder where he sat, pleased with his territory, his tah, his life. "Weather change coming," he said, after a good twenty minutes of silence, nodding toward the growing black fist on the horizon. There's often a series of thunderstorms in the area around Cormallon just before fall gets fully underway.

After a while, I said, "You know, I hope we don't get involved in any more investigations."

"I thought the idea appealed to your scholarly mind, tymon."

I shrugged. "The process is fine. I just don't like the results."

"Eliana was no friend of yours," he said, meeting my eyes.

"No, I know that. But it's still a great deal of responsibility to take for another human being." At least five other human beings, actually. As I thought about Jusik, Auntie, Leel, Coalis . . . the servants, the cats . . . the abandoned house and garden. . . .

A freshening wind came up, ruffling the sleeves of my tunic. I poured another cup of tah. The clouds were racing by now, autumn at their heels.

"It was good for our reputation," said Ran, giving me what he would consider comfort if it were given to him.

We'd discussed the idea of adopting a *trocha* child, but not, to my mind, exhaustively.

I said, "Speaking of training schools—"

"Great bumbling gods, haven't we finished that yet?"

"Really, Ran," I said, surprised. "When I think I've run through all my arguments, I'll let you know."

Two nights previously: Ran sitting on the bed, one sandal on and one off. "You don't understand the protocol, sweetheart. When *trocha* children get adopted, it's only as waymakers—an older sibling to help out with bringing up the firstborn."

"Great. Then he can be a waymaker. It'll buy us more time from the council, we can say we want to give him a year or two to grow before we start on our own kids."

"Tymon, are you listening? *Trochas* don't inherit. They grow up to be councillors, helpers-out, advisers, retainers. They don't take over the business."

"If we handle it properly, in a few years he'd be so ingrained into Cormallon people won't know where he came from. Don't you see, Ran, all this within-the-

family stuff the council harps on is just what your
grandmother wanted to avoid?''

He threw up his hands. "Only a barbarian would
even think she could get away with this!"

"That's exactly my point.''

Whereupon he gave up in disgust and went to look
for his other sandal.

It was growing darker. Suddenly the cool wind
turned cold, and burst down on us, picking up the
napkins Kursek had brought out and throwing them far
into the bushes. I grabbed the tahpot and burner and
Ran took the cups; we ran for the pavilion just as the
skies opened.

Sheets of water pounded against the roof. Lakes and
rivers fell around us. We started to laugh.

"What timing," said Ran.

"How will we get back to the house?" I asked.

We set our tah service down on the somewhat dirty
pavilion floor. "Kursek will show up eventually," said
Ran. "With umbrellas." I was standing against one
of the wide pillars that held up the roof. He leaned
over and kissed me. I kissed back.

It was a change-in-the-weather kind of kiss. *Not on
this floor,* I thought, though it wasn't a bad idea in
itself. . . . "Kursek," I said, at last. "Who knows
when he'll show up?"

"His hard luck," said Ran, paying no attention.

"Can't you see him . . . ? Standing in the down-
pour, waiting for us to finish?"

We started to laugh again and Ran stepped back.
"Should we drink our tah, then?"

"By all means."

Ran never asked me—*trocha* child or no *trocha*
child—what I planned to tell the Cormallon council
next year. Fortunately Ivoran years give you a little
more space to work with. As the old story of the con-
demned man goes—perhaps you know it? The man
reprieved by his king when he promised to teach a
horse to sing— "In a year the king may die, or I may

die, or the horse may die . . . or the horse may sing.''
Meanwhile, in my arguments with Ran, I stuck to the
practicalities; mainly because it was far too embarrassing to admit that I'd been slain by the charm of a
two-year-old.

Look, I'm only a barbarian who never got her doc-
torate. I do what I can.

I took my cup from Ran and thought of the capital;
it seemed lifetimes away. ''You know,'' I said, ''we
owe a debt of gratitude to those cats. When we go back
to the city, you should bring them a present. Silken
collars. A week of fresh fish.''

''A potful of mice.''

''Catnip. And don't forget to say thank you when
you go.''

He set down his tah-cup on the railing of the pavilion. ''You could go and thank them yourself.''

He smiled.

''No I couldn't,'' I said.

DAW

Doris Egan

The Ivory Novels

☐ **THE GATE OF IVORY (Book 1)** UE2328—$4.50

Cut off from her companions and her ship, attacked and robbed, anthropology student Theodora of Pyrene finds what began as a pleasure trip becoming a terrifying odyssey on the planet Ivory, where magic works. For all her studies and training are useless, and she is forced to turn to fortune-telling to survive. To her amazement, she discovers that she is actually gifted with magical skill—a skill, however, that will plunge her into deadly peril.

☐ **TWO-BIT HEROES (Book 2)** UE2500—$4.99

Drawn back to Ivory by her fascination with a world where magic not science holds sway, Theodora embarks with Sorcerer Ran on a mission into a province plagued by outlaws, where Ran is mistaken for the leader of a dangerous band long sought by the local law officers. Pursued by government forces, Ran and Theodora run for their lives—straight into the clutches of the outlaws!

☐ **GUILT-EDGED IVORY (Book 3)** UE2538—$4.99

When Ran and Theodora attend a gathering where the eldest son of one of Ivory's ruling families is killed by sorcerous means, all heads turn to Ran. Unless Ran and Theodora can find the true murderer, it will be the ruin of Ran and will destroy the family business. But when any number of people would gain from eliminating the leader of a powerful family, how can Ran and Theodora ever hope to unravel the many strands of intrigue and clear their family's name?

Buy them at your local bookstore or use this convenient coupon for ordering.

PENGUIN USA P.O. Box 999, Bergenfield, New Jersey 07621

Please send me the DAW BOOKS I have checked above, for which I am enclosing $_____ (please add $2.00 per order to cover postage and handling. Send check or money order (no cash or C.O.D.'s) or charge by Mastercard or Visa (with a $15.00 minimum.) Prices and numbers are subject to change without notice.

Card #_____ Exp. Date _____
Signature_____
Name_____
Address_____
City _____ State _____ Zip _____

For faster service when ordering by credit card call **1-800-253-6476**
Please allow a minimum of 4 to 6 weeks for delivery.

DAW

Cheryl J. Franklin

The Tales of the Taormin:

☐ **FIRE GET: Book 1**   UE2231—$3.50

Only the mighty sorcerer Lord Venkarel could save Serii from
the Evil that threatened it—unless it became his master. . . .

☐ **FIRE LORD: Book 2**   UE2354—$3.95

Could even the wizard son of Lord Venkarel destroy the
Rendies—creatures of soul-fire that preyed upon the living?

☐ **FIRE CROSSING: Book 3**   UE2468—$4.99

Can a young wizard from Serii evade the traps of the computer-
controlled society of Network—or would his entire world fall
prey to forces which magic could not defeat?

The Network/Consortium Novels:

☐ **THE LIGHT IN EXILE**   UE2417—$3.95

Siatha—a non-tech world and a people in harmony—until it
became a pawn of the human-run Network and a deadly alien
force. . . .

☐ **THE INQUISITOR**   UE2512—$5.99

Would an entire race be destroyed by one man's ambitions—
and one woman's thirst for vengeance?

Buy them at your local bookstore or use this convenient coupon for ordering.

PENGUIN USA P.O. Box 999, Bergenfield, New Jersey 07621

Please send me the DAW BOOKS I have checked above, for which I am enclosing
$_____ (please add $2.00 per order to cover postage and handling. Send check
or money order (no cash or C.O.D.'s) or charge by Mastercard or Visa (with a
$15.00 minimum.) Prices and numbers are subject to change without notice.

Card #_____ Exp. Date _____
Signature_____
Name_____
Address_____
City _____ State _____ Zip _____

For faster service when ordering by credit card call **1-800-253-6476**
Please allow a minimum of 4 to 6 weeks for delivery.

MARION ZIMMER BRADLEY

THE DARKOVER NOVELS

The Founding
☐ DARKOVER LANDFALL   UE2234—$3.95

The Ages of Chaos
☐ HAWKMISTRESS!   UE2239—$4.99
☐ STORMQUEEN!   UE2310—$4.50

The Hundred Kingdoms
☐ TWO TO CONQUER   UE2174—$4.99
☐ THE HEIRS OF HAMMERFELL   UE2451—$4.99
☐ THE HEIRS OF HAMMERFELL (hardcover)   UE2395—$18.95

The Renunciates (Free Amazons)
☐ THE SHATTERED CHAIN   UE2308—$3.95
☐ THENDARA HOUSE   UE2240—$4.99
☐ CITY OF SORCERY   UE2332—$4.50

Against the Terrans: The First Age
☐ THE SPELL SWORD   UE2237—$3.95
☐ THE FORBIDDEN TOWER   UE2373—$4.95

Against the Terrans: The Second Age
☐ THE HERITAGE OF HASTUR   UE2413—$4.50
☐ SHARRA'S EXILE   UE2309—$4.99

THE DARKOVER ANTHOLOGIES with The Friends of Darkover

☐ DOMAINS OF DARKOVER   UE2407—$3.95
☐ FOUR MOONS OF DARKOVER   UE2305—$4.99
☐ FREE AMAZONS OF DARKOVER   UE2430—$3.95
☐ THE KEEPER'S PRICE   UE2236—$3.95
☐ LERONI OF DARKOVER   UE2494—$4.99
☐ THE OTHER SIDE OF THE MIRROR   UE2185—$3.50
☐ RED SUN OF DARKOVER   UE2230—$3.95
☐ RENUNCIATES OF DARKOVER   UE2469—$4.50
☐ SWORD OF CHAOS   UE2172—$3.50

Buy them at your local bookstore or use this convenient coupon for ordering.

PENGUIN USA P.O. Box 999, Bergenfield, New Jersey 07621

Please send me the DAW BOOKS I have checked above, for which I am enclosing
$_____ (please add $2.00 per order to cover postage and handling. Send check
or money order (no cash or C.O.D.'s) or charge by Mastercard or Visa (with a
$15.00 minimum.) Prices and numbers are subject to change without notice.

Card #_____ Exp. Date _____
Signature_____
Name_____
Address_____
City _____ State _____ Zip _____

For faster service when ordering by credit card call **1-800-253-6476**

Please allow a minimum of 4 to 6 weeks for delivery.

DAW

Coming in HARDCOVER in October 1992:

WINDS OF CHANGE
Book Two of The Mage Winds
by Mercedes Lackey

In the MAGE WINDS trilogy, which began with the best-selling novel WINDS OF FATE, author Mercedes Lackey continues the epic that started with her first published book, ARROWS OF THE QUEEN. ARROWS OF THE QUEEN introduced readers to the remarkable land of Valdemar, the kingdom protected by its Heralds—men and women gifted with extraordinary mind powers—aided and served by their mysterious companions—horselike beings who know the many secrets of Valdemar's magical heritage. Now, in WINDS OF CHANGE, Valdemar is imperiled by the dark magic of Ancar of Hardorn, and Princess Elspeth, Herald and heir to the throne, has gone on a desperate quest in search of a mentor who can teach her to wield her fledgling mage-powers and help her to defend her threatened kingdom. But rather than finding a nurturing environment in which her talent can flourish, she is whirled into a maelstrom of war and sorcery as the Clan she has sought out to give her magical training is attacked by a mysterious dark adept from out of the Uncleansed Lands. And Elspeth must struggle to remember long forgotten magics, abandoning old ways, and risking the dangers of the unknown in a desperate bid to save her people. . . .

☐ **Hardcover Edition**   UE2534—$20.00

PENGUIN USA
P.O. Box 999, Bergenfield, New Jersey 07621

Please send me _____ copies of the hardcover edition of WINDS OF CHANGE by Mercedes Lackey, UE2534, at $20.00 ($24.99) in Canada) plus $2.00 for postage and handling per order. I enclose $_____ (check or money order—no cash or C.O.D.s) or charge my ☐ Mastercard ☐ Visa

Card # _____ Exp. Date _____

Signature _____

Name _____

Address _____

City _____ State _____ Zip _____

Please allow 4-6 weeks for delivery.
This offer, prices, and numbers are subject to change without notice.